RED BLUE S'

The CANZUK at War Series
Book 2

Dedication:

To my wife, Karen.
A patient supporter of her husband's distant dreams.

Definitions:
CANZUK:
A political and military alliance comprised of Canada, Australia, New Zealand, and the United Kingdom.

Battlefield Asset Management system or BAM:
This is a critical piece of Command, Control, Communications, Computers, Intelligence, Surveillance and Reconnaissance (C4ISR) used by CANZUK forces. It includes an earbud, a wrist unit (think an oversized Apple Watch), body and helmet cams, and a mouthguard. Pressing specific parts of the mouthguard enables the user to issue verbal commands to a near-AI system that seamlessly connects soldiers with other individual soldiers or units (e.g., a platoon, company, brigade, etc) and access various data applications that aid in the coordination of various battlefield actions and movements (e.g., artillery targeting software).

Near-AI:
Presently (in and around 2023), artificial intelligence as it now functions, is basically a software program that is hugely efficient and effective at scanning and retrieving information from available databases to provide human-like responses to a particular question or task (e.g., write me a blog post on topic A). In 2023, AIs are the equivalent of web browsers jacked up on steroids, amphetamines, and a six-pack of Red Bulls.

In the CANZUK at War series, I use the term 'Near-AI' to signal that artificial intelligence is something closer to Artificial General Intelligence (AGI), which, when it is achieved, will be or will be very close to, a sentient intelligence. "Near-AI" represents the final technology stage before a viable AGI is born.

Character Cast:

Canada
Merielle Martel, Prime Minister
Tessa Chong, Chief of Staff to Prime Minister
Paul Blanchard, Minister of Transport
Yvette Raymond, Minister of Health
Eloise St. Martin, Chief of Staff to the Minister of Health
Jonathan Weisman, Minister of Public Safety and Security
Irene MacPhail, Minister of Fisheries and Oceans
Sandy McNabb, Chief of Staff to Irene MacPhail
Colonel Jackson Larocque, Commanding Officer, Canadian Airborne Regiment
Madison Larocque, Wife of Jackson Larocque
Captain Zufelt, Captain, Pathfinder Company, Canadian Airborne Regiment
Warrant Officer Bear, Canadian Airborne Regiment
Major Kiraly, Surgeon, Canadian Airborne Regiment
General Kaplan, Chief of Defence Staff, Canadian Armed Forces
General Gagnon, Commander of CANZUK Expeditionary Army, North America
Asher Lastra, Staff Sergeant, Royal Canadian Mounted Police (RCMP), Protection Division
Corporal Coutu, Royal Canadian Mounted Police (RCMP), Protection Division
Constable Dupuis, Montreal Police Department (Service de police
de la Ville de Montréal - SPVM)
Stephane Martel, Inspector, RCMP, National Security Advisor, ex-husband to Merielle Martel

James Plamondon, Director, Canadian Security Intelligence Service (CSIS)

Colonel Azim, Commanding Officer, White Unit

Eric Labelle, Leader of Quebec Separatist Party

Mario Fortin, Fixer, Neo-Front de libération du Québec (FLQ)

Sam Petite, CSIS Intelligence Officer, Leader of Direct Action Team

Sarah Hall, White Unit Operative, Direct Action Team

Sergeant Jankowicz, Joint Task Force-2 commando, Direct Action Team

Master Corporal Sykes, Joint Task Force-2 commando, Direct Action Team

Kayed, CSIS Intelligence Officer, Direct Action Team

Douglas Jefferies, Reporter

Angie Jefferies, Reporter

Great Britain

Air Vice Marshal Robert Michaels, Commander, CANZUK Air Forces in North America

Wing Commander Harry 'Pony' Khan, Royal Air Force (RAF) Expeditionary Air Wing, North America

Flight Lieutenant Cheryl 'Petal' Robinson, RAF Tempest Pilot

Rampart (call sign), RAF Tempest Pilot

Rhino (call sign), RAF Tempest Pilot

Cypher (call sign), RAF Tempest Pilot

Rowdy (call sign), RAF Tempest Pilot

Australia

Colonel Bryan Rydell, Commanding Officer, 2nd Commando Regiment

Corporal Dune, 2nd Commando Regiment

France
    Marie-Helene Lévesque, President of France
    Pascal Charron, Minister of the Interior
    Pierre Besson, Director, Direction Générale de la Sécurité Extérieure (DGSE)
    Gabriel Besson, Son of Pierre Besson
    Colonel Bruno Corbin (aka "The Colonel"), Mercenary
    Henri, DGSE officer
    Commandant Dorian Elan, 13th Parachute Dragoon Regiment
    Chief Laroux, 13th Parachute Dragoon Regiment
    Lieutenant Roland Blondin, 13th Parachute Dragoon Regiment
    Lieutenant Roche, 13th Parachute Dragoon Regiment

United Constitutional States of America (UCAS) – The Red Faction
    Mitchell Spector, President
    Peter Parr, Chief of Staff to Mitchell Spector
    General John Spellings, UCAS Army
    General Hoffman, UCAS Air Force
    Major Trammel, UCAS Air Force, Coordinator, Operation Sunlight

Federation of American States (FAS) – The Blue Faction
   Valeria Menendez, President
   Andrew Morgan, Vice President
   Roberta Hastings Secretary of Education
   Dr. Janet Hastings-Moore, Daughter of Roberta Hastings
   General Sullivan, Chairman of the Joint Chiefs of Staff, FAS Armed Forces
   General Galway, Commander, Blue Faction Counter-Insurgency Operations

China
   Yan Jiandong, President, Peoples Republic of China
   Captain Zhang Bo, Captain, Peoples Liberation Army - Navy, Long March 15
   Captain Wu, Captain, Peoples Liberation Army - Navy, Long March 11

Ukraine
   Petr "the Fox" Mazur, Mercenary employed by the Blue Faction

Prologue

Eleven Months After the End of Take Whiteman
CBC News Report

As it had been for the entirety of the newscast, the face of the news anchor was sober. Her signature long black hair, cascading over one of her shoulders, contrasted starkly with the champagne-colored jacket she was wearing over a white blouse.

"And in the latest news out of the former United States, the Federation of American States has confirmed reports that its military has retreated from Pittsburgh.

"After two months of desperate, oftentimes brutal house-to-house fighting, the CBC has learned from several unnamed sources that the Blue Faction will make its next and perhaps final stand in Washington, D.C.

"With more from just east of Pittsburgh, we are joined by war correspondent Michael Devolin. Michael, what is the latest there on the ground?"

"Good morning, Grace." Wearing a flak jacket with the word PRESS stenciled on the front, the square-jawed male reporter stared into the camera and eagerly responded to the anchor's first question.

"The scene here in the City of Bridges is one of utter desperation. Reports are that two enclaves of Blue forces in the south and east of the city simultaneously fell late yesterday and that the sieging Red Faction forces have been ruthless in finishing off those defenders who for whatever reason did not flee the city.

"You will recall that last week the general leading the attacking UCSA forces had called publicly for the remaining Blue units to retire from the city, or else. As we are hearing now, the Red Faction is making good on the 'or else' part of that statement."

The female news anchor dominated the half-screen she occupied with a gravitas earned from her own time as a war correspondent and the streaks of gray she had allowed to frame in her face. "What are you hearing, Michael?"

"Grace, details are coming in dribs and drabs, but what we're hearing is appalling. As has been their practice throughout the war, the Red military has tried to suppress any information that might suggest their forces are acting outside the Geneva Conventions, but Pittsburgh is not yet locked down and we now have enough information to report that the Red Faction has once again engaged in a series of actions that could only be described as atrocities."

The news anchor nodded her head as though her colleague had just given her an update on the local weather.

"I understand you have some footage of these alleged crimes, Michael. Why don't you set that up for our viewers, and, as is our practice, we want to let them know the images they are about to see are unsettling in the extreme. If you have children in the room with you, you may wish to have them leave."

The correspondent nodded his head vigorously at the anchor's prompt. "That's right, Grace. Early this morning, we were provided with a four-minute video shot by a civilian who lives close to the area where the last of the Blue forces were positioned in the south of the city. I have been covering this war for nearly two years now, and I can tell you that what transpires on this video is as horrifying as anything I've seen. But, as much as it pains me to say it, it's also instructive."

The anchor's eyes narrowed. "Instructive. Really? Tell us more."

"Yes, quite instructive. As you'll see in the short clips we have selected for the broadcast, the Red military is at the height of its brutality. The actions of its soldiers are measured and deliberate. If you watch the video in its entirety, and I have several times, you will not see any kind of hesitation. In my opinion, the unit you are about to see has done this kind of thing before."

The newscast transitioned away from the split screen of the two reporters and became the single image of what looked to be the parking lot of a big box store. Charred and askew vehicles and debris littered the scene, but it was the group of people in matching fatigues that drew the viewer's eye.

They were gathered in what appeared to be ragged rows immediately in front of the store's entrance. To the right and left of the soldiers, concrete highway barriers worked to hem in the POWs.

"What are we seeing, Michael?"

"Grace, the information we've received indicates these are Blue Faction prisoners of war who have been captured or who have surrendered. In all, there are some two hundred men and women. As you can see quite clearly in the video, those that are unable to stand because of their injuries are laid down in the rows."

The person taking the video zoomed in on a man striding at the head of the gathered soldiers. Reaching the formation's far left end, the man turned as though he himself was on parade and began to walk in the other direction. The man's face exposed, he appeared to be yelling something in the direction of the captured soldiers.

While the man's walk continued, a still picture leaped into the top right of the news report. The image was of a mild-looking, middle-aged man wearing the standard field uniform of the UCSA military. On his chest, the viewers could make out the name "Lester."

"Grace, we've done some enhanced image work, and we can confirm the man that appears to be overseeing this operation is none other than Colonel Noah Lester."

"The Butcher of Cincinnati?" Whether for gratuitous effect or due to genuine surprise, the tone of the news anchor's voice was some combination of alarm and outrage.

"None other, Grace. And I can tell you in what follows, this man's grim moniker is well-earned. Again, the video we are about to show is graphic. We take no pleasure in airing it, but we owe it to our viewers to show them how barbarous this conflict has become."

"Thank you for the advisory, Michael, but remind us what is instructive about the video you are about to play?"

"Quite simply, Grace, this is the enemy Canada will face should it and CANZUK choose to intervene in this war. If Canada enters this conflict, as has been rumored, the soldiers you now see on the screen could one day soon be Canadian soldiers. And as you'll see in a moment, the UCSA is as ruthless as any government in the history of war. This is what Ottawa and its allies need to take stock of."

"Instructive indeed," the graying anchor said.

As the video started to play, the shot panned out once again showing the full gathering of Blue Faction prisoners. As the notorious American army officer began to walk away from the gathering of captured soldiers, a pair of armored vehicles rolled into the picture.

Without warning, the scene on the video lit up brightly in an orchestra of yellow and orange as streams of liquid fire began to eject from the turrets of the vehicles, saturating the collection of penned-in soldiers.

As the burning napalm began to consume the now-frenetic POWs, Red Faction soldiers marched forward from all sides of the square and began to shoot any Blue Faction soldier that managed to flee the inferno by running forward or attempting to leap over the concrete barriers.

Struck down by bullets, these few men or women were the lucky ones. Those caught in the hellish flames immediately collapsed, turning into writhing heaps of burning flesh.

The image of the carnage suddenly disappeared and was replaced by the split screen of the pair of newscasters. A look of shock marred the female anchor's face.

With no question or prompt, finally, the war correspondent spoke to break the silence. "This is humanity at its worst, Grace. If anyone thought the United States could find a negotiated outcome to end this terrible war, this is proof positive such an outcome is all but impossible. Madness has taken over this country.

"And it is this madness that Prime Minister Martel and the prime ministers of CANZUK are wrestling with as they contemplate involvement in this conflict. Whatever they decide, they and the people of the four countries that make up the alliance should understand the degree of awesome violence that awaits anyone or any country that decides to step into this conflict. Intervention, should it come to that, will not be pretty."

Recovered from the spell of horror that had been set upon her, the news anchor was once again projecting her usual professional self. "A sobering analysis, Michael. Thank you for this report and keep yourself safe.

"Now let's move on to developments in the South China Sea, where earlier today there was a collision of Australian and Chinese naval vessels."

Chapter 1

Paris

"Monsieur Besson, it remains the case that your son is hospitalized?"

"It does, Minister," replied Pierre Besson, the Director of France's foreign intelligence service, the Direction Générale de la Sécurité Extérieure, DGSE.

"And how does he fare?"

"It is a most peculiar thing, Minister. As you know, he is a young man of vigor and until this moment, he was a picture of health. Then, four days ago, he came down with what we thought was a case of the flu.

"On a whim, my wife had gone to visit his apartment and found him nearly comatose. After interrogating and then berating his roommate for doing nothing, she called an ambulance and had him brought straight to the University Hospitals Pitié Salpêtrière."

"Mon dieu!" the politician exclaimed, his face exhibiting a rare touch of emotion. "I had no idea he was that ill. What is his prognosis?"

"I appreciate your concern, Minister. Thanks to God and the intuition of my wife, the boy will survive. When he arrived, the doctors weren't so sure."

"I'm glad to hear it," offered France's Minister of the Interior. Childless himself, Pascal Charron nevertheless maintained a special place in his heart for the children of old-stock families that were doing their part to produce the next generation of Frenchmen. And Pierre Besson, a father of four stunning children, had more than done his share.

"And what made him so ill, my friend?" asked Charron. "I take it this wasn't a case of the flu. I recall your son quite well. He's a tower like you. Strong and a hell of a rugby player if my memory is correct. Boys like that don't get that sick unless it's something serious. I trust you informed the doctors of your profession and of who you are. We wouldn't want them treating your son as though he were some common riff-raff.

"You know as well as I, the hospitals in this country are a disaster. Every damn foreigner and their six kids that get a sniffle find their way into an emergency room, making it next to impossible for the good people of France to get the care they deserve."

As Charron's assessment of the French health care system left his mouth, Besson cracked his knuckles, working over his hand with the worry he felt for his son.

"After two days of not getting answers that would satisfy my wife, I did as you just suggested, and put a call into the chief administrator of the hospital, one Dr. Akerman."

"Ahh... Akerman. I know this man," Charron said, interrupting the intelligence officer. "A Jew and a most capable administrator. I trust he understood?"

"He did, Minister. After the conversation, things changed immediately."

"So you know what's wrong with him?"

"Not yet. I just heard from my wife. We have a meeting this afternoon. Apparently, there are results they'd like to discuss with us in person."

One of Charron's delicate hands came up to his mouth, and a single finger pressed against the thin and very French mustache that covered his upper lip. "And they told you nothing? No hints?"

"All they told my wife is that Gabriel's health would continue to improve and that we were both to attend the meeting this afternoon."

"Most peculiar, Monsieur Besson. In light of these events, I wonder if we shouldn't increase your security detail? Perhaps it should be extended to the whole of your beautiful family?"

"Not that I want to jump to any conclusions, but, in consideration of your role, perhaps a few extra people might be prudent. I take it you've advised your equivalent in the GDIS?"

Besson gave the Interior Minister, the second most powerful politician in France, a sheepish look. "I have not, Minister. Gabriel has been improving and the absence of results doesn't necessarily mean anything nefarious has transpired. It just means they haven't done the right test as yet. We'll know more this afternoon, and if something of concern is brought forward, I'll reach out to Madame Serrurier straightaway."

Charron smiled. "The last I checked, Monsieur Besson, I was this country's Minister for the Interior, and the Direction Générale de la Sécurité Intérieure reported to me. Despite the clashes between your two agencies, I know Madame Serrurier as a highly competent woman. You wouldn't know it by her conduct in the halls of government, but she's a mother of three, and, when it comes to children, I can assure you, the woman does have a heart."

Besson reciprocated the politician's smile. "While I appreciate the confirmation that the blood in Madame Serrurier's veins is in fact warm, I would respectfully ask that her agency not become involved. At least not until we have some indication that something untoward has happened to my son."

Charron pressed his lips together and nodded his head in agreement. "Of course. Of course. It shall be as you asked, my friend. You know better than I how to assess for risk. As always, I trust your judgment. It is unmatched among those who are doing the work that needs to be done to keep our country safe and on its current path."

"Thank you, Minister. Your interest as it concerns my family is touching. Should there be any developments with my son, rest assured the right people will be informed, including Madame Serrurier."

Charron nodded his head again and moved his hand in the direction of the saucer of coffee in front of him. Besson duplicated the action, and together, the two men, short and tall, enjoyed the blessing that was French coffee.

"I know it shall be as you say, so let us not discuss the matter any further. Instead, tell me of the latest from North America. How is it that our interests fare? I saw the news out of Pittsburgh. 'Ghastly' isn't strong enough a word to describe the most recent video that's making the rounds. This Spector fellow and his people - their savagery truly has no limits."

Paris, University Hospitals Pitié Salpêtrière

"*Bon soir*, my friends! I trust everyone is doing well. I am your duty nurse for this evening. Gabriel, you are looking better than ever. Rumor has it you will be leaving us tomorrow?" the nurse said cheerily.

The gaunt, but still exceedingly handsome young man beamed a warm smile in the direction of the nurse. "It's true. I'll miss you and your colleagues, Mademoiselle Leon, but I can't say I won't be glad to sleep in my own bed, even if it is in my parents' home instead of my flat."

"Well, that is good. Having now spent some time with your mother, I have all the confidence in the world that you'll be in the most capable hands." As the nurse said the words, she glanced in the direction of her patient's mother.

"Yes, he will be in capable hands, and hands that will not let him go for some time, I should say," the middle-aged woman said from across the room.

"Ah, mama, I'm not a baby. And I need to finish the semester. I've missed too much coursework already. I'm fine. The commute from our house to campus will be brutal. It's just not on. I'm twenty-one, *mon dieu*." As the words came out of the young Frenchman's mouth, they were firm and held a genuine tone of protest.

A new voice joined the conversation. "You will do what your mother says, and that is final, young man."

All heads in the room turned to the entrance to see the tall frame of the patient's equally handsome father. The younger nursing staff had enjoyed Gabriel's classic Mediterranean looks and subtle charm, while the older nurses had positively swooned over Besson, the senior.

It did not help in the least that the man was constantly trailed by a pair of dangerous-looking men who were obviously bodyguards. That no one knew the senior Besson's profession created a mystery and this mystery only added to the man's allure.

It was only the older man's wedding ring that had held the veteran nurses at bay, but even then, when the man was present, it was obvious, to the point of silliness, how much the level of care Besson the younger received improved when word got out Monsieur Besson was in the building.

"Ah, Monsieur Besson. Welcome to you. We haven't seen you for the past few days. You have been missed." As the nurse said the words, Madame Besson executed an exaggerated eye roll behind the nurse's back. No fool, and knowing her husband as only a wife could after twenty-five years of marriage, she had watched the cavalcade of nurses 'check in' on her son when her husband was present with equal parts amusement and pride.

"Nurse Lapierre, a good evening to you. It's been busy at work, and with my wife here, and with the likes of you and your colleagues, I knew Gabriel was in the very best hands."

Before the nurse could began to fawn at the compliment, the room was filled with the distinct sound of crackling electricity and distressed grunts from just outside in the hallway.

Instantly, Besson's demeanor changed. The veteran intelligence officer's posture tightened and in a quick movement, he placed himself between his son and wife, set his eyes on the door to the room, and reached one of his hands to the small of his back.

As every pair of eyes in the room turned to the entrance, a nurse with light brown hair and hospital green scrubs pushed a man in a wheelchair into the room too quickly. As the wheelchair came to a stop, the seated patient pulled back the blanket covering him from the waist down and fairly bounced to his feet.

Erect, the stern-looking man was holding a black matte handgun with a suppressor fixed to its barrel. The weapon was aimed squarely at Besson's chest.

For a long moment, the room was perfectly silent. Slowly, Besson removed his hand from the small of his back.

"A wise choice, Monsieur Besson." It was the nurse, who spoke French with the hint of an accent that suggested she was from the south of the country.

She walked forward into the room and stood a rectangular object of about eight inches in length on the narrow medication table at the end of the younger Besson's bed.

"Everyone, listen carefully," said the nurse. "This item does two things. First, it allows me to hear and see what is going on in this room. Second, when and if I want it to, it will fill this room with an agent that will severely affect your neurological systems, making you all but inert. In all but a few cases, the effects of this gas are short-term. In those cases where there have been long-term effects, my understanding is that they are stroke-like, but that that they can resolve themselves in a year or two."

The woman, who appeared to be in her twenties, narrowed her intense hazel eyes on the Director of France's external intelligence service. "You will be coming with us, Monsieur Besson." Gesturing to the wheelchair, she added, "Please, have a seat, won't you?"

Besson raised his chin into the air defiantly. "Go to hell. I'm not going anywhere."

The faux nurse tilted her head in the direction of her collaborator and said, "Do it."

The man quickly shifted his weapon in the direction of the nurse who had been doting on Besson's son and fired a round into the upper thigh. In the confines of the small room, the weapon's discharge was surprisingly quiet.

Struck, the nurse yelped and fell onto her bottom but apparently had the sense not to scream. Seeing the blood begin to pump out of her leg, the woman moved to put pressure on the wound, groaning in pain as she did so.

"I won't ask again, Monsieur Besson. The sooner you come with us, the sooner she can get help, and the safer your family will be."

When Besson said nothing, the fake nurse turned her head in the direction of her collaborator and said coolly, "The other leg, if you would."

This time, the man with the pistol took two steps in the direction of the wounded nurse, and, with a single hand, leveled the weapon in the direction of the nurse's other leg.

"Pierre!" Besson's wife said urgently.

Besson did not look in his wife's direction. Instead, he delivered a hard stare in the direction of the woman who had been giving the orders. "Enough. I will come with you, but know that you will not get away with this. In fact, you'll be lucky to get out of Paris. Whoever you are, you and everyone you care about will pay for this. France does not forget its enemies."

The woman's head tilted slightly as she seemed to consider Besson's assessment, and then she said, "Perhaps. But in this moment, you are coming with us and, from this point forward, it is imperative that you keep that handsome mouth of yours shut."

The nurse pivoted and again gestured toward the wheelchair. "Sit down, Monsieur Besson. Now!"

In three huge strides, Besson had placed himself in front of the wheelchair. With one final glare at the nurse, he lowered his tall frame into the waiting seat.

Once Besson's backside had made contact with the seat, the man with the pistol retreated from the wounded nurse and in a fluid motion made his weapon disappear underneath the hospital gown he was wearing. Getting behind the wheelchair, the man immediately began to turn Besson around to leave the room.

"Wait!" The voice came from Besson's wife. "Will we see him again?"

Still taking in the occupants of the room, the fake nurse, focused a look on Madame Besson.

"Remember what I said about the black object. In five minutes, you can call for help. One second before, I release the substance, and the nurse bleeds out. Understand?"

Her lips thin and a look of anger now on full display, Madame Besson nodded her head to confirm she had indeed got the message.

Taking her eyes off Besson's wife, the agent turned back to her accomplice and the wheelchair. "Move."

The order given, Besson's wheelchair began to move toward the door. On reaching the room's threshold, he quickly glanced back over his shoulder to get what might be his last look at his family. For a second, his eyes connected with his wife's. In that brief moment, his heart lurched as he recognized the look of terror in her eyes. As she disappeared, Pierre Besson promised himself that he would survive what was about to happen to him and that the people responsible for doing this to him and his family, would pay. They would pay dearly.

Besson could see nothing through the fabric covering his head. Moments after leaving the hospital in the back of an ambulance, he had been drugged. Fastened to a gurney and unable to move, he had watched the nurse drive a needle into his neck. Within seconds, a cold blackness had overcome him.

Somewhere over the Atlantic Ocean

Awakening sometime later, Besson perceived he was on an airplane. His hands were bound, he was seated, and he was desperately thirsty.

"Water," he said with a voice that sounded as though his vocal cords had been worked over with sandpaper.

Suddenly, the hood was pulled from atop his head and his vision was assaulted by the lights of the cabin. Everything was a blur. Blinking his eyes rapidly, two blobs eventually resolved into people.

The first he recognized as the nurse. As before, her face offered no expression. As he had noted then, she wasn't quite beautiful. As he did now with all young people he encountered, Besson gauged the young woman's looks through the prism that was his son. Had Gabriel brought her home, he would not have been unproud of him. Even seated, he could see the woman was a physical specimen. Black leggings showed muscled thighs while the top she was wearing showed sinewy arms that were the result of years of some kind of physical activity. She was a distance runner if he had to guess.

His eyes left the nurse to take up the man who was seated beside her. Easily twice the nurse's age, he had Mediterranean features like himself, and had one of the broadest chests he had ever seen. Besson wondered if the man did the bench press underneath a good-sized car.

The man offered him a warm smile, proffered a bottle of water, and then put it to Besson's lips. The moment the water made contact with his mouth, he gulped greedily.

On finishing the bottle, the thick man spoke in French. "Monsieur Besson, my name is Colonel Azim."

Though faint, Besson recognized the man's accent. "You're Quebecois. I knew CANZUK is being run by armatures but my capture goes beyond naïve to enter the realm of truly stupid."

His captor vigorously shook his head. "Let me correct you, Director. This was not a CANZUK operation. The British no hand in your capture. In fact, they're clueless about the events that just transpired. No, this mission was solely executed by the Canadian government. You will be our guest for several months, at least."

A sneer appeared on Besson's face. "Is that what I am, a *guest*? Allow me to bring you up to speed, Colonel. With my capture, you and your country have entered into a world you know very little about. France will not be kind to Canada once the Red Faction wins the war. And what you have done on this day will only make it worse."

When large man offered no reply, Besson continued injecting heat into his words. "And I might add that someday sooner than you might think, the people I work for will find you Colonel – you and everyone associated with my capture, and in your own country, you'll be hunted down like animals. And when it is you who is sitting across from me, I promise you will regret what you have done on this day."

Still silent, the Canadian shifted his bulk in his seat all the while his dark eyes continued to stare at Besson. The man appeared to be giving careful consideration to his next words.

Finally, when Azim spoke it was with a business-like tone. "Monsieur Besson, I had hoped the heat of operation that brought you into our care would have dissipated and you would have been in a more amenable state for our first conversation but I see this hope was misplaced.

"Indeed, the future that you speak of Director may come to pass, but I am not a man of the future. I cannot control or foresee what might happen six months from now. My actions can only impact the present. Right here. Right now."

Besson delivered a terrible smile in the direction of Azim. "You have no idea how badly you've cocked this up. It escapes you. I can see it your eyes. You may not believe it, Colonel, but a part of me actually feels sorry for you."

Azim shuffled forward in his seat, so he was within reach of tall Frenchman. As the Canadian next spoke, the knuckles on both his meaty hands cracked as he clenched them. "Your name full name is Pascale Phillip Besson. You are married and have been for twenty-seven years. Five years ago, you took up a mistress who is twenty-two years younger than you. Though a whore, she's is a delightfully pretty thing, and as a credit to your vocation, you've done a much better job of keeping her a secret from your wife than you have from us.

"I also know that in the years 2018 to 2021, you ran a kill team for Action Group Seven and under your leadership, you and your associates killed and tortured no less than fifteen men and women in Syria, Chad, and of all places, Flint, Michigan.

"But all of that doesn't matter to my government as much as the following Director Besson. Eleven months ago, we know that it was you or someone who works for you who passed along information to the UCSA about our operation in Missouri. And it was this information that led to the death of no less than 234 Canadian soldiers.

"But that fact unto itself is not why you are sitting across from me."

After a long pause, Azim released his clenched hands and continued. "You know all too well why you're in this situation, Director."

With as much disdain as he could muster, Besson said, "Are you asking me a question, Colonel? Because if you are, I don't have a fucking clue what you're talking about."

Azim moved like lightning.

His hands bound, Besson's was no physical match for the gorilla of a man that was now mauling him. Countless blows from softball-sized fists rained down on his face and body. Then, a well-executed slap landed dead center on his left ear causing his vision to blur. As a torrent of outrage flowed through his body, he couldn't recall the last time he had experienced this this kind of pain. Certainly, Besson had never experienced the degree of humiliation he was now enduring.

And then the assault stopped.

Azim, enraged and animalistic seconds before, stood over him breathing hard but looking as though he had done nothing more than shaken Besson's hand. To the right of the colonel, the nurse had not moved. Her hazel eyes had an intense and approving look to them.

One of Azim's strong hands reached down and with an iron-like grip, he wrenched Besson's face away from the young woman. "Eyes front you son of bitch. She won't help you. Had we left it up to her, you would have had your brains blown out in front of your wife and son back in the hospital.

"As it is, you get to spend time in a quiet place where you are going to tell us about why and how you killed my country's prime minister and what France's plans are for the referendum. We know you have people in Quebec. That's why you're here. You and your government crossed a line, Director Besson. And you and the agency you lead keep crossing it. We've had enough."

With a mighty shove, Azim drove Besson's head back into his seat. Despite the humiliation coursing through him, Besson issued a venomous stare in the Canadian's direction but before his brain could recover and issue the threat he desperately wanted to deliver, the nurse, the covert agent, the assassin, whoever she was, was beside him. He felt the familiar prick of a needle being driven into his neck.

As a cold blackness began to overwhelm him, the young woman whispered in his ear, "Welcome to Canada, Director Besson. I hope you enjoy your stay."

Chapter 2

Deep River, East of Canadian Force Base (CFB) Petawawa, West of Ottawa

Colonel Jackson Larocque sat at the kitchen table drinking his second coffee, as was his routine. Most of the windows of his modest home were open allowing him to listen to the morning's brouhaha that was the local birds. He loved the sound as much or more as seeing the birds feed from the various feeders he had strategically positioned around the house. His wife, who he had just heard rustling upstairs, was less enamored with the daily symphony.

As was their way, he got out of bed much earlier than her. Already, he had been for his third and final seven-kilometer run of the week and had spent another hour stretching and working the heavy bag he kept in their garage.

It had not always been like this. Madison Larocque too had been an early riser, but in her present condition, at least on weekends, she needed the extra time asleep to recharge.

He could hear her walking down the hallway. Larocque's eyes went to the kitchen's entrance. As his wife of nearly two decades breached the doorway, her hands were on her belly. She had a look of concentration on her face. Finally, her face lit up with a smile that suggested she was delighted with some secret development. "Whoa! He's bucking like a little cowboy," she said.

Looking at the woman with an arched eyebrow, he asked, "Good morning, my love. You slept well?"

Still smiling, Madison Larocque offered no reply. Instead, she moved across the kitchen whereupon reaching her husband, she gestured for him to give her one of his hands.

Complying, she gently slid his hand into her housecoat and guided it to the right of her navel. Larocque felt the movement right away.

"And you haven't even had your coffee yet. He's gonna be a handful this little man," he said.

His wife's face shifted from a rare look of benevolence to one of patented annoyance. "Oh, he's got energy all right. And don't think for one minute you get out of trying to wrangle him when he gets here, old man. Do you know that by the time he goes off to university, you'll be sixty-two?"

"As old as Moses," Larocque quipped.

"And I'll be fifty-eight. If you're Moses, who am I?"

"You, my love, will still be a hot piece of ass. Older, yes, but still smoking hot."

Madison scoffed and yanked his hand from her stomach. "Jesus, Jack, I hope you don't talk like that around your men. Careers have been ruined for much less. And don't think your connection with Merielle will protect you. Neither she nor your medals will save you if you go around objectifying women the way you do me."

"To be clear, my dear, I keep things on the up and up at work. At least when it comes to things like the big three. To do otherwise is to call down the EDI Gestapo."

"Is that what they call it now – the big three?"

Larocque nodded his head. "Race, Gender, Sexual Orientation. They are the big three, and they are supreme. With everything else, there's still some leeway. Transgress one of the big three, though, and you're right, not even the most powerful politician in the land could save me."

Madison's face darkened and then said, "Let's not talk about Ottawa and the snakes who live there. It turns out, your 'piece of ass' is in a rare good mood this morning. Did you get an update on that meeting you mentioned last night? When do you have to be at work?"

The question posed, she stepped into Larocque's immediate orbit and opened her housecoat. Fabric pulled back, Madison Larocque was naked.

A look of adoration lit up Larocque's face. "Word came in about an hour ago. There's a call with the brass from SOFCOM at 1100 hours. Details are sketchy, but there is some kind of development out of the US that is to be discussed. It's an all-hands meeting, or so I'm told."

She smiled down at him and offered a look Larocque instantly recognized. "So, you have time for your wife, then?"

Larocque firmly pulled her in closer to him with his left hand while his right reached upwards to cup one of her breasts.

"I believe we do have time, my love. More than enough, in fact."

Washington, D.C.

Valeria Menendez cast an exasperated look at the generals sitting across from her. Only one brown face, she thought, for what had to be the millionth time.

It had been just one of many problems she had been trying to solve since becoming president. Unfortunately, the military had been more intractable than the other institutions she had targeted in her tumultuous time as President of the United States and now the Federation of American States, the FAS.

As costly as it had been, the one thing you could say about the war is that it accelerated change.

To her own credit, almost every facet of American life had changed radically in the past six years. Guns outlawed. Check. Abortions on demand until birth. Check. Safe speech. Check. Slavery reparations. Check. Meaningful affirmative action programs.

Except for the white men in military uniforms now bloviating in front of her - check.

She had had enough. As was her way, her hand slowly rose into the air. As the red nails on her hand reached their apex, the general who had been making excuses for yet another lost battle paused his overview and allowed his voice to trail off.

While everyone's eyes in the room turned toward her, her dark eyes framed in on the five-star general sitting immediately across from her. He was a distinguished-looking man, but that might have been the end of his qualities. Her advisers had told her he was her most competent general, but since handing the man this war, he had done nothing but lose. And now the enemy was at the gates. Literally.

As she had discussed the matter with her inner circle, there had never been a doubt as to the angle that would be used to replace General Sullivan. Though he remained well-regarded in the military and across Washington, not even he would be able to resist what was to come. He wouldn't, because no one had.

General Sullivan's dead-looking, pale blue eyes were the last to meet hers.

"Madam President, you have a question?"

"General Sullivan, I appreciate General Smith's overview of our most recent failure, but I feel compelled to interject."

"Madam President, you may interject whenever and however you would like. What is it you would like to discuss?"

Menendez pushed her chair back from the boardroom table and slowly got to her feet. Tall for a woman, and in heels, she was now towering over the man she was about to fire.

"As General Smith has been explaining in detail for the past ten minutes, we are losing this war. That is inarguable. And as things go from bad to worse, it does so on the backs of the POC soldier. For every white soldier who dies, nearly three soldiers of color have died in the past two months. This was not acceptable when the war started and it's not acceptable now, General Sullivan."

"Madam President, as I've explained before, our ranks have swelled in recent months with refugees who've been fleeing the UCSA drive north. We've also heavily recruited from those encamped along the US-Canadian border. These camps are heavily populated by folks from minority communities. As I've said before, it's a question of simple math. The demographics of the FAS have shifted dramatically in the time our country has been at war."

As one of Menendez's eyebrows arched upwards, her hands uncrossed from underneath her breasts and fell onto her hips. "General, under your leadership, you have killed more black men in the past year than all of the police forces in America from the years of 1980 through to the past year. Six times as many in fact. The math might be simple, but it goes against everything my government stands for."

"Madam President -"

One of Menendez's hands flashed upwards. "Stop! I'm talking, General."

Doing as he was told, the man leading Blue Faction forces did not speak. Lifting his chin noticeably, General Sullivan proceeded to deliver what was most certainly a defiant stare back at his Commander-in-Chief.

Good, thought Menendez, the arrogant bastard knows what's coming. "General, let me remind you of the expectation we have discussed each and every time you have outlined this simple math to me. My government, which also means the military you lead, is living out the principle of equality. Equality is not a principle of convenience. It is not something I am prepared to shrug off at the expense of thousands of black and brown lives. This country and men like you, General, have been doing that for far too long."

"Madam President, I understand your concerns, but the numbers are the numbers," Sullivan interjected with his always calm voice. "We can't win this war by swelling the ranks of our logistics, mechanical and technical trades with untrained people. It takes months, if not years, to train a mechanic or pilot. After three weeks of training, we can field a capable infantry soldier. And that's what we need right now. We need people who can fire a rifle and as it happens, the people we have in numbers who can be trained easily are Persons of Color."

To the General's credit, the man had not taken the bait. Menendez had all but called him a racist. Sullivan might have an air of defiance about him but the man would not lose his cool and he definitely wouldn't explode, despite her charged insinuation. But Valeria Menendez had not become the first female and Latinx President of the United States and achieved the things she had because her opponents had acted as she had hoped. Change was hard, particularly when you were dealing with seasoned political operators, as General Sullivan most certainly was. But forcing change was her business.

"What have I said about principle, General? It is not something I am prepared to shrug off. Not for reasons of expediency or practicality. We have now had this conversation on two occasions, and you have twice thrown out this point of rifles instead of lug nuts. As before, I find the argument unsatisfying. More to the point, you have blatantly ignored my direction, and once again, as a man of privilege, you have made decisions to uphold the very system that brought war on this country in the first place. I abhor that system. Black and brown people are not expendable. Not under my leadership."

Menendez let the point stew for a moment, hoping that the politically astute man staring back at her would see the writing on the wall and fall on his sword. Instead, the man said nothing. He only stared back at her with those light-colored eyes that served to emphasize the racial supremacy she knew the man harbored deep within him as all white men did.

"General Sullivan, I no longer have confidence in your leadership to lead the war against the UCSA. Effective immediately, you are relieved of your command."

"Madam President, please. Now is not the time to sow division. We have a plan –"

Menendez's closed fist hammered down on the boardroom table. "'Sow division! Now is not the time? Please." Her voice was shrill. "Were we not just pushed out of Pittsburgh? How many died, exactly? Thirty-six thousand soldiers, never mind the civilian casualties. They're uncountable. If not now, when, General?"

Sullivan only stared back at his prosecutor.

"I take it no answer means you accept your resignation. Good enough for me.

"General, let me be clear. It is you and your callousness toward black and brown people that have created fissures in the military you claim to command. As I stand here and look at you, I can see the privilege oozing out of your pores and it makes me sick. You're dismissed. Get out of my sight. Now!"

Menendez's last word filled the room like the screech of tires.

Sullivan slowly rose out of his chair and to Menendez's relief, he made no effort to look down the table to catch the eyes of his fellow Chiefs of Staff. For the moment, he would go quietly. Just as she had predicted he would. Though respected by his peers, he was not beloved and there had been no indications Sullivan was interested in or able to duplicate the feat Mitchell Spector had achieved only eleven months ago when he had unexpectedly taken over the UCSA from Cameron Fitzgerald in a brutal and highly efficient coup.

Without a salute or one final look in Menendez's direction, Sullivan took up his Army service cap, placed it on his head, turned, and walked out of the White House's situation room.

After several long seconds, Menendez sat down, allowing her eyes to take up the man who had been giving the briefing. "General Smith, please continue. I'll announce a replacement for General Sullivan before the end of the day."

"Yes, Madam President."

Leaving the room and striding down the hallway toward the elevator that would bring him to the main floor of the West Wing, Sullivan's thoughts recounted a single conversation that he had with Vice President Andrew Morgan almost three months ago.

At the time, Morgan had only told him that no matter what happened he should remain loyal to the President and trust the process. When Sullivan had asked what the 'process' was, Morgan had only said it was best he did not know and that he should be patient and do his best to win the war.

He had known the Vice President for a long time. He had been in the last month of his second tour in Iraq when their deployments had overlapped. He had been commanding an infantry battalion on its way out of the wretched country, while Morgan had been coming in as the commanding officer of a platoon in SEAL Team 5.

In one of those great mysteries of life, the two of them had hit it off as though they were old college friends. In the years that followed, they had managed to stay in touch with the relationship culminating in both men being invited to their respective daughters' weddings. So when Morgan had advised Sullivan to be patient, he was prepared to do just that.

An hour later, back in his office, he hit send on his formal resignation letter to Valeria Menendez. Getting up from his seat, he walked to the door and left the office that had been his for all of America's second civil war.

It was just an office, and now, it was no longer his. His staff would box up his things and have them dropped off at his home.

And it was at home that he would wait. He would wait and see whatever process his friend and the Vice President of the Federation of American States would undertake to turn whatever was left of the country he loved away from the bloody cataclysm it was now racing toward.

Chapter 3

Undisclosed Location, North Carolina

Mitchell Spector held up the glass of Kentucky bourbon, swirled it around, and with an appropriate amount of deference, slowly brought the rock glass to his lips to take his first sip of the amber liquid.

As bourbon saturated his palette and did its good work, Spector exhaled with satisfaction. "It's as though Jesus Christ himself distilled this stuff. Goddamned magic is what it is."

"Mr. President, I would not be doing my job if I didn't remind you that putting Jesus Christ and the word 'magic' in the same statement is not something that's going to endear you to those of your supporters who are ardent practitioners of the Christian faith."

Spector raised an eyebrow and gave a hard look in the direction of the well-dressed man sitting across the room from him. In turn, the younger man reciprocated Spector's gaze with a look as uncaring as Spector's was hard. "Get bent, Peter. I've earned this, and I've earned the right to blasphemize however I see fit.

"Today was a big day for us. Pittsburgh falls and we no longer have to deal with Sullivan. It's like that woke shrew wants to lose."

This time it was Parr's turn to raise an eyebrow. "'Woke shrew'? Really. Perhaps we should go forward with that plan to tattoo 'magnanimous' and 'measured' on the back of both of your hands?"

Upon assuming the presidency of the United Constitutional States of America one of Spector's first orders of business had been to find someone that could help him navigate his new role and to better communicate with the people that were interested in what Spector was selling. Peter Parr had been that man.

Good looking to the point it was obvious to even the heterosexual men he encountered Parr had climbed his way up the corporate ladder of mainstream media meteorically. A journalist by trade, his skillset was better suited to the machinations of the boardroom, where in five short years before the war, he had radically turned around the fortunes of the nighttime lineup of one country's larger news corporations.

It was when Parr had agreed to Spector's offer to come to work for him that Spector fully accepted he could pull off his grand vision for a reconstituted and whole United States of America.

People shortchanged Parr because of his looks, but Spector had seen past these shallow or envious critiques. The man was incisive and hugely capable, but more important, he had been a winner his entire life. The bottom line was that a person like Parr would not have attached himself to Spector unless there was a better-than-good chance the Texan could win the terrible war they were fighting and reunite the country.

"Listen," Spector said after taking another slug of the bourbon. "You were in the same briefing I was. She fired her best general because he wasn't killing enough white people. That's what the briefing said. That's who we're dealing with. She and her acolytes caused this war with their crazed policies and for the life of me, I can't understand why half the country has stood behind her as long as they have."

"You know exactly why they continue to stand behind her, Mr. President. What happened in Pittsburgh has made my work more difficult." As Parr delivered his assessment of the Colonel Lester video, he levelled a hard stare in Spector's direction.

This is what Spector liked that about the man. Unlike most of the sniveling rats that were 'crisis communications' people, Parr had a backbone and only backed down from a debate when he felt he had done all he could to be heard.

"Horseshit," Spector snapped back at the man who had become his Chief of Staff ten months ago. "I told you I'm not going to discuss it anymore. You may not like Lester and his little fireworks display, but that's the war we've been fighting for the past three years, Pete. You're just late to the party. And let me remind you that only one month earlier, the Blues shot no less than forty-three of our people who made the mistake of taking a left instead of a right."

A grimace emerged on Parr's face as he recalled the images of the hacked-apart bodies that had been hung from a number of Pittsburgh's many bridges.

"No, my well-dressed friend, there will be no magnanimity. Not a pinch of it.

"We're going to win this war and when we do, I plan to stand over the shoulder of the man I direct to put a bullet in the back of Menendez's skull. And she won't be the only one. Everything I told you before you took this job will happen. This wokeness that still infects our country is a cancer and I won't rest until it's been cut out. Men like Lester have more work to do before this country can be whole again."

"And what does that make me? Your Heinrich Himmler?"

Spector guffawed loudly. "You'll be no more Himmler than I'll be the Fuhrer. To be sure, people will have to die but it will only be a few thousand. The D.C. elites, Ivy League academics, and a few thousand of the Blue's most radicalized 'influencers.'"

Spector almost spat out the name of this last group of operators. Of the three groups, he placed the most blame on the journos and TikTokers who had dominated and set the political discourse in the years leading into the civil war.

"The political and intellectual elites and their shills on social media will have to go, Pete. Those who don't leave the country will be found and taken off the board. The practice is as old as war itself but more important, it's effective. The United States needs a clean slate and I plan to give us just that."

"Mr. President, to be perfectly frank with you, I'm not disagreeing with the course of action you're suggesting. From what I've seen in the time I've been with you, I'm more convinced than ever that something like it is necessary. But what you might want to give thought to is getting more subtle than this last massacre by that Rottweiler of yours. Colonel Lester and his methods are not doing us any favors."

Spector gave Parr an annoyed look and then lifted the bourbon to his mouth in a quick motion and poured the rest of the liquid down his throat. Without warning, he lifted his heavy frame out of the chair he'd been sitting in.

"Hear me clearly, Pete. Menendez and her ilk have had twenty years to brainwash the 110 million people that inhabit the FAS. When we reunite this country, those people are going to need someone to remind them of the values that once made the United States the greatest country in the world."

Standing over Parr, Spector's huge mitt of a hand extended its index finger in the direction of his Chief of Staff.

"You, Mr. Parr – you and your many talents – are going to make America great again in those parts of the country that have been infected. Every city, every town, and every person. Call it propaganda, reprogramming, call it whatever you goddamned well like, but when it is all said and done, America's soul will be cleansed of the woke bullshit that has led us to ruin. And when we're done cauterizing every part of this country that needs it, we'll turn our attention to our neighbors to the north."

"You mean Canada, Mr. President. Is that wise? I feel as though we might have enough on our plate with the reconstitution."

Spector dropped his stabbing finger and set his hands on his hips, bringing attention to his gut in the process.

"Is it wise? No, I don't expect it is, but I haven't forgotten about them and what they did to us. And if that wasn't enough, many of

Menendez's people will go there, thinking they'll be out of reach. They'll think we're some kind of Gilead, and that we'll be fine to have this northern refuge where people can continue this war if only covertly and through social media. I'm telling you right now, Pete, that's goddamned fantasy. We won't be Gilead, and there won't be any place on this continent where Menendez and her ilk can hide."

As he finished his pronouncement, Spector's face was flushed, once again reminding Parr his boss was as much about emotion as he was calculation.

Letting out a deep breath, the huge Texan added, "I haven't forgotten about what they did to us in Missouri. Those pissants to the north have made everything harder for us, and, for that, Canada and the rest of that chicken shit alliance they belong to are going to pay, and pay dearly whether it's the right play or not. Mark my words Pete, we're going to teach the Canadians a lesson they won't forget, not for a thousand years."

Ottawa, Parliament Hill

Marielle Martel sat in her office on the second floor of Parliament Hill. It had been months since she had last sat alone in this space and had the time to marvel at the fact that she had become Canada's Prime Minister.

Exactly one month after the death of her mentor and predecessor, she had surprised her political opponents – those in her party and those not – by calling a snap election.

In her mind, she needed a mandate. She couldn't battle Eric Labelle and the separatist movement in Quebec and navigate a response to the growing disaster that was the American civil war without winning an election that solidified her role and her power.

The election had also served as a referendum on her party's decision to undertake the Whiteman operation. The effort to prevent the American Reds from gaining a new nuclear arsenal had been controversial, to say the least.

The idea that Canada would send troops south of the border and involve itself in the American civil war went against centuries of Canadian foreign policy practice, but that is what her Conservatives had done with their allies from Australia, New Zealand, and the United Kingdom.

In the end, Canadians from every part of the country lined up to support her. With the nuclear weapons from Missouri safely in the hands of the Colorado Neutral Faction and with the neo-FLQ exposed, her leadership and her proposed program became a political juggernaut that resulted in her securing the largest Conservative majority government since the first coming of Mulroney in '84.

But that had been seven months ago. With all that was going on in the world and in her own country, seven months might well have been seven years.

She hadn't realized she had placed her fingertips to her temples in a failed effort to relieve her most recent tension headache when she heard a soft knock at her door. Looking in the direction of the entrance, she took in her executive assistant and the look of concern on her face.

"You know, it's okay if we cancel a meeting or two," the woman said in the kind tone she reserved only for Merielle. "You are the PM after all."

"Not this meeting, Monique, but thanks. But there is an 8 am meeting this Friday that I'd like you to reschedule. I need to go for a long run and was hoping to do that in the Gatineaus. I'll need that time to make it happen."

"Consider it done. Are you ready for the next motley crew?"

Merielle smiled. Despite her headache, she had been keen on having this particular meeting. Late last night, she had been given a heads up that this next briefing would reveal a new and important development out of the US. "Send them in, Monique. I'm as ready as I'll ever be. For today, anyway."

Thirty seconds later, her closest advisors on security matters had arranged themselves around the small coffee table that was the centerpiece of the sitting area in her office. For reasons of efficiency and security, it was a small group made up of only six people, including herself. It made the meeting space tight, but because each person sitting around the table was well-practiced in the philosophy of 'just get it done', no one wasted any time suggesting that they should meet somewhere else.

Merielle offered a smile to the first person to enter the office. "Stephane, it's been a while. I missed you at our last session. Hockey again, was it?"

A grimace passed across Merielle's ex-husband's face. "You know the cat died, Mer. It was a disaster. I didn't know little boys could cry so much. They would go weeks without giving that animal so much as a glance, and then the next-door neighbor backs over Mr. T and it's the end of the world."

"I hate cats," Merielle said, with a look of delight on her face. "I told you not to bring one home and you did and look what you got for it. That thing was thankless and evil. It got what it deserved, not that you've asked me."

"Jesus, Merielle, I hope you don't let the public see this side of you," her former husband replied.

Merielle winked at the man. "Only this group gets to see the real me, Stephane. So as long as you don't leak to the press how delighted I am about your poor Mr. T being crushed to death, this won't be the issue that sinks my boat in the next election. Dead cat aside, I am glad to see you back at our little table."

Stephane Martel, now the PM's Special Advisor on National Security, reciprocated the friendly smile on his ex-wife's face. "Glad to be back, Madame Prime Minister. Shall we get on with the official business of today's meeting, or should we re-hash some more of my recent domestic bliss?"

"No more re-hashing. Send the boys and Anik my love," Merielle said while moving her brown eyes to take up the rest of the group. "I've caught the reports that Sullivan is out as the Blues' Chairman of the Joint Chiefs. I'm assuming that's at least part of why we've come together?"

"It is, Madame Prime Minister," said the Director of the Canadian Security Intelligence Service – CSIS. "For some months now, we've been having conversations with an individual in the Menendez Cabinet who is unhappy with how the FAS President has been conducting the war. We heard from that same person in the hours after the Sullivan resignation. He wants us to help him remove Menendez."

In what was her classic expression of annoyance, Merielle's lips pursed. "Interesting. And why am I only hearing now that your agency has been talking with someone from the Menendez Cabinet, Director?"

"Need to know, Madame Prime Minister," was the reply delivered without hesitation. In his fifth year as the agency head of Canada's combined domestic and foreign intelligence service, James Plamondon had demonstrated himself to be an entirely competent manager, who, when the circumstances warranted, was a problem solver that also had an imagination.

"And now I need to know?" On delivering the question, Merielle made a Herculean effort to keep her annoyance with CSIS out of her voice.

"We think so, Madame Prime Minister."

"Then please continue, Director."

The balding man passed over a document to Merielle. "Here's the full briefing, but the skinny is as follows. As soon as the war restarted, one of our Foreign Intelligence Officers – FIOs – was approached by an intermediary of Vice President Morgan asking for a meeting. Being skeptical at first, it took us the better part of a month to make the arrangements to connect with the VP directly. As soon as we were sure it was legit, Stephane and I met with him via a quantum feed."

Merielle lifted a finger. "Wait, I thought the Blues didn't have hardware for quantum comms?"

"They don't. We sent a team south with the needed unit. With all the compromises across the IT comms industry, it's the only way we were prepared to talk to him. It's allowed us to have a number of conversations with him since."

"Okay, so what does the Vice President want?"

"To cut to the chase, Madame Prime Minister, he wants us to help him invoke the 25th Amendment."

Merielle's face scrunched as she accessed that part of her brain that had allowed her to be half-decent at trivia in a previous life.

"The 25th Amendment, eh? That's ringing a bell." She snapped her fingers. "Got it! They wanted to use it to get rid of Trump back in the day."

"That's correct, Madame Prime Minister," the CSIS Director confirmed. "It's that part of the US constitution that allows the federal cabinet to set aside the president through a unanimous vote. Legal scholars will tell you that it was designed to deal with a president who becomes mentally incapable, but like everything with the American constitution, there's enough vagueness in the clause that it could be used in almost any circumstance."

"Right," said Merielle, "I remember now. And if I recall correctly, it was always wishful thinking that every member of Trump's

Cabinet would unify to get rid of him. All you need is one zealot, one true believer, and you go nowhere."

Being in sync as it was, the small group of advisors collectively let Merielle work through the question brewing in her mind. "He wants our help with the holdouts, doesn't he?"

One of Stephane's hands formed into a pistol. "Bingo. He wants our help with the two Secretaries he knows would never vote with him. He's confident he can win over the rest."

"And are we as confident?" Merielle asked, turning her attention back to the country's senior intel man.

"We could never be one hundred percent certain, Madame Prime Minister, but we think there's a very good chance he could bring along the others. With each passing week, Menendez is growing more erratic and isolated. The sacking of Sullivan is only the latest episode. But perhaps the most important consideration driving Morgan's actions is Spector and the Reds. With the fall of Pittsburgh, they are firmly on a path to winning this war. As Morgan sees it, it may be now or never."

The CSIS director turned his head toward the military officer on his left. "General Kaplan can speak to this better than I can, but our latest intel suggests that if something doesn't change soon, the Reds could be in Washington within the month."

Merielle took up the Chief of Defence Staff of the Canadian Armed Forces. Wearing the dark green service uniform, the CDS cut a whip-like figure who looked like he didn't miss many of the long-distance runs he was known for. "What's the latest, General?"

"Well, as Jim was saying, I can tell you things are not looking good for the FAS. Both Cincinnati and Pittsburgh were meat grinders, so both sides have burned through a lot of their best troops since the war restarted. But it's the French who've made the difference.

"Since they threw in fully with the Reds, Spector and his forces have an advantage that has grown with each passing week. While the Blues have had all of the advantages that come with defending major urban centers, the Reds have a near-limitless supply of munitions and the willingness to use them however they see fit. You've seen the pictures of Pittsburgh. They pulverized it block-by-block."

"The devastation of Pittsburgh is beyond words," Merielle said, offering her own assessment. "And they'll do the same to Washington? I would have thought they'd want to keep the city whole, seeing as Spector has talked about keeping it as their capital."

"We think they'll avoid destroying the most important historical sites, but Washington is a good-sized city, Madame Prime Minister. Due to geography, the Reds are going to have to attack D.C. from the west and south, and in both those directions there's a lot of city for them to grind through. No matter how you look at it, it should be a long slog for the Reds, who are themselves near exhaustion."

Merielle interjected, "I take it this is where the exit of Sullivan comes into your analysis?"

"Correct, Madame Prime Minister," the general replied. "As soon as Menendez took the Presidency, you'll recall that she implemented a swath of 'equity over merit' directives across the United States public service. The military was not exempted from these policies."

Merielle nodded her head. "I have a vague recollection of them, General, along with the implementation of the Firearm Possession Act and the expansion of the Supreme Court. I think historians will agree it was the packing of the court that tipped over the boat."

"Well, Madame Prime Minister, Menendez is now reaping the benefits of her vision on equity. The entirety of the Blue officer ranks are a morass of resentment where men and women don't know who to fear more – the Reds and their ruthlessness, or the ever-vigilant diversity and equity commissar that now infects every unit in the FAS military from the company level right up to General Staff."

Merielle whistled softly. As a visible minority herself, she was prepared to admit that at least part of her career in the RCMP had benefited from the longstanding affirmative action programming that existed in all parts of Canada's public service.

In her mind, a good and fair affirmative action policy opened certain doors to minorities. The door to first get in, the door to middle management, and then the door to upper management. You had to open these doors just a bit wider for POCs because of their smaller numbers, and, because whether Canadians wanted to admit it or not, data showed that all other things being equal, white Canadians were promoted at higher rates than non-whites.

But once you were through one of those three doors, everyone understood that you had to perform if you wanted to advance and do the important work within whatever management level you occupied.

"If things are so bad in the Blue military General, it's a wonder they've managed to resist the Reds as long as they have. Am I to take it that Sullivan was that good a leader?"

"He was, Madame Prime Minister," Kaplan said. "By all accounts, Sullivan was a hugely talented manager of people and had a solid grasp of strategy. It's been suggested by many that the man was Eisenhower come again. Most importantly, however, he was the last bulwark preventing Menendez's equity scheme from wholly infecting the Blue military. Now that he's been pushed out, the President's acolytes can carry out their work unopposed. It's been less than twenty-four hours since the Sullivan resignation and we've already seen four Army divisional commanders resign or receive transfer orders."

"Which brings us back to Vice President Morgan and this 25th Amendment plan, Madame Prime Minister," Stephane said, taking up the briefing baton from the CDS.

Merielle shifted her eyes to her ex. "You know my position on the war, Stephane. It hasn't changed. If Spector wins, Canada as we know it is done. For all the reasons we're familiar with, Cabinet and CANZUK were unprepared to support the Blues so long as Menendez was in charge. If Morgan is prepared to remove Menendez, I'm prepared to revisit our position."

She paused and looked down at her wrist to do a time check. Across her career, she loathed when people treated her time as though it was theirs. One of the few luxuries of being at the top of the political food chain was that no one got to do this to her anymore. In turn, she refused to misuse the time of others.

"Listen, gentlemen, we all understand why Valeria Menendez needs to go. It's the details of how we get rid of her that is the question. In the fifteen minutes before my next meeting, give me the rundown of the 'how,' and then clear your schedules for this evening. If things are as bad as we all think they are with the Blues, we need to move things along and fast."

Chapter 4

The Pontiac Region, Quebec, Northwest of Ottawa

For what might have been the twentieth time, Eric Labelle looked through the rear window of the Audi A7 he was a passenger in. One minute behind him, a second vehicle was following to ensure there had been no tail on the ground or in the air. CSIS, Canada's intelligence agency, had been noncommittal in their meetings with his staff as to whether or not they had an active file open on him.

He was well beyond furious with Canada's intelligence agency. Several points of data suggested CSIS had some kind of involvement in the death of his daughter in French Guiana. That this same agency, with blood still fresh on its hands, would then look to harass him in his capacity as a duly elected representative of the people of Quebec was a feat worthy of history's worst secret police. It was just one more reason he needed to pull Quebec out of Canada. Not that he needed another.

"We're making a turn up here," the driver and only other occupant of the vehicle said. "We'll be there in the next minute."

Labelle gave no reply to the man. Had he, he would have been curt. For the entirety of the trip, he had been reminiscing about his daughter and what the Canadian government had done to her.

When he had received a full briefing on Josee's role to undermine CANZUK's mission to remove the nuclear weapons from the American airbase in Missouri, he had been both surprised and pleased. The audacity of what his daughter had almost achieved had been nothing short of miraculous. That she had managed to create a double life as one of the neo-FLQ's operational leaders and function as an asset for France's DGSE were details he was still trying to wrap his mind around.

The Canadian government, hardly anxious to reveal the return of the FLQ to the country's political scene, had undertaken a cover-up of his daughter's murder that would have made the worst of the world's dictators green with envy.

France, on the other hand, had been all too helpful in providing the details of what had happened in the months leading up to Josee's assassination. They had laid it all out in a visit he had made to Paris. In accessing his own limited intelligence resources, he had been able to conclude much of the briefing had been accurate.

So, when the French had proposed a partnership that would see their intelligence service, the DGSE, actively work to support Quebec's legitimate separatist movement, Labelle had said yes without a moment's hesitation.

It was saying yes to the French that had brought him to the quaint cottage his Audi was now parked in front of.

Beyond the cedar-paneled building and through the trees, Labelle spied a good-sized lake that was, at this time of the day, a mesmerizing sapphire blue.

His driver, a recently retired Montreal policeman with years of experience on the department's Groupe Tactique D'intervention, opened the door for him. Exiting the vehicle, he inhaled deeply.

Somewhere close by, there was an open fire. He could smell it faintly on the breeze. The scene and smell somehow pushed back the foul mood he had been in moments before.

In better days, he and his first wife had brought their own children to a place just like this. Smiling wistfully, Eric silently sent a word of thanks to his daughter for the recollection.

As much as he was furious with Merielle Martel and the Canadian government for what they'd done to his daughter, the French had not been innocent in the affair. They had used his Josee, and when they were done using her, they had failed utterly in their commitment to keep her safe. But were she here now, his daughter would have no doubt dismissed his feelings of blame and advised him there was a much bigger issue at play – namely, freeing Quebec.

And so it was that when he entered the cottage and took in the two men standing behind the well-worn kitchen table, he was in a mindset to conduct business.

One of the two men gestured to the chair that had been set out for him. As he reached the table, Labelle extended his hand, and in turn, each man received the politician's well-practiced handshake. Neither of them provided their names.

"Please have a seat, Monsieur Labelle," the younger and more relaxed of the two men said. "Can we offer you anything to drink? Wine or perhaps something stronger? We have full use of the establishment, and I'm pleased to report it has a respectable selection of beverages to refresh or relax."

"No thank you," Labelle said while moving to take a seat. "I don't need to refresh or relax at the moment. I'll tell you what I would like, however."

"And what is that, Monsieur Labelle?"

"Names. You know mine, but I don't know yours. Even if they aren't your real ones. Indulge me, if you would."

"Of course," the Frenchman said with a warm smile.

"Indeed, as you say, they won't be our real names, which is why we didn't offer them, but since you have made this reasonable request, you may call me Henri, while my friend here is Louis."

Labelle nodded his head in the direction of the other man. "Louis doesn't speak?"

"He does, but he's more a man of action. It's my hope he'll have more to say in the latter part of our discussion."

"I see," said Labelle as he eyed up the man standing ramrod straight behind his own chair. Certainly not French intelligence,

Labelle thought to himself. The man's posture and style of mustache screamed military.

Labelle's eyes cast back to the speaker. "So, you called this meeting. What is it you would like to discuss?"

"Straight to business. This bodes well, Monsieur Labelle," the Frenchman said.

The two still-standing men took their seats.

"I'm a busy man, Henri. In case you weren't aware, I'm in the midst of running a campaign to have my province separate from Canada. In just under four weeks, I plan to win a referendum and become the first Prime Minister of Quebec. So, to be perfectly honest with you, I have little time to waste on any games your agency might want to play in my province."

The French foreign intelligence officer stared back at Labelle and, after a brief pause, said, "I appreciate the forthrightness of your comments but in this instance, I feel I must correct you. It is not France that is playing games. On the contrary, it is the Canadian government. New and dangerous ones, I'm afraid. Games that my country has played for generations."

"You mean games like killing its own citizens?" As the question left his lips, Labelle gave vent to the belligerence he had been holding in check.

"Indeed, you have my greatest sympathies, Monsieur Labelle. Canada crossed a line when they had your daughter killed on French soil. But regretfully, I'm making reference to more recent events. This Martel woman has transgressed my government again. I called you to this meeting to add details to the agreement you reached with my country six months ago during your trip to Paris. As you will no doubt recall, we left our agreement vague knowing that a time would come when we both might feel it necessary to put meat on the bones of our relationship."

"And that time is now? Your timing is impeccable," Labelle said irritably.

"Nevertheless. I have asked you here because I wish to discuss an opportunity with you that will assure you the one thing you want more than anything else."

"And that is?"

"A free Quebec. What else, my friend?"

"Perhaps you did not hear me correctly or maybe you haven't been keeping tabs on the news in this part of the world, but at the end of the month, Quebec will be free of Canada. I don't need your help, *my friend*."

The Frenchman's hands waved dismissively, ignoring the acid Labelle had injected into the final two words of his reply. "Yes, yes, we are familiar with your referendum, but just as you have been direct with me, Monsieur Labelle, I will not allow myself to treat you as though you are a fool. You and I both know you are going to lose."

"There is a month left," Labelle shot back bitterly. "That's a lot of time for things to change. We have rallies planned in Quebec City and Montreal and a massive campaign that will saturate television and social media. We're trending in the right direction. I believe in the people of Quebec. Now is our time."

One of the Frenchman's eyebrows crooked upwards. "Monsieur Labelle, I say what follows with the deepest respect. You are a man of intellect and wisdom before you are a man of dreams and visions. You know full well you are not going to win the referendum. We've run the models, just as you have. The numbers aren't there. Be rational. You owe it to the people of Quebec. But more, you owe it to Josee."

On hearing his daughter's name, Labelle could feel his internal temperature begin to rise. He rarely lost his cool, but when he did, it was volcanic. "You son of a bitch..."

But before he could unload the rest of what he wanted to say, the French intelligence officer doused him with the verbal equivalent of a bucket of ice water.

"Help us kill Merielle Martel. Help us with this task, and my government will do everything in its power to help you make Quebec a separate country."

At first, Labelle was unsure if he had heard the other man's words correctly. As he stared back at the envoy who still had a pleasant look about him, he eventually collected himself enough to confirm the statement. "Kill Martel. You're serious, aren't you?"

"Entirely serious. Your Prime Minister has decided to play a most dangerous game, Monsieur Labelle. She has taken something from us that she should not have. France will not let this stand."

"What has she taken from you that France is willing to undertake assassination?"

For the first time since walking into the cottage, the Frenchman's face took on an expression that suggested amiability wasn't the man's default personality. "I cannot say what she has taken. I can only say she has crossed a line and, in crossing this line, has set in motion events she will one day come to regret."

"And if I help you with this task, it is your proposal that France will lend its full power to my efforts to have Quebec leave Canada?"

"Yes," the Frenchman replied quickly. "Look to the south, Monsieur Labelle. As the Red Faction marches forward, France's power grows. In two weeks or maybe six, the United States' civil war will be over. Were I you, I might want to be on the winning side."

Labelle chewed over the man's words silently. Like everyone else, he had observed recent events coming out of the US with equal parts fascination and trepidation. He wasn't a warrior of any kind, but even he could see the American conflict was entering its final phase.

The French intelligence agent, if that's what he was, interrupted his train of thought. "Take your time. What questions I can respond to, I will. But know that I brought you here today because I need you to make a decision. If you leave this place without confirming your support for our objective, my offer is off the table, and you and Quebec will be on your own. We will not help you when Spector turns his eyes on your province, no matter how outrageous his demands or actions are."

Labelle's eyes locked onto the other man's. "I don't need more time. I can help but on one condition."

"And that is?"

"Whatever happens, it can't be linked to my party. If things don't go to plan, my people can't be caught up in it. It would ruin us. Perhaps forever."

"We understand," said the Frenchman. "It's not your party's support we need. It's your support and that of those people who supported your daughter. My colleagues are finding it difficult to connect with those who remain. In particular, there is a man we believe can help my friend Louis here complete the task he's been assigned."

"Fortin?" offered Labelle immediately.

The smile of the devil grew on the Frenchman's face. "Yes, Monsieur Labelle, Fortin is the one we're after."

"I know how he can be reached."

"We thought so. And will you make the connection?"

Again, Labelle did not hesitate. As much as he wanted Quebec to separate from Canada, he wanted much more for the Martel woman to pay for what she had done to his beautiful daughter. "Yes, I can connect you."

The intelligence officer nodded his head and after a pause, said, "Very good. There may be other things we need from you, but for now, connecting us with this elusive Fortin fellow gives us the start we need."

"When will you kill her? Before the referendum?" The questions spilled out of Labelle's mouth before he had a chance to think about it.

For the first time during the conversation, the military man with the oh-so-French mustache spoke. His voice was dry, sounding as though he had gone days without water. "For operational reasons, Monsieur Labelle, we cannot share the timing of our mission or any other details, for that matter. What I can say though, is that your help is what will make the difference – a difference that will change the course of history. A history that will assure our two countries' independence, and, dare I say, greatness for generations."

North Baltimore, Maryland

As Sam Petite pulled into the driveway of the good-sized home tucked into the trees of Oregon Ridge Park just north of Baltimore, he once again assured himself this location was as good as it was going to get for their op.

It was owned by an architect who had dual American-Canadian citizenship. A lifelong bachelor and a diehard Leafs fan, the man had fled to Toronto at the beginning of the war. Exhaustingly vetted to ensure he didn't have any connections with either side of the civil war, members of CSIS's newly formed Direct Action Group had secured the use of the property as a safe house for Petite and his small team.

As safe houses went, it was nearly perfect. The dense collection of maples, oaks, and ashes that dominated this part of Maryland, made it all but impossible for the neighbors to gauge the number of people or the level of activity taking place inside the spectacular nine-bedroom home.

Just as important, the neighborhood association to which the residence belonged employed a well-trained and discreet security firm to patrol and keep the community safe from the constant flow of refugees fleeing the war.

Any squatters or looters who scoped out the tranquil neighborhood had been dissuaded from entering into the forest-cosseted community by well-placed signage indicating the number of people that had been shot due to trespassing. Petite didn't wonder if the number of seventy-six was accurate. Rather, he was curious if the word 'shot' was synonymous with 'killed.'

However they defined their terms, the security service was running a tight operation along the community's perimeter and was by all accounts leaving the residents to live their lives. Whatever the architect was paying for the service, it was worth every penny.

As he reached the grand entrance to the home, one of the green double doors opened for him. Behind the door and holding it open, was one of the six Joint Task Force-2 – JTF-2 – operators that had been assigned to his team.

Dressed in non-descript jeans and a tee, Petite knew the man had a pistol at the small of his back and had access to an arsenal of weapons carefully hidden further back in the home.

"How'd it go?" the sinewy special ops man asked.

"Like a dream."

"How are things here?"

"Chill as ever, boss."

"Nice. Do me a fav, would you?"

"Name it."

"Gather up everyone in the kitchen. It's time for the gang to find out why we're here."

"Finally," the JTF-2 operator said.

"See you in five," said Petite.

"Copy that. In five." With one final look outside, the commando closed the door and moved to gather up the members of the team.

In under five minutes, the combined team of thirteen CSIS Direct Action officers and JTF-2 operators were seated or standing around the large island that dominated the center of the home's kitchen.

Petite took a moment to review the troops. They were thirteen of a larger team of twenty that had been training together for the past year. The Canadian public had no idea, but within weeks of the start of the second US civil war three years ago, Canada had quickly stood up three of these units. By the time of the resumption of the war just under a year ago, a total of eight teams were in operation.

The remaining seven members of the team were at other locations to the north. In ones and twos, they were managing a small portfolio of safe houses, vehicles, weapons, and on-the-ground contacts that might be needed should the mission Petite was about to outline go to hell.

"Alright, people, it's the moment you've all been waiting for."

"Bout time." The comment came from one of the JTF-2 spec ops guys, Master Corporal Sykes. "I'm getting sick and tired of listening to Janks moaning about his bees. Boss, we either get this done soon or you risk Janks going AWOL so he can race back home to tend to his bee city or whatever he calls them."

"It's a colony, man. And there's twenty of them actually, and they're delicate things. I got nearly two hundred pounds of honey out of them last year. All I'm saying is I won't get that much this season. My old lady is trying her best, but she just doesn't have the touch. Not like I do."

Suddenly, the commando's face began to turn bright red. "Wait, wait... that's not what I meant! She's got the touch, just not for my bees."

"Oh Jesus, Janks, stop digging already," Sykes said. "Everyone knows Mrs. Jankowicz has got the touch."

"Ouch," a female voice said further back in the group.

"Alright, alright. Zip it, you grade six jackasses," Petite said in a serious tone. "For the next fifteen, I don't want to hear anything about goddamned bees and old ladies. You feel me, Sykes?

"Solid copy, boss."

"Janks?"

"All good, boss."

"Good. Then everyone put an eye on your tac pads."

As one, the thirteen members of his team cast their eyes down to look at the BAM tactical pad each of them had in their possession.

The BAM, or Battlefield Area Management system was the agreed to Command, Control, Communications, Computers, Intelligence, Surveillance and Reconnaissance (C4ISR) platform used by CANZUK. Cloud-based and administered by one of the most powerful near-AI platforms in the Commonwealth, the system gave the Canadians and their allies a degree of interoperability that was science fiction only eight years ago.

"This is Roberta Hastings," Petite said, his voice level. "The FAS Secretary of Education. Somehow, in the next five days, we have to make Secretary Hastings disappear off the face of the earth without a trace."

Sykes' hand immediately shot into the air.

Petite's eyes met the commando's, but the face of a wisecracker had been replaced by that of a competent professional soldier. "Feeling it today, eh, Sykes? Shoot, Master Corporal."

"A snatch-and-grab of a Menendez Cabinet official ain't gonna be easy, boss. I mean you've seen the video coming out of Washington. It's a GD fortress."

"Good observation," replied Petite. "Washington is locked up tight, so we need to get creative and somehow find a reason to get our target out of D.C."

"Five days isn't a lot of time to come up with and then execute an op of this kind, boss. Surely, the folks back in Ottawa have some ideas?" It was a perfectly legitimate question and had come from the only professional anomaly on the team.

Sarah Hall had been the newest addition to the unit, but unlike the rest of the Action Group, she was neither CSIS nor JTF-2. In fact, to Petite, the woman, who was most certainly in her mid-twenties at most, was and remained a mystery. He'd had a hand in selecting the rest of his crew but in Hall's case, the directive to take her on had come from on high.

Bereft of a personnel file of any kind, she had joined the team only two months ago. Thankfully, the unassuming woman had acquitted herself well enough in their training that the rest of the team had readily accepted her. Whoever she was, she was scary talented at everything she did.

"There is no plan, Hall. I'm told that the need to move against Hastings is recent. So recent, in fact, the folks back home haven't had the time to pull together a full ops package. Because we're on the ground and because operations are what we do, they've kicked it down to us."

"Why don't we just take her out from afar?" This time the question came from Jankowicz, the most senior of the JTF-2 commandos on the team. People too quickly dismissed Janks because he looked like a meathead, but Petite and the rest of the group knew better. The Sergeant might have arms the size of Terry Bollea at peak Hogan, but he also had a shrewd operational mind. When he talked, the smart leader listened.

"Suggestions is why we're here, Sergeant. Shoot," Petite said.

"There's five of us who are long shot qualified. By tomorrow or the next day, we can come up with a plan to get into D.C. Just place us along her regular route to work and we'll do the rest. By the time they've figured out she's dead, we'll be on our way home. As I stand here, I can give you at least three different ideas to get us into the city. Remember, we look like them and talk like them. We just need a plausible story to get past the outer defenses."

Petite shook his head gently. "I wish it were that simple, Janks, but the bosses at Joint Ops Command need for Hastings and one other cabinet secretary to, and here I'm quoting directly from JOC, 'disappear in such a way that it looks like they've voluntarily left the Menendez administration.'"

"You mean like resign?" Sykes asked.

"Resigned, sabbatical, a health scare, a family emergency. Pick your reason, Master Corporal. Whichever it is, it has to look legit from the outside looking in. At least legit enough for the right parts of the media to buy into the idea that Hastings wasn't taken off the board by someone other than herself."

Sykes' face took on an annoyed look, "All respect to you, boss, but that sounds like mission impossible to me."

"Yeah, well, it's what JOC wants, and it's why I'm bringing you into the fold. Our best ops people have tried to shape this pile of shit into a workable plan, but everything they've come up with is hot garbage. We need a fresh set of eyes to pull together a plan that gives us a chance to succeed."

Hall spoke up again. "Hastings is one of Menendez's two political pit bulls. I take it the other target is Williams-Jordan, the Secretary of State?"

Petite made yet another note of Hall's astuteness when it came to politics. Despite her age, the woman had a keen understanding of a wide swath of topics, including the dynamics of both sides in the US civil war. He had been told not to reveal the name of the other target for reasons of operational security, but if confirming the information helped Hall and the rest of the team make better sense of the challenge they faced, he was prepared to confirm that particular piece of intel.

"Williams-Jordan is the other target. MI6 is working her. And I don't have any of the details of what their plans are, so don't ask."

As she stood there, it looked like Hall was forcing her brain to perform the intellectual equivalent of a bench press personal best. Others in the group had picked up on it and, as one, they looked in the young operator's direction.

"They want to isolate Menendez," Hall said eventually. "Hastings and Williams-Jordan are her staunchest allies in the Cabinet. Both are ruthless political assassins. Between the two of them, they've ruined at least as many political careers as there are people in this room."

"But what does that tell us?" interjected Sykes.

"If they want Hastings and Williams-Jordan gone, somebody – most likely a political opponent, must want to make a move on Menendez. With her two most fervent supporters out of the picture, Menendez will be vulnerable, at least politically speaking."

Once again, Petite was impressed by Hall. Her open musings closely reflected his own personal speculation, but in his case, he'd had the past hour to work it through. Hall's deduction had come in minutes, if not seconds.

"Good work, Hall, the wonks back in Ottawa would be proud. But figuring out the underlying reason why Hastings has to go isn't the challenge that lies before us. Making her disappear in the right way is."

Petite paused to look over the group. Four women and nine men. It was as solid a team as he had ever worked with. If not Hall, one of the others would see the path forward.

"I've sent each of you an intel file on the target. Review it, think on it, and come up with suggestions. At 2000 hours, I want everyone back in this room except those on watch, and I want ideas."

On giving the order, there was determination in every face looking back at him. "Save any more questions for when we regroup. The briefing I just sent will answer most of them. Whatever questions or concerns you still have we'll deal with them when we reconnect. For now, all you need to think about is Hastings and how we deal with her. Are we clear, people?"

As one, the assembled members of the Action Team gave a singular reply, "Clear."

"Good, and as you think through any potential solutions, know that the safety is off. Anything and everything that may be needed to get the job done right is on the table."

Chapter 5

Somewhere Along the West Virginia-Maryland Border

Commandant Dorian Elan of the 13th Parachute Dragoon Regiment had any number of extremely capable men under his command who could lead the mission he was now on, but against the wishes of his superiors, he had elected to get his hands dirty. The truth behind the decision was two-fold.

First, the men of his company needed to know their CO could and would risk his neck. While the men in the 13th knew full well that officers commanding the various units that formed the regiment were some of the best in the French Army, it never hurt a leader's standing if he could demonstrate abilities that were on par with the skills, he demanded from the soldiers he was commanding.

The second reason for his presence was the subject of his current hunt. The *Phew* or the "Fox" as it translated into English had been a terrible thorn in the side of the Reds in Pittsburgh. The Ukrainian mercenary had sharpened his teeth to razor-like proportions by fighting the Russians in his younger days. For the past five months, he had commanded a company of his countrymen that was both fearless and exceptional in all aspects of low-intensity warfare.

In the time the 13th had been helping the Reds eject the Blues from Pittsburgh, this Phew son of a bitch and his men had been responsible for killing no fewer than twenty-one of his men, including his 2IC, Second-In-Command.

The order to put the mercenary down had come from on high. Regardless of what it took, the Army could not let this man make it to another major urban center so he could again kill France's best sons and daughters.

A nearby soldier interrupted his ruminations with a soft tap on Elan's shoulder. "We've got him. He's riding in the lone black Ford F-250. It's missing its rear bumper."

"We're sure?"

"Ninety-nine percent. We have a visual and –"

He interrupted the man, "Visual means nothing, Chief. The man has at least a dozen similar-looking men dressed as he is."

Chief Julian Laroux, long used to the way his CO conducted his business, ignored the interruption, and when satisfied Elan would tolerate him moving forward with his update, he said, "And we've heard from our source in the unit, and the near-AI just picked up a voice coming from one of the phones in that convoy that is a match with Mazur's. As they say, sir, three's the charm."

"Normally I'd agree, Chief. But this Mazur fellow wasn't named the Fox for nothing."

Elan brought the binoculars back to his eyes and through the thick vegetation that dominated this corner of West Virginia, he took in a dozen or so multi-colored pickup trucks, each laden down with men and war-fighting equipment. They had stopped at a quarry that until recently had been in the business of digging up and processing silica. He zeroed in on the black truck third back from the lead vehicle.

Anticipating the Fox would head west to Washington, Elan had sprinkled his company along the many possible routes between the two cities in the hope that when they did get a bead on the Ukrainians, one of the teams would be able to get a visual on France's most wanted man.

"And what did your source tell you about why they've stopped? I see jerry cans everywhere. It can't be because of fuel."

"Greed, Commandant," the Chief replied.

Elan slowly dropped the binoculars from his eyes and looked at the other man. "Tell me more, Chief."

"If you can imagine it, sir, he's renegotiating his deal with the Blues. He won't come into D.C. until they've met his new price."

"Interesting," offered Elan. "And how have we come across this development?"

"The near-AI, Commandant. In the last gasps of defending Pittsburgh, the Ukrainians, and others, lost access to whatever comms gear they'd been using. They're now onto some older kit. It was only about twenty minutes ago, but the SIGINT near-AI managed to breach his encryption and localized him. That is the Fox. Everything says so."

"Excellent work, Chief. Make the call to the flyboys. They should be close. I want an airstrike on these bastards ASAP and I want every team that's close to us to converge on this location to set up choke points at all points entering and leaving this position. I won't have him escape us this time."

"Yes, sir," Laroux said. "And what about us?"

"Give the word to the men to be ready. The moment the fireworks go off, we advance. I want to look into this man's dead eyes before this day ends."

"Yes, sir."

As the Chief began to slither away from their concealed position a few meters back from the tree line, Elan gently grabbed the other man's uniform, halting the non-com's departure.

"Yes, Commandant?"

"Tell Lambert I will paint the target."

Laroux smiled at his CO and nodded his head as though he fully expected the order. "Copy that, sir."

Elan released the other man and with barely a whisper of sound, the reconnaissance paratrooper stalked away to relay his CO's orders.

Just as quietly, Elan raised the targeting scope that had been lying on the forested floor. Bringing it to his eye, he zeroed in on the man leaning against the black pickup that was missing its bumper. In seconds, the scope had automatically adjusted its lens. There he was. Petr Mazur in the flesh. And just as Laroux had foretold, the allegedly too-greedy man was talking in an animated fashion on a phone.

Elan moved the reticle of the targeting device back to the center mass of the pickup and pressed the button on the targeting laser that would be the conduit to unleash hell on this man who had caused his country so much pain.

Three minutes later, Elan triggered his throat mic. "Falcon lead, this is Viper Actual. Confirm your distance from my position?

"Viper, we're twenty klicks from your position and we're hot."

"Good, I need you to wipe clean an area seventy-five meters square. My mark is the center of the kill zone. Do you copy?"

"Viper, I have a solid copy on your data. HAMMERs are on their way in one mike. Continue to hold the target. Falcon lead out."

Fifty-seven seconds later, the thunderclap of destruction that struck the gravel pit where the Ukrainian mercenaries had gathered had been nothing short of God-like.

In total, the Falcons, a pair of Block 4 Rafaels, had launched eight Highly Agile and Manoeuvrable Munition Extended Range, or HAMMERs at the roughly formed collection of vehicles.

Using the Fox's pickup as the epicenter, the combined power of the air-to-ground missiles hitting the ground milliseconds apart had created a colossal explosion that eviscerated two-thirds of the vehicles. Around those pickups that were not burning wrecks, men lay strewn dead or on their way to departing this world.

As Elan and his men closed in on the circle of hell, they had been twice required to fire their weapons, but these exchanges had been short one-sided affairs. Despite their well-earned reputation as cagey and fierce fighters, those few men that had survived the strike were still human. Concussed or broken in some other way, their attempts to fend off the encircling French paratroopers were half-hearted, at best.

As Elan's squad of men maneuvered around yet another shredded and burning truck, he laid eyes on his prize, and in a miracle that would have rivaled the second coming of God's only son, he stared at the barely damaged black pickup. Were he not the professional he was, his jaw would have physically struck the gravel-covered ground.

In his fourteen-year career in the French Army, Elan had never once panicked, but in that moment, he could feel his already speedy heart rate begin to transition from a trot to something approaching a gallop. If that son of a bitch had survived and escaped this nightmare, he swore he'd…

"Sir!" The call came from the right side of their formation. Immediately, Elan turned and as he did so, he took in the paratrooper furthest out on their flank. His rifle at the ready, the soldier was advancing toward a body.

As he pivoted, the formation of men around Elan shifted as one ensuring their commander remained at their center. Together, they prowled in the direction of their comrade who had pulled up short of an unmoving mercenary.

To Elan's delight, as he neared the person of interest, he realized that the man was in fact still alive and dragging himself on his stomach. Elan could not see the man's face, but the clothing was a match with what he had seen from afar only minutes earlier.

"Laroux."

"Yes, Commandant?"

"Turn the bastard over, would you?"

"Yes, sir."

On snapping out the order, a pair of soldiers moved forward, and together, they roughly flipped over the injured mercenary so he was looking into the sky.

Stepping forward, Elan gazed into the face of the man he had been desperately chasing since his government had ordered the 13th into this cursed civil war.

And in what was the day's second miracle, Elan could see that the only indication of a wound on the mercenary's body was the still-wet blood seeping out of the man's nose and ears.

Standing casually above the Ukrainian, Elan produced an extra water bottle he carried on his person, opened it, and poured it on the man's face from on high. As the last few drops of the liquid struck, the Fox's eyes sputtered open. Dazed, the man's eyes blinked rapidly as he tried to make sense of the cataclysm that surrounded him. After several long seconds, his eyes narrowed in on Elan.

As the two men's eyes locked onto each other, the French special forces officer turned his torso slightly and tapped the regimental patch on his shoulder.

In a remarkable demonstration of fortitude, the Ukrainian mercenary gathered himself to say something. When he spoke, the Fox's voice was strained. "Fuck you, you fascist son of a bitch. Fuck you and France."

The Ukrainian capped off his defiance by spitting dark red saliva onto Elan's filthy boots.

Elan smiled at the other man's pitiful effort. Despite the certainty the Ukrainian wouldn't be able to hear anything, he said, "What a hunt you have been, Monsieur Fox. And despite all that you've done, you have earned a modicum of my admiration. My men and I will remember this day well."

Elan's eyes left his quarry. "Chief Laroux."

"Yes, Commandant."

"Get this piece of filth on his feet."

"Yes, sir."

In seconds, the same two soldiers who had flipped over the wounded mercenary had him up. Wobbly at first, the Ukrainian merc eventually got his bearings. Elevated, he took the opportunity to survey the destruction that surrounded him.

Eventually, his eyes reacquired Elan, and as he did so, he saw there was a pistol pointed at his chest.

"This is much better than you deserve," Elan said, his voice absent of any emotion.

Pulling the trigger of his Beretta 92X, Elan sent two rounds into Ukrainian's chest. Stumbling back into the truck, for a brief moment, France's most wanted man offered Elan a defiant glare.

Casually, Elan aimed his pistol at the Fox's forehead and pulled the trigger. The contents of the man's brain destroyed, the mercenary dropped to the ground in an uncontrolled heap.

Without hesitation, Elan stepped toward the body and in doing so began to work up a healthy amount of saliva in his mouth. Standing over the mercenary he spat into the bloody mess that was Petr Mazur's face.

It was hardly the professional thing to do, but the men who had observed the disrespect would speak of it to their mates, and in a short enough time, the whole of the regiment would know just how personal this hunt had been for Elan. More important, it would reinforce for the dedicated soldiers of the 13th Parachute Dragoon Regiment that to kill any of them was to be killed without remorse of any kind.

"Chief!" Elan snapped.

"Yes, Commandant."

"Find a tree and hang this bastard from it."

"And the card?"

Elan reached into his pocket and handed Laroux the thirteenth card of the standard tarot deck – the Death card. "Post it online,

Chief. Let us remind the world that the 13th, on behalf of France, always repay its debts."

University of Buffalo, New York

"And so, I am exceedingly proud of this policy announcement. As we have done since coming into office, my administration has made reparations a key priority. The Advancement of Equity In Education Act or, as it is otherwise known, the 50-20 bill will ensure colleges and universities in the Federation of American States pay their fair share."

As Menendez stared out at the crowd gathered in front of her, she had made a point of raising her voice an octave or two as she said the words "pay their fair share."

As though on cue, the crowd of mostly young faces cheered her on vigorously. And so they should, she thought. Of all constituencies in this country, it was young adults she and her party had courted most aggressively. Before and during the war, young people in the university system had been instrumental in cowing those who had not been fully behind her program.

Critics had called the youth-oriented movement America's own "Cultural Revolution," but Menendez thought that comparison was both sloppy and unfair.

For instance, when Mao's Red Bands had finished their work, it was estimated that some 250,000 intellectuals had been killed or had killed themselves. An exaggerated number to be sure.

Whatever the figure, Menendez's own effort to recalibrate the country's post-secondary system and how it treated American history had only ruined a few hundred careers. It was not a comparison worth making in her mind. Not a single person had been shot and, to the best of her knowledge, not a single 'struggle session' had come to pass. It had all happened organically and voluntarily.

As the cheering relented, Menendez continued with her speech. "With the passage of this bill, any post-secondary institution with an endowment that exceeds a quarter of a billion dollars will be required to pay fifty percent of their endowment's annual investment gains to the National Slavery Reparations Fund.

"Further, these same institutions which, over the course of their histories, have profited and built corporate empires on the shoulders of black slaves and then cheap black labor, will be required to reserve twenty percent of their enrollment for black students."

Menendez again paused to allow the cheers of the crowd to fill the confines of the U of B auditorium.

"Friends, students, faculty. While I am the president and it is my responsibility to lead our country through the difficult times that confront us, I could not do this work without the support of my Cabinet. And in my Cabinet, I have no greater advocate than Secretary Hastings."

With her million-watt smile on full display, Menendez shifted her gaze from the audience and gestured grandly with her hand to the tallest of the women standing to her left on the stage.

"Please, everyone, give the Secretary a round of applause. It is Secretary Hastings, her vision, and her tenacity, that have been instrumental in transitioning our colleges and universities away from the elites that have made it their life's mission to suppress this country's racialized communities and the working class.

"Secretary Hastings, please come forward to say a few words."

Despite every word and gesture being rehearsed in advance, Roberta Hastings acted surprised when the President invited her to the podium.

Wearing a pair of heels that added two inches to her six-foot-one-inch height, the Secretary gracefully strode across the stage to take up the proffered hand of the FAS President. They had talked about an embrace but had decided against it on the count of Hastings being so much taller than Menendez.

"I set 'em up, Roberta. You knock 'em down," Menendez said to the other woman away from the microphone.

"Will do, Madam President. I won't be long."

With that, Hastings glided to the podium and quickly adjusted the mic, all the while projecting her own smile at the audience.

"Thank you, Madam President. I appreciate your words and I would echo them back to you. Without your leadership, none of this could have happened. Your perseverance in the face of the patriarchal menace and racial hatred that confronts you and your administration is historic.

"Every day you inspire us to keep moving forward with those necessary changes that will make our country more equitable. I will not stop, Madam President. The people in this room will not stop. We will continue to run this race until the tri-supremacies that are whiteness, men, and wealth, can no longer dominate our society."

An unseen female voice in the back of the auditorium, screamed out, "No more men!" and then began to repeat the phrase until a few others took up the chant. Within seconds, the entirety of the audience, with the exception of those who held positions where it would have been uncouth to join, was shouting, while simultaneously punching one of their fists into the air. "No more men! No more men!"

As she surveyed that part of the audience she could see from the light drenched stage, Hastings noted that the few men that were in the crowd were as animated as anyone in the room. One young man in the second row was seen to be gesticulating so hard as he drove his fist upwards, she wondered if he might hurt himself. He was quite handsome, she thought.

As the chant died down, Hastings, buoyed by the energy coursing through the room, leaned forward into the podium. When she spoke, the auditorium was again silent. "Just as we will win the war against the bigot Spector and the Red Faction, with the 50-20 policy, we will win the battle against white supremacy and the anti-progressives that still lurk in our post-secondary system. We must root these deniers out, my friends. And we must be ruthless in doing so."

Hastings paused, allowing her words to briefly hang in the air of the filled-to-capacity room. She took another look at the young man she had peeked at moments before. He was enraptured.

Raising her voice another octave, Hastings delivered her final verbal ministration. "My friends, go forward and do the important and good work that you have been doing. Whether you are a student leader or an administrator, you know what needs to be done. But as you do this hard and necessary work, know that the Secretary of Education and the President herself are behind you. The state and all the powers that we can bring to bear are behind you. Every step of the way."

Chapter 6

Undisclosed Location, North Carolina

Spector turned away from the screen and the speech that had just been given by the Blue's Secretary of Education.

"Turn that horseshit off," Spector said, making no effort to hide his disdain.

"Not impressed, Mr. President?" Parr remarked.

"The sooner this war comes to an end, Pete, the sooner I don't have to listen to that drivel from Menendez and that freak show Hastings. We are moving on Washington and we are about to win this war and these two are pretending like things couldn't be better. How in the name of Christ himself have we not won this war already? Riddle me that, won't you?"

"It's a great question, Mr. President, and a terrific segue into the topic of this meeting."

Parr turned his seat away from the large Texan who was President of the UCSA to focus on one of the many generals sitting around the table.

"General Spellings, what's the latest on the ground in the northeast? Then let's talk about your proposal to end this war. We're all very interested."

"Thank you, Peter," Spellings said, in response to the handoff.

Given his fourth star on the same day Spector had executed his coup against his predecessor, Archie Cameron, the general had been the President's go-to man since the war with the Blues had restarted.

An entirely unlikeable person, anyone that engaged with the military was forced to ignore Spellings' complete absence of humor and seemingly unquenchable ruthlessness because the man got results.

"Mr. President, with the fall of Pittsburgh, we have begun to consolidate two army groups in preparation for taking Washington. As you're aware, in Richmond, Army Group Four is ready to go. When we give the word, all four of its divisions will drive into Washington from the south.

"In Pittsburgh, Army Group Three is reconstituting. Because of our losses in taking the city, we've had to consolidate from six to four divisions. As you know, sir, Pittsburgh was a bloodbath. It was every bit as bad as Cincinnati. Worse in some ways."

Spector exhaled loudly on hearing the assessment. "Which is why I'm prepared to hear your proposal, John. The idea that I'm going to lose another forty thousand soldiers taking a city is no longer a part of our equation. But before we get to that, tell me what we're up against?"

"Yes, Mr. President." On acknowledging Spector's request, Spellings got to his feet and walked over to the huge LCD at the head of the converted briefing room.

On arrival, the screen came alive with an aerial map labeled "District of Columbia."

"Image Alpha," Spellings said to no one in particular. On giving the command, the map of D.C. zoomed in and a series of blue squares appeared.

"Mr. President, in taking Washington, we are facing four professional fighting divisions. They are equally divided between the west and the south of the city. Throw in the Blue's militia in and around the capital and we're looking at a force of approximately one hundred thousand fighting men."

"To our one-sixty. So not great odds, then?" Spector said, interjecting.

"They are far from ideal, Mr. President." Turning his back to the map, Spellings ordered, "Video three, please."

The screen again shifted. Upon resolving, the meeting's attendees began to take in what was most certainly a video from a reconnaissance drone.

"Mr. President, this is what awaits our brave soldiers in Washington."

Parr whistled. "Dear Lord, it's a fortress. Where is this?"

"This, Mr. Parr, is Richmond Highway in Groveton. It is exactly one-half the distance between where the Blue's defenses start and the White House. Fortifications like this exist across the city. The Blues have taken every bit of learning from Cincinnati and Pittsburgh and have created a gauntlet so severe that I could not stand here in good conscience and tell you we could take that city with the forces we now have."

A second video started. This time, the landmark was recognizable as the former grounds of RFK Stadium.

In the late '20s, the D.C. government had spent billions to build a new urban campus. Due to cost and its prime location, the development had been controversial from the start. But it had only become a focus of national scorn when the developers had announced they would allow the Washington Islamic Centre, WIC to relocate to the campus and take up a full fifth of the available space.

Spector, who had been living in Washington at the time completing an obligatory Pentagon staff posting, remembered the political storm well.

Then and now, he had thought the Wokeists had taken things too far. He hadn't been opposed to the WIC's relocation. What he and so many others had been upset about had been the size of the structure they had built and then the expectations they had placed on the other organizations that had populated the new urban oasis.

Among other politically correct concessions, the involved politicians had acceded to the requirement for female athletes to dress modestly on the various playing fields. In the grand scheme, it had been a minor thing, but along with everything else, it was this kind of decision that had led to the country's fracture.

"As you can see in this video, Mr. President, the fortification of the RFK Urban Area makes crossing this part of the Anacostia an all but impossible task. Every bridge across the Potomac is the same. Even with the help of the French in the air, it's my best guess we're a hundred thousand soldiers short of what we need to take the city."

"And that doesn't include what CANZUK might send across the border," said Spector again interrupting.

"It does not, Mr. President," replied Spellings. "Would you like the update on CANZUK now or after my proposal for what to do about Washington?"

This time, it was Parr who interrupted the briefing. "General, go ahead and weave CANZUK into the big picture analysis if you would, and then move to your proposal for D.C."

Everyone in the room was well aware that Parr had Spector's full confidence, so when the dapper man from Miami gave direction, it was followed as though the President himself had made the request.

"Of course, Mr. Parr," Spellings said, his tone respectful. "As it pertains to CANZUK, their posture along the border hasn't changed. They have three divisions on the Canadian side of the New York border, and our human and satellite intelligence inform us that upwards of two hundred strike fighters are also in that part of the country.

"Altogether, it's a well-equipped force, Mr. President, but as it stands at the moment, there are no indications they're getting ready to move south."

"A part of me wants them to try," Spector growled. "Depending on the day, I'm of the mind we bypass Washington and drive up to

Toronto and do what we did to Cincinnati. Except worse. We take care of the Canadians, and then we're free to do as we please with the Blues."

"I'd recommend against that, Mr. President," Spellings replied. "All indications out of Ottawa and London are that they are finding it difficult to deal with Menendez. As best we can tell, she has refused all of their entreaties."

Spector harrumphed loudly. "Goddamn, that woman is spiteful. Say what you will about Menendez, no one holds a grudge like her. Even now, she can't bring herself to get past the fact they didn't bring her into the Whiteman operation."

"She's the primary reason we're in a civil war in the first place, Mr. President," offered Parr. "The woman simply cannot bend from her principles. It's why even now, as Washington is being surrounded, she's implementing her agenda in an effort to further cement her control."

"Like Hitler in his bunker. In denial and unrepentant until the bitter end," Spector pronounced of his political rival.

On laying out the analogy, he turned from Parr back to Spellings. "So CANZUK isn't a factor at the moment?"

"For now, they're keeping their collective noses clean."

Spector grunted. "Fine, we'll deal with them another time, but mark my words, people, the moment we fold in Washington, you're going to have to give me one hell of a good reason for us not to roll north into Toronto and then Ottawa."

Spector delivered hard stares at Parr and then Spellings. "Are we clear on that point, gentlemen?"

"Perfectly clear, Mr. President. This was always the plan," Spellings said.

"Good, then tell me how we're going to take Washington without a pyrrhic victory."

Spellings nodded soberly. "Of course, Mr. President. As directed by you and thanks further to the ingenuity and hard work of our people at what remains of the Pantex facility in Texas, we now have nine nuclear weapons that can become operational the moment you give the order, sir."

On hearing Spellings' pronouncement, Spector's meaty fist pounded on top of the conference table. "Hell of a job, John. I knew you could get this done. Nine of them, eh? That's two more than I was expecting. What are we looking at in terms of size?

"Six are tactical, ranging from two to three kilotons. Three are strategic. There's a single twenty-kiloton unit and two with a forty-kiloton rating. All units are gravity bombs. Mr. President, I'm pleased to let you know, we can now get as mean as you want us to be."

Spector nodded his head vigorously. "Forty, you say. That could flatten all of D.C.?"

"It's four times the power of the bomb dropped on Nagasaki, Mr. President. It wouldn't rival the strikes on New York and Chicago, but Washington is a smaller city. If we detonate it above the city, the results would be similar. It would be incredible devastation. Historic Washington as we know it would cease to exist."

The Texan's big hand came down on the conference table again in jubilation. "Terrific work, General. Just Terrific. This capacity is a game changer. I take it we're going with the original plan to use the tactical nukes on D.C.?"

"That is the plan, Mr. President."

Spector leaned back into his chair and once again took up the screen that featured the battlements the Blues had constructed in and around the WIC. Looking satisfied, he called out, "Someone get the cigars. This is a moment worth celebrating. By my guess, the end of America's second civil war is now two weeks away at most. Well done, team."

There was a shuffle at the back of the converted Ops Center and as if appearing by magic, an orderly was suddenly standing beside the President, holding a box of what Parr recognized as Cohiba Lanceros.

Two minutes later, with his cigar lit, Spector took a deep and satisfied drag on the refined tobacco. Turning the cigar over in his hand, he pointed the wetted end of the Lancero at Spelling, who himself had refused to take up the celebratory smoke. "Show me your plan, General. I promise I'll keep my mouth shut as you tell me when and how you're going to give me Menendez, a mostly intact Washington, and an end to this damn bloody war."

Ottawa, Parliament Hill

After the assassination of her predecessor and mentor, Bob MacDonald, Merielle had elected to keep the seat she had always sat in for Cabinet meetings. Bob's seat at the center of the long oak table had remained empty as a stark reminder to everyone in the room what the cost of leadership could be.

Three seats down from this empty chair, Merielle had mostly listened to a fiery debate that had been taking place between two factions in her Cabinet. The debate focused on the upcoming referendum in Quebec and to what degree Canada's federal government should involve itself in the final stages of the "No" campaign.

Expertly manipulating the fallout from the Canadian Prime Minister's assassination and the Whiteman operation, Eric Labelle and his separatist party had worked a miracle and convinced enough of the right people, including Canada's supreme court, that the country should have its third referendum on Quebec's sovereignty. And all of this had been done in record time.

In 1995, the country had avoided political ruin with the slimmest of majorities. In a vote where nearly five million people in

Quebec had cast a ballot, only fifty-four thousand individuals, or one percent of Quebecers, had saved Canada.

Merielle had been a child at the time of the referendum, but she could remember events leading up to the vote as though they had only played out last week.

Living in Montreal, her parents had been staunch federalists. Her aunt and uncle, who lived in rural Quebec an hour east of Montreal had been lukewarm supporters of the separatist cause.

Fairweather separatists they may have been, but she could remember the blow-up her father and uncle had in the week leading up to the vote. While blows hadn't been thrown, the words exchanged had been far worse than any punch. It would be another twenty years before the two men would agree to be in the same place, never mind exchanging words.

Today's media pundits and the talking heads of the Laurentian elite had convinced themselves that should a national divorce happen, it would mostly be an amicable affair. But her own experience, still fresh in her mind from decades ago, told her otherwise.

To think that Montreal and other parts of Quebec could not devolve into the Balkans or some version of Northern Ireland was as stupid as it was arrogant. Despite what her critics would have the public believe, Merielle was confident she was neither of those two things.

While the possibility of Canada having its own civil war needed to be contemplated seriously, the solution to that awful outcome was to win the upcoming referendum. And handily, if possible.

It was the "how" of winning that was driving the emotional debate playing out in front of her.

Yvette Raymond, the Minister of Health and easily Merielle's strongest rival in Cabinet, had been sparring with Paul Blanchard, the most loyal of her ministers. As the leaders of their respective factions in Cabinet, the two politicians rarely took each other on, but with the fate of the country on the line, they had discarded their respective proxies and were now clashing directly.

"Look at the polls, Paul," Raymond said, her voice as cool as ever. "We are going to win. Every single poll has us up by one full percentage point. That's less than one hundred thousand votes. With all due respect to Merielle, if she goes to the rally in Montreal and there is a misstep of some sort, that's not much of a cushion. Let me remind you, we're just over a week away from the vote. That doesn't give us enough time to recover if we encounter disaster. We are positioned to win because we have kept Merielle above the fray. At this point, she is a liability, not an asset."

The blonde from Quebec City sported a heavy accent, but her command of the English language was stronger than most of the Anglophones in the room.

A trial lawyer who had made a name for herself before getting into politics, Raymond had never been close to Bob MacDonald. Seven years earlier, she had battled Merielle's predecessor for the leadership of the Conservative Party and had lost in a close race.

To many opinion makers, had the circumstances of MacDonald's death been different, and had it not been the case that Merielle was the defence minister during the Whiteman affair, many thought that Yvette Raymond would have been the most likely person to become Canada's next prime minister.

When Raymond again spoke, she raised her chin slightly and looked directly at Merielle. "The country is at stake, so somebody has to say it. Merielle is a problem. As much as she may be able to seal the victory, she also has an uncanny ability to inflame the separatists."

Raymond paused, allowing a long silence to grow in the room. Still staring at Merielle, the woman used her striking looks and consummate poise to good effect. When she next spoke, the verbal dagger she had been using to filet Blanchard sliced in the direction of Merielle. "We still don't have good answers as to how Josee Labelle was killed. Every time Eric Labelle sees or hears from the prime minister, it's like a bull seeing red. I've seen the videos, colleagues. When the matador is taken, it is not a pretty sight. It is my strongest recommendation for the prime minister not to attend the rally in Montreal this coming Saturday."

"Outrageous!" roared Blanchard in the seat beside Merielle.

A bear of a man, he had a temper that matched his physical description, when provoked. Merielle quickly placed a hand on Blanchard's forearm. Raymond had challenged her directly, so it must be her who addressed the insinuation. "Paul, keep your powder dry."

Merielle slowly released her hand from the big man's arm. "Yvette, I thank you for putting your concern on the table. As a Cabinet and as colleagues, it is better we are open with our disagreements. Too many governments have floundered and fallen because of power struggles such as this."

The other woman snapped, "This is not a power struggle, Merielle. This is about keeping the country together. Your job is not my motivation. Unity is."

"Do not interrupt me again, Yvette," said Merielle, her tone matching the other woman's iciness. "You have your allegation, indirect though it might have been. It sits on the table in front of us like a piece of shit on a sidewalk. You will give me my due and you will listen. Do that, or you can leave this room and you can hand me your resignation."

Raymond's jaw visibly clenched, but the woman did not offer a reply.

"First, let me address the rumor that I or someone in the Canadian government had something to do with the death of Josee Labelle. This is a pernicious accusation that I have left unaddressed in the confines of this room because it is a rumor so outrageous it does not merit a response. It is a rumor, I would add, that is being fomented by a government that is a staunch ally of Mitchell Spector, and a government we know had a hand, if not a leading role, in the assassination of my predecessor.

"France, the same country that has re-armed the Red Faction giving them the tools needed to win the American civil war. France, the same country that has allied itself with petty dictators and war criminals the world over. France, the very same country that has, in the past two years, evicted more than two million North Africans, some of them French citizens, out of their country. Are you prepared to accept the disinformation of France, over the assurances that have been provided by officials in your own country, Yvette?"

On hearing the question, Raymond's eyes narrowed and became prosecutorial. "Do not invoke the boogieman of France, Merielle. You know full well that the bi-partisan investigation of the Labelle murder did not offer conclusive evidence that the Canadian government was not involved in Josee Labelle's death. In fact, Madame Prime Minister, many questions remain."

"What would you have me do, Yvette? Establish a Royal Commission? Now? As war rages to the south? While France continues to plot against us? You've seen the very same reports I have. You've been in the same briefings I've been in. We're treading water in an ocean filled with sharks, and you want us..." As Merielle said the word "us," she gestured to the whole of the room. "...to pour buckets of our own blood into the water? To what end?"

The blonde politician now stared daggers back at Merielle. "Are you that enamored with power that you would risk the fate of this country? I'm not asking you to resign or start a Royal Commission, though both of those outcomes are not without merit. I'm only suggesting that instead of playing with fire, Madame Prime Minister, you check your ego for only the next few days, and let those of us that do not carry the taint of this country's only ever extra-judicial killing do the work of saving the country."

Raymond's proposal delivered, the two women stared each other down until Merielle ripped away her eyes. With a deliberate effort, she slowly pushed her chair back from the huge oak table and got to her feet. Standing, she looked up and down the room, her eyes connecting with the thirty-six politicians that made up her Cabinet.

"Colleagues, on the matter of the Montreal rally, I will be attending. The objections put forward by Minister Raymond have been noted. I have every confidence that should the vote not go our way the entire country will be informed that I was told not to attend. It is in this moment that those in this room who gave that advice will have the opportunity to gloat and recriminate."

Her gaze fell back on Raymond. As cold as ever, the woman's ice-blue eyes stared back at her, brimming with defiance.

"If the past nine months have taught you anything about me, it is that I'm a fighter. If I'm standing in front of a burning building, I could no more prevent myself from going in to save its occupants than I could avoid going to Montreal to try and help us win this referendum. Eric Labelle and the separatists can be damned. I am this country's prime minister until I'm not, so I will go to Montreal and I will speak with the people."

She counted to three as she waited for Raymond to give some indication that she would continue with her putsch, but the woman remained silent.

So be it, Merielle thought. The rift between her and Raymond was now in the open for all to see. The timing was horrendous, but she preferred this type of fight to the one the woman had been covertly waging since Merielle had won the election.

"We'll end this meeting on this note," Merielle said, taking up the rest of the room. "When I stand on that stage and I take the podium to address the crowd in Montreal in five days, it is my hope all of you will be with me. It is my wish the people of Quebec will see a Conservative Party that is united, just as they would like to see a united Canada.

"But as I stand here before you, and I make this ask, I understand we might not be as united as I would like us to be. I understand that some of you might have concerns similar to those voiced by Minister Raymond. If you feel that way, let me say that now is not the time for you to act on these concerns. They can be addressed after the referendum. After the referendum, we can address these concerns fully, so that those of you who have doubts can put these concerns to rest. But now, more than ever, we need to be united."

Still standing, Merielle turned away from addressing the full room and again zeroed in on her challenger. Merielle's index finger was raised to point at Raymond, who remained seated. "That includes you, Yvette. You might control the party in Quebec, but I'm the prime minister. You're with me, or you can resign. What is it going to be?"

For a long time, Yvette Raymond didn't reply to the ultimatum, but in the woman's thoughts, she saluted herself in grand style. The accomplished solicitor that she was had foreseen the outcome of this debate. With the right kind of encouragement, the political neophyte and simple woman standing before her had walked straight into the web that had been laid out for her. Her new ally had foreseen this outcome. Together, they would make a fine team and would save the country that had served them both so well.

"Well, Yvette. What's it going to be?" Merielle said, her voice lowered to the point of nearing a growl.

"I'm with you, Madame Prime Minister. I'm with you and a united Canada."

Chapter 7

Quebec, Gulf of St. Lawrence

It had taken three weeks since his meeting with the Quebec separatist leader to organize his team. He had pulled heavily from his old unit, the 13th Parachute Dragoon Regiment.

Though it had been almost ten years since he had been the CO of France's most capable conventional force, Bruno Corbin had been sure to carry with him indications of his former command, including his rank of colonel and his beloved mustache.

That both made him more recognizable in the hazy world of international covert ops it didn't matter to him in the least. The spies and their ilk were free to change their appearance and skulk in the shadows.

Not him. He commanded men and would always command men. Let those he was contracted to deal with know that it was "the Colonel" who had been paid to see to their end.

Yes, this made him notorious, and yes, it made it more likely that on some random day in the future he would be killed unexpectedly, but heart attacks and cancer were equally unexpected.

Regarding his current enterprise, he had been exceedingly pleased that there had been no resistance to drawing on the active soldiers of the 13th Dragoons to form the core of his team. Indeed, he had been promised he could have France's best soldiers, and in his mind, that is what the men of the 13th Dragoons were.

There were others on the kill team, of course. A dozen operators from the DGSE's Direct Action Division would form the core of his planning group while another dozen or so operators with specialized skills had been drawn in from across France's intelligence and special operations infrastructure.

But for the mission he had been asked to deliver on, he needed brute force in numbers. He needed a critical mass of shock troops he knew he could rely on. And just as important, he needed the right type of man to lead these same soldiers.

In the dark and with the cool breeze of the Gulf of St. Lawrence blowing across his shorn scalp, the Colonel had taken a knee beside the neo-FLQ man that Eric Labelle had connected him with.

Within three days of meeting with the Quebec separatist leader, he had spoken in person with the man who was as much responsible for the rise of the FLQ as Josee Labelle. Now thirty-six years of age, Mario Fortin had served twelve years in the Canadian military, and all twelve of those years had been in the Royal 22nd Regiment, Canada's sole French-speaking regular force infantry unit.

Based on his personnel file, the highly intelligent and reserved man had been an exemplary soldier. The only mar on his record was a series of entries suggesting Fortin might have had links to one of Canada's white nationalist organizations.

To hear it from Fortin, it had been after his fourth harassing conversation with a pair of CSIS Intelligence Officers that he chose to resign from the military and life he loved and take up a quiet existence off the grid two hundred klicks north of Montreal.

It had been Josee Labelle who had identified Fortin as a potential collaborator and drawn the man out of his seclusion and into the leadership ranks of the reformed terrorist movement.

Based on everything the Colonel knew about Josee Labelle, it was clear Fortin did not have the woman's vision or ambitions. Instead, the man was an exceedingly competent 'doer' who seemed to have a gift when it came to navigating the notoriously close-knit and complex waters of Quebec's underworld.

Be it, white supremacists, the Hells Angels, or the scores of crooked cops who worked in the province's various police forces,

Fortin seemed to know them all, and in short order, had secured their services masterfully.

"There they are," said the separatist, pointing out to the water. "Just past the point."

With a clear night sky and the silver light from a waning moon bathing the water in front of them, the Colonel could easily see the two small fishing boats that were bringing him his last batch of commandos.

Ten minutes later, he and Fortin were a dozen feet from the waterline waiting for the first of eight heavily laden Zodiac boats to slide onto the rocky shore. Black and powered by ninety horsepower electric outboard motors, the watercraft silently carved through the waves that were gently rolling inland.

As the first of the boats approached the shoreline, figures in each of the Zodiacs carefully disembarked and waded onto the rocky shore.

As had been the case with the previous drop-offs, all the soldiers were wearing civilian attire. As the commandos worked to unload their equipment, a single man strode in their direction. On reaching them, the squared-jawed soldier came to an abrupt stop, executed a parade ground-worthy salute, and then jutted out his hand. "Colonel. Good to see you, sir. I was hoping it would be you waiting for us."

Taking the younger man's hand, the French mercenary quickly drew the soldier into an embrace. "It's great seeing you, Dorian. I can't tell you how pleased I was you agreed to take this on. We need a man of your caliber to get this done."

"When I was told it was you running the op, I couldn't say no. I owe you too much, my Colonel."

"You owe me and France nothing, Dorian. The only ones that have done more for our great country than you are already across the great divide, where they wait for you in the pantheon of our country's great patriots."

A sheepish smile lit up the soldier's face showing off perfect teeth that fairly glowed in the moonlight. "Still fancying yourself a part-time poet, I see, Colonel. It's that type of spirit that got me to take this mission."

The Colonel's hand reached forward to slap the commando on his muscled shoulder. "Whatever the reason you came, Commandant Elan, I am glad of it."

"And who's this?" Elan said, gesturing in the direction of the Quebec separatist.

"Of course, my apologies. I lost myself in your arrival," the Colonel said as he rounded on the other man.

"Commandant Dorian Elan, allow me to introduce the man who has been helping us in-country. This is Sergeant Mario Fortin, once of the Van Doos. Now he is of the Front de libération du Québec, and he has been invaluable to our cause. It has been some time since I've met a fixer of his capabilities. He has opened many, many doors for us."

The Quebecer and Elan stepped toward one another to shake hands.

"Sergeant Fortin, meet France's most capable soldier and the leader of the team that is going to force Canada to its knees."

Ottawa, National Defence Headquarters

"How's Madison doing?" Colonel Bryan Rydell of the Australian 2nd Commando Regiment asked his friend.

On hearing his wife's name, a smile crossed Larocque's face. "Ready to get on with it and just a touch salty as a result. Just the other day, she was reminding me that I'll be many years retired when the kid ships off to university."

"Ah, no worries, mate," the Aussie officer replied, matching the Canadian's good energy. "It's practically the norm nowadays. Take me for example. I'll be fifty-six when my youngest heads off to uni."

"How is Ms. Rydell, by the way?"

"Ship-shape, but also a touch nervous. The whole bloody country is truth be told," replied the Aussie.

"China?" asked Larocque. "I see they just launched their fourth carrier. To be honest, I'm surprised your government hasn't recalled you and your boys. Any day now, you'll be in as much shit as we are."

The Australian CO nodded his head affirmatively. "You're spot on, my friend. In concert with the Japanese, I'm told we're preparing to designate any part of Vietnam, Thailand, Brunei, or Malaysia as red lines. If the ChiComs move against any of these countries, it's on. For us and the alliance. The British task force should be in the region sometime next week. The *Queen Elizabeth* will be a welcome sight."

Larocque's fingers drummed the leather chair he had been sitting in for the past twenty minutes. Things were getting more real and complex by the day, he thought. Between Madison and making sure the regiment was back in fighting shape, he'd mostly turned his brain away from the bigger picture.

"What about California?" Larocque asked suddenly. "They have to make a move at some point."

"You would hope that's the case, said Rydell, his voice sounding frustrated. "But as best we can tell, they aren't even looking in the direction of the Pacific. "They're focused on the Reds like a targeting laser. Rightly or not, they see Spector as more of a threat than the Chinese, who are half a world away."

"You think that's why you're still here, then?" asked Larocque. "If the Blues can hold on, I guess there's the possibility it could free up California to send the Third and Seventh Fleets to take up the cause against the Chinese. But that's a big 'if' at the moment."

For the first time in the conversation, the third and last man in the waiting room spoke up. Where Larocque and Rydell were whip-like in their respective builds, Colonel Luke Wright, the CO of the British Parachute Regiment, was a squat war hammer of a man.

"Everything turns on Washington, gentlemen. If the Blues shit the bed, everything gets more dangerous for each of our countries. I betcha that's why the three of us have been called in. We're off to Washington, lads. I can feel it in my stubby bones."

Before Larocque or Rydell could prod the Brit on his prognostication, a female voice interrupted their conversation. "Gentlemen. They'll see you now. Ops room five, if you don't mind."

"We don't mind, not one bit, eh, lads?" the Brit officer gregariously called back to the master corporal that had passed along the order.

The man bounded to his feet and quickly took up a position beside the pretty brunette. Turning to face Larocque and Rydell, the man wore a shit-eating grin on his face. "Come now my friends. Let us not keep the good generals waiting."

After exchanging a look, the Canadian and Australian officers slowly pried themselves from their seats and moved to follow the soldier who would guide them to where they would find out what had brought all three COs to Ottawa.

A minute later, the three men were seated in one of the half-dozen operations rooms that were located in this part of Canada's National Defence Headquarters – NDHQ.

General Gagnon, the man who had commanded the operation that had successfully removed the nuclear weapons from Whiteman Air Force Base just eleven months ago, sat at the head of the table flanked by several other high-ranking officers from each of the CANZUK nations.

"Good to see you, gentlemen. Grab a seat if you would." Gagnon said gesturing to the only chairs in the room that weren't yet occupied.

Completely unremarkable in appearance, Gagnon pushed back from the table and got out of his seat, and walked in the direction of the large screen that dominated the far end of the room. On his arrival, the screen lit up with a map of what looked to be a good-sized city.

"Gentlemen, this is Washington, D.C. and from this moment forward, our conversations are to be treated with the utmost operational care. Your 2ICs can be brought into the know about what I'm about to tell you, but that's where it ends. Everyone else down the chain doesn't find out what we're about until I give the say-so. Is that clear?"

Larocque and the other two colonels immediately affirmed Gagnon's directive.

"As we speak, efforts are underway to facilitate the removal of President Menendez." The Canadian general let the extraordinary statement hang in the air for a moment.

"By whom, General?" Rydell finally asked.

"By CANZUK, Colonel, but the why and how of this effort is not our concern. What is our concern is being ready to act when the change happens. And for your units specifically, that means D.C."

Gagnon again let this second statement ferment for a moment allowing the three COs to make comment, but when none came, he continued. "As you're aware, on losing Pittsburgh, what remained of the Blue Faction 3rd Army retreated back to Washington. Effectively, D.C. is their last stand. On the condition that

Menendez is no longer the President of the FAS, CANZUK will officially throw in with the Blues."

"About bloody time," the British Para CO said.

"Many will agree with you, Colonel, but many others will not. But that's not our concern. We have been given our orders, and I and the people in this room are going to do our best to affect them."

"So when do we leave?" This time it was Larocque who posed the question.

"That, Colonel, is the trillion-dollar question. As you know, we have three divisions waiting on the Ontario side of the New York border. The British 3rd, the Canadian 2nd, and what we've taken to calling the CANZUK 4th Division. Altogether, it will be the CANZUK 1st Army."

As the General laid out the structure, Larocque recalled there had been discussions about the Canadian Airborne being folded into the CANZUK 4th.

Five months back, the 4th had been a hodgepodge of Canadian reservist units, an Australian light infantry brigade, and a smattering of Kiwi units. Larocque had fought hard to keep his regiment free of the outfit and had won the argument, but not without pissing off more than a few of the brass, some of whom were seated in the room.

"Once the 1st Army gets the call," Gagnon continued, "it will be their job to pick up a reconstituted Blue division at Fort Drum and then make their way to Washington. What the strategy and order of attack will be is to be determined. There are too many variables in the air at the moment, but you can bet your last dollar, Spector and his people will send at least some of their forces to meet us."

Colonel Wright whistled. "That's a hell of a hammer and anvil, General."

"It is that, Colonel. Based on our current count, Spector has something in the range of 120,000 to 160,000 soldiers moving in the direction of D.C. And that doesn't include his militias. With them, you're looking at what might be a quarter of million men under arms."

His elbows on the table, Rydell's hand went into the air.

Gagnon's eyes took up the Aussie. "Question, Colonel?"

"More of a comment, sir. You say each of our units is to be sent to D.C., but that assumes the Blues can hold the city. How many soldiers does the FAS have left? It can't be more than a hundred thousand. At least not frontline units. What's to say the Reds don't end this war before our lads along the border start their engines?"

Gagnon nodded his head. "Excellent question, Colonel. This is where your units come in. When the call comes, all of 2nd Commando, the Airborne Regiment, and 1st and 2nd battalions of the Parachute Regiment will be flown into Washington, whereupon, if things go to shit, each of you and your regiments will help the Blues hold off the Reds until our forces from the north can begin to engage."

"If?" said Larocque.

"Yes, 'if,'" Gagnon said promptly. "The Blues have fortified nearly every square inch of Washington and those soldiers that are in the city will be veterans of both Cincinnati and Pittsburgh. If the Reds do move to take the city, it'll be a slog. In fact, if I get it my way, outside of any forward air control missions you might need to conduct, it's my hope you and your soldiers won't be involved in any fighting. Once the four divisions arrive from the north, it might be that we can stop the attack on Washington altogether."

"When do we leave, sir?" asked Wright sounding eager.

"Tentatively, you'll be wheels up on the day of the referendum. Everyone will be focused on what's happening in Quebec. All three of your units will be flown into Dover Air Force Base in Delaware.

From there, the Blues will get you into reserve positions in Washington proper."

Larocque interjected, and when he spoke this time there was a hint of annoyance in his voice. "Wait, 'tentatively'? This plan isn't set already? Tell me the Blues know we're coming?"

On hearing the question, Gagnon's face took on the look of someone being caught doing something they shouldn't. "Officially, the Blues aren't in the know. At the moment, Menendez is still running the country. Until she's out of the picture, everything is up in the air. As we speak, we're quietly feeling out the right people to make Delaware happen. Assuming things develop as we intend them to, we need your outfits to be ready and wheels up within six hours."

Gagnon took a moment to lock eyes with Larocque. "We're good, Colonel?"

"Yes, sir. Sorry to be a dick. I'm just a bit gun-shy. The last time I got into the shit, our plans didn't last thirty minutes. I don't have any of the details, but isn't removing a president a bit of an uncertain endeavor?"

"To say the least, Colonel," Gagnon said, his tone sober. "And were I you, I'd be feeling the same way. Just know that we're leaning on your units because what we need for this mission are experienced operators who can adapt. This is what all three of you did in Missouri, so we're sending you into D.C. And I stand by my earlier statement, there's every chance you'll see minimal action."

Gagnon removed his gaze from the Canadian Airborne CO to once again take up all three men. "Assuming there is a new FAS president and our side wins the referendum, the PM and the other CANZUK leaders will announce to the world we're in Washington and we're throwing in with the Federation of American States. The next day, our three divisions will cross into Upstate New York.

When it all goes down, it should be a powerful moment and will hopefully boost the morale of the Blues in D.C."

"So we're finally getting into this war," Larocque said, his voice neutral.

Gagnon nodded his head. "It looks that way. I know the timing is terrible for you, Jackson, but we need you leading the Airborne more than ever. It is mission-critical to make sure the Blues don't collapse. We need all three of you to go. As I said, with what you collectively achieved in Missouri, it's going to be a hell of a shot in the arm for all involved. You three and your units in Washington are our insurance policy against disaster."

Far from a heartless man, Gagnon looked at Larocque with an obvious kindness in his eyes. Every officer in the room knew what Larocque had been through in Missouri, and most would know the status of his wife. As the General began to open his mouth, Larocque moved to squash any more talk of him and his situation. "I'm good, sir. The boys and I are all in. We always were."

Months ago, Larocque had been given the chance to walk away from his command and hadn't because he knew something like this was coming. His country was going to war and now, more than ever, his special set of skills was needed. The only question that remained was whether or not Madison would find it within herself to support what the government was once again asking him to do.

Chapter 8

Ottawa

Merielle exhaled contentedly. Her lovemaking with the man lying beside her had been intense. It had been over two weeks since they had been together in this way, while still being in each other's presence. It had been maddening.

When they had finally got time to be alone, they had all but devoured one another. It was a terrible thing to be in love and not be able to do the things that new couples did, but that frustration was well compensated for when they finally got the chance to be intimate. Fireworks were not an exaggeration.

"I've asked for a transfer," said the man lying beside Canada's Prime Minister.

"I know. I was advised this morning," Merielle said.

"By who? I only just told the Inspector yesterday. Jesus, you would think in this day and age, people would do a better job of holding their secrets."

Merielle reached across the bed and placed her hand on Staff Sergeant Asher Lastra's muscled and hairy chest. "Does it matter? Likely it should have happened after the first time we did this."

"It should have but you've been busy and that's made me busy. You don't sit still for a moment, woman."

She smiled in his direction. "I'm still busy, Staff Sergeant. What's changed?"

Lastra gave her a sheepish look.

In response, she elevated an eyebrow and after a few seconds of staring finally said, "Out with it. We don't hold back. It's the only way we are going to survive the craziness that is our lives."

Lastra pushed himself up from under the covers, so his full upper body was exposed. For a man in his late forties, he was in terrific shape, Merielle thought, not for the first time.

"Well, out with it." As the words left her mouth, it was clear the afterglow of their physical intimacy had fizzled away.

"Alright, alright. Last week, I overheard a few members of my team talking about us."

Seeing the look of alarm spread on Merielle's face, he quickly continued. "It wasn't anything bad. In fact, they all seemed happy for us."

"But?"

"But, it clearly wasn't the first time they'd been talking about it."

"So, they know. That was bound to happen sooner or later. What of it?"

"It's procedure Merielle. You of all people should know there are rules and regs to follow."

"Most times but not always. Sometimes, you have to break the rules."

Lastra shook his head. "We have a great team protecting you, Madame Prime Minister. I mean it's as good as any outfit I've worked with. One of the reasons it's so good is that we follow procedures. I mean every 't' and every 'i' is crossed and dotted without fail."

"With the exception of our relationship?" Merielle offered.

"Bingo. What makes me so special? I'm breaking the cardinal sin of protection work. I'm emotionally involved with the asset. Christ, I'm sleeping with her."

An angry look leaped onto Merielle's face. "Just sleeping with?"

"No, Jesus, Mer. It's more than sex and you know it. You're the first person I've been with since Catherine. It's taken me five years to get past her. On top of that, with this thing we've got ourselves into, I've altered the course of my career, and most likely not for the better. There are people in the Force who won't take kindly to what I've done, and it won't matter one iota who you are. In fact, it'll work against me, and I'm not ready to retire."

Exhaling loudly, Lastra reached out to Merielle and pulled her in his direction. Allowing herself to be dragged across the bed's sheets, she slipped her arm underneath his back and laid her head across his stomach.

"Depending on where I get transferred, I could be back in a uniform pulling over miserable bureaucrats who get their thrills out of going thirty over on the parkway."

"I would never let that happen," Merielle said, as she began to kiss his skin just above his navel.

"It's good of you to say, Merielle, but I don't want you getting involved. God knows you have enough on your plate as it is. The Inspector says she'll have the transfer worked out by the end of the month. There's no sense worrying about it until I see where they're going to send me."

"So, you'll be able to run the team in Montreal, then?"

"Montreal?" As he said the name of the city, one of Lastra's hands enmeshed itself with the hair on the back of Merielle's head.

"Yes, Montreal. I made the decision this earlier today. I'm surprised you haven't heard about it. It's all over the news. Can you imagine a scenario where I don't go to the rally? What kind of leader would I be if I didn't attend?"

"Maybe they're not wrong," Lastra said quietly.

Merielle's kissing stopped immediately and she pulled her head away from Lastra's hand. Released, she rolled off him and propped herself on the bed's headboard, exposing her naked upper body.

"Not you too?"

"Mer, c'mon. You've seen the same reports I have. How many death threats do you have to receive before it sinks in? For Christ's sake, you saw what happened to MacDonald. You were there."

Merielle's eyes narrowed and her lips thinned as she took a moment to reassess the man lying in her bed.

When she next spoke, her words held an icy tone. "I will not let Labelle steal the referendum from me, Staff Sergeant. Not when we're so close to winning. That separatist bastard has something up his sleeve. I can feel it in every fiber of my body. If I'm not in Montreal doing everything I can to fight him, I won't be able to live with myself. I have to be there."

"But you're winning, Merielle. Every poll has the 'No' side up. If you go to Montreal, you're going to work the separatists into a lather. If the rally goes badly for whatever reason, it might be all Labelle needs to win over enough of the undecideds who don't like what you did in Missouri, and because of…"

"Because of what?" Merielle snapped. "Because of Josee Labelle?"

Lastra reached out a hand toward Merielle, but she slapped it away. "Merielle, I don't care what happened to Josee Labelle. And most Canadians don't care either. The world is a dangerous place and by all the available evidence, Eric Labelle's daughter was playing a dangerous game.

"But you're a Quebecer, Mer, and Quebecers think differently on such things. They've given you a pass on Missouri, but Labelle is forcing them to think about his daughter. It's political opportunism of the worst kind, and I loathe the man for it, but it is what it is."

Lastra's hand, thick with coarse hair, reached out and firmly took in Merielle's. This time she didn't slap it away.

"Montreal is a bad idea, my love. And Eric Labelle is not Josee Labelle. There is zero evidence he had anything to do with his daughter's actions and there's nothing to suggest he has any plans beyond trying to win the referendum. If the neo-FLQ still exists, Monsieur Labelle isn't involved. That's been proven. Let it go."

Merielle suddenly jerked her hand from his. "I think I'm going to go for a run. When I get back, I'd like for you to be gone."

"Merielle..." Lastra said in a pained voice.

She cut him off. "Don't Merielle me. Just be gone by the time I'm back."

With that, Merielle gathered her clothes and made her way out of the guest room she had occupied since first moving into Prime Minister's residence. As she walked past the master bedroom where she had found Bob MacDonald and his wife on that terrible night months ago, she steeled herself.

Asher Lastra had not been working the MacDonald security detail on that evening, so he had not seen the butcher's bill. She had, and it haunted her every day since.

It was the French who had killed her friend and mentor and she knew it was the French who had urged Josee on. And it was the French who continued to lurk in the dark political waters that confronted Canada in the former United States. That they were not somehow involved in the coming Quebec referendum was inconceivable.

They were here in Canada. She knew it and damn anyone who told her otherwise.

It was this private supposition more than anything else that was driving her to make the extraordinary decisions she had made in recent weeks. As she began to put on her running gear, she reminder herself that France was not the only country that could operate in the shadows. Canada, now a country of fifty million people strong, could and must do the hard things.

Somewhere in Connecticut

It had been Hall who had come up with the plan to capture the FAS Secretary of Education. The woman seemed to have an encyclopedic knowledge of the Menendez administration, which when combined with a flair for ops planning had produced the workable plan that the Joint Operations Committee back in Ottawa had approved.

Hall's plan hinged on the fact Hastings and her daughter were estranged. Hall had not been able to identify why the estrangement had occurred, but that particular tidbit wasn't critical for her plan to work. They just needed to leverage the broken relationship to draw the Secretary out of the fortress that was now Washington.

The Model R Tesla they were riding in quietly pulled off the rural highway onto a heavily treed road that the team's near-AI had told them led to a secluded power relay station. As the vehicle came to a stop a short distance later, Petite turned in his seat and faced Hall. Sitting in the back seat of the sedan, she hadn't said more than two words during the three-hour trip. "This is the place," he said.

Hall nodded in confirmation. "The daughter's house is one klick north. It's a straight line through the bush from here to her backyard."

Petite turned his head to the vehicle's driver. "Thanks for the lift, Janks. If all goes well, we'll see you back here in a few."

"Copy that, boss. You're sure you don't need a few more hands with you? Sykes and Collette can be here in five."

Before Petite could respond to the JTF-2 operator's offer, Hall interjected, "We're good, Janks. We stick to the plan."

Catching the authority of the younger woman's reply, the Canadian special operations soldier said nothing. Instead, he locked eyes with Petite and waited.

"We're good, Sergeant. We follow the plan. Just like Hall says."

"Then we're good," the big commando replied. "Good luck to you both."

Petite thrust out his fist to which Janks reciprocated with a fist bump. "Thanks, Janks. We'll keep you updated as best we can."

Hall's door opened. A second later she was at Janks' window, offering him her own clenched fist.

Janks didn't hesitate. Gently, with a closed hand that looked like a holiday ham, he pounded the woman's much smaller fist.

"Sorry, to be a bit of a dick, Janks," Hall offered. "When I get zeroed in, I can get intense."

"It's all good. I'm no different. We'll be waiting for your first update. Good luck."

With that, Janks engaged the vehicle and slowly turned it in the direction they had come from. Turning away from the departing car, Petite locked onto the enigma who was the young woman standing beside him. "Back at the house when you pulled me aside and told me that it could only be you and me who goes in, you said you'd tell me later why. Now is that time. Who are you really, Sarah Hall, and what exactly have I got myself into?"

Hall, dressed as though she was about to head out on a hike, stared back at Petite. That her light brown hair was in a ponytail high atop her head only served to accentuate her youthfulness.

But Petite had learned early on in their relationship that Hall used her appearance as a tool. She would let you think she was too young and inexperienced. That she was pretty didn't help matters.

But it was all a ruse. Since arriving, the woman standing in front of him had worked the façade brilliantly. Task after task, Hall's doubters had come to find out they were dealing with someone much different than they appeared.

"I'd like to start with an apology, Sam. While I've seen your full personnel file, you have not seen mine. You've only seen the parts of my service that the people I work for want you to see. It's a necessary if regrettable thing that is done to protect who I really work for."

Petite grunted. "So, I don't know who you are but know all about me. You don't need to apologize for that. I'm proud of my career. I've always done the best I could and done what I thought was right. Even when those things were hard."

"Yes, you have," Hall offered, her tone neutral. "I'm a part of a small group of people in our country that are operating within the confines of what has been described to me as an 'undisclosed writ.' A writ you had a hand in creating, by the way."

Petite's eyes narrowed. "You mean Haiti?"

"Yes, Haiti is exactly what I'm referring to," offered Hall.

"I did what I had to do to achieve the mission I was assigned." As the words came out of Petite's mouth there was a clear bitterness to them.

Hall nodded her head quickly in response to Petite's statement. "I'm aware that your legal status was precarious after you came back from your Haiti posting. That won't happen again, Sam. I can promise you that."

Hall paused for several seconds, giving the impression she was considering her next words carefully. "The fact you and I are standing here indicates that something has changed within our country. After Afghanistan, Ukraine, Haiti, Whiteman, and the assassination of MacDonald, Canada has finally decided to unbind the one hand that has always been behind our back."

"And what does that mean? For Christ's sake, Hall, stop being so cryptic. Say what you gotta say. If we need to do some hard things, then let me hear what they are. I'm not a child and I'm no fool."

Hall unflinchingly took up Petite's brown eyes as they stared at her. "Can count on you to do the hard things, Sam Petite."

The months that followed his service in Haiti had been a touch-and-go period of his life and career. Then, Petite had been a field officer in an agency that didn't give its people a license to kill. The weeks of interviews and waiting while the Canadian Security Intelligence Service tried to figure out what to do with him had finally come to an end when Robert MacDonald's Conservatives won their first majority.

Within a month of the election's end, he had been taken off administrative leave and had been given his next assignment, and not so much as one more word had been mentioned to him about the man he had killed as a part of Canada's effort to rescue a female CAF officer from Haiti's most notorious gang, the Alpha-7s.

That his career had resumed as though the previous eight months had not happened had been an unsolved mystery that to this day bothered Petite in the extreme.

As Hall awaited his reply, Petite finally concluded that this woman and whomever she worked for might have answers as to why he was standing here and not sitting in a jail cell with a conviction for murder. More than anything, he wanted an answer to that question.

"You can count on me, Hall. Whatever thing needs to be done, I'm all in. It's why I agreed to lead an Action Group team and it's why I'm here now. But before I take one step in the direction of this house we're about to visit, you better level with me.

"People in our business don't like surprises, and I'm no different. I want to find out exactly what I've got myself into and what these *hard things* I have to do might be."

Setting his hands on his hips, Petite delivered an unremitting stare in Hall's direction. "Whoever you are Hall, you dish now, or I'm not going anywhere."

Chapter 9

Undisclosed Location, North Carolina

Parr walked down the long hallway that led to Spector's private quarters. It was well past midnight. As was his habit, he had been awake perusing the previous day's social media. It had been a quiet day, with all of the usual players weighing into the Blues' education announcement out of Buffalo.

Arriving at an open, double-door threshold, Parr stopped and looked into the confines of a cavernous bedroom where only half of the lights were on. It was one of the many impressive spaces in the well-kept property that the President's inner circle had been occupying for the past three weeks.

Spector, a man who had been subjected to no fewer than three assassination attempts since becoming the UCSA's leader had mandated they move their base of operations periodically. Earlier in the day, Parr had received an update on their next location. That they would be heading back to his home state of Florida thrilled him.

"Come in, Pete."

Parr zeroed in on the voice. The Texan was to his right, tucked into the corner sitting underneath a colonial-looking sconce providing light to whatever book the man had been reading.

"Good morning, Mr. President. Burning the midnight oil per the norm, I see."

Spector gestured to the chair across from him. "Take a seat."

As he took the proffered seat, Spector leaned forward and gently tossed the King James version of the Bible he had been reading onto the floor.

"The Bible, eh? Contemplating some weighty stuff are you, Mr. President?"

Spector took in a deep breath, held it briefly, and then exhaled loudly. "It doesn't get more weighty than nuclear weapons."

"So you've made a decision, then?"

"I have. We'll move forward with the plan discussed today."

"It's the right call, Mr. President. In the end, you'll save tens of thousands of our soldiers' lives. And by now, most of Washington has cleared out. Civilian casualties will be minimal. And we can always rebuild. But unlike the Blues, 'build back better' won't be just a slogan."

"Always looking for the right angle to sell, aren't you, Parr?"

"It's why you pay me the big bucks, sir."

"Yeah, well, let's see what those big dollars have to say about what I'm about to tell you."

"That's foreboding. I didn't think things could get more serious than tactical nukes."

"You might not think that once you hear what I have to say."

Parr crossed his legs and made himself more comfortable. To his surprise, the conversation that had taken place a few hours earlier about dropping low-yield nuclear weapons on D.C. had not fazed him in the least. The overriding thought he'd had while he listening to the conversation was what would it matter if another forty thousand or so people died when millions had already been slaughtered.

"Mr. President, I'm already all in with what you are trying to achieve. We both know if we somehow manage to lose this war what the consequences will be for someone like me. The only question will be whether or not I'm hung with dignity as was done with the Nazis at Nuremberg or like a barking dog à la Saddam Hussein."

"Astute, Mr. Parr," Spector said quietly. "But keep this in mind, if you would. No American general or soldier was tried for laying waste to Dresden or Tokyo. It won't be any different once we settle things with the Blues. The victors write the histories of the wars they win."

Parr made no reply to the statement. Instead, he waited to hear why he had been called to the President's suite at this late hour.

"Pete, I will not give Menendez a platform once we take Washington. She's as much responsible for this war as Fitzgerald and Cameron were. In some respects, she has more responsibility. Her ideologies ruined this country, so the notion that I'm going to give the woman and her people the opportunity to spout off through some trial with a pre-determined outcome just isn't going to happen."

"Smart, Mr. President. She'll only be made into a martyr by those who continue to resist."

"I'm glad you see it that way because it's you who are going to erase Valeria Menendez, her people, and all the things they believe from this continent the moment we move on Washington."

Parr arched an eyebrow. "How is that, Mr. President?"

"A purge, Peter. A purge the likes of which the world hasn't seen since the Soviets took Russia from the Czar. With your help, I want to sterilize the Blue population of every notion of equity, white supremacy, critical race theory, and the rest of that horseshit drivel they spout off each and every day. We go back to the way things were circa 2010, if not earlier."

Parr stared back at Spector for a long moment and finally said, "You're serious about this?"

"Son, I just gave the order to use nuclear weapons on Washington, D.C. It doesn't get more serious than that. We can't take that city and continue this war of attrition with the Wokeists. It all has to end. Whatever country we're to become, we need a fresh start. Can you do that for me?"

Parr didn't hesitate with his reply. "I'll need names. And I'll need access to the right kind of people. People who won't flinch when the time comes. This won't be pretty. At least in the first month or so."

Having given the idea of a societal purge considerable thought, Spector had replies ready. "There are names from the militias I can provide and there are others in our ranks. You'll need hundreds if not thousands of men. This will need to grow, Peter. I want this effort to touch every city and town from here to the top of Maine. Treat it like the cancer it is. There can't be one stitch of this disease left in our country or it'll grow back."

"And the list of names of people that need to go? We have one?" asked Parr.

"We do. When we talked about this casually a few months back, I had asked for a list to be built. The last I checked, it had over nine thousand names, of which two thousand are critical."

"Nine thousand?" Parr said, with a hint of incredulity in his voice.

"It's a big job," Spector said quickly. "But if we're going to reconstitute the United States and secure its future for the next fifty years, it has to happen. Purges are never pleasant or easy. And when it's all said and done, there's every chance polite society will turn its back on you. You'll do your best to hide what has to be done of course, but enough people will know what you did for me. Can you live with that? You're what –forty-five?"

"Forty-three, Mr. President."

Spector nodded his head. "What if you live to ninety, Mr. Parr? That's a long time to live as a pariah."

Parr's reply was again prompt. "Robert McNamara lived forty-one good years after his stint as Secretary of Defense and that man oversaw the slaughter of fifty thousand American soldiers and hundreds of thousands of Vietnamese civilians. Bush Forty-Three invaded and destroyed Iraq under false pretenses and to the day he died, huge swaths of the country adored the man."

"So, you'll do this for me?" Spector asked the younger man point blank.

"I agree it has to be done and that it has to be done well. Since our conversation on this topic months ago, I've given a lot of thought to the process. In many ways, it fascinates me." As Parr related the last part of his statement, his eyes and voice became distant as his mind began to race through everything that would need to be done to prepare for this new part of the war.

Spector nodded his head appreciatively. "I knew it was the right decision to bring you in, Peter. You'll have my administration's full support. No matter how bad things get, you can count on the entire weight of my team and myself. So, you will lead the effort?"

Parr's eyes refocused and again connected with Spector. "I will, Mr. President. I think I have to."

"Good. Very good. This is big, Pete, and it's the last piece of the operational puzzle."

Without notice, Spector hefted his bulk up from his chair. Despite his age and waist size, the man rose quickly. Parr, younger and in decent shape, moved to follow the other man to his feet.

"It's time I got a bit of shut-eye. Thank you for coming to meet with me at this late hour. By the time you get back to your office, the list of names will be in your email. Have a look at it and after we meet with the generals for the daily briefing in the morning, I'd like to hear your initial thoughts on how we tackle this problem."

"I'll have several, sir."

As Parr turned to leave the room, Spector spoke again. "Remember, Pete, it's us who are going to win this war."

Stopping his turn to the door, Parr again took up Spector's face. Though their conversation had only taken a few minutes, the man appeared more tired than when he first entered the room. Long days and weighty decisions, took their toll on any man. "I understand, Mr. President. And just as not a single person on their most forgiving day would show stage four cancer mercy, neither will I with this task. This has to be done thoroughly and completely."

Spector nodded his head gently in response to Parr's reply. "Then you understand precisely, Peter."

Washington, D.C.
Despite being the Secretary of Education, Roberta Hastings had insisted to the President that she be included in that part of the Cabinet dedicated to informing how the war was conducted.

And it was a good thing. In the four years the war had been raging, Menendez had needed people committed to her vision. On more times than she could remember, senators, cabinet secretaries, and at least two generals had attempted to remove Hastings from this circle of power, and on each occasion, the President had backed her up and set people straight or more often, sent them packing.

It looked like another attempt was in the offing. Hastings had been forced to bite her tongue repeatedly as Vice President Andrew Morgan had finally begun to show his true colors.

In truth, she had always suspected the man. White, middle-aged, and an Ivy Leaguer, he had always been soft on Menendez's program. While she and a few others in the Cabinet had undertaken to implement the President's diversity and equity initiatives with alacrity, Morgan had relegated himself to economic issues and the occasional foreign policy challenge.

This morning, Morgan sat across and at a slight angle from the President, and as always, everything about the man's communication style was measured. "Madame President, I understand General Sullivan's plan, and I understand that it is likely to be months of hard fighting before the city is at risk. But what I don't understand is why you insist on staying here in Washington. With the front so close, you are at risk at each and every moment. A single artillery strike or a lone sniper who gets a lucky shot. They're all just a few kilometers away. You can oversee the war just as easily from Boston."

Sitting beside the President and practically vibrating with fury, Hastings had heard enough. "The President has addressed this point already," she said, refusing to employ Morgan's VP honorific. The plain-looking man with greying hair shifted his attention in her direction. Until this moment, they had never tussled.

"Madame Secretary –"

"Let me finish," Hastings snapped across the large boardroom table.

"The President has addressed your point. She's not leaving the capital, nor is anyone else from the Cabinet. The people and our soldiers need to see that we are standing firm. As a former soldier yourself, I would think you would have understood the symbolism, if not the practicality of this approach."

"Madame Secretary, I appreciate the practicality of staying here, but the proposal is at odds with how we've conducted the war to date. Since the outbreak of hostilities, we've been directing the fight from afar. I don't see why that should change now."

To signal the Vice President was done with Hastings, the man shifted his attention back to Menendez.

Hastings felt a blaze of indignation rise within her. She hated men. More, she hated men of privilege. In the years since the start of the war, she had tolerated Morgan because he was a controllable version of the type of person Menendez needed to keep her hold on power.

"I'm not done speaking." As the words slowly came out of Hastings' mouth, they held a tone everyone in the room was familiar with.

Valeria Menendez would recognize it too, and in that instant, the woman would signal the fate of the person Hastings had set her sights on by heading her off, or by letting her gallop toward what was the beginning of the end of someone's political career. Menendez said not a word.

For a split second, the room remained completely silent as the Vice President turned his attention back to Hastings. The look on the man's pasty face suggested he understood exactly what had just transpired.

As their eyes locked and just as Hastings was about to unleash a barrage of accusations, her phone on the table in front of her lit up indicating a call was coming in.

She risked a glance at the number. With the exception of her Chief of Staff and a handful of the people in the room with her, only one other person had her number.

Her eyes flashed away from the phone and locked onto Menendez. "I'm terribly sorry, Madam President. I have to take this call."

Not waiting for a reply, her hand snatched the phone and got up from the table. Turning, she bee-lined for the Presidential Emergency Operations Center – PEOC – entrance, and on exiting the secure conference space, she toggled the phone and brought it to her ear.

"Hello, Janet, honey, is that you?"

There was only silence in response to the question.

"Janet, is something wrong? Is everything okay?"

"It's me, Mom," the other voice said. It sounded exhausted.

"My goodness, it's good to hear your voice. It's been so long. The babies? How are the babies? Oh my goodness, they're not babies anymore, of course. It is so wonderful to hear your voice. Are –"

The voice on the phone cut her off. "I have cancer. I'm dying, Robbie. I need to see you. I need to see you soon. We need to discuss what to do with the kids."

Now down the hall, Hastings darted into an unoccupied office and closed the door. Her heart was pounding in her chest. "What do you mean, you're dying? What do you mean you have cancer? When? What? Jesus, honey, what's going on?"

There was a pause and then Hastings heard a deep exhalation travel through the phone. "It started in my ovaries, but now it's everywhere. We caught it too late. The doctor tells me I might have two months, but I think it'll be sooner. Much sooner."

As her eyes began to well, Hastings surprised herself by letting loose an audible sob. It had been three years since she'd last spoken with her one and only child. As she carelessly wiped her nose with the sleeve of her jacket, she couldn't have cared less if anyone heard her burst of emotion. She had held herself together throughout this entire terrible war but the idea that her daughter was near death was a bridge too far.

When her daughter next spoke, there was a hint of desperation in her voice. "How soon can you be here?"

"To Hartford?"

"Yes, I'm just outside the city now. I moved a year after the war started."

"I can be there first thing tomorrow. Does that work? I can get there tonight if you need me to?" Hastings said, her words sounding urgent.

There was a slight pause, and then her daughter replied, "No, tomorrow morning is fine."

"Okay, it'll allow me to make arrangements this afternoon. As you can imagine, things are kind of crazy around here."

"What kind of arrangements?" her daughter asked.

"Oh, security mostly. They won't let anyone from Cabinet leave the city without a detail."

Again, there was hesitation on the phone. When her daughter next spoke, Hastings caught the anxiety in the woman's voice. "Security?"

"Yes, security, honey. Is everything okay? Are you safe?"

Her daughter's reply was immediate but more important, whatever anxiety had been there seconds before departed. "Everything's fine. You know I don't like guns, and the drugs they have me on have made me an emotional wreck. Things will be better when you get here."

"Okay. However, I can help, honey, I'll help. I'm so glad you called. I'll be there tomorrow morning. Noon at the very latest." As Hastings spoke, she made no effort to tamp down the delight she was feeling. Even if it was terminal cancer that had forced her only child to reach out to her, it was an opportunity for Hastings to correct this small but important part of her life. Maybe now, her daughter be would open to trying to understand the difficult choices she had made in the years since their estrangement.

"Okay, Robbie, I have to run. Thanks for picking up. We'll talk tomorrow."

"Oh, honey, I'm glad you called. I -"

Hastings heard the connection drop.

For several long moments, she stayed moored in the chair of the borrowed office and thought about the conversation she'd just had. With all that was going on, her daughter's timing could not have been worse, but the chance of reconciliation, even if would be for a short period, was an opportunity she could not pass on. And the kids. Janet's husband had been killed in the first months of the war and she had never been particularly close to his family.

For all intents and purposes, her daughter was alone in a dangerous world, and if she was dying that made her grandchildren and their future her number one concern.

No doubt Valeria would understand, Hastings thought. The question was, could the woman survive politically with her out of D.C. for a day or two? She was certain she would. Morgan may have found a spine, but no one would ever accuse the man of being decisive. No, Andrew Morgan was a creature of Washington, and like all such creatures, they were slow to act.

Whatever his plans, they would still be in lethargic motion two days from now. And in those two days, she would have her people find out what Morgan was up to and when she was back in D.C., she would remind the Vice President who the big players in this town actually were.

Somewhere in Connecticut
Dr. Janet Hastings-Moore slowly placed the phone on the kitchen island and looked at the woman seated at the kitchen table with her two children.

"Well done, Doctor."

"Yeah, well, I didn't have much of a choice, did I?"

"No, you didn't. As I told you, this is serious business, and I'm not messing around."

As the woman delivered her message of control, she let her hand slip from Hastings-Moore's daughter's delicate shoulder.

"I'd like to bring my children to the washroom, and I'd like some time alone with them. I need to help them understand what's happening."

The woman who called herself "Jennifer" rose from the kitchen table chair she had been sitting at and took a step away from her daughter. As the distance increased between her oldest child and the woman, the vise-like pressure within Hastings-Moore's chest bled off, if only slightly.

"One at a time. That's the deal."

"Why not both? Did you not just listen to the conversation I had? I'm doing what you asked. She'll be here tomorrow."

Jennifer nonchalantly moved back in the direction of her daughter and again placed her hand on the girl's shoulder. As the woman's hand reconnected, she lowered herself onto her haunches so her head was level with Hastings-Moore's daughter's face. The girl, more than bright enough to understand the dynamic that was playing out, was no longer terrified. Instead, her angelic face featured a look of exhaustion. As a mother, it broke Hastings-Moore's heart.

"Taylor, go with your mom," Jennifer said, her voice as unemotional as ever. "I'll stay here with your brother and we'll have some ice cream. And when you come back, it'll be your turn. Can you do that for me, young lady?"

The girl looked to her mom and seeing a nod of confirmation, she replied with a firm sounding, "Yes."

Still hunched, Jennifer prodded the young girl in the direction of her mother. As the eight-year-old crossed the kitchen to arrive in her mother's arms, Jennifer languidly stood and locked onto the displeased eyes of the woman she needed to manage for the next dozen or so hours.

"It bears repeating Dr. Hastings-Moore. Do what I ask when I ask it. Do these things and this transaction of ours will go perfectly. Don't do what I ask, or ask questions that you already know the answer to, and I'll put a round into the back of both of your kids' heads while you watch."

Despite the ghastliness of the threat, the woman delivered the commitment without any hint of aggression or malice. It had been that way since she and the man had casually walked into her kitchen an hour ago.

"I'll do whatever you ask. Just don't hurt my babies. They're all that matters to me. I could care less about Robbie. She was and is a terrible person. If I didn't see her again, it would be too soon."

The Red Faction agent, or whoever this woman was, took a step in the direction of her son. It wasn't clear the happy-go-lucky kid, who had just turned four understood what was transpiring. As the woman loomed beside him, he looked in his mother's direction with his kind, bright eyes and began to cry. As her instincts as a mother flared, she took a step in the direction of her son.

Before she could take a second step, the woman produced a handgun in a flash. Matte black and menacing, the barrel of the weapon was leveled at the back of her son's still-soft skull. The boy couldn't see the weapon, but as a look of terror leaped onto his mother's face, some evolutionary principle of self-preservation asserted itself and he suddenly became silent.

"Look at me, Doctor," ordered Jennifer, her voice cracking off the walls with authority for the first time.

Her feet rooted into the kitchen floor the moment the weapon appeared Hastings forced herself to tear her eyes from her son. When they connected with her hazel-eyed captor, she shot the woman the kind of look a mother bear would deliver to anyone that got between herself and her cubs right before she mauled that person to death.

When the woman called Jennifer next spoke, her words were low and laced with menace.

"I don't give a damn that your children are children. What's happening here and now is so much bigger than you. I swear to you, I will kill them if you don't do what I ask when I ask. Do you understand?"

As the threat registered with Hastings-Moore, she lowered her chin and softened her face so it didn't look like she wanted to commit murder. "I understand. I believe you."

"Good. Now take your daughter and do what you need to do."

As she said the words, Jennifer casually removed the pistol away from the back of her son's head, and, just as quickly as it had appeared, the weapon vanished somewhere at the small of her back.

When Jennifer next spoke, the young woman demonstrated she could in fact smile. She took a step around her son, turned to face him, and as though she were a camp counselor, in a sing-song voice, she said, "I scream, you scream, we all scream for ice cream." Then, she slowly held out both of her hands to the boy. "What do you say, James? Can you show me where your mom keeps the ice cream?"

On realizing the prospect of ice cream was real, her son's face lit up. As he slid off the chair he had been sitting in and darted his way to the freezer, Hastings-Moore forced herself to turn away so she could gather up her still-distraught daughter.

As they left the kitchen, she bowed her head close to her daughter and whispered, "It'll be alright, princess. When Robbie gets here, this will all go away. I promise."

"Who's Robbie, Mommy?"

Hastings-Moore should have expected the question, but with all that had been going on, she hadn't seen the inquiry coming, so it took her a moment to decide on the answer she wanted to give. In the end, she decided her daughter deserved the truth.

"Robbie was my dad, sweetie. But now, I guess he or she would be your grandmother. No, she's definitely your grandma," Hastings-Moore stated firmly.

"Oh, so she's a trans person? Is that why you've never talked about her before?"

"No sweetie, that's not why. Robbie, your grandmother, is easily one of the meanest people I've ever met and were it not for this Jennifer lady and her friend, you and James would have never met her. At least not while I was alive."

"But we're gonna meet her tomorrow, right?" Excited by the prospect of meeting the grandparent she hadn't known she had, her daughter seemed to forget their predicament.

"You will," Hastings-Moore said, relieved her daughter was finding some positive aspect of the nightmare they had suddenly found themselves in.

"And will grandma make the bad people go away?"

"She will, sweetie. I promise. One way or another, she's going to make the bad people leave us alone."

Chapter 10

Undisclosed Location, North Carolina

The giant screen at the end of the boardroom flickered and, an instant later, the seal of the President of the United Constitutional States of America was replaced with the image of the Chinese President, Yan Jiandong.

"Good evening, Mr. President," Spector said in a respectful tone.

Within a year of the first near-AI being produced, instant translation had become ubiquitous the world over. And in the years since the software had first come on to the market, it had become so good human translators were only needed for the most obscure languages.

"Good morning to you, President Spector. I trust the sun is shining on you and your family on this day?"

"It is Mr. President, thank you for asking. My family is well. I hope the same for you and your loved ones?"

"It is the case for my family and for the people of China, and so it is a blessed day, Mr. President."

Spector, having spent nearly two years in China a lifetime ago as the United States senior military liaison spoke his next words in Mandarin. "May China, her people, and her leader be forever blessed."

As the words left his mouth, the border of the language software changed from red to green to signal to those on the call that the near-AI didn't have to translate the last words.

Yan smiled grandly and when he next spoke, the software remained green as the Chinese leader delivered his reply in near-perfect English. "Ah, that's right. You were posted here for a period of time, weren't you?"

"For two years, fifteen years ago. Mandarin is a hell of a puzzle, but I managed to fit together a few of the pieces. I enjoyed the challenge at the time, as I recall."

"Indeed, it is a challenging language, Mr. President. Your pronunciation was excellent, but more important, I appreciate the gesture. How can I help the United Constitutional States of America today?"

"President Yan, I first want to start by offering you my own personal apology and an official apology from my government for the unapproved use of the J-31 fighter planes that your government so graciously put on loan to us for the purpose of defeating the Federation. They should not have been used in the brief struggle against the CANZUK alliance.

"What my predecessor did was duplicitous in the extreme, and while I took no pleasure in removing President Cameron from power, I want you to know that my predecessor's actions, as they pertained to China, factored into the action I took."

After an extended pause, Spector added, "Mr. President, I have a place in my heart for China, its history, and its great people. With today's conversation, it is my sincere hope we can once again work toward our mutual interests."

China had been beyond furious with the UCSA when it commandeered and put the J-31s into action against CANZUK. In part, it had been in response to this fury that Spector had chosen to execute Cameron in the humiliating fashion he did. Now, as he stared back at the man who was the most powerful person on the planet, Spector hoped the terribly defiled body that had turned up on a rural highway in the backwaters of Tennessee would carry enough weight.

"President Spector, despite his actions, your predecessor was a man and leader of one of the world's great nations. We should never take delight when such a person suffers but it is also a very dangerous world. And when people do not honor their agreements, it is a fact of history that powerful, even great men can suffer outcomes such as the one that befell Archibald Cameron."

Spector nodded his head gravely at the other man's words but offered no reply.

Yan continued. "President Cameron's death was a timely reminder, and therefore a gift to myself. For that, President Spector, you are to be commended for your bold action and you have my thanks. It is my position that you and I can begin to walk down the path of forgiveness."

With this overture made, Spector mentally pounded his fist into the table in victory. Yan had signaled that a reconciliation between their two governments could happen. The question now was, what was 'forgiveness' going to cost him?

Despite his many public dismissals of the Commonwealth alliance, CANZUK was a problem. A problem that Spector calculated the UCSA couldn't solve on its own, at least not in the short term.

France had been playing its part, but her role was limited to helping the Reds defeat the Blues. To do more and truly rock CANZUK back on its heels, he needed the help of the man on the screen looking back at him.

He and his planners had made their decision. Once the war with the Blues was over, they would turn their attention to California and the American west coast. With the Great Lakes, the St. Lawrence River, and three divisions of soldiers waiting across that river, it would not be an easy task to drive his exhausted army north, as much as he wanted to teach the Canadians a lesson.

A much easier task would be to re-integrate California and pressure the various American neutral states back into the constitutional fold and then, as one re-united country, cut Canada in two. Controlling the oil sands would be their first order of business.

Without access to Alberta's oil sands and with a naval blockade of Canada's ports in the east, the governments of Ontario and Quebec would fall within a year's time. Laying waste to what history called Upper and Lower Canada would please Spector to no end, but these swaths of territory were the industrial heartland of Canada, and he would need their manufacturing capacity if he was going to rebuild a United States that could once again face off against the Chinese.

But for all this to happen, Spector needed to give CANZUK a reason not to send its forces across the 49th parallel into Upstate New York. If the Chinese could put pressure on CANZUK in the Pacific and preferably, Canada's west coast, Spector would have the room he needed to reunite his country. The remaking of North America would come shortly thereafter.

Hoping that President Yan understood at least some of this calculation, Spector leaned into the diplomatic strategy he knew best.

"Mr. President, I take it you are aware that the CANZUK alliance is on the cusp of supporting the Federation of American States?"

"I am aware. As you would expect, we are keeping a close eye on events in North America. Satellite imagery suggests at least three divisions are getting ready to move south. This is backed up by other sources we have access to."

"We can't let that happen, Mr. President," Spector said hotly.

One of the Chinese leader's eyebrows arched upwards. "We, President Spector?"

"President Yan, we are both busy men, and from everything I have seen and read of you, I know you are an intelligent person, who operates with integrity. In my world, one of the characteristics synonymous with integrity is honesty. I would like to be honest with you, if I may?"

"President Spector, I would not have taken this call if I did not believe you too were a man of respectful character. It is because of this respect I am open to your words."

The perimeter of the display turned green as the Chinese leader next spoke. "There is an English expression I believe is held in both of our countries. Honesty is the best policy. It is something I strongly believe in, particularly when it comes to my country's relationship with others. President Spector, with perfect honesty from us both, tell me what is on your mind?"

This time, when Spector nodded his head at the other man's words, it was to signal his satisfaction. He had played his cards right. "Mr. President, I take it you are familiar with Vancouver Island?"

"Quite familiar. My dearest mother had vacationed in British Columbia several times in her final years. If I remember correctly, she was particularly enamored with Vancouver Island. One of Canada's crown jewels, she had called it. I also had a cousin who did her Ph.D. at the University of British Columbia. She visited the island many times and spoke of it as though it were a magical place."

Spector smiled in response to the Chinese President's words. "It sounds as though you might be more familiar with the place than I am, Mr. President."

Continuing, Spector said, "And, of course, President Yan, you will most certainly be familiar with the 99-year lease the British forced on your country for the control of Hong Kong?"

For the first time in the conversation a frown emerged on the Chinese leader's face. "I am, Mr. President. It was and remains an ugly stain in my country's history, but full credit is due to the British - they used this arrangement to tremendous political and economic effect. But why do you ask of this arrangement?"

Spector leaned forward into the camera so that his body took up more of the frame, and after a nine-month pregnant pause, he rolled the dice that had been spinning in his head from the moment the Chinese dictator appeared on his screen. "Mr. President, how would China like to own a part of North America for the next 99 years?"

Chapter 11

Deep River, East of CFB Petawawa

His wife's red-rimmed eyes stared back blankly at him. Over the past two hours, Madison Larocque had cycled through the full range of raw emotion she posessed. Not once but twice.

"You do know it's a miracle that we got back together and we're having this baby, don't you?"

Larocque had answered this question already. His first response had sent his wife into a five-minute spiteful rant. This time around, he chose silence.

"Fine, don't answer me. It's your go-to, isn't it? Things get hard in our relationship and you shut down. You go quiet, you leave, you turn on your drinking." These last words oozed with bitterness.

"I'll come back," Larocque said, in a voice that sounded exhausted. "The chances we'll be involved in any fighting is small. We're gonna fly in, show the flag, then wait for the reinforcements coming from the north, or maybe the Reds don't attack. Maybe, when they see us, they go back to the negotiating table."

His wife threw up her hands. "For Christ's sake, Jackson, you're not an idiot. Open your eyes! Even I can see that the FAS is backed into a corner. And I've heard you say it a hundred times. This Spector bastard is ruthless. No one believes he's going to negotiate anything. Look what they did to those poor people in Pittsburgh. He's an animal leading a bunch of savages. And what do we care if the Americans slaughter each other? Do you want to know my opinion, Jackson Larocque?"

Again, Larocque decided it best not to say anything.

"Well, I don't need your permission to speak, Colonel. Tell your friend Merielle this war is none of our fucking business! That's my opinion and the opinion that most people in this country hold."

Larocque winced visibly as his wife mentioned the PM's name. To say that she was not a fan was an understatement.

He and Madison had got back together immediately upon his return from the Missouri mission. In the months since he had been required to make numerous trips to Ottawa. For most of those visits, the PM had made a point of having some type of interaction with him. They had even gone out for dinner on one occasion.

He had understood the attention and in truth, had welcomed it. He and the PM had both been through an extraordinary experience. In the effort to secure the American air base, they had talked a couple of times but these conversations had been short and under duress. With the successful end of the mission, there had been a mutual need to talk through the events and understand one another and the decisions they had both made. In the process of these conversations, he and Canada's prime minister had formed an unlikely bond.

When he next spoke, Larocque decided it wouldn't be helpful to engage on the topic of Merielle Martel. "I'm going to Washington because that's where General Gagnon needs me and the regiment to be. This is what I do, Mads. This is who I am. I love you with all my heart but I can't not go to D.C. any more than a fish can breathe out of water."

His wife took a step forward and slowly placed a hand on her stomach. When she spoke, her words were absent the raw emotion she had been projecting. "This baby inside me is a sign, Jacks. That we got back together, that I got pregnant so quickly, and at forty-two. How is that anything but a sign?"

Madison moved forward again. Entering his physical orbit, she moved to take up his hands. Gently, she placed them on her belly. Slowly, she guided his hands across the t-shirt she was wearing until he arrived at the spot where he could feel the tiny person inside his wife prod the perfect enclosure surrounding his new son.

"We are getting a second chance. We need to do this right this time. You can retire, Jackson. No one is going to fault you. You're a national hero. Everyone in the country – your boys, Merielle, every single member of the CAF – everyone will understand. You've done so much. I know you love me, just as I love you. We can do this together. Do it for me. Do it for our daughter. Do it for Lauren, my love. She hasn't left us, honey. She's still with us, and I can't help but think she's played a part in all of this."

On hearing Madison invoke their daughter's name, Larocque swallowed hard and felt the beginnings of moisture gathering in his eyes. In the time since their only daughter had taken her life, he had only heard Madison mention Lauren's name on the rarest of occasions.

The sudden and unexpected death of their daughter had been devastation beyond measure for Madison as it had been for him. It had broken their marriage and sent Larocque down a path of self-destruction.

It had been Missouri and his command of the Canadian Airborne Regiment that saved his life. The struggle that had been Whiteman AFB had given him purpose, just as it had given him the courage to fix things with his wife. And whether it had been real or not, he remembered the conversation he had with his daughter at what had been the lowest point of the fight to hold the American airbase. In his moment of need, she had come to him like an angel.

As he felt the baby kick again, Larocque was struck with a clarity of thought that Madison was right. Not one miracle, but several, had happened to bring him to this moment.

He pulled his gaze from his wife's belly and reconnected with her brown eyes. "I'm back in Ottawa on Tuesday. I'll let Gagnon know I want out and that I won't lead the boys into Washington. You're right. He'll understand."

As tears began to fill Madison's eyes, she pulled him closer. "Everyone will, Jackson," his wife said, in a relieved voice. "Everyone will."

Somewhere in Connecticut

Roberta Hastings was in a foul mood.

Late yesterday, she had been furious to find out that she would not be ferried to her daughter's home by helicopter as requested.

With the Reds so close and dominating the air south and west of the city, The Office of Protective Operations, that part of the U.S. Marshals Service that provided protective details to members of the Menendez Cabinet, advised that no one could fly anywhere unless it was urgent and had the approval of the right person in the White House.

Piqued that her authority wasn't good enough for the unrelenting marshal she had been speaking with to get her close to her daughter's home, she had called the President's Chief of Staff and demanded that the woman make the necessary calls to get her up north the next morning.

Those calls made, Hastings, along with a pair of heavily armed U.S. Marshals, had spooled into the air while the darkness of early morning still dominated the sky above Washington.

Her annoyance from the evening before had returned with a vengeance as she had found out that she would be making the trip north in an Air Force MH-138A helicopter and not one of the much more comfortable VH-92 Patriots that the President flew in. Up early, anxious about her daughter, and set to travel two-plus hours north in Spartan-like conditions, Hastings had already found two different opportunities to tear a strip off the senior ranking pilot flying the helicopter and the two marshals assigned to guard her.

Intentional or not, Hastings had caught their looks of mild disgust as they responded to her early morning hounding. She knew what they were thinking and hated them for it. Men, and in particular the alpha males that were shepherding her to her daughter's home outside Hartford, would never understand or accept her. It was this misogynistic intolerance – this privilege of being born inside the body you were meant to have that had driven her into politics and made her into the unflinching change agent she was.

These men, and men like them, didn't have to like her and what she stood for. They just needed to do what they were told and keep their prejudices in a dark, deep place where she couldn't suss them out. Long ago, she had come to the realization that this was the best she could hope for as it pertained to most of the male gender.

To gain a full conversion of mind, such that a man truly believed Roberta Hastings was a woman in mind, spirit, and body, you had to mold that man's thinking when he was a boy.

It was this education, this societal transformation, that had been her life's work for the past fifteen years. But it was only with the arrival of the Menendez government that her efforts had been given the authority and resources needed to make a wholesale change. The two men now driving her to her destination were too old to have benefited from her policies. But the day would come in her life when such bigots were all retired relics of another era. This above all other things is what drove her to do the work she did.

As the unmarked vehicle they had picked up at the small private airport outside Hartford began to slow down to make a turn, she pulled her eyes from the picturesque scene that was this part of the Constitution State. From the front seat, the senior of the two marshals said, "After this turn, we'll be taking the next left, Madam Secretary. It's just another kilometer after that."

When Hastings said nothing in reply, the marshal spoke again. "Ma'am, when we arrive, I would ask that you stay in the vehicle so that Deputy Brown and I can clear the area around your daughter's home. Once we're satisfied everything is in order, we'll ring your daughter and then we'll proceed to clear her home. Then – ."

Hastings cut him off. "You'll do no such thing, Deputy. Look around you. We're in the middle of nowhere and this little trip you've been forced to join me on was hardly advertised. My daughter and her children don't need you traipsing through her house for the sake of inflating your egos."

"Ma'am, it's protocol."

"Don't 'Ma'am' me. You will address me as Madam Secretary and you and your partner can stay right where you are, thank you very much."

When the senior deputy next spoke, he injected a level of authority into his voice that Hastings had not yet heard from the man. "Madam Secretary, I will order Deputy Brown to stop and turn this vehicle around if you don't let us do our jobs. I don't know what your problem is and I don't care who you are. It's our job to make sure you're safe and I'm not going to be the first marshal in the history of the Service to lose a cabinet secretary because said secretary didn't do what she was reasonably asked to do."

Hastings stared back murderously at the man but chose not to reply. In that moment, her daughter's need trumped her burning desire to verbally castrate this power-tripping piece of garbage who dared speak to her as though she were some unimportant junior staffer.

With a colossal effort, Hastings dropped her eyes from the senior deputy marshal and turned back to the tranquil green-and-gold fields that lay outside the car's window. Far in the distance, she could see a single farm home. It gleamed white in contrast to the green fields and the sizeable forest that backstopped the property.

A few minutes later, their car pulled up into the long gravel driveway of that same quaint-looking homestead.

As the vehicle came to a stop, Hastings was almost vibrating when she heard the doors unlock. As the two deputies extricated themselves from their seats, the cheerful-looking yellow front door of the two-story home opened, allowing her daughter to walk into the brightness of the morning sun.

Quickly, Hastings flung her door open and stepped out of the vehicle. As her eyes locked with her daughter's, she heard the older marshal too harshly order her back into the vehicle. Imperiously, she ignored the man and started to walk towards the house.

"Honey, I'm sorry I couldn't get here sooner," she said with genuine angst in her voice. "And don't worry about the men. They're U.S. Marshals. They just need to take a look around your house. I told them everything would be fine, but they insisted."

Hastings stopped her movement as the senior marshal intersected her path. His hand was elevated and was in the universal position of 'stop.' "Madame Secretary, I need you to get back in the vehicle. Please."

Hastings looked at the man incredulously and when she spoke, her voice lacked the high-pitched timbre of its normal self. Instead, it was low and laced with menace. "Get out of my way. Get out of my way now, or I will drop you where you stand."

As the marshal's eyes widened in surprise, Hastings caught a flash of movement in the direction of the house.

To Hastings' left, the other marshal, the one named Brown, barked out a short curse while his hand darted to the holster on his hip. No sooner had the man's hand gripped the weapon, Hastings heard a crack and saw the marshal's head snap back. Inexplicably, a chunk of something left the back of the man's head.

As the marshal soundlessly keeled backward and fell to the ground, Hastings instinctively shifted her eyes to her daughter. She hadn't moved, but she was no longer alone. A man and woman, each carrying an assault-style weapon of some sort, were advancing from the porch in the direction of the remaining deputy.

In the burst of chaos, the remaining marshal had managed to turn himself around to face the threat, but unlike his partner, had not gone for his side-arm.

The two figures prowled forward, their weapons aimed squarely at the federal officer. Both were dressed in practical clothes that looked like the couple had been out on a hike.

Without warning, the female broke left so that Hastings and the marshal were no longer aligned.

Hastings saw a burst of fire spit from the end of the woman's weapon. Simultaneously, she heard a wet discharge as a single round connected with the senior marshal's skull. Knees buckling, the man Hastings had been arguing with only seconds before collapsed on himself, his body forming a contorted heap on the ground not six feet in front of her.

As blood began to pour out of the marshal's destroyed head, Hastings began to feel an unfamiliar pressure in her throat. As quickly as the sensation had come, she doubled over and vomited the contents of her stomach onto the gravel of the driveway.

After her third, now fruitless, heave, she caught sight of booted feet entering her downcast vision. Slowly, Hastings removed her hands from her skirt and stood while wiping her mouth.

As she took in a deep breath to steady herself, she inhaled the pungent combination of acidic bile of vomit and the coppery smell that was present with too much blood. The woman who had killed the marshal stood calmly with her weapon still pressed into her shoulder.

Out of the corner of her eye, Hastings picked up movement and then heard the sound of feet moving across granulated stone. She shifted her gaze to take up the woman's accomplice. Well-built and of average height, Hastings was struck by how much the man looked like Denzel Washington in his prime. Arriving, he unceremoniously tossed a pair of running shoes at her feet.

"Put them on." It was the woman who spoke. Her voice had an unmistakable edge to it.

Hastings didn't look at the woman or acknowledge the order she had been given. Instead, she looked to find her daughter. She was still on the porch of her house, standing where she had been when Hastings and the two marshals had first arrived. Though some thirty yards apart, she could easily see the streaks of tears on her face.

"Honey, are you okay? The children. Is everyone all right?"

"We're fine. Everyone is okay. But I need you to listen to them. They're..." Her daughter was unable to finish the sentence as she started to weep.

The Secretary rounded on the lead assassin. Her angst as a parent and the confidence that came with the authority she wielded in Washington combined themselves in that instant to fill her with white-hot outrage. "Whoever you are, you've made a huge mistake. What do you think's going to happen when the two men you just killed don't call in in the next five minutes? The State Police know we're here. Whatever you want and whoever you are, I won't cooperate."

As she offered words of defiance, she stood at her full height, crossed her arms, and stared at the woman as though she were some inconsequential intern who had just brought her the wrong order of coffee.

The woman who had just ended the life of two federal marshals lowered her weapon and called over her shoulder, "Dr. Hastings-Moore, please bring out your children, if you would."

On making the request, Hastings' gaze darted back to her daughter. Though her eyes were still wet with tears, at the mention of her children, she caught the all-too-familiar look of defiance on her daughter's face. Good, thought Hastings. The same stubbornness that had driven her daughter away from her was something they would need if they were going to survive.

"Now, Dr. Hastings-Moore!" the woman snapped.

When her daughter remained unmoving, one of the woman's hands went into her pocket at which point she began to calmly count backward. "In five, four, three..."

On "three," Janet Hastings-Moore turned and scampered back into her house.

A minute later, she returned, leading her two small children. Both had been crying, though at the moment, Hastings saw that her only two grandchildren were both doing their best to put on brave faces.

Around each of their necks, looking grotesquely out of place, was a dark choker of some sort. On their innocent little bodies, the item was an ugly affront.

Hastings turned on the female terrorist or whatever she was. "You bitch. I'll kill you. I swear, I will!"

The woman's reply to Hastings' threat was immediate and nonplussed. "In fact, Madam Secretary, you will cooperate. You'll cooperate because as I've just demonstrated to you, my colleague and I are entirely serious about our business."

The woman paused, took a step closer to Hastings, and when she next spoke, her words were low while her green-brown eyes shined with bright intensity. The combination gave the young woman an unhinged feel.

"I don't care about your grandchildren, Madam Secretary. In my mind, they are but two of the hundreds of thousands of children your government has killed already. What are two more?"

"We didn't start this war," Hastings said indignantly and then quickly added, "and I won't cooperate. Who sent you? That bigot, Spector? Both of you can go to hell!"

"The reality is, Madam Secretary, that it doesn't matter who sent me. Right now, the only thing that does matter is that you understand that I'm prepared to set off those rings around the necks of those beautiful children in front of their mother."

The young woman reached into her pocket and pulled out a small device. As she held it, her thumb moved to cover the unit's single button.

"Look at me, Madam Secretary. Look me in the eyes."

Hastings removed her gaze from the woman's hand and stared back at the person who had dared to threaten her and her family.

"Hear my words, Secretary Hastings. I just killed two men in cold blood. I will kill your grandchildren, and I'll leave you and your daughter alive to work on the relationship you rushed here to try and mend."

Hastings' jaw tightened visibly. "You evil bitch."

"Just practical, Madam Secretary. But even if I was evil, it doesn't mean we can't work together. I know who you are, Roberta Hastings, and I know all of the terrible things you've done. This being the case, think of what happens in the next hour as just one more time you have to make a deal with one more devil."

"What do you want?" Hastings snapped.

Her captor turned and gestured to the shoes that had been thrown at Hastings' feet by the Denzel look-alike.

"First, I want you to put on those shoes. And then we're going for a short family walk."

"And then?" Hastings, asked her voice now a growl.

"And then, Madam Secretary, you are going to resign from the Menendez Cabinet. And happily so."

Chapter 12

Undisclosed Location, North Carolina

Parr strode down the hallway of the colonial mansion ignoring the building's historic and exceptionally maintained beauty.

Spector, a man who in the past ten months of working for him had never sent a text had just sent him a single message, "parlor room. now."

In the two days since his conversation with the President about the de-politicization of the Northeast United States, he had been working feverishly on the task of finding the people they would need to make the plan happen.

To Parr's relief, this element of the plan was advancing far quicker than he'd anticipated. In the short time he had been working the problem, he had come to learn that he had underestimated the amount of psychological venom that had been pumped into the governmental types he was bringing onto his ops team.

His quiet conversations with the first two men he thought would be interested in the project had immediately turned into what the corporate world would have called a full-fledged Tiger Team. In the hours that followed, no fewer than thirty men and women from both the military and civilian sides of the government had come together to put flesh on the bones of a plan to strategically neutralize thousands of people.

When he had first been given the task by Spector, he had been unsure if he would be able to meet the challenge. Now, as he heard his people work through the logistics of things like re-education camps and the number of kill teams it would take to hunt down and liquidate thousands of academics, lawyers, and high-level bureaucrats, his confidence was brimming.

To be sure, it was unpleasant and un-American work, but not a person in the room doubted the task's necessity. The death toll of America's second civil war was approaching a staggering twelve million people. If another ten or even twenty thousand needed to die to prevent this madness once and for all, this is exactly what this group of people was prepared to do.

On receiving Spector's extraordinary text, Parr had ordered the planning group to take a break. They'd been at it for six hours straight. A late lunch and period of recharge would do everyone good.

As he turned a corner, his eyes took up the entrance of the room he had been ordered to attend. Without hesitating, he walked into the room to find Spector and several officials standing in front of a pair of large screens that were used in support of the more intimate meetings the President liked to have in the space.

Catching Parr's entrance out of the corner of his eye, Spector turned to face his Chief of Staff and thumbed in the direction of the displays. "Hastings has resigned."

Parr rounded on the screens and took in the ticker rolling across the bottom of the newscast.

As he read the update, his cheeks puffed out as he exhaled a long breath. Parr finally said, "I didn't see that coming."

"No one did. Just like we didn't see the resignation of Williams-Jordan yesterday," Spector said of Menendez's Secretary of State.

"And what reason did Hastings give for her departure?"

Spector chuckled at the question. "You wouldn't believe it if I told you. Apparently, she's defecting to us."

When one of Parr's eyebrows shot up, Spector continued, "It's horseshit, of course. Her statement, which was delivered by her or was it him? I can never tell with these people. Whichever, they looked more than a little ragged from whatever ordeal they had been put through."

Spector scoffed. "Jesus, would you listen to me? 'They!' The woke bastards even have me using the right pronouns."

"A month from now, Mr. President, a person's pronouns aren't going to matter anymore," Parr offered in a matter-of-fact tone.

A short officer with hair more grey than red stepped into their orbit. "Mr. President, I have news that's connected to the resignations. Critical news, I believe."

Spector, above all things a practical man, pretended as though the officer had been a part of their conversation from the get-go. "General McCaul, let's hear it."

"I've just been advised that Vice President Morgan and a coalition of the FAS Congress are about to invoke the 25th Amendment. We're still working through the analysis, sir, but we think Morgan might have the votes."

Spector looked back at the officer as though the man had just told the President to get bent.

"That son of a gun," Spector said softly to himself.

"That son of a goddamned gun," the big Texan repeated, this time loud enough for most of the other heads in the room to be turned in his direction.

"I take Morgan is making a move? I didn't think he had it in him," Parr asked, guessing at the meaning of his boss's utterances.

Looking pensive, Spector's eyes found Parr's "I didn't think so either, but it looks like he finally found the balls to do something about his batshit-crazy boss. Just six months too late to save his own hide."

The UCSA President turned his gaze back to the red-haired general. "You're sure about this?"

"We have it from several sources, Mr. President, and they're all saying the same thing. Once something like this gets out there, it'll spread like wildfire. Truth be told, sir, I'm surprised the media isn't reporting it already."

Spector's eyes left the man and then without warning, he took a few steps forward so he was in the middle of the room. He looked around the space and after confirming who was present, glanced at the officer closest to the parlor's double doors. "Colonel Olds, shut those doors if you'd please."

As though he were a cadet, the man sprung to comply with Spector's request.

As the doors shut, Spector moved again, but this time to the front of the room. Reaching the south end of the space, he turned to face the team helping him run the war. At a height of six-five, the man towered over the room.

As Parr took the president in, he could see that the man had just been flushed with renewed energy. While moments before, he had looked weary, he now had the look of a man whose horse had just separated itself from its competitors on the final bend.

"Gentlemen," Spector said, his voice loud enough to easily fill the room. "General McCaul has just advised me that Vice President Morgan is in the process of invoking the 25th Amendment. For those of you who don't know, the 25th is that part of the Constitution that allows the Cabinet to remove the President from power. Morgan needs two-thirds of the Senate and House to make this happen, and because I am a betting man, I'm prepared to put all of my chips on the possibility Morgan will get his way. While he may be a reserved man, he is no fool."

Spector paused and then said, "I'm happy to be corrected, but my gut and my head are telling me we're about to see the end of President Menendez."

"Praise Jesus," someone behind Parr exclaimed. The man's voice sounded entirely earnest.

"Praise Jesus, indeed," Spector echoed the words of the brief prayer. "All of you know that I am a work in progress when it comes to my faith, but at this very moment, I feel as though I'm filled with God's favor. There is a path before us, and I can see it as clearly as I can see each of your faces.

"Now, in this very moment, we can remake our country so that it is never brought to its knees again. Those of us in this room are united in this desire and just as importantly, we are united in how this remaking is to be done."

Spector again paused, placing his hands on his hips and jutting out his chest a bit more than normal. It was a power pose of supreme confidence. Parr, ever the PR man, noted the subtle movement with a professional appreciation.

"We cannot take our foot off the gas, people. In fact, we need to press down on the accelerator. If we give Morgan time to consolidate his hold on power, all we'll hear from the media, the diplomats, and those who don't have the backbone to do what needs to be done is to go back to the negotiation table."

After a brief pause, Spector's voice boomed within the confines of the room. "Like hell are we negotiating anything!

"The enemies of American greatness want nothing more than to see us remain divided and to negotiate eternally. Our enemy is as weak as it has ever been. Hear my words – we are going to crush the Blues, and with your help, we are going to remake our country, from sea to shining Goddamned sea."

His hands still on his hips, Spector looked at every man in the room, seemingly sizing up each one to gauge their willingness to undertake the task. His assessment of the room ended with his eyes landing on Parr. "There is no turning back from what we are about to do. Is this understood?"

To his surprise, Parr was the first to answer the question. "We're with you, Mr. President. All the way."

Spector gave him a resolute nod. "And the rest of you?"

Every voice in the room gave some type of confirmation. While some delivered a solemn promise, others delivered an assent of the F-bomb variety.

Spector then looked in the direction of General Spellings. "General, you told me as recently as yesterday, we could launch our attack on Washington in a week. You now have two days."

"Mr. President..." began the taciturn four-star general.

Spector cut him off with a raised hand.

"General, I don't care how it gets done. It does not need to be pretty. The foundation that underpins our enemy is weak. We cannot give them time to reset their footing. Speed is what we need. I want more Patton and less Eisenhower."

"Yes, Mr. President. We'll make it work," Spelling replied.

"I know you will. And I know you're going to lead us to great things, General. I just know it."

Spector turned his eyes back to Parr.

"Pete."

"Yes, Mr. President?"

"It's the same for you. In two days, you and your people will be ready to go. And that's not a question."

"We've made excellent progress on the plan, Mr. President. We'll do our best for you and the country."

Spector nodded his head with satisfaction at Parr and then turned his gaze to take in the rest of the room. "People, the tasks of General Spellings and Mr. Parr are our everything for the next forty-eight hours. Whatever they need, you make happen. Does everyone understand?"

Again, the voices in the room delivered a clarion affirmation of their leader's direction.

"Good. Unity of purpose. That's what I like to hear. In two days, people, we take Washington and with our convictions and God's own blessing, we will officially begin the work of making this country of ours great again."

West of Ottawa

Larocque was halfway between Ottawa and CFB Petawawa when the wrist unit of his BAM system vibrated telling him a call was incoming.

"Who is it?"

Connected with the sound system in his truck, the alluring female voice that he had selected for his BAM oozed, "Merielle Martel."

"Accept the call," Larocque said instantly.

"Jackson. It's Merielle."

"Madame Prime Minister, thanks for the call," Larocque replied formally.

"Cut the shit, Colonel. It's Merielle and that's that."

Larocque chuckled. "Just wanted to make sure the Ottawa bubble hasn't gone to your head. It's been a few months since we last chatted. Things change, you know."

"Don't I know it," Merielle said, her voice now sounding tired.

Larocque, a mere colonel, had not wanted to bother Merielle with his news, but upon getting to know her since the events of Whiteman, he knew beyond a shadow of a doubt that the right call was to advise her personally of his decision.

Were she to find out about his retirement by way of some random briefing, Canada's prime minister would not have been pleased. And though Larocque was confident that Merielle's displeasure wouldn't amount to anything, he was loyal to those who were loyal to him.

"What's up, Jacks? Your email said I shouldn't worry, so I'm going to assume all is well with Madison and the baby?"

The question put a smile on Larocque's face. With all the woman had going on, and with hints Madison was not on Team Martel, the question confirmed the PM was, in fact, a well-practiced politician.

"Madison and the baby couldn't be better – thanks for asking."

"Then I assume we're going to be talking about you. What's the news?"

"I wanted you to hear it from me first, Merielle. I just put my papers in to retire."

"Bravo, my dear Colonel," Merielle said, in a tone that suggested she was delighted by the news. "You were right to let me know with a call. Had I not heard it from you, I would have been pissed."

"It means I won't be going to Washington, Merielle. My 2IC is a capable man and by the sounds of it, all we'll be doing down there is show and tell."

There was a pause over the connection and just as Larocque's anxiety began to elevate at the delay, the PM said, "Jacks, this is the right call. Right now, your wife and baby need you more than your country does. And if anyone in this country has earned the right to turn in their kit, it's you, my friend."

Larocque exhaled loudly. "I'm so relieved to hear you say that. I know you told me never to mention it, but I'm in your debt for what you did after Whiteman. If you asked, if you needed me to, I'd go to D.C. It would be difficult for Madison, but I would make her understand."

"Well, there's no need for that. Whoever your 2IC is, they'll be soldier enough to handle whatever is waiting for them in Washington. No doubt you've seen the same intel I have. The Blues have turned the place into a fortress, so the chances the Airborne will need to get their hands dirty is almost out of the question. This was always meant to be a show-the-flag op. With Menendez gone and Morgan as President, we can finally move to help the FAS," Merielle said, making an unsaid reference to the three CANZUK divisions waiting positioned along the New York border.

"So, the divisions are going to cross into the States?" asked Larocque.

"They will. Assuming Morgan consolidates power, it'll be the day after the referendum. Gagnon and the generals would like it done sooner, but the idea we'd cross the border before the referendum is a non-starter."

"In four days, then?" said Larocque

"Thereabouts. The opposition parties are going to howl, but if we don't prevent Spector from winning the war or at least give us leverage to negotiate with the man, it's the beginning of the end for us, even with CANZUK. It's now or never, as they say."

As the PM said the words, a pang of regret started to grow within Larocque. In a few short weeks, Canada and its allies were going to war, and he was choosing this moment to leave his soldiers.

Perhaps sensing his disquiet, the prime minister moved to slay the growing kernel of doubt in his thoughts. "It's the right call, Jackson. You've done enough. More than enough. No one – not me, not Gagnon, and not your soldiers, is going to say anything other than you did right by your country and that Regiment of yours. The Airborne is what it is today, because of you. That's no small thing. Pass the torch, Colonel, and raise that new son of yours. That is your new mission."

"Thank you, Madame Prime Minister. Your words mean a great deal to me," Larocque said, his voice beginning to crack.

Thankfully, intentional or not, Merielle moved to end the conversation. "Listen, Jackson, I have to go. My Chief of Staff is actually tugging on my sleeve if you can believe it. I'm off to barnstorm in Quebec for a few days and then it's Montreal for the final rally. Wish me luck, Colonel, and send my best to Madison. For what it's worth, tell her I'll be thinking of her."

"I will, Merielle, and good luck."

Chapter 13

East of Quebec City

Yvette Raymond had elected to drive herself to the meeting location about an hour east of Quebec City. She was familiar with the area, having regularly visited Le Massif, the ski resort of the well-heeled that formed the main economic piston of this part of the province.

Tonight, however, she had not been given the luxury of being able to pick out landmarks or familiar stretches of highway to guide her travel. The late summer weather was horrendous. Rain was coming down in sheets while the saturated clouds did their determined best to make the night as foreboding as possible.

Because of the weather, she had elected to pilot the SUV herself. Without a doubt, she could have left the journey to the near-AI that inhabited her vehicle, but at nearly fifty years of age, she had grown up and learned to drive when self-driving cars had still been something out of science fiction.

"In six hundred meters, take the next right," the near-AI said in the warm male voice Raymond had designated for it.

Continuing, the voice added, "After that, Ms. Raymond, you will drive another five hundred and forty meters and your destination will be on your left. As you make the next right, note that the road you will be traveling will quickly transition to gravel. As I note the weather conditions, it is my recommendation that you drive this last part of your journey below the speed limit."

While the few friends she had might engage with and even thank the near-AI for its perfectly reasonable driving advice, she ignored the semi-sentient software. Like most things Raymond encountered in her life, the near-AI guiding her to her destination was a tool to be used and nothing more.

Minutes later as she pulled up to the forest-ensconced villa, the home's owner, one Marc-Antoine Trembly, could be seen waiting for her. He was protected from the torrent of rain by a gigantic veranda that jutted out from the building at some avant-garde angle.

The Quebec billionaire was flanked by a man on his left whom Raymond did not know. The rain still pounding her vehicle, that same man suddenly produced an oversized umbrella and began walking toward her door.

At his arrival, Raymond opened her car door and was instantly struck by a wall of thick moist air infused by the rich smell of the nearby sopping forest.

"Minister Raymond, please come with me," the large man said.

Without a word, she slid out of her vehicle and walked in step with the man toward the incredible chateau.

As she reached the protection of the overhang, Trembly met her with open arms. "Yvette, my friend. It remains the case you are more stunning in person than you are on TV. It's been too long. Thank you for coming. I'm terribly sorry for the weather."

As was their culture's way, the two Quebecers exchanged an embrace with faux kisses to each of their cheeks.

As they pulled away from one another, there was a bright flash followed a millisecond later by the crack of thunder.

"Tabarnac. What a night!" Trembly cried. "Let's get inside, shall we?"

Gesturing to the massive, all-glass door, Raymond saw another man she did not recognize. This one was taller and broader than the one still standing beside her.

As the three-person party reached the entrance, Raymond gestured to the hulk of a man holding the door open. "I don't remember your help being so intimidating the last time I was here?"

"The world has changed, Yvette. Truth be told, I'm more than a bit surprised you're here on your own. These are dangerous times we live in. Even here in Quebec."

If the billionaire's reply was an attempt to elicit some kind of response from her, she ignored it. She was used to controlling conversations, even with wildly successful businessmen like Marc-Antoine Trembly.

She stopped the group's collective march and fixed her eyes on the home's owner, Trembly. "I take it Monsieur Labelle is in the kitchen?"

"He is."

Raymond stepped forward, entering Trembly's personal space. When she spoke, her voice was low. "Marc-Antoine, I'd like for you to stay here."

On hearing Raymond's request, Trembly slowly reached out to take up her petite hands. As she let him take hold of her, she fixed her intense eyes on his.

"Yvette, you may be one of the smartest people I know and a senior cabinet minister, but it is more important to me that you are a friend. A close one. I wouldn't have let you leverage our personal history if I didn't trust you. And just as I have placed my trust in you to arrange this meeting, you have to trust me. It's my one and only condition."

Trembly squeezed her hands. "You know me, Yvette. I'm no separatist. And I know you aren't, either. But fate and necessity have forced our hands. Let me help you with this difficult path."

Raymond continued to bore into Trembly's unflinching eyes for another long moment. Indeed, the path she was about to walk down was a dangerous one. One that this man and his money and connections could make easier if she let him. But conspiracies, if they were to be successful, were best done with the smallest number of people possible. Marc-Antoine Trembly was one man, but behind him was a corporate army, never mind whatever else the man had his claws into. It was the question Raymond had wrestled with since the moment she had reached out to him – could he be trusted?

Trembly released her hands and stepped back. "This war Martel is planning is madness, Yvette. It has to be stopped and if that means we have to throw in with someone like Labelle, then so be it. Better the devil you know as they say."

On hearing Trembly's unvarnished assessment, she quickly glanced in the direction of the titan of a man who, by sheer proximity, had to be listening to their conversation.

Catching her eyes on the large man, Trembly said, "Don't worry about the Commandant or his men. I pay them well but more, I trust them with my life and with my secrets."

Raymond's gaze reconnected with the billionaire. "If things don't go as planned my old friend, it may be the end of us. What I have to lose Marc-Antoine is significant, but in your case, the risks are incalculable. That is what my trust could cost you."

Trembly nodded solemnly. "Then so be it, Yvette. Martel has to be stopped. Jesus Christ, you just told me she's going to send soldiers into the US. If that's not madness that has to be stopped at all costs, then I am at an utter and complete loss as to how to proceed."

"You know what Labelle will want. Are you prepared to give it to him? As a federalist?" Raymond asked.

The billionaire did not hesitate with his reply. "By any measure, it is the lesser of two evils. So yes, I'm prepared to make that deal. It's that, or there is no Canada."

Raymond nodded her head. He had it right. Merielle Martel might win the coming referendum, but the moment this cursed Anglo alliance that Canada was a part of crossed into the US, the PM would be signing the country's death warrant. Of that, Yvette Raymond was certain.

It was madness of the highest order, and it was her and only her, who had the good sense, the connections, and most importantly, the wherewithal to stop events before things got out of hand.

Raymond took a step in the direction of the kitchen where the separatist leader, Eric Labelle awaited them. "Then you have my trust, Marc-Antoine Trembly. With your eyes wide open, come with me, and let us meet with Monsieur Labelle. Together, let us see what kind of arrangement can be made to save our country from the fool that is Merielle Martel."

CFB Petawawa, West of Ottawa

General Gagnon, the three-star general that had overall command for the CANZUK army that would cross the border into the Federal States of America, had taken up one of the two seats that sat in front of Larocque's desk.

That he was sitting in Larocque's office and not back in Ottawa attending some high-level planning session was both a surprise and, for the moment, a mystery.

The man had flown by helicopter to Petawawa, the army base that was home to the Canadian Airborne Regiment and the 4th Canadian Division. Whatever his reason for being here, the time-conscience senior officer had given up a good part of his day to see Larocque in the flesh.

"So, you submitted the request?" Gagnon said.

"Yes, sir. SOFCOM accepted the paperwork, and General Day is supportive of Greene taking on command of the Regiment."

"Well, there was no doubt about that, Colonel. Everyone is thrilled for you and Madison so that he would accept your retirement request was never in doubt. The only question is whether or not he would agree to let your 2IC take command."

"He did, and on my recommendation," said Larocque, his tone firmer than might have been warranted with an officer of Gagnon's stature.

"So, you think Greene's up to the task? Because, if I'm going to agree with Day to promote a lieutenant colonel to full colonel under the circumstances that face us, I need to know he'll be up to the task in Washington. People tell me he's more bureaucrat than an operations man."

"He is a bureaucrat." This time, the curtness of Larocque's reply was blatant.

He had fought under Gagnon's command during the Whiteman operation and had come to like the man. He would have thought the extent of their service together would have made his recommendation of Greene a done deal. That this appeared not to be the case had quickly set Larocque's temper in the direction of simmer.

"Sir, with all due respect, Greene is more than up to the task. But more to the point, there is no damned way the Reds will be able to take Washington within the month. That gives our divisions more than enough time to get where they need to be."

Larocque leaned forward in his chair and tented his hands on his desk, all the while keeping his eyes locked on the three-star general. "The way I see it, General, Greene's bureaucratic talents make him all the better for the task. Apparently, D.C. is still awash in Blue bureaucrats. I know Greene well enough to know the man will be like a pig in shit. You'll be well served by him."

For a long moment, Gagnon said nothing. Finally, he let loose an exhalation that belied his wiry, even slight, frame. "I didn't want to tell you this, but we just got some new intel. That's why I made the trip from Ottawa to see you in person."

On hearing Gagnon's statement, both of Larocque's calloused hands rose to his face where they began to grind his skin. A bad habit, Madison gave him the gears every time she caught him doing it. After one vigorous cycle of kneading, Larocque finally asked the question Gagnon was waiting for him to ask. "What's the new intel?"

"Before I tell you, I want you to know that I spoke to General Day about thirty minutes after you left his office. As of right now, he's one of the very few that have been given the information I'm about to give you. And for what it's worth, based on that information, he's still of the view Greene should assume command."

"But you still came here in person to give me information. So I'm gonna take it you don't agree with General Day."

As the words left Larocque's mouth, he could start to feel the anger rise within him. He had given this man and his country the lives of over two hundred of his soldiers, never mind the dozens of others who had lost limbs or were wracked with the terrible effects of PTSD.

Before he realized it, Larocque was standing. And though his desk separated him from the still-sitting general, his physical height and the emotional energy coursing through him made it seem like he was a giant towering over a small child.

"Are you here to pull my retirement papers?" Larocque said, his voice filled with something approaching menace.

Before Gagnon could reply, there was a sharp knock at Larocque's door. Turning his head in the direction of the entrance, he all but yelled at his attendant. "Corporal Niveau, what part of we are not to be disturbed do you not understand?"

The door flew open. It was Lieutenant Colonel Greene.

Larocque had worked with the man intimately for almost a year and, in that time, he had not seen the expression his 2IC was now wearing. If he had to guess, Greene, a mostly unflappable and entirely boring man, had a look of panic stitched onto his face.

His eyes darted from Larocque to Gagnon.

"You've got your BAMs on silent, don't you?"

Before Larocque could confirm he had shut off his comms system, Gagnon was out of his seat. "What's got you in a state, son?"

"It's on the news, sir."

When Gagnon next spoke, his voice held the air of command. "Colonel Greene, what's on the goddamn news?"

"The Reds, sir. They've just nuked Washington."

Chapter 14

Ottawa, National Defence Headquarters (NDHQ)

Merielle swept into the operations room that was one floor underground in the east building of NDHQ. The choice of meeting location had been selected to assuage the nerves of those in her Cabinet. The understanding that there were a couple of feet of concrete and steel above their heads would be the psychological tincture they would need to be able to focus on the conversation about to take place.

What had taken place in Washington just an hour earlier had the potential to dramatically alter the alliance's plan to send its militaries across the border.

Merielle strode intently to the head of the large boardroom table, stopped, and began to survey the room. With her best poker face in play, she gave no hint of the vexation she felt on seeing Yvette Raymond.

She should have asked for the woman's resignation, but the fact of the matter was that Raymond held more power in Quebec than she did. Until the referendum was in the past, Merielle had decided to play out the ancient adage to keep your friends close and your enemies closer.

Directly across from Raymond was Paul Blanchard, the Minister of Transport. He had already messaged Merielle pledging his full support for whatever direction she wanted to take. Despite the confidence the large man had expressed through his texts, Blanchard looked worried.

And he wouldn't be the only one. The entire Cabinet would need a heavy dose of confidence injected into them as soon as the discussion got underway.

On that count, Merielle held news that should put control of the conversation in her hands. The trick would be to maintain control of the field of play as long as possible so that enough of the Cabinet Ministers present would go in the direction she needed them to.

"Colleagues," she offered in her most reassuring voice. "Thirty minutes ago, myself and the leaders of CANZUK spoke with President Morgan of the Federation of American States. He is alive and well and wants us to know he greatly appreciates the support of the alliance. Despite the barbarity of Mitchell Spector and the Red Faction, he wanted us to know the Federation of American States remains intact and is determined to hold Washington. And..."

"And what of President Menendez?" Yvette Raymond interjected, her question sounding like an accusation.

So, the confrontation would take place immediately, Merielle thought. That was unlike the Minister of Health. In most other clashes, the woman would lie in the grass allowing others to draw out Merielle's position, and only when she felt she had the fullest picture of her rival's strategy, would Raymond strike like the snake she was.

But before Merielle could answer the question, Paul Blanchard entered the fray.

Raymond's opposite in every way, he was all strength of personality with the physical stature to back it up. If Raymond was the cold-blooded viper who lurked, Blanchard was the vigilant bull who kept a close eye on his herd, ready to do battle anytime somebody meant to do it harm.

"For Christ's sake, Yvette," Blanchard said, his voice already too loud for civilized conversation. "The 25th Amendment was ratified by the Blue Congress. Menendez isn't president anymore, so who cares where she is and what she thinks? And further to that, why don't you give Merielle the courtesy of letting her finish her first few sentences? Or did I miss something and you were voted in as the leader of the party?"

To the surprise of no one in the room, Raymond coolly ignored Blanchard's verbal broadside. Instead, she held her penetrating blue eyes on Merielle. "The 25th was ratified, but in the American Constitution that the FAS continues to operate under, Menendez has the right to offer a written rebuttal to Congress. That hasn't happened, and because it hasn't, Valeria Menendez remains the President of the FAS.

"So, my question remains, Madame Prime Minister. Where is President Menendez and under what authority does Vice President Morgan speak for the FAS?"

Not for the first time, Merielle sent her large friend a mental thank-you. His intervention had allowed Merielle to regain her footing so she could reply to Raymond as cool and collected as her rival.

"According to President Morgan, former President Menendez is missing, possibly lost in one of the strikes. They do not know where she is and because of this, President Morgan, his new Cabinet, and a majority of Congress have signed a declaration confirming Morgan's authority. Andrew Morgan is the President of the FAS, Yvette. Full stop."

To Merielle's surprise, Raymond pushed her chair back and stood. She was not a tall woman, but from her years as a corporate lawyer, she knew full well how to manage a boardroom. When she next spoke, her voice was several octaves higher. "A majority of Congress or the required two-thirds set out by the Constitution? Because if we're talking about a simple majority of fifty percent plus one, whatever authority Morgan thinks he has, I can assure you President Menendez will tell you it's not enough."

"Sit down, Yvette," Blanchard growled across the table. "You're not some queen holding court. Let the Prime Minister speak her piece."

The Quebec City MP ignored Blanchard and continued to stare in the direction of Merielle.

"Madame Prime Minister, not including yourself, twenty-six of your thirty-one Quebec MPs are prepared to resign from caucus if you do not undertake to do the following.

"First, if you still had any intention of attending tonight's 'No' rally in Montreal, you will now excuse yourself, and in light of today's developments, you will postpone the rally by one week.

"Second, whatever plans you have concocted with CANZUK to involve yourselves in the madness that is the United States' second civil war, you will cease and desist immediately. Further, you will enter into discussions with CANZUK with the aim of taking on a position of neutrality relative to the conflict."

As she delivered the ultimatum, Raymond's red, lacquered fingers were steepled in front of her sternum. The contrast of her dark red nails and lips with her pale skin gave the woman a vampiric-like quality.

"You will do these things, Madame Prime Minister or I will call a press conference and I will make public these demands along with a formal call to those Conservative MPs outside Quebec to join us in our protest."

Raymond stepped forward, placing both of her hands on the conference room table.

"Let me do the math for you, Merielle. We only need five more members of our caucus and we can bring down the government and force a constitutional crisis the likes of which this country has never seen."

A terrible smile then surfaced on Raymond's face. "You have three hours to make your decision, Madame Prime Minister. Accede to our demands, save Canada, and save yourself from the embarrassment of having to resign in ignominy. Canadians don't want the country and the war you are trying to sell them."

Stepping back from the table, Raymond slowly pulled her eyes away from Merielle and turned to face the rest of the Cabinet. "To those of you who I have not yet spoken with, ask yourself if you are prepared to support the madness this woman is trying to sell you. Ask yourself, what business is it of Canada to get involved in another country's war? The moment our first soldier steps into the US as this woman proposes, there will be a target on our country's back. I will not condone this terrible decision, just as the vast majority of the Quebec Caucus will not stand by to watch our country commit political suicide. The US Civil War is not Canada's war. Choose wisely, colleagues."

On finishing her pitch, Raymond's eyes fell on Paul Blanchard. "And do not let warmongers and sycophants tell you that Canada's independence is on the line if it does not intervene in the disaster that is the United States. Instead, ask yourself this question: do you want to be part of a government responsible for a mushroom cloud over Toronto?"

The big Minister of Transport ejected upward from his seat. "It's you who's mad, Yvette. What you're doing right now is no less than treason." As Blanchard issued the pronouncement, his voice was low and ominous.

Raymond issued a quick laugh. "Ha! Treason? I don't think so, Paul Blanchard. And in the next three hours, we'll see who the party thinks is sane and not. Until that moment, we will leave you. In the time that remains of your meeting, I trust you will carefully consider our proposal. I daresay the future of the country depends on it."

With this statement, three other members of the Cabinet – all Quebecers – got to their feet and turned to follow Raymond as she began to move to the boardroom's exit.

As Merielle watched them leave, she felt the hand of her Minister of Finance come down gently on her forearm. Quietly, the woman pleaded, "Merielle, don't let her leave the room. We have to work this out. Please."

Merielle had never been the bare-knuckles political street fighter that Blanchard was. Nor could it be said she was an incisive backroom operator like Yvette Raymond. But, the one thing that she brought to the table that made her a really good cop and perhaps a good enough politician was her instincts.

As Raymond reached for the handle to the boardroom entrance, Merielle rose from her chair and called out, "Yvette!"

Flanked by her allies, the striking blonde released her hand from the door and turned back to look back at Merielle. The look on her face was one of contempt.

Glowering at her rival, Merielle said, "Minister Raymond, I would have thought that in the crisis created during the Whiteman mission you would have learned I do not take kindly to threats and deadlines."

"I have given you a deadline, but I have not made a threat, Madame Prime Minister. I have simply offered an alternative policy prescription that is in contradiction to the direction you wish to take our country. This is how democracy and the parliamentary tradition work. I am exercising my rights as they've been given to me. That's hardly a threat."

"Then let me exercise my own right," Merielle retorted. She gestured widely to the other politicians in the room.

"We don't need three hours to consider your offer. When you walk out of this room, you and those with you are no longer cabinet ministers. Further, by this time tomorrow, if you have not reconsidered the folly of what you're about to do, you'll be out of the party. You and every MP that chooses to stand with you."

A look of what might have passed as sadness spilled onto Raymond's face. "There you go again. You are not a dictator, Merielle Martel. Even now, as your world begins to crumble around you,

you are making decisions without consulting your Cabinet. Perhaps you should speak with them before you take another step toward disaster."

Merielle pulled herself to her full height and set her hands on her hips as though she was wearing a tactical belt. Her right hand itched to be atop her service pistol.

"If you walk out that door, Yvette, you and your fellow travelers will not be able to come back. I implore you to think carefully of what you're about to do."

Continuing, Merielle gestured to the whole of the room. "But if you do leave it might be that some of us can't or won't hold back. There are some powerful, well-connected people in this room Yvette Raymond. Is that what you want? To sit alone in the House of Commons? To have no power? To be a political lepper? To have people whisper you're no different than Josee Labelle? A traitor to Canada?"

Raymond scoffed. "Does that mean I'll suffer the same fate as that woman? Or would you still have this room believe you had nothing to do with Labelle's death?"

When the Quebec City MP next spoke, her voice was low and laced with contempt. "You don't deserve to be Canada's Prime Minister. For what you've done and what you're doing, you deserve to be in a cell block."

Merielle took a step in the direction of her rival but before she could hit full stride, a pair of hands gently grasped her from behind. Allowing herself to be stopped, she leveled glaring eyes in Raymond's direction.

"Leave, Yvette. Get out of my sight and go do what you think you have to do. But whatever that is, know you and your demands, and those who have chosen to stand with you can go straight to hell."

Montreal

The phone vibrated in Elan's pocket. Immediately, his hand searched out the untraceable comms device.

"Oui," he said.

"We have received final word that she'll be attending the rally this evening."

"And we're sure? Even with what's happened in Washington."

"It's one hundred percent. Your target will be there."

"Then we move forward as planned?" said Elan, his voice level.

"Yes, we execute as planned. You have my full confidence, Dorian. Tonight, you will change the course of history."

"Thank you, Colonel. Your support will be appreciated by my people."

"Quickly, Elan added, "Sir, may I ask you a question?"

"Of course. What's on your mind?"

"Director Besson, sir. What of him?"

"Ah...I wondered when you might ask. In truth, my young friend, I do not have any information I can share with you about your uncle. To their credit, the Canadians have done a remarkable job of tucking him away."

"So we know it's the Canadians that took him?" Elan said with more emotion than he had intended.

"Of that we're certain. As to where he is, our best guess is that they have him somewhere up in the north of the country. We don't know where precisely. Otherwise, we would have gone after him."

Elan paused for a moment to consider his next question. Soldiers of his rank did not advance in their careers by questioning the authority or wisdom of their superiors, but in France, family was at least as important as country – perhaps more so.

"Sir, by going after the target, are we not putting my uncle at risk? I mean, if we're successful or not, might he be the one to suffer for it? He is the Director of the DGSE after all."

There was an extended silence over the connection, and just as Elan thought his appraisal of his career was about to come true, the Colonel spoke.

"Though it is not for you to ask this kind of question, I will answer it because of all people you should know."

"Thank you, Colonel. My uncle and I are not particularly close, but he is my mother's brother and as you know, the blood of family runs thick in those of us who are old-stock French. For better or worse, we must stick together."

The Colonel grunted in affirmation. "More true words have not been spoken, and it's all the more reason you are the person to do what must be done."

There was another bout of silence over the connection, while the Colonel took a moment to choose his words. "Dorian, our country is playing a complex game. You and what you will do tonight is but one move on a larger board. And though you cannot see it, your piece is intimately linked to that of your uncle. Success tonight brings us much closer to getting him home safely. Of that, we're confident."

"And if we do not succeed?" Elan said.

"There is one simple answer to that question, my most capable friend, and that is, just do not fail."

Chapter 15

MSNBC, broadcasting from Los Angeles

"General Morrison, please walk us through what we are seeing on this clip."

"Well, Amanda, this footage is approximately fifteen thousand feet to the west of Washington and from this vantage, you can clearly see the five mushroom clouds. Two are to the northwest and hit North Bethesda and Bethesda proper. Each strike was tactical and likely between two and four kilotons.

"Along the I-95 corridor that leads into the city from the southeast, you can see another pair of strikes. These, too, were tactical.

"The last strike that was dropped on Pentagon City was the largest by some measure. My sources are telling me it was approximately four to five kilotons. Still a tactical weapon, but, as you can see from the video image on the screen, its effects are magnitudes greater than the other bombs that were dropped."

"And why were these tactical nuclear weapons dropped where they were, General?"

"Well, the answer to that, Amanda, would appear straightforward. The UCSA will be driving their forces up through the corridors they've created with these weapons. It was no secret that the FAS forces had spent the past six months feverishly building up their defenses. The Red Faction, having made the calculation that the taking of the city through conventional means would have meant weeks, if not months, of terrible fighting elected to do what the Russians did to end the war in Ukraine."

"But what about the radiation, General? Won't the use of nuclear weapons make Washington unlivable? Is this not a pyrrhic victory for the UCSA?"

The gray-haired man shook his head in the negative. "It's a great question, Amanda, but the truth of tactical nuclear weapons detonated as air bursts are that they produce a short-lived amount of radiation. While the soldiers and people that were caught in the initial blast would have been saturated with lethal doses of radiation, within as few as twenty-four hours, Red Faction forces employing the right types of protection will be able to advance into these areas with little to no effect on their health. Within forty-eight hours, the radiation will be negligible.

"Truth be told, Amanda, with the butcher's bill the Red Faction paid in Cincinnati, I'm surprised these weapons weren't employed in taking Pittsburgh."

Despite the apocalyptic nature of the interview, the brunette news anchor offered her guest a pleasant smile. "General Morrison, we greatly appreciate your expert analysis of the events that have played out in Washington, D.C. They are shocking, to say the least."

"Any time, Amanda," the retired military man replied.

"Audience, stay with us as we give you more breaking developments out of the former United States.

"When we come back, we'll be joined by long-time contributor, Neil Zimmer, who'll speak with us about President Morgan's brief and only comments on the nuclear strikes, the whereabouts of former President Menendez, and Morgan's legitimacy as the new president of the Federation of American States."

Somewhere in Connecticut

Through the video, Roberta Hastings looked exhausted. And when she spoke, her words sounded equally tired.

"And so it is with a heavy heart that I am resigning effective immediately from my position as the Secretary of Education. As I have already outlined in detail, I can no longer stand with President Menendez. We need new leadership in Washington. Leadership that can come to an agreement with the UCSA. Our countries must come together and heal. I regret it has taken so long for me to act on this sentiment, but I have been feeling this way for many months. This ends my statement."

The streaming video cut to a news anchor with raven-black hair. "That was former Secretary of Education, Roberta Hastings. CNN received this video only an hour ago and based on our preliminary analysis, we can confirm that the video is authentic."

The anchor's eyes shifted to another in-studio camera.

"To help us understand this message, let's bring on CNN contributor Wendy Mills-Holten. She has covered education and Secretary Hastings for years and, by luck, we're able to have her in our studio here in Boston. Wendy, thanks for being with us today."

"Thank you, Lillian. I'm glad to be here."

"Wendy, with the Secretary's sudden resignation and the disappearance of the two marshals that were her protective detail, what are we to make of this statement? When you put all of it together and look at the political developments in Washington, this statement raises a host of concerns. You know Secretary Hastings personally. What are we to make of it?"

Hall clicked off the screen on the laptop and turned to Hastings. The Secretary's face looked as though she wanted to commit murder.

"Good enough work, Madam Secretary," the operative said.

"Good enough? You piece of garbage. There's a special place in hell waiting for you. You're not going to get away with this. You heard the report – anyone with half a brain can see I was coerced."

Hall said nothing. Instead, she turned back to the laptop on the table in front of Hastings. "Show clip eight," Hall directed the computer's near-AI.

Over the next three minutes, Hastings watched a BBC report on the attack on Washington. Somewhere in the middle of the piece, the look on her face transitioned from homicide to one of skepticism.

"What? You expect me to believe this? The Reds nuked D.C.? I don't know what game you're playing at, 'Jennifer,' or whatever your name is, but I'm done being jerked around. I've done what you wanted. I want to see my daughter. That was the deal."

Hall stared back at the Blue Faction official. "You don't have to believe it, Madame Secretary, but it's true. Your country's walk to national suicide continues apace and it is in this mess that your resignation will play out. Yes, people will be skeptical but it will be enough for our purposes."

As Hall moved to close the laptop, Petite entered the office where they had been keeping Hastings since their arrival at the safe house three hours ago.

Looking at Hall, Petite said, "You showed her?"

"Just now. She doesn't believe it."

Petite turned to face Hastings. "Your daughter and grandchildren have been given a vehicle to drive back to Connecticut. I have a pair of team members following them, but only to ensure they make it home safely."

"Lies and more lies," spat Hastings. "You've killed them just like you're going to kill me. How can you two live with yourselves?"

Petite's gaze left the American and connected with Hall. "I just got off the BAM with Azim. I guess you convinced him to read me into this program you're a part of?"

"We need more people like you, Sam. There's not enough of us who are willing to do what needs to be done to keep our country safe."

"That's exactly what Azim told me," Petite said as his eyes left Hall's and his voice became quiet.

"So you're in?"

"Yes," the CSIS officer confirmed. "Along with Sykes, Jankowicz and Kayed. They're the only ones I'm confident can do the type of work this colonel of yours is suggesting will need to be done."

"Kayed, eh?" asked Hall. "She doesn't strike me as the type."

"She's the type. Trust me. She grew up in Yemen during their civil war. She knows how savage things can get. She's as prepared as anyone to do what it takes to make sure the Reds don't come north."

"If you say so," Hall said. "What's next?"

"The five of us are to drive north where we'll be picked up by chopper. As Azim tells it, we're needed in Ottawa ASAP. He's to give a full briefing once we're on the road."

"What do you mean 'in Ottawa'?" Hastings interrupted the conversation.

"You're Canadians?" The woman's voice sounded confused. "If you're Canadians, why would you make me give that statement? And why would you do this? You people are supposed to be nice. You're supposed to be our friends."

Petite's gaze turned back to Hastings. As he looked down at the seated cabinet secretary, Hall thought she saw a look of sadness come onto his face. "Sam, let me do this. One more won't make my cross any heavier."

Petite shook his head. "We're a team now, and I'm its leader. It's on me. In any event, from everything I know about her, I'll be doing the world a favor."

Hastings suddenly rattled the chair she was bound to and issued a terrible scream in the direction of her two captors. "Talk to me, you bastards! Tell me what's going on. I want answers. I am a member of the Menendez Cabinet. You can't treat me this way!"

On finishing her statement, Hastings began to sob.

In the midst of the fit, Petite had drawn a suppressed Beretta 92FS and now had it casually pointed in the direction of Hastings' chest. On seeing the weapon, the American's sobs quickly died down.

"Please don't kill me," Hastings moaned. "I did what you wanted and I meant what I said. All of this. All of it will stay with me. I won't say a word to anyone. Whatever your government has planned, I promise, I won't say anything."

Petite pulled the trigger of his weapon sending a pair of 9mm rounds into his target's chest. Hastings bucked as each bullet struck her sending mini geysers of bright red blood into the air.

A grim statue, Petite slowly raised his weapon and leveled it at Hastings' head.

"My daughter." Hastings simultaneously shuddered and wheezed. "I need to know if she's safe. Please. It's all I ask."

As the question registered with him, Petite brought his second hand to the butt of his weapon so as to steady the shaking Beretta. When he spoke, his voice was barely audible. "Your daughter did not want to see you, Madam Secretary. But whatever your outcome, she wanted me to pass on a message."

As blood filled her lungs, a sick, gurgling sound emanated from Hastings' mouth when she next spoke. "What… what was her message?"

"That sometimes, bad people get what they deserve, Madame Secretary."

Hastings clenched her jaw and then with a supreme effort bellowed, "Liar!"

As the word left her mouth, Petite felt blood-drenched spittle hit his face. He pulled the trigger and sent a third bullet into the politician's forehead. The Secretary's head snapped back violently, forcing the rest of her body to lean backward to the point where the chair passed its apex causing it and Hastings to clatter onto the floor.

Lowering his weapon, Petite silently observed his work.

"She was poison, Sam," Hall quietly offered behind him. "And we don't know where Menendez is. For all we know, she's holed up somewhere in D.C. If we kept Hastings alive, there would always be the risk she would revoke her resignation, and then Morgan's status as President would be up in the air. This was the only option."

Petite raised his eyes from the body and turned to look at Hall.

"This is the work we do, Sam," said Hall while gesturing at Hastings. "This is what you've signed on for. We're only doing what other countries have done for generations. I know it's anathema to everything our country stands for, but we live in a time where millions are killed at the push of a button. We have to fight with our gloves off and our eyes open. It's that, or we start singing the Star Spangled Banner or whatever anthem Spector's redneck posse comes up with."

"Azim calls it the White Unit," Petite said somberly. "It doesn't look very white. It's more red or even black if you ask me. White is sterile and clean. What I just did is none of those things."

"On our flag Sam, white is in the background. It's unnoticed. It's the unsung tableau that holds our country together."

Hall took a step toward Petite and placed a hand on his shoulder. Someone has to be a counterweight to the Reds, the French, the Chinese. Hell, even the Germans are getting their hands dirty. The Brits can't do this work on their own, and the Aussies and Kiwis are half a world away. It's a radically different world than it was five years ago."

Still looking at the executed body, Petite pulled away from Hall's touch. "But cold-blooded murder?"

Hall nodded her head and after a moment, quietly said, "We let Hastings' daughter and grandchildren go, Sam. We're not the bad guys. We just play the bad guy's game when the moment calls for it. The White Unit and the things we have to do are temporary. It is a moment in time that will pass. If you want to leave, you can, but that's not going to stop the work from getting done."

Still looking at Hastings, Petite shook his head slowly and began to unscrew the suppressor off the end of his pistol. "No. I know what I signed up for."

Finally, he looked in Hall's direction. "I had Sykes and Jankowicz dig a hole a few klicks from here. We'll dispose of her and the Marshals there, and then move to the rendezvous to catch our ride home.

"I know what I signed up for, Hall. And now, like you, I'm all in."

Chapter 16

Deep River, East of CFB Petawawa

Larocque stared at his wife sitting on the living room's sofa. The moment he had walked into the house, she had burst into tears. Now she was staring despondently into a void that Larocque himself could not perceive.

"I'm leaving, Madison. I have to." His voice was soft as he delivered the news. "The whole Regiment is lifting off in eight hours. It's not enough time for a transition and the situation has changed. It's going to be hot down there. I can't leave the boys hanging. Greene is a good officer but not in a million years could I not lead this mission. My love, you have to understand this."

His wife continued to stare into whatever nothingness had a hold of her.

Larocque took a step forward and took a knee beside his wife. Gently, he placed his hand on her knee and squeezed. "Maddie, I don't want to leave without hearing your voice, even if it's to say you won't be here when I get back."

After a long moment, Madison's eyes fluttered. Slowly, she turned her head toward her husband.

"I've never told you this before, but I talk to Lauren. Not often, but every now and again."

Larocque made no reply.

"The conversations are so vivid. She's so beautiful, Jackson. If you could see her, you'd wonder where her wings are. She loves you more than anything."

"I know, my love. I love her too. With everything I have." Larocque's voice began to crack as he gave his reply.

Madison placed her hand on top of Larocque's. Despite being ice cold, the essence of Larocque's soul swelled at her touch.

"I haven't told you this, but when I left you, I started going to church. I had to. I had to find something to help me deal with the pain. It was that or it was joining our baby. I chose God, Jacks. And I don't regret it because he's given us another chance. He's given us another miracle." As she said the words, her free hand moved to her stomach.

"I had no idea, my love," Larocque said. "Why didn't you tell me?"

"Because I know you don't believe. You are a practical and down-to-earth man."

For a second, she offered him what seemed to be a genuine smile. "Jesus is bullshit magic and make-believe. Isn't that what you say?"

"Something like that," Larocque said, keeping his tone neutral.

"Well, you don't have to believe but I do. He's guiding us, Jacks, and as much as I don't want you to go to Washington and as much as I resent Merielle and the country for how they've used you and the regiment, he works in mysterious ways. God has a plan for you, just like he has a plan for our baby."

"And what about you, Madison? What's the plan for you?"

She pulled her hand off Larocque's and moved to stand.

Still on one knee, Larocque looked up into Madison's liquid brown eyes that were still moist from crying.

"I left you once before, Jackson Larocque, and I was miserable. We got back together, and I immediately became pregnant. God has made his intentions abundantly clear. I'm going to have this baby, Jackson, and you'll survive this war or you won't. It's God's plan and I don't have a say."

Larocque slowly rose so he was once again looking down at his wife. "I'll come back, my love, and when I do get back, we can talk through all of this. Whatever journey you've taken, I want to learn more and I want to be with you."

Larocque's wife said nothing. Instead, she reached behind her neck and unclasped the crucifix necklace she had on.

"Give me your hand."

Larocque reached out with one of his hands, palm up, callouses exposed. Gently, Madison pulled him in close to her so that his hand was on top of her protruding stomach and with great care placed the dangling crucifix at the center of his hand.

"You've done enough for Canada, Jackson, but I also understand I can't stop you from being with the Regiment. I understand that now and I accept it."

Larocque stared at the dainty-looking piece of jewelry. "Help me put it on."

"No," Madison said quickly.

"No?"

"When you believe, then you can put it on. Until then, keep it with you and keep it safe."

Larocque closed his hand tightly around the necklace and could feel the crucifix bite into his flesh. "I'll be back, Madison. And I love you."

His wife locked her eyes on his. "I know you do. Now do what you have to do. I'll be here when you get back."

Montreal

Staff Sergeant Asher Lastra took in the assembly of RCMP and Montreal police officers and the half dozen staff from the Prime Minister's Office.

He had called in several favors and been able to double the Prime Minister's protective detail, but in his opinion, they would never have enough officers. In all, there would be sixty RCMP officers from the National Division for Protective Operations and hundreds more from the Montreal police and several other local police agencies.

More bodies were what he wanted, but with the additional firepower and eyes came the headache of making the logistics of the operation work. It was this factor that had prevented him from reaching out to Canadian Special Forces.

The thought of having a squadron of JTF-2 commandos and some of their toys riding shotgun as Merielle went to and from Olympic Stadium had been an attractive idea but it would have meant layering over yet another bureaucracy making the whole affair even more unwieldy.

Lastra didn't have the patience for it and, unsurprisingly, the brass in the RCMP was of the same mind. As it was, Canadian Special Operations Forces Command had its hands full with everything going on in Washington.

Since the Reds had dropped tactical nukes on the city, he had been hearing all sorts of rumors that various CANZUK special operations units were getting ready to head south, if they weren't there already.

The one and only conversation he'd had with Merielle on the subject of ditching the rally had been a fruitless attempt. When the images of mushroom clouds over Washington hit the news, he had elected to make one last attempt at getting her to see reason about Montreal.

But the woman would have none of it. She had listened to each of his points and for each of his objections, she had a response as to why the rally needed to move ahead.

Merielle's final words on the matter had been gentle but firm. "Asher, I know you're doing your job and your job is to keep me safe but I'm not some trust fund drama teacher and you'll never, ever, find me hiding in a closet should bullets start to fly. It's who I am. Washington only makes the unity of the country more important. If the Blues fall, a separated Canada is as good as the 51st state of the union. I'm going to Montreal so what I need from you now more than anything else is for you to get me there safe and back again."

As she said those words to him, he could see the same level of passion she had when they made love. There was no way to turn away Merielle when she had both her heart and mind set on something.

And so here he was, addressing two hundred-plus police officers in an air hangar at Pierre Elliot Trudeau International Airport.

"People, to reiterate one final time - from here it's down Highway 40. We off-ramp at Pie-IX Boulevard, which brings us straight to Olympic Stadium. Both the 40 and Pie-IX will be shut down to local traffic. As we move to the stadium and back to PET, we'll have eyes in the sky. And remember, if you see something, no matter how insignificant, report it. Communications and vigilance are paramount."

Lastra slowly scanned the officers gathered in front of him. To the last, they were focused and serious. "Do we have any final questions on getting the asset to and from the event?"

No hands went up. A good sign, Lastra told himself. Both the Montreal Police and Sûreté du Québec, the province's version of the state police were quality outfits. Not perfect by any stretch, but they had enough competent people in the room that somebody would say something if they had a concern.

"Seeing no questions, colleagues, here's my last reminder. At all times and most importantly in the stadium, the chain of command starts and ends with me. If for whatever reason, I am unable to provide direction, Staff Sergeant Mellon will assume command. If Mellon is unavailable, Staff Sergeant Nguyen will take the lead. RCMP will retain command and control of the operation at all times."

As he surveyed the collection of cops one final time, he assured himself everyone was on board. There were no glazed eyes, no whispering of complaints in the back rows, and as best Lastra could tell, there was no indication the jurisdictional bullshit that usually infected this type of operation was lurking in a corner somewhere.

On this one occasion, cops from at least three different outfits had elected to play nice with one another. Lastra didn't know who to thank for this blessing. Whatever the reason for his good fortune, he was an experienced enough cop to know that he should take the win.

"Time check is now 1817 hours. Our VIP, call sign Outrider, puts down in twenty, so you have that amount of time to make any final preparations. If there are any adjustments, advise Mellon or Nguyen ASAP. The moment Outrider steps off that plane, things get real, we're locked in, and we move like clockwork."

Lastra gave the room one last opportunity to ask a question. He counted off two long seconds. When no hand came up, he barked loudly into the wide-open space of the hangar, "Briefing dismissed."

Undisclosed Location, North Carolina

Parr had elected not to be with Spector to watch the live feed of the strike on Washington.

Where Spector and his generals had obsessed over the exact placement of the low-yield nuclear weapons, he had invested as much or more energy into final preparations for Operation Sunlight.

The two-day deadline had sent him and his team into a planning session of epic proportions. Had it not been for the periodic visits from the President's medical team offering a range of pharmaceutical pick-me-ups, they would not have achieved half of what they had.

Though it was far from their original goal, they provided the names, pictures, addresses, and, in some cases, active geo-locating data for the top two thousand elites to the nearly three hundred kill teams they had managed to pull together since his planning team had first been given their mission.

The kill teams were a mixed bag of anyone within the planning team's network of contacts they knew to be competent and morally flexible. After almost four years of bitter civil war, it turned out that finding this type of individual wasn't nearly as challenging as Parr had thought it would be.

Ranging from dozens of lone wolves to groups of up to twenty, each hastily gathered unit had been given a list with one to half a dozen names, with those names at the top of each list being given the highest priority.

The instructions they had received had been necessarily simple: *The FAS is collapsing. Find the people on the list using the information provided or through your own means. Eliminate these individuals through whatever means necessary. Immunity for all actions is assured with UCSA victory. Payments for validated eliminations will be made through your respective contact.*

Their 'respective contact' was the highest-powered near-AI that Parr could get his hands on. With guidance from the planning team, the near-AI virtual planner would stay connected with and coordinate each of the teams through whatever comms or near-AI device each assassin had on their person.

Using publicly available data or by accessing information it could get through various back channels in the ether, the virtual planner would feed each team a constant stream of information on their respective targets. As best it could, it would also monitor police and other emergency outfits to help them respond or avoid detection as they moved down their respective lists.

Although the strike against Washington had only taken place nine hours ago, Parr had been surprised by the results achieved thus far. In those communities that were close to the frontlines, just over two hundred targets had been eliminated and, as yet, not a single team had become inactive.

The nuclear strikes and the collateral damage they sowed combined with the huge movement of people fleeing out of fear of what would come next, had made the task of infiltrating into Blue-held territories an easier task than the planning team had anticipated. It was chaos of the highest order throughout the FAS.

Parr walked into the planning team's operations room. With a few exceptions, everyone was present and working away on a laptop or some other device.

"Peter," he heard a voice call his attention.

His head snapped in the direction of the voice. His eyes locked with the baby-faced Major Trammel. Youthful he might look, but the Air Force Academy graduate had been one of Parr's most effective team members. He strode in the direction of the man.

"What's up, Major?"

"Not sure if you're the squeamish type, but it looks like we've got our first big fish and they've got a live stream going."

"Let me see it," Parr said without hesitation. He had made this decision early on. He couldn't be the leader of this operation and avoid seeing at least some of the mess. Corporate leadership 101 was that you sometimes had to get close to the action. Let the team see that you're invested. That you're prepared to do the hard things you're asking them to do.

"Who is it, Major?"

"Dr. Angela Merkley. She's a Professor of Communication and Social Influence at Temple University. On the list, we have her at number twenty-five. As university professors go, she has an outsized social media following due to her longstanding participation on the Resist and Radicalize podcast. I've never once listened to it, but I guess she's one of the leading firebrands for the Menendez Administration. She has no less than five million followers."

"Oh, I'm all too familiar with Professor Merkley," said Parr. "Firebrand doesn't do her justice. Among her other accomplishments, she was one of the early proponents of Shame.com."

"White, Racist, Fascist. Out'em all at Shame.com." The Air Force officer employed what Parr thought was a not-too-bad radio voice to invoke the life-ruining website's tagline.

Parr pointed to the bank of displays in front of Trammel. "What are we looking at?"

"A lecture hall in the Kline College of Media and Communications."

"You're kidding," Parr scoffed. "With all that's going on, this woman is still holding lectures? Jesus, we just nuked D.C., and these kids are sitting in a classroom in Philly, not a hundred miles away? Ignorance truly is bliss."

"The Blues are telling people to go about their normal business, sir," said the Air Force officer. "They're advising only that folks stay off the major highways. Looks like a good number of the sheep are doing what they're told."

"Sheep, indeed," said Parr. "Well, it looks like they're going to be less one of their shepherds. Who do we have in the room?"

"Two members of the East Choctaw Nation Militia, if you can believe it. They went straight to Philly as soon as the order went out. This will be their first action."

"And they're live streaming?" Parr asked a hint of disbelief in his voice.

"It's their MO, sir. Our file says they're two brothers. They have a huge following on 8Chan and quite the library of videos, I'm told.

It's sad so many sick people in the world are willing to watch this kind of thing live, but this is the society we live in."

Parr nodded his head in agreement and then pointed to the screen. "Looks like it's show time."

A woman, with purple hair and a pair of thick-rimmed glasses, marched into the room and placed herself behind the lectern. Based on the feed, it seemed as though there was a fair distance between the person taking the video and the target. As the academic began to settle in, the videographer slowly increased his magnification.

Parr watched with increasing fascination as the woman calmly organized herself to the point of finally setting both her hands on the podium. Without saying a word, she slowly panned her eyes across the room.

Her voice filled the room. "I see a few of you are recording this morning." With a lingering New England accent, Merkley's jarring voice was instantly recognizable to anyone who kept tabs on that part of the ecosphere that influenced Blue Faction politics. In this world, Dr. Merkley was a veritable star.

"Well, this morning, I give you my explicit permission. You can record or stream all you like because we won't be getting into any of the course material. Instead, I'm going to give you a little preview of what I'm going to talk about on the pod this afternoon. And I've got a lot to say."

Merkley moved from behind the lectern to the middle of the speaker's dais. "I'm proud of all of you. With all that is happening, you chose to come to class today to learn about the things that make a difference. And you can see, by the ongoing events in Washington, that everything I've said about the patriarchy and white supremacy is correct. Spector and his cronies are the archetypes. They are so threatened, so unwilling to lose control, they've used nuclear weapons. I didn't think it possible, but here we are."

The short, wiry professor took two steps forward so she was on the edge of the platform where she proceeded to canvass the entirety of the lecture space with bespectacled eyes. "What have I been telling you? You and everyone who listens to me online. The patriarchy and white men will not let go. They cannot. Even in the FAS, we now see that a man – a fucking white man – has replaced a woman of color. They won't, they cannot lose control. The white patriarchy will not let it happen, no matter the cost. They need it so badly, they'll use the ultimate weapon, not once, but twice. Mark my words, people – they'll use it as many times as they need to assert their control."

The lecture hall was perfectly silent. As the professor stared forward, her next statement ready to unload, Parr started to feel his heart beat faster in anticipation.

The person controlling the camera panned outwards and to the right so that the academic was now sharing the screen with one of two entrances that led to the floor of the lecture hall. Quietly, the person operating the recording device spoke a single word: "Now."

The door opened and a lanky man strolled into the lecture hall. While dressed like any college student, the interloper's face was covered by a rubber mask sporting the visage of the 45th President. With a practiced hand, the camera operator zoomed in on the figure.

In the masked man's right hand was a semi-automatic pistol. Parr, an avid shooter, instantly recognized it as a Glock 34, a weapon designed for hitting targets at longer distances. The handgun, fully extended out from the man's body, had an oversized magazine protruding from the grip.

The professor, a long-time creature of the lecture hall, instantly picked up the change in the room's energy and turned to face the intrusion that all eyes in her classroom had shifted to.

For a quick second, the professor and the gunman stared each other down, and then Merkley, while moving in the direction of the lectern, screamed at the top of her lungs, "Of all days, how dare you wear that mask into my classroom. Leave! This is a gun-free campus! Leave my classroom, NOW!"

"Does she not see the gun?" Major Trammel asked in disbelief.

Reaching the lectern, Parr watched the professor scramble to reach for something, and then, as if by magic, the purple-haired academic had a snub-nose revolver in her hand and opened fire.

"Whoa! He didn't see that coming," Parr said excitedly.

As the first shots left the professor's gun, the Trump-masked gunman staggered backward, but then let loose with his own weapon, unleashing a hail of bullets.

As the sound of gunfire and the screams of the female-dominated classroom began to fill the operations room, Parr sensed others begin to gather around Trammel's workstation. Good, he thought. He'd show them he could stomach what needed to be done. It was one thing to watch a mushroom cloud from afar, it was something else entirely to sit front row at a public execution.

As his people gathered, they witnessed the woman with the purple hair laid out on a blood-smeared dais. She was propped up on her elbows, desperately trying to wriggle away from the masked man. In the intense exchange of gunfire, the professor had somehow become weaponless. Reaching the edge of the speaker's platform, she finally gave up trying to escape, and, with whatever life she had left in her, stared forlornly at her executioner.

Now standing over his target, the gunman pointed his handgun in the direction of Merkley's face and without word or warning, pulled the trigger.

As the back of the academic's head exploded making an unsightly mess across the vinyl-tiled floor, Parr forced himself to continue to take in the gory act. Staring intently at the high-def broadcast, he watched as the masked agent of chaos turned to face the camera and unleashed a keening war cry.

As the man's howl came to an end, the camera pulled back from the blood-soaked scene so that much of the rest of the lecture hall was now in view.

While many students had fled the classroom, a few remained sitting or standing in place, for whatever reason, their eyes glued to the fate of the popular instructor.

Stepping away from the body, the gunman raised the nightmare of a weapon and trained it on a pair of young women huddled together in the first third of the seating. Again, without warning, the masked man unloaded with a sustained barrage of rounds.

As new screams of terror filled Parr's ears, he calmly said, "Shut it off, Major."

Instantly, the stream of mass murder was replaced by a benign program being run somewhere else on Trammel's computer. As Parr's vision pulled back from whatever inconsequential data lay on the screen, he purposely exhaled a gust of air from his lungs, hoping the display would draw whatever eyes in the room were not already on him.

"Good work, Major. The task that's before you is not easy, but it is precisely the work that needs to be done. For the moment, it's our job to extend the despair and chaos the Blues are feeling in Washington to the rest of the FAS."

Parr turned away from Trammel to face the rest of the room. "Let there be no doubts about it what needs to be done, people. For the next several weeks, we are the purveyors of an intimate and terrible chaos, and without a doubt in my mind, we are playing a crucial part in our country's effort to win this war. It is through our efforts that we will shatter the society that has caused our country and families so much pain. And shatter it we must, because if we are going to rebuild the FAS into the vision that is held by the President, we must be ruthless and complete in our efforts to wipe away all resistance. Without hesitation or quarter given, we must sterilize the body politic that is the Federation. This is our mission."

He quickly scanned each of the faces looking back at him and the word that came to mind was "resolute." This group could do what needed to be done, as could he, Parr thought with satisfaction.

"Back to work, people, and keep your foot on the gas. Operation Sunlight doesn't stop until the President says so."

Chapter 17

Dover Air Force Base, Delaware

The British brigadier general giving the overview of the current situation in Washington was standing beside a huge LCD display that had been flown in as a part of the CANZUK air mobile brigade HQ still in the process of setting up on Dover AFB.

On the east coast of Delaware, Dover was a two-hour drive from D.C. and well outside the cloud of radiation dissipating several kilometers east of the US capital.

This far from the fighting and with F-35s from the *HMS Prince of Wales* patrolling the sky above there had been no need for Larocque and the Airborne to arrive via airdrop.

With the help of CANZUK air traffic controllers, the American air base had been accepting a steady stream of Hercules and Globemaster flights dropping off hundreds and then thousands of soldiers and their needed supplies and equipment.

The brigadier pointed out a location on the satellite image the display was projecting. The remnants of the mushroom cloud towered over the area the officer had just placed a green laser on. "This satellite image was taken twenty minutes after the attack. The southernmost strike hit the D.C. enclave of Arora Hills. Based on what we've been told by our new friends, it was a direct hit on the Blues' command-and-control node for this part of their defense."

The brigadier's laser then shifted north. "The strike here hit a similar node centered on America University. As you would expect, both areas – nearly one kilometer in radius – have been utterly devastated. Whatever command and control existed is off the board."

The brigadier touched the screen and the image shifted to a video. "Since arriving in-theater, we've sent in recce drones to get a firsthand look at the damage. Ladies and gents, the images speak for themselves."

Larocque took in the scene from the slow-moving drone. It must have been at the heart of one of the strikes because for hundreds of meters in each direction, all he could see were eviscerated or shattered buildings of various shapes and sizes. Those buildings that had managed to stay erect were actively burning or charred shells of their former selves.

Suddenly, the video cut to another angle. The drone was now high above the epicenter of the destruction. At about five hundred meters out from the blast's center, Larocque noted the damage didn't look all that bad. Certainly, it was nothing like the devastation from the city-ending strikes the Reds had hit New York and Chicago with two years earlier.

To his immediate right, Colonel Luke Wright of the UK Parachute Regiment must have been thinking the same thing because aloud he said, "If you ask me, General, it seems like the neighborhood has held up pretty well. I mean, those brownstones on the periphery of the blast, well, they look as solid as the day they were built."

Before the brigadier could respond, from somewhere behind the gathered group of assembled CANZUK officers, a female voice full of authority spoke. "It's the radiation that's the problem."

Larocque and the other senior officers turned in unison to see a FAS three-star general flanked by a pair of colonels. All three of them were in their battle rigs, though unlike the two grizzled men flanking her, the general had removed her helmet. She was tall, with close-cropped hair now more grey than black. More obvious, however, was the black patch that covered her left eye. It was the patch that identified her to the group.

"General Galway, welcome to our briefing. I'm thrilled that you saw fit to come to us in person," the brigadier said, his voice echoing in the corners of the busy hangar.

Larocque took in Galway. In the special forces community, she was a walking, talking legend. Early in her career, she commanded frontline infantry during the latter years of the Afghanistan conflict. After completing two tours outside the wire as a Special Forces liaison, she had been one of the first women to successfully complete the US Army's Special Forces Qualification Course and become a full-fledged Green Beret.

From that point on, her career had become necessarily obscured until the outbreak of the civil war, when she was given the high-profile responsibility of running the Blues' counterinsurgency program.

That she had been good at the job had been validated by the fact that the only person in the FAS with a bigger bounty on their head was President Menendez herself.

Galway set her one eye on the British general. "If we're going to get the right people out of D.C., General, you're going to need my help. Yesterday, I would have told you that we could have held Washington for six months at least. Now, we'll be lucky if we make it the next 24 hours.

"The Reds knew exactly where to put the nukes to maximize their damage. It's the radiation that's put us over the edge, General. Every soldier that was west of the Potomac is now dead or dying from radiation poisoning. East of the river is hardly better."

Larocque watched Galway as she walked around the seated CANZUK officers. She stopped in front of the brigadier at which point the Brit special operations commander snapped off a sharp salute that Galway returned.

She gestured in the direction of the seated officers and said to the British general, "May I address your soldiers?"

"Of course, General. The floor is yours."

Galway turned and with her one good eye, surveyed the gathered officers from each of the four countries that made up the alliance. When she got to Larocque, there was a subtle narrowing of her eye.

"Colonel Larocque, isn't it?"

"Yes, Ma'am," the Airborne CO's reply was prompt.

"I'm glad you're here, Colonel," she said, offering a smile that seemed out of place on her battle-scarred face. "You and everyone else. It's a sad day that the FAS needs outside help, but that time has come and I, for one, am glad it's CANZUK that has answered the call."

Galway thumbed in the direction of the paused image on the display behind her. "Washington is lost. Nothing we do can stop that now. But with your help, we can find and pull out the man that can turn this war around. We lost contact with President Morgan and his Secret Service detail two hours ago. Because of the catastrophic damage caused by the strikes, digital communications across Washington are a hot mess.

"The last we heard from President Morgan's people directly, he was getting ready to leave Pentagon, where by coincidence he had been when the first three strikes landed. As the brigadier was about to tell you, the fourth of the five strikes hit Pentagon City. The epicenter of the attack was about a half mile from where the President was located.

In response to the revelation, there was a wave of murmuring from the assembled officers. It was Rydell of 2nd Commando that put a voice to the question every officer in the room was thinking. "All respect, General, but I reckon that's a bit close. How do you know President Morgan survived the blast? I mean, you just mentioned the radiation. It would have been pretty intense at that distance."

Galway's eyes took up the Australian. "Thankfully, the Pentagon was built to resist exactly this type of scenario, Colonel. Further, we received multiple on-the-ground reports of a convoy leaving the Pentagon heading east across the Potomac twenty minutes after the last bomb hit."

Galway turned her attention to the brigadier and gestured to the display that still held the image of the destroyed neighborhood they had been reviewing. "May I?"

"Of course. What would you like to see, General?"

"Put up a map of the city. The White House and everything south of it."

The British general made the necessary commands to the near-AI and a tactical map of the area Galway had requested was birthed onto the display.

Walking over to it, Galway set her finger on the George Mason Memorial Bridge. "The President's motorcade was seen crossing the George Mason going north into D.C. proper. However, in addition to the nuclear strikes, the Reds have also been lobbing in artillery and conducting air strikes across this part of the city.

"In the event of an evacuation from the Pentagon, standard protocol would have been for the President to be moved north across the George Mason and then straight up 14th Street to the White House, where he would have been placed in a bunker or flown out of the city by helicopter."

As Galway recited the plan, her finger ran south to north along the escape route. Once her finger landed on the White House, she turned to face the seated officers.

The look on her face was one of concern. "14th Street and most of the other avenues across old D.C. have been made all but impassable by the Reds and their artillery. And, despite the radiation, the Reds have sent thousands of irregulars into the city with orders to kill anyone and everything on sight. As I stand here before you, there is a human slaughter taking place in Washington."

"And it's because of this shitstorm you don't know where your president is?" It was Larocque who had posed the intemperate-sounding question. As Galway had been painting the picture of the falling city, it had struck him what the FAS general was going to ask them to do.

Slowly, Galway turned her single eye onto Larocque. "Indeed, it is a shitstorm, Colonel and as I stand before you, we still don't know where President Morgan is, as impossible as that might seem. Worse, I don't have the forces I need to find him. Truth be told, I don't like it one little bit, but the reality of the situation that faces myself and my people is that need your help, Colonel Larocque. I need all of your help. I need an organized, well-armed force that I can communicate with to go into Washington proper to track down and pull out my president. That's why I'm here."

As a look of genuine concern spread across the American general's face, Galway took a step in Larocque's direction. For a moment, the ambient sound of soldiers readying equipment in other parts of the hangar was the only sound in the officers' walled-off briefing area.

Finally, the FAS general broke the silence. "I stand before you Colonel, as a fellow soldier with my cap in hand. Were I you, I would think twice about sending my men into the disaster that is D.C. Nevertheless, that's just what I'm here to ask of you. My question for you, Colonel, and your fellow officers is this – are you willing to help me find the one man that can save my country?"

Montreal

Olympic Stadium, or the Big O as it was known in Montreal, was vibrating with energy. Some fifty thousand people had made their way to the same massive concrete sprawl that had made the likes of Nadia Comaneci and Caitlyn Jenner household names three generations earlier.

Merielle felt vindicated by the crowd's size and its engagement. With all that had transpired south of the border, she had been worried that people would have passed on the rally, but her instincts had been right. In today's world of disastrous conflict and social media isolation, people were desperate for something, anything, to bring them together.

In a last-minute concession to Lastra, she had agreed that she wouldn't sit on the massive stage for the duration of the rally. Instead, she had taken in most of the event from a second-level suite on a right angle to the stage.

In hindsight, it had been the right call, as it had allowed her to get a feel for the dynamics of the moment. Whoever had decided to bring in the DJ to work the crowd between speeches had been a genius. The Big O was roaring.

Now on the move and surrounded by her protective detail, she could feel the bass of the music as it assaulted the predominantly young faces that made up the crowd. As she walked the floor of the stadium to the stage, everywhere she looked she saw ecstatic faces screaming and waving the Canadian flag.

Ahead of her, Merielle caught sight of Lastra. As the overall lead of her protection team, it had been his job to observe, direct, and coordinate the hundred or so police officers exclusively dedicated to ensuring her safety.

He had made his way to the stage and positioned himself at the top of the stairs she was about to ascend. Head completely bald but wearing a neatly trimmed beard, he cut quite the figure as he stood imperiously looking out onto the crowd awaiting their country's prime minister.

As she reached the stairs that led onto the stage, the front end of her detail opened up, allowing her to negotiate the steps to where Lastra was waiting. He finally took his eyes off the animated throng that was the audience and looked at her with the Mediterranean brown eyes she had come to adore.

Despite the stress recent events had placed on their relationship, Merielle was thrilled he was here. With all that was happening, the man was an immovable rock she could grab onto to steady herself whenever she might need it.

But now was not one of those times. They both had jobs to do. The moment her feet set upon the stage, the capacity crowd roared as though she was the world's most popular pop star.

Wearing a power suit and flats that would allow her to move quickly if needed, Merielle brushed past her lover onto the stage proper and thrust both her hands in the air.

Responding to her appearance and raised hands, the crowd somehow increased the ferocity of its cheering.

Despite Lastra's direction not to delay her movement to the reinforced podium that awaited her at center stage, she felt compelled to stand unmoving, basking in the pulsating energy of the moment.

Merielle knew full well her pause would make Lastra apoplectic, but something in that moment would not let her move. For all her recent difficulties politically, it was moments like this that made it all worth it.

Suddenly, to her left, she sensed a presence. Turning away from the glare of the lights and the screaming, she turned to see that Paul Blanchard had somehow made his way onto the stage.

The Minister of Transport's speech had preceded Merielle's and the big man from the Pontiac had delivered a barn burner. He had gone ten minutes over his allotted time, but no one in her entourage had offered a hint of concern or complaint. Blanchard, a seasoned political brawler and a first-rate orator had not held back on Eric Labelle and the separatists.

Standing beside her, Blanchard put his arm across Merielle's shoulders. Despite feeling like a child beside the colossus that was Blanchard, together they waved at the sea of humanity that lay before them.

After a full minute of engaging with the crowd, Blanchard leaned down to Merielle and, over the noise, said, "Your beau thought you might get lost on your way to the podium, so he asked me to escort you safely to where you need to be. He's going to kill me if I let you linger any longer."

With a huge smile, Blanchard then extended the crook of his arm in her direction. "Would you give me the honor, Madame Prime Minister, of escorting you the rest of the way?"

Placing her arm in Blanchard's, she allowed him to walk her in the direction of the podium.

Reaching center stage and without warning, her big friend enveloped her in a full hug. With no choice but to allow it to happen, Merielle gave a silent word of thanks that Blanchard had the good sense not to pick her up off the stage.

Finally, he let her go. With a massive grin on his face, he winked at her and turned to the crowd to give it one last wave.

As he turned to walk off the stage, Merielle took a deep breath and took a step onto the dais that would align with the podium's singular microphone.

As she settled her hands on the lectern and scanned the mass of people arrayed in front of her, she could hear the stadium begin to become quiet.

She counted from ten and by the time she hit one, the only sound she could perceive was the natural, unavoidable thrum that was present with crowds the size of the one now staring at her.

Merielle zeroed in on one particular woman. Like most of the crowd, she was young. She had a beautiful face and was wearing a hijab. With her right hand, Merielle reached into the inner pocket of her jacket and grasped the document she knew was there. Slowly, she pulled out the black rectangle embossed with Canada's coat of arms.

Slowly, she raised her Canadian passport into the air. As she did so, she saw the young woman reach down somewhere onto her person, and, with a million-watt smile, hold up her own passport.

Merielle reciprocated the woman's smile and then pulled her gaze back so she could take in the sea of people in front of her as fifty-thousand-plus individuals collectively reached into their pockets, jackets, or purses to retrieve and hold aloft that document Canadians cherished as much as any national binding symbol.

"*Mons amis*, my friends," Merielle said as she began to lower her passport. "*Je suis Canadiens. Vous etes Canadiens.* You are Canadian, we are Canadians. This is how it must be. For forever and a day. Tonight, as I stand before you, let me assure you that destiny serves a united Canada."

Primed to respond to anything she might say, the capacity crowd delivered its first roar of approval.

"My friends, I have the honor and duty this evening to tell you all the reasons why you should vote 'no' to the referendum the separatists have unnecessarily thrust on us. To those of you who are watching and are still not convinced of how you should vote, or to those Quebecois who appreciate the benefits of a united Canada, but have concerns about the state of affairs in our part of the world, I say to you all, give me the next twenty minutes of your time.

"Open your heart and give me this one short moment to tell you the facts as to why this century belongs only to those countries that have the fortitude to stand united in the face of global tyranny, nuclear holocausts, and economic devastation."

Hands still on the podium, Merielle leaned forward, bringing herself closer to the electrified audience.

"Will you give me this time?" she fairly yelled into the microphone.

Instantly, the crowd responded to the question with thunderous applause and with close-by screams of "yes," "*oui*," "go for it," or "we love you, Merielle."

She beamed back to the crowd. "My friends. My fellow Canadians. Let me take you on a journey that only a united Canada can take. Let me show you why it is only through Canada that we maintain the very things that make us great as a country. Democracy. Diversity. Prosperity. And, most importantly, freedom."

On Merielle's pronouncement of "freedom," the stadium erupted into an extended bout of cheering.

"*Bon!*" she proclaimed loudly into the microphone. "Then let us start with freedom, shall we? Let us start with what binds us. Freedom more than anything else is what makes us Canadians. The freedom to choose your religion, your politics, where you live, where you work, who you love, what you do to your body, and perhaps most importantly, what you say."

She looked in the direction of the media tower at the center of the stadium floor and waited for the camera's red light to turn on.

"My fellow Quebecers. Hear my voice. The people that stand to win the terrible war that is to the south of our border do not understand and do not revere freedom as we do in this province. Do not think for one moment that a separate Quebec, an island of French in what is an ocean of English, will be able to grow or even guard the freedoms all of you hold dear.

"We Quebecers are a proud and distinct people, but on a continent of nearly five hundred million, Quebec amounts to just two percent of the population. I'm sorry, my friends, but two percent doesn't even make the appetizer section on the menu that is international politics today."

There were two huge screens behind Merielle and until that moment, they had only featured her. As she delivered the next line of her speech, the four flags of Canada, the United Kingdom, Australia, and New Zealand filled the two screens.

"Friends, freedom for Quebec is not eleven million people. It is one hundred and sixty million people. In the unity of purpose and in an unwavering commitment to the freedom the CANZUK nations hold dear, Quebec, united and strong within Canada, can and will withstand the storm of tyranny that confronts the distinct society we as a collective have labored so hard to build."

Montreal

They had debated eliminating the Canadian Prime Minister inside the stadium, but Elan had nixed the proposal.

As he had entered the Big O to attend the rally and passed by the various layers of security, his decision had been vindicated. The RCMP and the Montreal police had done an admirable job of securing the massive building. In the aftermath of the assassination of Canada's most recent prime minister, Robert MacDonald, the country appeared to be taking the matter of protecting its leader more seriously.

Metal detectors, individual searches, dogs, dozens of near-AI-controlled surveillance drones, and vigilant-looking police officers in the dozens, had created what was almost certainly an impregnable shell around the Martel woman.

Inside the stadium and close to the stage, even more security had been brought to bear. Of particular interest to him was the VIP screen the Canadians had set up in front of the podium.

A smooth gray rectangle surrounded the elevated dais that Canada's leader now occupied. Run by an advanced near-AI, the Israeli-designed and highly secret VIP protection unit contained various sensors that continuously scanned the crowd and the air particles around the person it was protecting.

In the event someone pulled anything that looked like a weapon or should the product's highly attuned sensors perceive anything moving faster than thirty kilometers an hour, the screen's near-AI would identify, assess, and neutralize the threat in a fraction of the time a human being could.

Elan had seen a demonstration of an earlier version of the technology and had been amazed as the unit neutralized six high-velocity sniper rounds from no less than 150 meters away.

What the unit had done to protect its charge from an exploding suicide vest had been even more impressive. Not a shred of shrapnel had made its way through the device to impact the unhinged product rep that had agreed to stand in as the demonstration's VIP.

No, Elan thought, ending this woman's life on the streets of Montreal had been the right call. Outside, they had room to play with if their first effort didn't go according to plan.

He looked at his watch. Martel had been at it for fifteen minutes and if he was any judge, she would be wrapping up within the twenty minutes she had promised. It was time to go.

Taking pains to ensure the enamored look on his face remained in place, he turned and began to make his way through the thick collection of people that stood between him and the exit.

As he left the stadium floor and entered the vaulted concrete lobby that was the Big O's main entry point, he caught the eyes of two of his team members masquerading as a pair of young lovers.

Hand-in-hand with Canadian flags tied across their shoulders, he sensed them pull in behind him as he made his way to the doors that would lead him into the humid night air that had been accosting Montreal for the past two weeks.

Outside, twenty thousand more people had gathered to watch Martel's speech on several gigantic outdoor screens. As he walked through the overflow crowd, every person he saw seemed to be spellbound by the words of the Canadian prime minister.

He had to give it to the woman. For all the talk that Merielle Martel was inept as a politician, she had delivered what was perhaps one of the best speeches he had seen in person. On her last night alive, Elan had no doubt that she would be remembered as giving the performance of her life.

As he finally cleared the last gaggle of young people and strode onto the boulevard that ran parallel to Olympic Stadium, Elan felt a buoying of his confidence.

A van pulled up beside him and opened its door. Stopping, he turned in the direction from which he had come. Only the two faux lovers seemed to have taken any interest in him. Without saying a word or making eye contact, the pair released their hands and jumped into the waiting vehicle.

Taking one last look to see if anyone had taken more than a casual look in his direction and seeing no one, he too entered the van and closed the door behind him. The moment the door shut, the van was on the move. Two men, both young, but with serious looks on their faces, sat in the front seats.

Together, they were five out of two hundred and twenty men and women the Quebecois terrorist Fortin had helped to smuggle into the province.

"Gilles," Elan said, the tone of command unmistakable in his voice.

"Yes, Commandant?"

"My comms unit, please."

The man in the passenger seat turned around and passed Elan a wrist unit and earbud, which the French commando set about putting into place.

With his finger, he pressed the appropriate app on the wrist unit.

The near-AI comms software that the French Special Forces employed immediately came to life and asked Elan for the code that would give him access to the network of operators that stood ready to carry out the night's mission.

"Charlie-Three-Alpha-Zulu."

"Access code confirmed," the near-AI intoned.

"Open channel Delta-Niner."

"Channel open."

"All units, all units, this is Archer Actual. Operation Revel Anger is a go. I repeat, Revel Anger is a go. We execute Plan Alpha on my mark. Stay ready, people. Archer Actual, out."

Chapter 18

Somewhere in Connecticut

To her surprise, Hall had found the drive from the safe house to the location where they would offload the former Secretary of Education and the two US marshals less stressful than she might have imagined.

As Petite drove their van, she concentrated on streaming in various newsfeeds to get the latest on what was happening in D.C.

Now, some eight hours after the strikes, the media narrative was coalescing around two main points.

First, the Blue forces in Washington were in the midst of collapse while Red Faction forces had begun to push into the city.

True to their doctrine, Spector's generals had unleashed thousands of their militia into the still-burning and irradiated city to amp up the havoc.

Having achieved direct hits on at least two of the Blues' command and control nodes, one journo after another was confirming that the remaining defenders were in a sorry state of confusion and one D.C. neighborhood after another was falling like dominoes. A nightmare of a nightmare thought Hall.

The second overriding point concerned the FAS political leadership. In the wake of the five different strikes, no one knew what had become of either former President Menendez or Morgan. Speculation was that Menendez had been killed in the one and only strike that landed on the east side of the Potomac.

A two-kiloton bomb had been dropped between Howard University and the Washington Hospital Center, making useless the multiple hospitals located in that part of the city.

There had been reports that Menendez and elements of her inner circle had descended on Howard to consult with a law professor who was an expert in the 25th Amendment. If this had been the case, there was little chance the woman was alive.

Reports about Morgan had been harder to come by. The FAS's new president had managed to issue a mostly garbled statement from an undisclosed location in the first hour after the strike, but since that time, there had only been rumors about the politician's whereabouts.

The Reds, entirely prepared to take advantage of their atomic ruthlessness, had managed to infiltrate some number of kill teams in and around the White House and other key buildings in the city's core.

Despite the threat of radiation, Hall had seen multiple clips of pitched battles between what looked like Secret Service agents and D.C. police and armed-to-the-teeth civilians that seemed intent on getting into buildings and killing as many people as possible.

From everything Hall had been able to glean during their drive north, if Morgan was still alive, the man appeared to be at the center of a red blue storm that rivaled anything she had experienced in the final terrible battle to hold onto Whiteman AFB.

"We're here," said Petite.

Hall pointed ahead. "There's Sykes. Look, he got himself a tractor. A resourceful one, isn't he?"

Petite gave no reply. He had been quiet for most of the trip.

Hall had let the veteran CSIS intel officer make sense of his thoughts in peace.

Years earlier, Petite had killed a man with his bare hands in Haiti, but Hall's understanding of that brutal death was that it had been seen as necessary for Petite to complete his assigned mission.

The execution of Hastings, because that is what it had been, had been something else entirely.

Whatever the man's feelings, Hall hoped that he was smart enough to put them in the context of recent events. Their efforts had contributed directly to the invocation of the 25th Amendment *and* the Reds had dropped five tactical nukes on Washington. If that wasn't justification enough for Petite to do what he had done, perhaps Azim had been wrong to bring the man into their circle.

Petite stopped the van in front of the dilapidated machine that Master Corporal Sykes had somehow got his hands on.

On getting out of the vehicle, Petite walked up to Sykes and the two men gave each other a fist bump.

"What's the good word, boss?" the JTF-2 commando asked.

Petite's reply was immediate and nonchalant. "You've got that hole dug?"

"Yes, sir. Six feet deep as requested. Janks is there waiting for us."

"And Kayed?"

Sykes pointed to a nearby hill. "Somewhere up there. She's keeping an eye on things." As the commando's hand dropped away from pointing in the direction of the hidden CSIS officer a green dot appeared on the center of Hall's chest.

As she looked down at the targeting laser, she felt what could only be an imagined burning sensation across her chest. She looked up from the wavering dot and connected her eyes with Petite.

"Tell her to cut the shit, Sykes," Petite said.

"Sure thing, boss."

A second later, the targeting laser disappeared.

Petite motioned a hand to the tractor. "That fossil works?"

"Like it's brand new. Our man the farmer was gracious enough to offer it. He says the piece of land where we've put the hole is as remote as remote gets in this part of the State."

"Good. Then fire it up and bring it over to the back end of the van. Hall and I will get our packages ready."

"Copy that, boss."

As Sykes turned and took a step in the direction of the tractor, Hall snapped, "Hold up, Sykes."

The commando stopped, turned, and again took up the two newly arrived operators.

Hall put one of her hands to her ears and canted her head slightly. After a pause, she finally said, "Chopper, out of the north. Sounds like our ride is early."

Petite looked in the same direction as Hall and, after a moment of his own careful listening, tapped his wrist unit and said, "Cardinal One, this is Bronco Actual. Confirm that you are north of pickup point Bravo?"

On hearing the pilot's confirmation, Petite replied, "Copy that, Cardinal. We'll be ready for you in fifteen mikes. We need you to delay your arrival. Find somewhere to chill. We'll be as quick as we can."

Petite turned his attention back to the JTF-2 operator. "Get that tractor over here pronto, Sykes. Hall, help me with the packages and then I need you to scrub down the van. Make it like Mr. Clean himself worked the thing over. Sykes, tell Kayed to do the same with your ride."

"Copy that, boss," Hall and Sykes said simultaneously. For a split second, Hall eyed the fit commando and he in turn shot her a quick smile.

For his part, Petite was already on the move. Hall moved to follow, and as she did so, there was a slight uptick in her confidence in the man as a leader.

As Petite opened the doors to the back of the van and took in the three wrapped bodies, he didn't hesitate in grabbing the first lump's feet and yanking it hard. A regular lifter of heavyweight, Petite easily pulled the first body free and clear from the back of the van, the package making a solid thump when it struck the ground.

For a brief second, he looked down at the body and then moved his eyes to meet Hall's. "We do what we have to do. Isn't that right, Hall?"

She nodded. "This shit is for real, Sam. We do the things we do and face the potential consequences of our actions because each of us has a keen sense of the bigger picture. Right now, we're just one more tool in our country's toolbox to survive."

"So it's about survival for you?"

On the other side of the vehicle, they heard the tractor engine start. Together, they stooped down and grabbed the two ends of the wrapped body and lifted it into the air. She looked into Petite's eyes.

"I don't owe you an explanation for why I do the things I do, Sam. My reasons are my own, but if it helps you, every time I have to do something like you did today, I ask myself whether or not the action will help to prevent the madness of today's world from flooding into the lives of the people I care about."

Hall pulled her eyes away from Petite's to take in the approaching tractor. On its arrival, together, they heaved the body into the ancient John Deere's shovel.

When she looked back at Petite, he had already turned to grab the next body. She didn't need the CSIS officer to rebut or agree with the rationale she had offered him. He would have to find his own way.

Her path had been made clear to her in a blood-soaked theatre in the middle of nowhere Missouri. With her country about to go to war, she hoped the man would find his own reasons, because if he didn't, Sam Petite too would become a liability Hall wouldn't hesitate to deal with.

Montreal

As Merielle walked at the center of a gauntlet of police officers, she fielded dozens of well wishes from those people permitted in this part of the stadium.

Her speech, though not as long as her Minister of Transport's, had hit the mark. It seemed a blur now, but she was certain the ovation she received at the address's conclusion had gone on for a solid five minutes. It had been thorough and rousing.

Blanchard, again at Lastra's request, had been sent on stage to prompt her departure. Joined by the rest of those cabinet ministers who had come to the rally, they had spent another couple of minutes engaging with the voracious crowd. On two occasions, Blanchard had to casually grab her arm and guide her back into the protective rectangle that surrounded the podium. Practically punch drunk that she had delivered her speech as well as she had, she had let her friend move her to and fro on the stage as though she were a clueless child.

Off the stage, Merielle immediately began to recover her senses, and she, Blanchard, her Chief of Staff, and a couple of other key officials from the Prime Minister's Office were swallowed up by her protective detail, which promptly whisked her and the entourage to that part of the stadium that contained her motorcade.

"Things have escalated in Washington, Merielle. General Gagnon wants to brief you as soon as possible," Tessa Chong, her Chief of Staff, said as they turned a concrete corner and the nine vehicles of her motorcade came into view.

"I'll speak with him as soon as we're settled in and on our way back to the airport. Did he give you any hint of what he wants to talk about? Our people only just arrived in Washington."

"He wouldn't say. He was rushed on the call. He only said that he needed to speak with you ASAP."

Merielle shook her head in annoyance. She would have to have a word with Gagnon. Tessa had been her Chief of Staff for almost a year and in that time the woman had won over Merielle with her competence and loyalty. The general and a few others would need to be told explicitly in the coming days that speaking with Chong was like speaking with her directly. She could not be all things to all people simultaneously.

As they approached the line of up-armored black SUVs that formed her motorcade, Lastra appeared to her left near the head of the nine-vehicle convoy. He was flanked by a posse of police officers Merielle recognized as the rest of her protective detail. With the exception of Lastra, each was now openly carrying the latest version of the Heckler & Koch MP7 submachine gun, the RCMP's standard weapon for VIP work.

As they moved toward her, Merielle didn't need her twenty-plus years of experience as a cop to see that her protective detail was more primed than usual.

"Good job on the speech," Lastra said, his tone entirely business-like.

"Thanks. I think you owe Paul a beer, though." As Merielle delivered the reply, she thumbed in the direction of Blanchard.

Lastra's eyes took up the Minister of Transport. "I think I owe him more than a beer, Madame Prime Minister. Maybe a steak dinner and that still might not be enough."

After months of intense intimacy, Merielle could tell from Lastra's tone that the man's comments were made out of relief and not consternation. In hindsight, it had been beyond stupid for her to leave the protective bubble offered by the defensive technology surrounding the podium. In the hours leading up to the speech, Lastra might have told her half a dozen times not to leave the confines of the gray rectangle except to leave the stage. That Lastra was handling her stupidity as gracefully as he was, was one of the reasons she had fallen for him. He was a most reasonable man.

Blanchard, who had been speaking with Merielle's Chief of Staff, was approached by a female RCMP officer in tactical gear who pointed in the direction of one of the SUVs near the head of the convoy. "Minister Blanchard and Ms. Chong, you'll be riding in unit three, if you please."

Chong, who normally rode with Merielle, was about to protest when Lastra said, "Madame Prime Minister, you're going to ride with me in vehicle five."

"Ride with you?" Merielle said the words louder than she might have wanted.

"Yes, you're going to ride with me. Until we're wheels up and out of this city, you're not getting more than five feet away from me for the rest of the night. You will survive without Ms. Chong for the twenty minutes it will take us to get to the airport." As the words came out of Lastra's mouth and their eyes connected, it was abundantly clear his earlier reasonableness had transformed into another trait Lastra had in spades – stubbornness.

Dropping her eyes from the man she loved, she looked at her Chief of Staff. "It's okay, Tess. I'll be on my phone. Text me the items you want to discuss, and we'll get into them on the plane. And I have to connect with Gagnon in any event. I have his number so I can call him direct."

Scrunching her mouth to signal her annoyance with the idea that she would be separated from her boss, Chong finally nodded her head and allowed herself to be directed to an SUV toward the front of the line of bulky black vehicles. Blanchard, as easy-going a man as there might be when it came to who rode with whom in a VIP motorcade, tossed Merielle a smile, shrugged his massive shoulders and moved to follow Chong.

Turning back to Lastra, Merielle saw that he had moved and was holding open the door to the fifth vehicle in the convoy, a Mercedes V-Class armored limousine. Called a limousine, in reality, the thing was a minivan. In all her time in Cabinet, she had not ridden in the vehicle, nor had she seen her predecessor, Bob MacDonald, do so.

Taking her eyes off the entirely un-prime-ministerial-looking machine, Merielle shot Lastra a curious look. When their eyes connected, Lastra offered her nothing but the look of a determined staff sergeant intent on doing his job.

Not for the first time, she chided herself for falling for another cop. Despite all the changes that had been made in society over the past fifty years, that combination of man and police officer still produced one of the more frustrating personality types that her gender could encounter.

On reaching the door to the van, she stopped in front of Lastra and placed a hand on one of his forearms.

"You really know how to make a gal feel special, Staff Sergeant. It's been a long, long time since I rode in a minivan."

Lastra deadpanned his reply. "Technically, Madame Prime Minister, it's a limousine. And at the moment, it is this humble chariot that's been selected to ensure your safety. Rest assured, there is a method to my madness."

"I see." Merielle pulled her hand off Lastra's arm and moved to step into the waiting van.

Taking her seat, she took in the driver and a second officer in the passenger seat. Both were in plain clothes.

In the rear seating of the van were another two officers but they were in their tactical grays. One was wearing goggles, while the other was staring intently at a laptop on her lap. On the bench seating between the two officers was a black box the size of a laundry basket with various glowing panels on it.

Merielle turned her gaze back to the sound of the closing panel door to see Lastra take the last available seat to her right.

As he settled into his seat, she thumbed to the two tactical officers seated behind them. "Are they the real reason I'm riding in a minivan?"

Lastra gave a quick look over his shoulder. "No. I told you the real reason already. Until we're back at 24 Sussex, you're not to be five feet away from me."

He then looked ahead and without making eye contact with anyone, said, "All units, this is Shiver One. Outrider is on board. We're a go for location X-Ray. Move out and keep it tight everyone. Shiver One out."

Within a few seconds of Lastra's order, their vehicle began to move in the direction of the same pair of huge shipping doors they had used to enter the stadium.

As they left the concrete monstrosity that was the Big O, Merielle leaned back in her seat, inhaled deeply, and took in the last vestiges of daylight. Montreal's skyline to the west was a canvas of black featuring various shades of blue overtop a soft thin line of orange. It had been a good day. She had given the soft separatists and fence sitters the most compelling reasons to stay in Canada she could possibly give.

It was out of her hands now. Quebec would vote and Canada would remain united or it wouldn't.

Closing her eyes, she immediately dismissed the idea of taking a cat nap in the few minutes it would take for the motorcade to make it to Trudeau International. She needed to connect with Gagnon to see about the disaster that was playing out in Washington. What a cluster-fuck that had become, she thought.

A minute later and with a huge effort, she forced her eyes open as she felt their van begin to negotiate the on-ramp that would take their convoy onto the Metropolitan, the expressway that was the quickest route to the airport.

No doubt to the consternation of those out and about this evening, the Montreal Police had blocked off the central artery giving the motorcade an unfettered route to their destination.

Just as Merielle's hand went for her phone so she could connect with the general, the police officer in the rear seat with the goggles spoke. "Boss, we have three Montreal PD cruisers approaching us from the rear. They're moving fast."

Together, Lastra and Merielle shifted in an attempt to put eyes on the three vehicles racing to close the distance between themselves and the motorcade.

"They're not supposed to be there," Lastra said, the tone of his voice neutral.

"Sergeant." This time it was the female officer that was sitting beside the glowing box.

"Go ahead, Angie," Lastra said.

"I'm picking up multiple airborne objects to the north and south of us. They're drones, for sure."

"How many and how close?"

Suddenly, the black box in between the two tactical officers began to vibrate urgently and several of the unit's panels turned various hues of red.

"We have incoming!" the female officer announced urgently. "Countermeasures are engaging. Jesus, I can't tell who they're targeting!"

Lastra's response to the update was immediate. "All units, all units. We have incoming. Evasive maneuvers…"

All of Merielle's senses were drawn to the front of the van as the SUV immediately in front of them exploded into a massive ball of orange and yellow. As the driver of their vehicle hammered the van's brakes, she felt pain bloom across her chest as her seatbelt engaged. Over the screeching of tires on asphalt, a second explosion rocked the expressway. This time, the flash of light and concussive boom came from behind.

Before Merielle could turn her head in the direction of the second blast, she heard a series of sharp cracks to the left of her face. Shifting her eyes to where the jarring sound was coming from, she saw the window beside her was quickly filling with a random pattern of small white craters.

She felt something jiggling at her waist and was surprised when she felt her seatbelt disengage. As her brain tried to make sense of what was happening to her window, someone grabbed her from behind, and with a tremendous demonstration of strength, she was ripped from her seat and shoved to the vehicle's floor.

"Stay down!" Lastra roared at her.

Tapping his wrist unit, Lastra began to give orders in a even keel tone, "Unit five, engage the Montreal PD hostiles. All remaining units, we are getting off the expressway. We're moving into the city. We need buildings between us and those drones. Take Papineau and then Sherbrooke. Unit one, take the lead. Now, people!"

On the floor, Merielle felt their vehicle begin to rush forward, even as more bullets continued to pepper the van's armored paneling and ballistic glass.

As the van began to make speed, she heard another blast. Intense white light flashed from in front of their vehicle and the officer driving their van violently jerked the steering wheel to avoid whatever debris had just materialized in front of them.

Beside her, Lastra was berating someone in French. "I don't care how many of your officers are engaged across the city, I need you to put officers you can trust on this motorcade right now, or so help me God, Gaetan, I will make it my life's fucking mission to make sure you own as much of this disaster as is possible."

Lastra paused to listen to the voice in his earbud and then said, "Just get me some people you trust, ASAP. Shiver One out."

He looked down at Merielle and then thrust out his hand. She grabbed hold and he pulled her up to put her back in her seat.

"There are still half a dozen drones tracking us. We don't know how many of those are armed. We're going to put ourselves into the taller buildings of downtown. It'll make us harder to target. Montreal PD tells me their officers have been ambushed across the city. It's chaos everywhere."

Back in her seat, Merielle caught sight of the exit off the expressway. The three vehicles of the motorcade that were ahead of them raced down the off-ramp at speed. Their lights blaring, they muscled themselves into the intersection and turned onto the busy avenue that would bring them into the heart of the city.

Merielle felt a tap on her shoulder. Turning to Lastra, she saw that he was holding a ballistic vest. "Put this on."

Reaching for the armor, she said, "Tell me things aren't as bad as they seem?"

"It's a cluster fuck of epic proportions, Mer. If I had to guess, there are kill teams all over the city looking for you. We lost four vehicles of the convoy, including the counter-assault van. 'Bad' is nowhere near a strong enough word to describe what's going on."

"Hold on!" the officer driving yelled suddenly, just as the van bucked wildly as it negotiated a curb to get around a snarl of traffic.

As the van settled back onto the street and raced forward, Merielle's eyes again took up the vehicles that were now in the lead of her motorcade. She could see three identical-looking black Chevy Tahoes. It dawned on her she couldn't tell which of the three SUVs contained her colleagues. She rounded on Lastra. "What about Tessa and Paul?"

Lastra's face transitioned from grim to sad. "They were hit, Mer. They're gone."

Chapter 19

CTV News Report, Montreal

"The scene here in Montreal is one of extreme chaos," the brunette, twenty-something reporter said with a serious look cast across her face. "The Montreal Police have indicated they are not in a position to comment on the status of the prime minister. They will only say an unknown number of their service members have been injured and killed. They have no idea who the identity of the attackers are and they refuse to speculate."

"And any word from the Prime Minister's Office, Stephanie?" asked the news anchor.

"None, Anoushka. All calls to the PMO and the RCMP haven't been returned. The only thing we know for sure is that the Prime Minister's motorcade was attacked on Highway 40, which is known as the Metropolitan here in Montreal. In that attack, four vehicles of the motorcade were hit by some type of explosive device, most likely missiles from drones that had been reported in the vicinity."

The images of the anchor and reporter disappeared and were replaced with raw video footage of a group of Montreal Police officers trading automatic weapons fire with some off-camera assailant.

"And what is the latest about the reports of gunfire across the city, Stephanie?"

"As I said, Anouchka, it's chaos as I've never seen before. At various points in the past thirty minutes, I've heard sustained gunfire coming from all directions. It's not an exaggeration to say Montreal has turned into a warzone."

As the two journalists reappeared on the screen, the on-the-scene reporter looked at someone off-camera and nodded her head vigorously. "I'm sorry, Anouchka, but I'm being told we have to leave this area now."

As the words left the reporter's mouth, the sound of close-by gunfire erupted, overwhelming the dampening technology that prevented the audience from being exposed to unexpected, jarring sounds. Through the sustained crackle of weapons fire, the reporter shrieked and suddenly stumbled out of frame.

"Stephanie, are you okay?" the anchor asked urgently. "Stephanie?!?"

As it continued to capture the sound of automatic weapons and the nearby screams of people, the floating camera drone that all roving reporters used to file their reports slowly panned down and adjusted its lens to reframe its subject.

On the ground, it found the female reporter lying astride a curb. The young woman's eyes were wide open and unblinking and at the center of her chest was a large blot of red that had soaked through the fitted sky-blue blouse she had on.

The image suddenly cut away to reveal the face of the stunned studio anchor. One of her hands was covering her mouth. Dropping it slowly, her eyes shifted beyond the camera, a tell that the broadcast's producer was talking in her ear. She shook her head once, and then again.

"No, I can't. I don't care!" she insisted, without looking into the camera.

Finally, after a long silence, the anchor's eyes re-connected with the millions of people that were riveted to the incredible live broadcast. "Ladies and gentlemen, stay with us through this next message from our sponsors as we look to provide more breaking news from Montreal."

Montreal

Elan stared intently at the various large displays affixed to the wall of the cargo van his team had converted into his command center.

Like everything else, they had done a superb job. Looking at the vehicle from the outside, there was nothing to suggest that the van had enough near-AI firepower to easily control fifty different drones each conducting fifty different missions.

To his right and left, were those soldiers he trusted to implement the plan as it had been meticulously crafted over the past week. Aside from the fact that their target continued to live, their effort had progressed as well as he might have hoped. Montreal was bedlam.

The best plans were simple. The moment they had moved on Martel's motorcade, unsuspecting police across the city had been set upon by a dozen kill teams. Plugged into the Montreal PD's communications network, he had listened firsthand as dispatchers and their supervisors melted down in real-time as the reports of "officers down" flooded into the call center.

"Commandant, the target is turning onto Papineau."

Mentally, Elan pumped his fist. Martel's motorcade had done exactly what he had thought they would do if they survived the attack on the expressway. Move into the city and find cover.

"We're still at five surviving vehicles?" he asked calmly.

"Yes, Commandant. Four SUVs and a van."

The fact that the motorcade was moving could only mean one thing. Martel was alive.

As he had predicted, they were going where it would be more difficult for his remaining tactical drones to target and attack the fast-moving convoy.

He had been genuinely surprised that the initial ambush had not destroyed all the vehicles in the motorcade. The intelligence

Elan had been given was that the RCMP didn't operate a VIP air defense system but clearly that information had been wrong.

The moment his Turkish-designed tactical drones had launched their first salvo of short-range anti-vehicle missiles, whatever system the Canadians operated went into action. The two tactical trucks positioned near the front and at the end of the motorcade produced dozens of small drones that zipped to intercept the incoming projectiles.

Of the ten missiles they set upon the convoy, only three hit their targets. A fourth vehicle was destroyed a minute later by a second salvo that had also mostly befallen whatever air defense programs the Canadians were operating.

With five vehicles left, Elan had only two tactical drones armed with a total of four missiles remaining.

As he continued to stare at the screens in front of him, he reminded himself for what must have been the tenth time that the current series of events had been discussed and planned for.

Only the greatest fool would have counted on the entire motorcade being destroyed by the drones. So much in war went sideways the moment the killing started. And luck – both the good and bad kind – was always something you needed to account for, even if you couldn't forecast how such luck would play out.

It was for this reason he had brought in the size of the force he had. Sixteen eight-person teams were placed strategically across the city waiting for whatever eventuality would come their way.

And whether it was his own good luck or a product of good planning, he'd guessed correctly that Martel's people would evacuate the expressway and take the very first exit to move south into Montreal's core.

As he watched the camera feed of the unarmed surveillance drone tracking the five remaining vehicles, Elan tapped his wrist unit and said, "Connect me with Archer Three and Four."

"You are now connected," the near-AI comms software advised.

"Archer Three and Four, the target is heading south down Papineau and will be on your position in less than a minute. There are five vehicles. The target is in one of them. Stop the convoy, identify the target, and neutralize it. Use whatever means necessary. We're sending a Dragon in your direction, but as of this moment, you two are on your own. Copy my order."

"This is Archer Three, I copy your order, Archer One."

"Archer Four here. I also copy your order," another voice said.

Elan tapped his wrist unit to cut the connection between the two teams and turned to the man sitting beside him.

"Lieutenant, advise Archers Six and Seven they need to be at rally point Bravo as quickly as they can get there without drawing notice of the police."

"Yes, Commandant," the junior officer replied promptly.

Elan then looked in the direction of the man sitting in the darkness of the driver's seat. "Chief Laroux, get us underway. Rally point Bravo is where we need to be, and be mindful of that lead foot of yours. I would imagine the Montreal PD is a bit on edge at the moment. They may be too occupied to pull you over, or they may be pulling everyone over for whatever reason. Just make sure you get us there."

The tough-looking noncom flashed Elan a grin. "Rally point Bravo, don't get us pulled over. Solid copy on that, Commandant."

In seconds, they were underway. As the electrified van quietly left the dark corner of the parking lot they had been occupying, Elan turned his attention back to the tactical displays and locked onto a drone stream that was showing an island of vegetation surrounded by residential buildings. The surveillance drone's map overlay labeled it "Parc La Fontaine."

Switching to infrared, he could see the glowing specters of perhaps a dozen individuals darting among the trees on that side of the park that ran parallel to Papineau. Again, he applauded his team's planning. As though put there by a premonition, Archer Six and Seven were exactly where they needed to be to affect a devastating ambush on the approaching convoy.

So far, it appeared that Canada's prime minister had been served by some combination of competent people and a healthy dose of luck. As the five-vehicle motorcade raced across the street that marked the north end of the park, Elan reminded himself that in war competence had its limits and at some point, a man, or in this case, a woman's, luck had to run out.

To his left, another soldier spoke. "Sir, Dragon One-Three has arrived on the scene. It has a single missile remaining. Should we take the shot and if yes, which vehicle?"

Elan didn't hesitate. "As soon as the ambush starts, take out the last vehicle. That will box them in. Advise Archer Four they should concentrate on the lead vehicle. It's up to them to firm up the south-end of the kill zone."

"Copy that, sir. And what about Dragon one-five? It still has half of its outlay. We can have it on location in three minutes."

"Keep it away and put it somewhere it can't be found, Corporal. If our prey survives this next attack, we'll want its punch."

Washington, D.C.

For the second time in less than a year, Larocque was leading the Canadian Airborne Regiment into what had the potential to be a blood-soaked shit show. Only this time around, the show in question was already well underway, and unlike the effort to remove the nukes from Whiteman AFB, they would be operating with little to no plan.

With the arrival of General Galway and the news that President Morgan was missing, the three CANZUK Regiments' mission had changed from arrive, organize, and figure out how best to support the faltering Blues in Washington, to a rescue mission, where ten companies of commandos would enter the confused disaster that was Washington D.C. to try and find a man who might not be alive.

On top of everything else, Galway had advised that the Blues had nowhere near enough military vehicles for them to mount the operation. Instead, Galway's people had scoured the communities around Dover AFB and pulled together a hodgepodge of trucks, flatbeds, and even cars to help Larocque and his British and Australian counterparts make the two-hour trip west into Washington.

In a testament to the insanity of the moment and the professionalism of the CANZUK special ops regiments, within an hour of the American general's arrival, nearly two thousand soldiers in nearly six hundred vehicles were on the road racing west across the state of Delaware.

It was in this rapidly unfolding situation that the BAM showcased why it was more important than any weapons platform operated by the CANZUK militaries.

As Larocque rode west in the passenger seat of an almost extinct, fifteen-year-old diesel-chugging Ford F-250, himself, Colonels Rydell and Wright, along with the CANZUK brigadier and Galway, worked collectively to divide Washington into a grid that each of their companies would search upon arrival.

In turn, via the BAM, Larocque, Rydell, and Wright doled out orders to their respective chains of command about how the search would begin and what actions would be taken if resistance was encountered.

The situation was not without precedent. Almost every officer in each of the CANZUK militaries had studied in some form what had happened in Kabul when the Americans had pulled out of Afghanistan.

Canada, the UK, and Australia all had special forces in the city as it was collapsing. The situation had been chaos personified, but in that disaster, small, well-led units of soldiers had excelled.

In closing out his orders to the men and the handful of women that were riding into the still-irradiated American city, Larocque had been clear. First, operate at platoon strength at a minimum. Second, the safety is off so use as much lethal force as you need. Finally, communicate, communicate, communicate. The BAM's near-AI will be your best friend if you let it do its job. So let it do its job, he had reiterated to his people via a Regiment-wide channel not five minutes ago.

Larocque looked at his own BAM wrist unit. It had been ninety minutes since leaving Dover. They had made excellent time.

To his relief, there had been very few vehicles on the road leaving the city to delay them, and those few people they saw trudging in the direction of the eastern seaboard were in no shape to do anything but shamble forward. The fleeing residents of Washington were filthy, tired, and more often than not, exhibiting physical manifestations of radiation sickness. Terrible burns and clothes covered in dried vomit created a trail of sadness Larocque and his soldiers would not soon forget.

As the sprawl of the city grew denser and the predicament of the refugees became more apparent, he had twice been required to beat down the suggestion that some number of the Airborne's medics be left behind to help the sorry-looking folks they were passing.

"Helping these folks is not our mission, people," he had ruthlessly broadcast across the BAM. "We focus on our objective like a laser so we can prevent this from happening in Toronto or Montreal. If I hear of or see anyone stopping to help any of these poor bastards, mark my words people, it'll be MP handcuffs and a court martial waiting for you when we get home."

The jump-off point for his four companies was FedEx Field. The long-retired football stadium loomed ahead of him as a massive silhouette blotting out the still-raging fires across the western half of the city.

It was from the stadium that his nine hundred soldiers would leapfrog from objective to objective into the capital as they looked to pick up a signal from the Secret Service team that had been guarding Morgan.

In her briefing back at Dover, Galway had indicated the combination of nuclear and unrelenting conventional attacks on the Blues' communication infrastructure was the most likely reason why no one had heard from the new FAS president beyond his first limited broadcast after the strikes. If Morgan was alive, it was Galway's opinion that the Secret Service agents protecting him would be moving their charge east in the direction of Delaware.

When it was suggested by Colonel Rydell of 2nd Commando that the right play for the Secret Service would be to find one of the many bunkers in Washington and hunker down to wait for things to calm down, Galway's response had been unequivocal. "Washington is lost, Colonel. Whatever organized defense existed before the strikes has disappeared and, as we speak, the city east of the Potomac is crawling with Red militia and kill teams. They all have the same orders: create havoc and find and eliminate by any means necessary those politicians on the Reds' hit list. If Morgan hunkered down as was suggested, the man was dead, or soon would be."

Galway had added that, in a flare of American military tradition, the Reds had assigned playing cards to their top fifty-two targets. As the Ace of Diamonds, she had advised Morgan was only behind Menendez as the UCSA's most wanted target.

That had been the context of the maelstrom he and his soldiers had been asked to drive into by the FAS general.

As the old Ford Larocque was riding in came to a halt, the voice he had selected for his BAM, a chilled-out replica of Scarlett Johansson, spoke in his earbud. "Lion Actual, your presence is requested for a conference call organized by Ajax Actual, do you accept?"

"I accept," Larocque said as he positioned his tac pad to frame in his face.

Seconds later, he was looking at a screen with the same half-dozen officers he had been speaking to back at Dover AFB.

"Good, we're all here," advised the British brigadier, Mick Brown, call sign Ajax. "General Galway has an urgent update for us. General, the floor is yours."

"We've heard from President Morgan's team," Galway advised.

She had been cool as a block of ice back in the hangar, but with this update, the American special forces officer spoke with obvious urgency. "We've heard from Morgan's detail and they've told us he's alive but barely. As we speak, his legs are caught under some unmovable rubble. The agent I was speaking to thinks they need to be amputated if he's going to be moved."

"If we can secure the location, we can send in a surgeon to take care of the legs if it turns out they have to go," the brigadier offered in a matter-of-fact tone. "Both the Paras and the Airborne Regiment have field surgeons with them here at Dover."

"Good to know, General. The question is, can we get to and secure the location," Galway said.

A map of Washington suddenly appeared on Larocque's tactical pad. The map quickly zeroed in on that part of the capital east of the Potomac River.

At this elevation, the last and largest nuclear strike was marked off. The Reds had dropped a single bomb east of the river. According to CANZUK intel, the strike's purpose had been to sow chaos in the rear guard of the Blues' defenses.

The weapon had been dropped just north of Howard University, where there were four hospitals along with one of D.C.'s main arterial roadways. According to the map, each of the hospitals and Rhode Island Avenue had been caught in the weapon's estimated three-kiloton blast radius, meaning they were no-go zones for at least another twenty-four hours.

The map narrowed and shifted again, this time moving to the southeastern quadrant of the city. An arrow suddenly appeared over a large rectangular building. The map narrowed still further and from the image now on Larocque's screen, he could see the structure in question had a convex roof. It wasn't a barn, obviously, but that was the look of the structure from what he was seeing on the screen.

"This is the D.C. Armory," said Galway. "At the time of the strikes, President Morgan had been at the Pentagon. Within half an hour of the last detonation, the President ordered his protective detail to drive in the direction of the White House in an effort to connect with his wife. That the Secret Service permitted this course of action is an outrage for another day, but it was in this effort to collect the First Lady that the Presidential motorcade was set upon by several pre-positioned kill teams. Hounded from all sides and being bracketed by artillery fire, the Secret Service was forced to drive east. They made it as far as the Armory."

Galway paused her update as Larocque's tac pad shifted to a video feed. Instantly, he could tell it was the same building he'd seen on the map, but in this image, he could see parts of the building had been severely damaged or collapsed altogether.

The camera zoomed onto the eastern side of the building, where the main parking lot of the Armory was located. Here and there, Larocque could see flashes of weapons being fired in the direction of the building's main entrance. The feed again zeroed in on a section of the parking lot that held about a dozen different vehicles. At this magnification, he could see scores of men firing weapons and scurrying from place to place.

Galway's voice interrupted the scene. "This is a real-time feed from one of your drones. As you can see, the building is in rough shape because the Reds have hit it twice from the air. It was the second strike that immobilized the President. With the arrival of the F-35s from the *Prince of Wales*, things above Washington are now touch and go instead of desperate."

"But not on the ground evidently," Larocque said in reference to the on-screen fighting.

"On the ground, things have gone from bad to worse. The Reds know Morgan is inside the building, so with each passing minute, more and more of these kill teams are showing up. Inside the building are the President's Secret Service detail and perhaps eighty soldiers from the Armory's garrison. Together, they're holding off the Reds, but just barely."

The original static map of D.C. reappeared on Larocque's tactical pad, but this time it had centered itself over FedEx Field, the Airborne's current position. A blue line appeared marking out the route between the stadium and the location of the Armory.

The next voice he heard over the BAM was that of the brigadier. "Colonel Larocque, you and the Airborne are the closest to the Armory by far. I'll be sending Rydell and 2nd Commando in your direction to establish an escape corridor, but it's you and your lads who will need to get to that location and secure the Armory."

"Copy that, sir. The boys and I will be rolling within ten mikes."

"Good, and don't think I don't appreciate what I'm asking you and your soldiers to do, Colonel. Our count of the men around the Armory already exceeds your force count and as General Galway said, that number is increasing by the minute. This is gonna be a real knife fight, but if anyone can get to that building and get Morgan out, it's you and your boys. Rydell and 2nd Commando won't be far along in joining you and the Paras won't be long after them. Everything we've got on the ground and in the air will be dedicated to you getting in and out of that building."

As the brigadier mentioned air power, Larocque heard the unmistakable boom of a nearby fighter plane break the sound barrier. It was close enough that the concussive sound wave overcame the workman-like chug of his truck's diesel engine. "Good to hear, General. I'll pass along the vote of confidence to my people. I take it we'll be able to lean on the *Prince of Wales* if we need CAS?"

"Air support will be spotty, Colonel. For the moment, the Reds are giving us all we can handle in the sky. As soon as the PoW's F-35s began to engage the Reds, the French Air Force joined the fray. The bloody French haven't declared war officially on CANZUK, but you wouldn't know it by the actions of their pilots. Until more of our fighters from up north have arrived, it'll be a draw in the air."

Rydell broke into the conversation. "Sir, if I may?"

"You may, Colonel."

"I just got word from my heavy weapons company with a pleasant surprise. Looks like someone prioritized a Swarm for us. They're being unloaded in Dover as we speak. They'll be ready to go within the hour."

"That is a pleasant surprise. Well done, Australia," The brigadier said.

"Colonel Larocque, they may be a controversial option, but should you need them, as you just heard, we'll have some extra punch for you."

"Let's just hope we don't need them, sir," Larocque replied, as his memory dug up a demo video of what the South Korean-manufactured anti-personnel drones had done to a field of unsuspecting watermelons. 'Vicious and inhumane,' had been the words he had used to describe the weapon at the time.

"Hope we shall, Colonel.

"Gentlemen and General Galway, we have a loose plan, but it's a plan nonetheless. We'll adjust as needed. Colonel Larocque, get your people on the move and keep us posted. As things stand, it appears you should only encounter light resistance en route to your objective."

"Copy that, sir. We'll be rolling ASAP. Lion Actual out."

Chapter 20

Montreal

Lieutenant Roland Blondin stood to the right and behind the two men on his team who were armed with the GM6 Lynx fifty caliber sub-compact rifle. At twenty-five pounds each, he had assigned the killing machines to his two strongest men.

The two beefy commandos had weapons shouldered and were looking north down the tree-lined street in the direction of the approaching motorcade. To Blondin's relief, the Canadian Prime Minister's convoy had not yet been joined by any vehicles from the Montreal PD.

He and his team of seven other men were near the southern end of the park, while Archer Three and his team were at the midpoint of the multi-block green space.

Necessarily, their plan was simple. Once his team stepped out and unleashed hell from their position near their end of the park, Archer Three's team would advance and set upon the left flank of the convoy, whereupon the two teams would come together to conduct a final envelopment of whatever remained of the motorcade.

Blondin looked down the avenue. Unsurprisingly, their quarry was moving at a breakneck pace. The emergency lights from each of the vehicles were casting spasmodic shadows on the trees and the brownstone buildings that ran parallel to the park.

As the lead vehicle, a hulking Chevy Tahoe crossed into the designated kill box of their ambush, he snapped at the two men with the fifty cals, "Fire!"

Already aiming at the lead SUV, together, the two large, civilian-attired French commandos pulled the triggers of their weapons and unloaded the entirety of their fifty caliber ten-round magazines.

At the mid-point of the barrage, Blondin shifted his eyes from the firing soldiers to take up their target. In the few short seconds since his men had opened up, they had managed to pulverize the front end of their target.

The Tahoe's windshield was filled with holes that had been punched clean through, while the front end of the SUV was shredded and smoking, the twenty rounds of the two devastating weapons having ripped through the vehicle as though it were paper mâché.

Despite the onslaught, the SUV continued to move forward, if much more slowly. Under such conditions, doctrine demanded the drivers of the remaining four vehicles push past the wounded member of the herd in an effort to clear the ambush.

Expecting this tactic, Blondin pivoted to where he should see two more of his soldiers driving a pair of vans onto the street to cut off the motorcade's escape.

On cue, the two vans were where they were supposed to be. The commandos driving each vehicle would remain behind the wheel and as needed would ram or cut off any of the convoy that tried to get past them.

Turning back to the ambush, he was greeted by a follow-up salvo from the fifty cals, though, on this occasion, the rate of fire was more deliberate as the two commandos became more precise with their second barrage. From further ahead, other weapons from the remaining soldiers on his team opened up to broadside the convoy that was trying to navigate past their wounded comrade.

Blondin raised his weapon and placed its reticle on the passenger-side windshield of the closest SUV. As he cut loose with a burst of fire from his sub-machine gun, he allowed himself to feel a dose of sympathy for the men inside the vehicles he and his soldiers were trying to destroy.

As he sent another long burst of 7.62mm rounds into his target, his mind urged the Canadians to stop their vehicles and surrender. Though some of his men would think differently, he certainly didn't take pleasure in killing more than he had to. This could all be over in seconds if they would give up their charge. Not everyone had to die.

But in defiance of his telepathic plea, one by one, the tires of the four remaining vehicles in the motorcade began to squeal in reverse as they tried to evade his team's unrelenting barrage.

He tapped his comms unit. "Archer Three hit them now!"

"Copy that, Four. We're in position. We're..."

BOOM! A mini sun replaced the last SUV of the reversing convoy. The strike by the Dragon tactical drone had been perfectly timed. Through the reverberations of the explosion, Blondin heard the screech of tires as the remaining three vehicles came to a disorganized halt.

Blondin called into his mic, "Archer Three, advance, advance, advance."

"Copy Four, moving now. Have an eye for us."

In the distance, Blondin heard the wail of police sirens. Close, but not close enough, he thought. He issued a sharp whistle, drawing instant looks from the five members of his team that surrounded him.

He chopped his hand in the direction of what was left of the Canadian Prime Minister's motorcade. "Move in. Keep an eye out for Archer Three. We finish this now!"

Montreal, Papineau Avenue

Merielle flinched as the reversing SUV immediately ahead of them detonated into a ball of fire.

Instantly, the driver of their van, one Corporal Coutu, slammed on the brakes, painfully driving Merielle's torqued body into her seat.

"Into the park, Coutu!" bellowed Lastra. "Move, move, move!"

As Coutu's hand darted to the gear shift, bullets began to impact the van from multiple directions.

Since Merielle had become prime minister, on two different occasions, she had attended exercises run by the RCMP's Protection Division to run through various scenarios of people trying to kill her. In these sessions, it had been explained that each of the vehicles in her convoy had armor and bullet-resistant glass that could withstand rounds of up to 7.62mm and direct hits from a grenade.

Rounds any bigger, she was told, would cut through the vehicle as though it had no armor at all. But such ammunition, Merielle had been advised, was all but impossible to find in Canada. The country's strict gun laws and their ruthless enforcement made weapons like the fifty-caliber sniper rifle the firearms equivalent of Bigfoot.

So, it was with a sense of foreboding and surprise that a grouping of large holes suddenly appeared in the passenger side windshield of their van. Whatever their caliber, the bullets easily punched through their van's ballistic glass to drive into the officer sitting in front of Lastra. Bright red blood exploded outward from the impact, saturating the van's console and dash.

As bullets continued to hit and enter the van, she shifted her eyes to her right to take in Lastra. On his face, she instantly registered a look of terror and shock. His eyes met hers and, as they did so, he raised his left arm. From his bicep down, there was nothing but jagged strands of flesh.

Whatever had resulted in the slaughter of the officer in the van's passenger seat had also grievously injured Lastra. So close to his heart, blood was spurting from the limb.

Instantly, Merielle struck out with her hands to encircle Lastra's upper arm.

On making contact, Lastra groaned in pain.

As she felt the warmth of his blood cover her hands, Merielle could feel the anger within her starting to build. In a rush, the fury that began to surge within her galloped over whatever confusion and fear she had been feeling only seconds before.

With a mighty effort, she tore her eyes from the man she loved and turned in the direction of the driver's seat. With bullets still peppering the van, Corporal Coutu was staring blankly at the body of his colleague beside him. His face was awash with fresh red blood.

Still with a vice-like grip on Lastra's arm, Merielle roared in the direction of the 20-something RCMP officer, "Corporal!"

When he did not respond, Merielle tried again, "Corporal Coutu, you son of a bitch, look at me!"

Like an enraged tigress, she lunged in the direction of their vehicle's catatonic driver and with both of her blood-soaked hands, grabbed him by the collar of his ballistic vest and viciously shook the man like a rag doll.

On what might have been her fourth shake, the RCMP officer's eyes transitioned from the realm of stupefied back to the reality of the moment.

As Coutu's eyes locked onto Merielle's, another burst of heavy-caliber rounds tore into the van. Merielle heard a scream of pain from the female officer that had been operating the near-AI countermeasures box in the van's final row of seating.

When Coutu's eyes moved in the direction of the scream, Merielle's right hand delivered a wicked slap to the side of the man's face.

"Right here, Corporal! That's it, look at me, not her."

His eyes blinking rapidly, he yelled at her, "I'm here. I'm here."

"Good. Then get this fucking van moving, Corporal. Get us into that park and drive this thing like you stole it." Merielle released the policeman's vest and turned to take in the scene in front of them.

Through that part of the windshield not covered in blood or shattered, she could see the surviving officers from the remaining SUVs had extricated themselves and were desperately exchanging fire with their attackers. They were sacrificing themselves to protect her. They were going to die so she could escape.

Merielle turned from the nightmare, moved back to Lastra, and re-clamped her hands on his destroyed arm. His face was terribly pale.

Another short burst of high-caliber ammunition entered the van, causing Merielle to flinch. From behind her, the officer who had been responsible for managing the motorcade's drones yelled, "We have multiple men approaching us from the rear. For Christ's sake, Coutu, get us outta here!"

Suddenly, Merielle was thrown backward as the van started to reverse. As her grip strengthened on Lastra's arm to prevent her from falling to the floor, the man screamed in pain. Just as quickly, she was thrown again as the Mercedes darted forward, hopped a curb, and raced into the waiting darkness of the green space.

Stabilized, she called to the Corporal, "There's a hospital on the other side of the park. Drive three hundred meters south past the tennis courts and then take a left. If my memory is right, the emergency department is on the south side of the complex. Get us there pronto."

The driver jerked the van right, avoiding something Merielle couldn't see, and then called back, "But that's not far away. They'll follow us there. We have to get you somewhere safe."

"Newsflash, Corporal, there's nowhere in this city that's safe. Just get us to the ER. Now!"

Montreal

Elan heard a police vehicle scream by their van. Undoubtedly, it was headed to the scene of the ambush. On one of the four screens in front of him, he saw his van half a dozen streets south of Parc Fontaine. Through the van's shell, he could easily make out the sound of gunfire echoing throughout this part of Canada's second-largest city.

To his right, the lieutenant said, "Vehicle number three is moving into the park."

"The van?" Elan asked as he took up the display relaying the surveillance drone feed overhead Archer Teams Three and Four.

"Yes, Commandant."

Calmly, Elan asked, "Where's that last Dragon?"

"On its way."

"Get it here, ASAP."

"On it, sir."

Elan pulled his eyes from the moving van as it sped through the park and scanned ahead of the vehicle. According to the tactical overlay on the video, kitty-corner from the location of the ambush was a hospital. The van and whoever was in it were headed in that direction.

"Lieutenant, I want that last Dragon to put its eyes on the emergency entrance of *Hôpital Notre-Dame*. When the target arrives at that location, you will take out the van or you will make the hospital unavailable to the people in said van. I would prefer the former if at all possible."

The lieutenant, a man Elan admired for his well-honed planning skills, was also a member of his HQ team because he was utterly ruthless in his willingness to conduct war. So when the younger officer promptly confirmed his order to slag the hospital's emergency department if necessary, Elan was unsurprised.

He turned his attention back to the van weaving amongst the trees of the urban park. As it reached the edge of the green space and began to negotiate the sidewalk and curb to cross the street to reach the massive health complex, Elan gave full credit to whoever had trained the unit protecting the Canadian Prime Minister. Getting to this point in the game had been a remarkable achievement. But the unit's run good fortune had come to an end.

Quickly, Elan's index finger moved to the center display and designated two locations in the immediate vicinity of the hospital. He then activated his comms unit.

"Archers Six and Seven, move to points Echo and Foxtrot respectively, and wait for my order."

As the leaders of both teams quickly acknowledged the directive, he tapped the tactical display a third time and called out to Chief Laroux at the wheel of their van.

In what was a modern-day rarity, the senior noncom had a half-done cigarette hanging out of his mouth. "Chief, take us to rendezvous point Lima if you would. It should be on your screen."

"Copy that, Commandant. I see it."

"And, Chief," Elan quickly added.

"Yes, Commandant."

"Your cigarette. Do you have more of them?"

Though one of the noncom's eyebrows raised questioningly, the man knew well enough not to reply to his CO's inquiry with his own question. Instead, he took a quick drag on his smoke, exhaled in the direction of the window, and said, "I have half a pack left."

"Good, I'll take one."

As the older man's raised eyebrow was exchanged for a devious smile, he reached into his shirt pocket, grabbed at a cigarette, and tossed it across the length of the van.

Elan easily caught the expertly thrown projectile and quickly set it onto his lips. Lighting it, he took a deep and satisfying drag and felt all the better for it.

With the same hand holding the cigarette, Elan's middle finger tapped on the van now making its way through the parking lot that serviced the emergency department. "Where's that Dragon?"

"Ninety seconds out, sir," said the Lieutenant.

"Good," Elan replied, his voice sounding confident. "It's past time we brought this hunt to an end."

Chapter 21

Upstate New York

As the Royal Canadian Air Force – RCAF – Bell 525 medium-lift helicopter began to put distance between itself and Fort Drum, Hall did her best to pick out the various collections of Canadian and British armor that had been arriving at what was still the home of the 10th Mountain Division.

As night had fallen, the task of identifying the columns of army green fighting machines and their logistical brethren had been more difficult than when they had first arrived at the American army base two hours earlier.

As Colonel Azim had told her, it was 10th Mountain along with the 1st Canadian and 3rd British Divisions that would form the vanguard of the force that would race south to lock horns with the Red Faction units presently storming Washington.

A year ago, when CANZUK had undertaken its effort to take Whiteman Air Force Base in Missouri, the alliance's various mechanized battlegroups had only been able to fight the Reds to a draw and then only because the combined air forces of Canada, Britain, and Australia had managed to take control of the skies.

This time around, the battle to control the air space across the American northeast would be more difficult because of the French Air Force.

France and its goddamned meddling thought Hall. She hated the country. Since the arrival of its President Marie-Helene Lévesque, the French through the DGSE had taken to agitating nationalist movements the world over. Quebec, Josee Labelle, and the neo-FLQ had just been one of their more dazzling attempts. That they now had their claws deeply into Spector and the UCSA was a testament to the guile and foresight of Lévesque and her advisers.

France's President had read the situation in the United States exceedingly well and had committed to the Red Faction at the right time. With a nationalistic-oriented partner like Spector controlling large swaths of North America, France's anti-immigrant and anti-progressive program would be able to mount new heights in Europe and further afield. An engaged and confident France would make everything in North America more difficult than it needed to be, mused Hall.

A kick to her shin brought her analytical wallowing to a quick end. Across from her, Petite was holding up a tactical pad with its screen projecting in her direction. "I take it you haven't seen this?"

"Seen what?"

"Hot off the wire. The PM's motorcade was attacked after the rally."

Hall jumped out of her seat to get a closer look at the display and asked urgently, "Is she alive?"

"Details are fuzzy. It sounds like Montreal is a warzone. Shit is still going down. The only thing for certain is that four vehicles in her motorcade were destroyed while the rest were able to get off the Metro and head into the city."

Petite turned the tac pad back in his direction and tapped the screen a couple of times. When he flipped it back to her, a video being shot from somewhere above Montreal's busiest expressway showed a swarm of emergency vehicles positioned around one of the still-burning SUVs of the PM's motorcade.

Hall stared at the image with a growing sense of anger. She had a deep connection and was fiercely loyal to Merielle Martel.

She pulled her eyes off the tac pad and locked them onto Petite. "Tell the pilot we need to get to Montreal ASAP."

Petite arched one of his eyebrows questioningly but said nothing.

"Listen, Sam, we both know the Montreal PD is as shady as hell, and we also know we haven't rooted out all the hardcore elements of the FLQ. If Montreal is a warzone as you say, she's gonna need people she can trust."

"No way," Petite shook his head emphatically as he said the words. "This little team of ours completed our mission, Hall. We've got our orders and we're gonna follow them. Other people can sort out what's going on in Montreal. We've done our bit and then some."

"Sam, I know today's been rough, but think through the situation. With all that's going on, here we are, the five of us, in a helicopter, a mere forty-minute ride to Montreal. I know this is gonna sound woo-woo, but fate is staring at us straight in the face, and it is screaming for us to get into the game. I can feel it."

"No," Petite said, this time loud enough to draw the attention of the other members of the team. "We've got orders, but more than that, we've pushed things far enough for one day."

"Sam, listen to me. That bullshit world of CSIS and following orders to the letter is behind you. We work for Azim now and have been given operational flexibility because quick and well-executed tactical moves are what win wars. We can be in Montreal before anyone else." When these last words came out of Hall's mouth, they sounded close to a plea.

Suddenly, Petite's left hand flashed upwards, his palm out, signaling for Hall to pump her brakes.

"Accept the call," he said.

For a too long moment, Petite looked forward staring into the depths of the helicopter's cabin as though he were in a trance.

Finally, when his eyes moved back to Hall's face, he spoke. "Solid copy, sir. We'll get there ASAP. Bronco Actual out."

Petite started nodding his head slowly. "That was Azim. Someone has mortared the hell out of the heliport at Dwyer Hill and the runways at CFB Trenton and there have been multiple explosions at Petawawa. Everything has gone batshit crazy. Azim wants us in Montreal."

Hall only nodded her head at the intelligence officer's update.

Petite stood up and grabbed a fabric handle attached to the cabin's ceiling. "Listen up, everyone. We've got new orders. CANSOFCOM needs someone they trust to be in Montreal ASAP. Apparently, that's us."

"Tell me they know where the PM is?" asked Sykes.

"They don't, but they're working on it," said Petite, his eyes taking up the special ops commando. It'll take us forty minutes to get there. As soon as they get a fix on her position, we'll know. In the meantime, if you have personal channels, start working those."

"Copy that, boss," Sykes said. "I've got a few solid connections in the Montreal PD I can work."

"Good, I've got a couple myself," said Petite. His eyes shifted to the big Polish-Canadian from Saskatchewan.

"Janks, bomb up and make sure we're ready to rock and roll once we set down. Everything that can kill something comes with us."

"Sure thing, boss," the more senior of the two commandos replied.

"Kayed."

The quiet, thirty-something CSIS operator only raised her chin to signal she was ready for whatever task she was about to receive.

"Get online and see if you can't get a solid bead on the current location of the PM's motorcade. I know it's mass confusion at the moment but try your best. If I remember correctly, you spent some time doing counter-cyber work."

"I did. It was a five-year slog, boss, but I know my way around the dark web. If something is there, I'll find it."

"Good. The moment you find anything useful, let me know."

Finally, Petite's gaze returned to Hall. "That's some kind of woo-woo you've got access to."

"Coincidence is what it is," Hall replied in an entirely neutral tone.

"No, it's not a coincidence. It's looking at the facts as you knew them to be and it's listening to your gut. In my experience, that's what good operators do. I'm just sorry I didn't see it for what it was."

"What do you need me to do, Sam?"

"Got any contacts in Montreal?"

"None that would be helpful."

"Then hang tight and analyze the information as it comes in. My bet is that if there's anyone that can make sense of it and point us in the right direction, it's you."

"Copy that, boss. I'm down."

Washington, D.C.

As his pickup truck pulled up to the eastern side of the Robert F. Kennedy Urban Campus, Larocque could hear the ferocious gun battle taking place along the western length of the modern-day oasis that had replaced RFK Stadium and the blight of parking lots that once surrounded it.

The trip had been uneventful. Galway had sent with them a handful of Blue Faction soldiers who had been able to quickly talk their way past and through the few FAS defenses still manned along their route into the city.

Because of their civie mode of transportation and because he hoped the Reds wouldn't be expecting an organized force to counter their efforts to assault the Armory, Larocque had held onto an ambition that the Airborne would find the Reds unsuspecting and ripe for a quick and one-sided ass kicking when they arrived.

In reality, the Reds had posted a rear guard so when the regiment's Pathfinder Company hit the mid-point of the Campus, they had rolled headlong into a firestorm of waiting enemy lead.

That had been fifteen minutes earlier. Since that time, he had ordered A Company forward to reinforce the Pathfinders and had listened to the Regiment's reconnaissance company call in a pair of air strikes to put down the Red's strongest points of defense.

Followed by members of his HQ staff, Larocque dodged out from behind a public washroom that stood between him and the officer leading the Airborne's recon company.

Dashing between cover, he instantly perceived the tear of bullets as they cut through the air at supersonic speeds around his person. Pumping his legs, Larocque zig and zagged several times as he covered the distance between the washroom and the Pathfinder CO.

Breathing hard but otherwise untouched, he and his small team of planners reached the large urban art display of colorful geometric shapes that had been their destination.

"Captain Zufelt," Larocque managed to yell between gasps for air. "What's the ETA on that air strike?"

"You're just in time, sir. According to my BAM, the RAF should arrive in about three minutes."

The younger man thumbed over his shoulder. "If you're up for it, sir, it's a quick jaunt to get a front-row seat."

"Lead the way," Larocque said without hesitation.

Without saying a word, the stocky officer turned and darted past half a dozen more colorful shapes until he arrived at a yellow rectangle that demarcated the end of the display.

"Make a hole, you bastards!" Zufelt barked at his men. Larocque watched the Pathfinder captain, as strong as any man in the entire Regiment, grab the back of one of his soldiers and hoist the man off his feet to make enough space for the two of them.

"Hey, what the fu-" the soldier terminated the curse the moment he saw who had grabbed him. "Captain, Colonel," the corporal said while nodding his head to both officers. "Good timing. These pricks are about to get what's coming to them."

As Larocque and Zufelt cozied up beside the corporal, they took in the structure that had been the Regiment's bane for the past twenty minutes.

The Microsoft Cultural Performance Center was the architectural crown jewel of the RFK Urban Campus. The massive bandshell was known the world over for its sail-inspired roof and for the dozens of precise human sculptures of American cultural icons that blessed every surface of the building.

Sadly, the structure was now saturated with Red Faction soldiers that had erected hard points along the bandshell's stage and at various points along the base of the majestic structure that crowned the top of the building.

The American media was going to have an uncontrolled fit when images of the soon-to-be-leveled work of art hit the news, but Galway had been explicit in her orders. *'Do what you need to do to find and rescue President Morgan. If buildings or civilians are in the way, they're of no consequence. Extract Morgan, period,'* had been the American general's exact words.

As Larocque shoved away whatever regret he was feeling about the spectacular building, the shape of a person suddenly emerged from one of the hard points on the bandshell's roof. Whoever the idiot was, rather than run to where he wanted to be, he undertook a casual saunter toward what Larocque presumed was the next closest hardpoint.

From somewhere behind him, he heard the unmistakable crack of one of the Airborne's Winnipeg-manufactured LRT-3 .50 cal sniper rifles.

Instantly, the man moving atop the bandshell's roof stumbled, performed a sloppy kind of pirouette, and then fell off the roof's edge. Over the gunfire, he didn't hear the impact of the body as it connected with the concrete stage, but his brain unhelpfully went on to imagine the sickening sound.

Turning away from the gruesome death, Larocque took up the Pathfinder CO. "Captain, where's the RAF?"

"Just got word it's been delayed, Colonel. Word across the BAM is that the French have engaged the fighters delivering our package."

"Impeccable timing. What's the new ETA, then?"

"'Soon' is all I got from Haymaker."

While a look of annoyance spread across Larocque's face, he made a special effort not to admonish the Pathfinder Captain about something he couldn't control.

"Haymaker" was the designated call sign for the Australian AWACS plane flying within the protective confines of the CANZUK naval task force off the coast of New Jersey. On that plane, a small group of officers acting in concert with the BAM system's Target Management App, TMA, collectively managed all air activity in the skies in this part of America.

As a burst of automatic gunfire found their position, Larocque and the rest of the soldiers jammed tightly behind the yellow block and lowered their profiles.

As heavy caliber bullets began to chew through the concrete of the display, he contemplated giving the order to move locations, but before he could, his ears picked up the faint but distinct clacking sound of more than one precision-guided munition adjusting their targeting fins. Contrary to Haymaker's update, at least one of the Royal Air Force's F-35s had gotten through.

With the bullets still pounding their position, Larocque quickly raised his head above the outline of the artwork and took in the scene.

As though the bandshell had become a stirred-up anthill, Red militiamen were scrambling in every direction as they tried to escape the coming danger. They too had heard the approaching smart bombs' clacking precursor.

As Larocque took in the unfolding chaos, the incoming machine gun fire from the Red defenders all but stopped. Standing, he reached into his pocket to grab his wife's crucifix while at the same time issuing a silent prayer. Despite their name, 'smart bombs' were far from perfect weapons. Not when they were dropped by a pilot who was being harassed by enemy fighters. He and every soldier around him knew full well even with all of today's modern tech, guided weapons missed their targets all of the bloody time.

Still erect, the thought of Madison and their final conversation comforted him. So much death had confronted him in the past two years. Both in quantity and quality. As Zufelt bellowed for his paratroopers to take cover, Larocque moved to cover his ears, but he did not stoop or take a knee.

Because it was impossible to do otherwise, his eyes were closed when the two pairs of Mk 82 five-hundred-pound bombs struck the bandshell. At nearly two hundred meters away, the pressure wave from the four simultaneous explosions rocked him backward but with only the top half of his body exposed, he easily remained on his feet.

Opening his eyes to take in the scene, Larocque saw only a giant cloud of grey and black smoke where the bandstand had been. It would be a few minutes at least before he could properly assess the damage. He turned to Zufelt.

"Captain, your way is now clear. Advance. I want us at the Armory in ten mikes. No excuses."

"Copy that, sir," Zufelt replied quickly.

As Larocque turned away from the Pathfinder captain, he activated his BAM. "Open Channel, Lion Command Team, priority Alpha-Red-Zulu."

"Channel open," the near-AI voice advised.

"Airborne, this is Lion Actual. Pay attention. Here are your new orders. The Pathfinders are advancing to the Armory. Company A, you will move up and you will join them as they look to connect with the waiting friendlies. Companies B and C, you will move into our current position where you will stay until 2nd Commando arrives. Will figure out what to do with you once we get a sense of what's happening at the objective. Be primed for anything. Questions?"

Larocque counted to three. "Hearing no questions, execute as ordered. Lion Actual out."

Larocque turned to find Zufelt already giving orders to his soldiers. In small groups, commandos from the regiment's recce company were quickly gathering so they could begin their advance through the destroyed bandshell.

"Priority incoming call from Watchtower Alpha. Do you authorize?" the near-AI of his BAM asked via his earbud.

"Authorize," Larocque said promptly.

"Colonel, I trust your men are beginning their advance?"

When he heard Brigadier Mick Brown's voice, Larocque instantly understood something was up.

"Yes, Sir. I should have two companies in the building within the next ten to fifteen."

"Good, because you've got company coming your way. SIGINT has picked up lots of chatter from the Reds. Regular Red Faction army units from across the city are bee-lining it to your location, Colonel."

"Armor?" Larocque asked.

"Yes, and lots of it, I'm afraid," the British general advised.

"How big are we talking, sir?"

The brigadier paused for a moment, no doubt to get the latest estimates.

As Larocque waited for the intel, the lead elements of Zufelt's Pathfinder company advanced past his position in the direction of the Armory. As the heavily armed paratroopers passed, his eyes locked onto each young man that looked in his direction. In every case, his look of assurance was met by a look of determination.

The pride that began to swell up in him as he continued to watch more of his soldiers march forward was interrupted by the brigadier's well-heeled accent.

"It's at least a full battalion, and Abrams are leading the way. And if the armor wasn't enough, scads of militia are with them. Their numbers are uncountable."

Larocque's response to the update was business-like. "General, make sure the surgical team is ready to go when we give the word. Which doc are you sending in?"

"Your man, Kiraly, but we have another on standby if she's needed."

"Kiraly was with us at Whiteman. The man works well under pressure."

"Indeed," said the general, in agreement. "As soon as you make the call for him, we'll have him at your position in ten minutes."

"Good. Is there anything else, sir?"

"No, Colonel. Just know we'll be doing everything we can to help you hold that position for as long as it takes."

"Solid copy on that, Watchtower. Lion Actual out."

Chapter 22

Undisclosed Location, North Carolina

As Parr stood beside Spector, he could feel the malice rolling off the man like a tropical storm charging landfall from the Gulf.

Fifteen minutes ago, he'd been briefing the president on Op Sunshine and its early payoffs, when they'd been interrupted by one of the officers helping run the operation in Washington.

"Mr. President, we've got confirmed reports CANZUK soldiers are in Washington," was all the man had been allowed to say before Spector launched out of his seat to race to the Washington-focused ops space.

Now, Parr was standing beside the UCSA President as he took in a bank of large displays. Each of the screens was projecting a different piece of real-time data from the hundreds of inputs available to the Red Faction generals.

The display that was the focus of Spector's current ire was at the center of the collection.

"When did they arrive and how many are there?" The President's question was posed in a neutral tone.

"Our best guess, Mr. President, is that they touched down four, maybe five hours ago. And they're still arriving. We now have people in the area and we can say with certainty that CANZUK has either a Herc or Globemaster landing every twenty minutes or so. If that's been their operational pace for the past five hours, they could have well over two thousand men on the ground. However, in the time we've been watching, most of what we've seen being offloaded is equipment and supplies. Intel reports those soldiers that have left Dover are mostly getting around in civilian vehicles."

"I see. And what's your best guess, General, about who our CANZUK friends sent our way?"

"The intel is still fresh, Mr. President, but multiple assets are telling us it's the same units that were involved in the Whiteman operation."

"And those units were, General? Say their names for me." On issuing the question, Spector's voice changed. The neutrality from moments ago had been replaced with a tone verging toward menace.

To the man's full credit, the two-star general raised his squared-off chin, looked at Spector directly, and gave his response. A much braver man than himself thought Parr.

"Again, we're on this late, Mr. President, but we're estimating one or perhaps two battalions of the UK's Parachute Regiment and some number of Australia's 2nd Commando."

The general paused ever so briefly before committing the name of a third CANZUK outfit. Finally, he said, "And what looks like the entirety of the Canadian Airborne Regiment, sir."

"And is he with them, General?" The question left Spector's lips as a half-growl.

The major general said nothing. Instead, one of the screens behind him shifted its image to show three soldiers wearing a camouflage pattern Parr didn't recognize. The image zoomed in and focused on the man at the center of the trio.

For a long moment, Spector stared at the image of the soldier, his face impassive. He then took a step in the direction of one of the antique chairs that littered the converted operations room. Leaning forward, he gently placed his two meaty hands on the chair's backing.

When the President of the UCSA next moved, Parr could hardly believe his eyes. Like an enraged bull trying to eject an unwanted rider, Spector drew the antique piece of furniture into the air, swiveled, and with all of the might of his huge frame shattered the piece of furniture upon the rock-hard plastered wall to his left. The room went deathly quiet.

Facing the wall, Parr watched Spector's back rise and fall as the huge man's lungs did their best to take in enough oxygen.

After perhaps half a dozen deep breaths, Spector finally turned back to face the various senior officers that were responsible for running the war. His face still glowing, he slowly looked around, seemingly measuring every person in the room.

When his wide eyes passed over Parr, the earlier malice he had heard in the Spector's tone had leveled up into something physical and dark.

Spector pointed a sausage-like finger at the screen. "Something bigger than these CANZUK clowns or the even United States stands before us people. Call it fate. Call it God. Call it whatever you damned well, please. That man. That son of a bitch has been sent to save the person who we need to kill more than anyone else on this planet."

After a pause, Spector bellowed, "What are the odds of that? C'mon, don't leave me hanging people. What are they!?!"

In no surprise to Parr, no one in the room took up the question. Like him, every other person in the room was hoping the next words out of Mitchell Spector's mouth would signal their leader was steering away from whatever insanity now had a grip on him.

"My friends, mark the following words," Spector said, his voice no longer a yell. "Our destiny is bigger, more powerful, and if you like, more divine, than whatever fate is driving the hands of our enemies. It pales in comparison. They are a candle to our pillar of flame."

In his right hand, he was still holding a piece of the chair he had just eviscerated. He tossed it onto the ground.

"Hear my words, people, and hear them well. The next thousand years belong to a renewed United States. Andrew Morgan will not stop us, and as sure as hell is a million degrees, I won't let a bunch of goddamn Canadians stop us either. Not a second time."

Spector moved forward and placed himself beside the screen that was still projecting the image of the three middle-aged soldiers. Raising his hand, he placed a finger beside one of the soldier's heads.

"This man beat us once before. It will not happen again. And if losing my shit is what it takes to convince you I'm serious about what I'm about to say, then give me another chair. Give me every chair in this room if you need to."

Spector's index finger loudly pounded the display. "This man and the alliance he's a part of extended our country's war. Tens of thousands more brave Americans have died because of CANZUK's meddling.

"Before the sun sets on this day, this man is dead, his unit is extinguished, and that son of bitch Morgan is hanging from a tree. Is this clear?"

The general who had been the initial focus of Spector's ire responded with a mild, "Yes, Mr. President."

Spector drew up his large frame and exploded, "I said is this clear, people?!?"

As one, each of the military officers in the room responded with a "Yes, Mr. President!"

"Good, then we're now on the same page. Today, we will not fail the citizens of the UCSA. They have risked much and suffered more. We do what needs to be done so that it is we who write the history of this conflict. It is our destiny that awaits us, so if we do nothing else on what remains of this day, you give me Morgan, and you give me that son of a bitch, Jackson Larocque."

Ottawa

"The Prime Minister is dead. And so is Blanchard. You saw the videos. No one could have survived that. Someone has attacked our country and our party needs a leader. Right now. Not in eight hours and certainly not in twenty-four."

As Yvette Raymond delivered her pronouncement regarding Merielle Martel and her continuing absence, her words were as calm as her mannerisms were self-assured. When it came to the power play she was in the process of making, she was thankful that the well of confidence she had access to was all but endless.

"And has that been confirmed by the RCMP, Yvette? Where is the Commissioner and why isn't she here with us to give us an update? Why is it just you briefing us?"

The questions came from Martel's Minister of Fisheries and Oceans. From Newfoundland, Irene MacPhail was as feisty as the Atlantic storms that lashed her province.

But with everything that had transpired, MacPhail was alone in her willingness to fight for the Prime Minister. The rest of the Martel Cabinet, most of them still in Montreal, were scared. Scared of the prospect of losing yet another prime minister to some shadowy element, and scared of developments coming out of Washington. It was an avalanche of unknowns and dire news.

The fear that had been created during the past three hours had manufactured a power vacuum that was now churning above Ottawa like a hurricane. To fill that vacuum, Yvette Raymond knew she would need to move fast and be daring. She was eminently capable of both.

"The Commissioner is dealing with the disaster in Montreal and I suspect will continue to be preoccupied with her agency's failure for several more hours."

"Poppycock, Yvette," MacPhail exclaimed, her face beginning to match the fiery color of her hair. "The last I checked you were the Minister of Health. The RCMP reports to the Minister of Public

Safety. It's not for you to make any pronouncements on the RCMP. I want to hear from that portfolio directly."

Along with MacPhail and most of the rest of Cabinet, the Minister of Public Safety was in Montreal, so when the impassioned Newfoundlander asked the question, she took her eyes off the webcam at the head of the boardroom to look in the direction of the person responsible for Canada's federal police service. "Jonathan, what's the RCMP saying, and where the hell is the Commissioner?"

Inwardly, Raymond smiled. MacPhail might have a backbone, but the woman was also terribly predictable.

Within minutes of the attack on Merielle's convoy, she'd had Jonathan Weisman on a quantum connection, and in less than ten minutes had reached a deal that would see the young and ambitious politician from Vancouver assume the Foreign Affairs Cabinet portfolio if he could manage to run interference with the RCMP.

Raymond had foreseen Weisman's political opportunism, just as she had predicted that MacPhail would be the most difficult of the bastions that guarded Martel's hold on power.

Jonathan Weisman looked like the slick political operator he had been before running for office. Thin, with a man-bun and tailored clothing that screamed he was most certainly not of the common people, the MP from Surrey-Newton had been silent in the conversation thus far.

To Raymond's growing dismay, her collaborator did not immediately intervene to respond to MacPhail's question. Instead, he sat up, slowly pulled his phone out of his suit jacket, and stared at the contents of some message no one else in the room was privy to.

Finally, without looking at MacPhail, Weisman looked into the camera and said, "There are no updates further on the report that Paul Blanchard and the PM's Chief of Staff were killed in the initial attack that took place on the Metro. The status of the Prime Minister is unknown."

MacPhail jumped on the reply. "So, we don't know if Merielle is dead? And for Christ's sake, Jonathan, you didn't answer my question about the Commissioner."

Raymond didn't give her ally the chance to engage with Merielle's self-appointed proxy. While Weisman might be a capable enough political operator, he was no Paul Blanchard when it came to political fisticuffs. "It's been three hours, Irene. If she's not dead, where is she? Kidnapped by whatever terrorists attacked us? Or perhaps she's floating up the St. Lawrence? We need to act. It's now 2 am. In four hours, the people of this country are going to want leadership and just as Merielle took up the mantle when Robert died, we must do the same."

MacPhail's retort came fast and hot. "We or you, Yvette? At least when Merielle became PM, everyone knew she was Robert's right hand. No one could argue that he wouldn't have approved of her. But more important, until that point, Merielle had not coveted the leadership like you. Shame on you, Yvette, and shame on any of you that have it in your mind to support what she is trying to do. We must wait on some kind of word regarding the PM's status."

In her mind's eye, Raymond tipped her hat to MacPhail. In politics and drinking, one should never underestimate the boldness of the Newfoundlander. The province was a hard land, occupied by hard people who made little hesitation when it came to a scrap, political or otherwise.

It might be that, if MacPhail was allowed to continue with her righteousness, Raymond's carefully thought-out plans might not come to pass. So, in that very moment, she calculated it was time to put all her chips on the table.

Admittedly, she did not have the hand she wanted, but her years of boardroom machinations and political dustups were telling her that she could bully the pot on the table.

"By way of provision 4.6 subsection 2A of our Party's constitution, in the absence or death of a leader of the party, I hereby call a vote of the members of Cabinet to designate an interim leader of the Party, who will, in no less than four months, administer a leadership convention to elect a permanent leader of the Party.

"I hereby make a motion to invoke said provision and to nominate myself, Yvette Raymond, to undertake the responsibility of interim leader of our Party and, by dint of this position, to assume the role of Prime Minister."

After a brief pause, Raymond continued, "Do I have a seconder for this motion?"

"I second the motion," Weisman said.

"Then we shall take a vote. A two-thirds majority is needed for the motion to pass. Minister Weisman, would you please count the votes of those of you in Montreal."

A minute later, Weisman finally said, "Seventeen yeas and twelve nays."

On hearing the numbers, a long-buried corpse of anxiety began to claw its way to the surface of Raymond's brain. Two more people than she had anticipated had voted against her. Quickly doing the math, she needed eight of the ten people sitting around the Cabinet table with her in Ottawa. She knew she had seven.

With long-mastered savagery, Raymond mentally drove a stilettoed heel into her rising anxiety and with all her normal iciness, asked for the count of those with her in Ottawa. "Raise your hands if you support the motion."

Seven hands rose quickly, while one pair of hands folded in on themselves. When Raymond's eyes met with the man who had called her bluff, he raised his chin and glared at her.

Too bad she thought. Mr. Oyinlola was not only exceedingly handsome, but had been one of Martel's more effective ministers. Her Cabinet would miss his competence, while she herself would miss his smile and how the man looked in a suit.

Her gaze shifted to the two remaining people who had not yet cast their votes. The two junior ministers, one from New Brunswick and the other from Ontario had their eyes locked on one another. Slowly and together, the man and woman each raised their hands into the air.

It was all Raymond could do not to smile in triumph. Instead, with her façade of coolness intact, she said in a sober tone, "We have nine of ten votes here in Ottawa for a total of twenty-six of thirty-nine votes. The motion passes."

Chapter 23

Montreal

As the bullet-riddled van approached the emergency entrance of the hospital, Merielle took in a scene of chaos.

Ambulances were positioned haphazardly, while bloodied but determined medical staff and paramedics were running in every direction.

Outside the entrance of the emergency department, Merielle spied a Montreal police officer administering chest compressions to a grievously wounded colleague. Another pair of cops stood close by watching the desperate scene play out, a female officer seemingly crying into the arm of her male counterpart.

With the lights of their van flashing, no one moved to stop their vehicle as it maneuvered as close as it could get to the emergency room entrance. Finally, their van screeched its tires to stop directly in front of the Montreal cops.

On their arrival, the two unoccupied police officers tore themselves away from one another and together, cast a pair of furious looks at the unmarked van that had intruded on the intimacy of what looked to be their colleague's final moments.

Realizing the half-destroyed state of Merielle's van, the two cops immediately drew their pistols and aimed them squarely at Corporal Coutu in the driver's seat. Through the many punctures in the vehicle's armor, Merielle could easily hear their shouts for Coutu to take his hands off the wheel.

With one look at Lastra's pale face, Merielle moved herself across his body and laid one of her hands on the van's sliding door, yanking it open. A second later, her feet were on the pavement, and she was striding in the direction of the two officers.

Seeing someone had exited the van, the female officer pivoted and aimed her pistol at the center of Merielle's chest. "Stop moving! Stop moving or you're fucking dead. Stop, now!"

Despite the unhinged feel of the officer's commands, Merielle had no intention of stopping. Lastra needed medical attention and for all she knew, the same people that had ambushed her motorcade were following her. In fact, it was that assumption driving her forward.

Slowing her pace, if only slightly, she zeroed in on the officer's name tag.

"Constable Dupuis, look at my face. Take a deep breath and look at my face, woman," Merielle said in French.

Finally, with only a few feet between her and the muzzle of the officer's weapon, Merielle stopped. "Look at me, Dupuis," she said again calmly. This close, she could see the officer's pistol was wavering and that Dupuis had a charged look in her eyes.

To Merielle's left, she heard a level voice call in the direction of the agitated policewoman. "Stand down, Sylvie! Stand down!" It was the other officer.

When Merielle's gaze turned to take him in, he was slowly moving in the direction of his partner. Reaching her, he gently placed his hand on Dupuis' forearm and then said something to her that Merielle did not catch.

Whatever the man had said, the female cop's pale blue eyes blinked rapidly and then opened widely.

As she lowered her weapon, all she said was, "Jesus Christ."

Disaster averted, Merielle turned on her heels and raced back to the van.

To her relief, Lastra had already managed to extricate himself. His good arm was around Coutu while the male officer from the back row was carrying the female RCMP officer that had been operating the countermeasures box. She was unmoving. The look on the man's face and the amount of dried blood on his uniform confirmed the woman was dead.

Merielle ripped her eyes from her people to reacquire the male Montreal cop who had helped settle down Dupuis. "Constable, get on the horn with your people and get as many of them as you can to this location. Whoever shot up my motorcade is still out there, and my bet is they're not done."

"Yes, ma'am," the police officer said without hesitation.

"And you," Merielle said to Dupuis. "Take Staff Sergeant Lastra off the hands of Corporal Coutu. You're coming with me to find a doctor."

She rounded on the driver of their van. "Coutu."

"Yes, ma'am," he replied instantly.

"You're now in command of the protection detail. Bomb up with whatever you can get your hands on and make sure nothing and nobody comes through the front entrance of the Emerge who isn't one of the good guys."

"Copy that, ma'am," said the RCMP officer.

She walked up to Lastra who was now leaning heavily on Dupuis. He smiled at her. "I just can't stop you from being a cop, can I?"

Merielle returned his smile and then moved to kiss him on the cheek. As she did so, her hand slipped down to Lastra's waist and in one quick motion, she released his sidearm.

Taking a step back, she held up the Sig Sauer P320 XCompact so she could take a good look at it. Satisfied she could manage the weapon's key features, she tucked the handgun into the waistband of her pants. "Once a cop, Staff Sergeant Lastra, always a cop."

Her eyes moved to the female officer helping Lastra stay erect. "You good, Dupuis?"

"Good enough, Madame Prime Minister."

"Be strong, Constable. We're gonna get through this." As Merielle delivered the encouragement, she nodded her head in the direction of the officer that had been doing chest compressions when they first arrived. The cop had stopped his efforts at some point during their arrival and was now sitting astride the body. A thousand-yard stare occupied the older officer's face.

"You," Merielle called in the direction of the seated cop.

When he didn't respond, she tried again this time with a voice that cracked like she was on parade giving commands to a platoon of cadets. "Constable!"

Finally, the policeman looked in her direction.

"Yes, I'm talking to you," Merielle said. "On your feet, man. Now! I need bodies who can shoot guns."

The Montreal cop, who might have been in his late forties, looked at Merielle and blinked several times, coming to the realization as to who was barking at him. Slowly, without looking in the direction of his deceased comrade, he got to his feet and squared himself to face Merielle.

"You're the prime minister," he said as if he was trying to convince himself of what he was seeing.

"I'm sorry about your colleague, Constable, and yes, I am. I need you to stay here with Corporal Coutu and between the two of you, you can't let any of the bad guys get past you. Can you do that for me?" Knowing full well what the man was feeling, Merielle made sure to inject a healthy dose of sympathy into her voice as she asked the question.

The cop's eyes quickly found Coutu and then returned to the politician. "I'll do what I can."

"Thank you. I know you will."

Releasing her gaze from the police officer, Merielle turned to the rest of the group and raised her voice to speak to her newly formed entourage. "Everyone else, let's move!"

Montreal

Through the gen-eight night-vision camera of their on-station surveillance drone, Elan watched the van leave the park and dart across the thoroughfare that ran east-west along the hospital's frontage. Reaching the northwest of the good-sized facility, the driver of their target's vehicle took a hard left and raced his machine in the direction of the hospital's emergency department entrance.

As the van expertly negotiated the ambulances that clogged the emergency department's parking area, Elan's mind played the sound of screaming tires when it finally came to a stop.

Scanning the feed, he noted only two police patrol SUVs among a random herd of emergency vehicles near the entrance. More cops would be coming, to be sure, but if things went to plan, his men would be gone before large numbers of the Montreal PD arrived. Their attacks across the city still had the local police on their heels and it would remain that way for an hour at the least.

Via the drone's camera, Elan curiously watched the drama of two police officers drawing their weapons on their target in high def.

The angle of their surveillance drone relative to the action on the ground gave Elan the perfect angle to see the broad side of the van when its panel door began to open.

"Magnify on that door," Elan ordered, his voice full of command.

Instantly, the camera of the drone transitioned to the spot he wanted. As he watched the person remove themselves from the vehicle, he began to experience something approaching ecstasy. As the image on the camera clarified, it was as though he was standing in the parking lot looking at the Prime Minister of Canada.

"Lieutenant, I'm not going to ask again, where is that Dragon!"

"Just over a minute out, sir."

Elan gritted his teeth as he watched his target dialogue with the two police officers who had since lowered their weapons.

"Pull the camera back," Elan ordered. With his finger, he tapped the entrance to the emergency department and a designation point appeared on the tactical overlay on the screen. He then activated the comms software. He had kept a channel open to the two vans of commandos he had positioned close to the hospital. "Archers Six and Seven, get yourselves within one hundred meters of the target, and then you are to advance into the emergency ward on foot and find the target. You are to confirm the target has been neutralized or you will neutralize the target if she is not already off the board. Copy those orders."

In quick succession, the leaders of the two teams, a captain and sergeant, acknowledged what was to be done.

Elan turned his attention back to the surveillance drone's streaming video. Martel and a casualty who was being supported by one of the Montreal cops began to walk toward the entrance of the emergency department.

"The Dragon is in range, Commandant," said the lieutenant.

In the lead, Martel disappeared through the large glass entrance. As the Canadian PM left the screen, a pair of what could have been nurses stepped into view. He watched as one of them produced a white sheet, which she proceeded to lay over the prone policeman who had been receiving first aid only a few minutes earlier.

"Sir, the Dragon is ready," the Lieutenant repeated, his voice absent any hint of emotion.

"Fire both missiles, Lieutenant. There's no sense holding back at this point. We need to finish this, now."

"Copy that, sir. Dragon is firing. Missiles are away."

Chapter 24

Washington, D.C.

Larocque strode into the domed vehicle depot and parade ground space at the heart of the D.C. Armory. His eyes immediately went to a pair of jagged holes at the dead center of the massive convex ceiling.

In the hour after the nuclear strikes, the Red and French air forces had conducted a sustained bombing campaign that targeted key structures that weren't impacted by the tactical nukes.

Particular attention had been paid to the eastern half of D.C., where the Armory was located. Re-occupied by the Blue military near the beginning of the war, the Reds had struck the Armory with no less than four separate attacks – two artillery and two air strikes.

As Larocque stopped to briefly take in the huge open space, he immediately picked up on the craters where two bombs had struck. Around them, were blackened and, in some cases, still smoking vehicles. Thankfully, whatever bodies had been part of the destruction were no longer present. Slashes and trails of dry-red blood marked where the most serious of casualties had been felled.

The reason for the Airborne being here was across this open space on the east side of the facility. Another pair of bombs had struck the administrative wing on that side of the building. The subsequent collapse of various parts of the one-hundred-year-old structure is what had immobilized the FAS president.

Approaching the east side of the drill square, there was a pair of strapping men, each attired in a dust-ridden dark blue suit, waiting for him. One of the men had a sub-compact assault rifle in the crook of his arm, while the other was holding open the door.

Arriving, the man holding the door offered his hand, which Larocque accepted.

"Colonel Larocque, I'm Special Agent Mike Phillips. I'm in charge of the President's protection detail. Glad you could make it."

"I was told a Billings was in charge?"

"Billings is dead, sir. Hit by a sniper not twenty minutes ago," Phillips said in a matter-of-fact way. "I don't see a doctor with you. I got the impression from your men he would be coming with you."

"Just me for the time being, Agent Phillips."

The Secret Service agent gave Larocque a hard stare, not making any effort to hide his displeasure.

"He's not far away, Agent, but before I make the call for my surgeon, I need to put my own eyes on your President and I need to assure myself this place can be held. The Reds know your President is here, and they want him real bad."

"Sir, with all due respect, you're wasting time. We've been holding this place for nearly four hours. We're solid."

Larocque pointed past the Secret Service agent. "He's this way?"

Larocque took a step toward the open door, but Phillips grabbed him roughly by the arm and growled, "I told you we're good, Colonel. Make the call for your doc. Make it now."

Larocque forced his eyes to calmly meet the American's. The big Secret Service agent had two inches on him, at least thirty pounds, and a face that looked like thunder.

"Agent Phillips, let me make something perfectly clear to you. My soldiers and I are here because your country can't get its act together. Now, I want to save your President, but if in the attempt of trying to save him, my boys get slaughtered because this place turns into a modern-day Alamo, then my country is prepared to leave your President right where he is."

The man's grip tightened on Larocque's arm. "I'm telling you, we're solid. We can hold as long as we need to."

Larocque lowered his voice and shifted his stance just enough that the other man could sense something had changed. "Listen closely Agent Phillips. Half the Red army that's in Washington is on its way to this location. Things are gonna get real tight, real soon, so until I see your President and the layout of your defenses with my own eyes, my doc and the rest of my boys won't so much as take a step in the direction of this place."

Larocque's gaze held the other man, but his right hand came up where he firmly placed it atop the agent's hand still holding his arm. "And for the record, Agent Phillips, my after-action report will now officially document you've wasted at least two minutes of my time. I hope, for your sake, that's not the difference between us getting your President flown out of here and him dying in this pending deathtrap."

This time the Secret Service man growled something inaudible and then released Larocque's arm. Stepping into the doorway ahead of Larocque, he said, "He's this way. Follow me."

Larocque paid close attention to the lefts and rights that had been needed to get to their destination. Like most buildings of the era when the Armory was built, it was a rabbit warren of hallways and single offices.

As they approached the outermost wall of the structure, the sound of soldiers making their defense began to ring in his ears. As he walked down a long corridor, he took in room after room of what had to be Blue Faction soldiers manning machine guns and other defensive weapons yelling over the sound of gunfire for one thing or another. Larocque nodded his head. He liked what he had seen so far from the defenders.

They turned another corner and in twenty steps was a pair of oversized doors that had a couple of disheveled Secret Service agents standing guard. Unlike the stoic facades that Larocque was used to seeing in news reports, the two men had obvious looks of worry.

Stopping in front of the shorter of the two agents, Phillips turned to face Larocque.

"Through the doors and to the right. He's under a pile of rubble. You can't miss him. We've tried everything to get him free, but.... Well, you'll see."

Larocque nodded his head at the agent's assessment, and then said, "Lead the way, Phillips."

Without another word, a Secret Service agent opened one of the doors and Phillips dodged into the room.

Following, Larocque walked into what at one time had been the building's substantial officers' mess. The room was cavernous with a ceiling at least twenty feet high.

Standing pat and taking in the entirety of the space, he quickly surmised what had happened. An air strike had hit the adjacent room causing the wall between the two spaces to collapse. The explosion had also brought down one of the two massive concrete pillars that kept the ceiling of the huge space erect.

It was a good-sized chunk of that pillar that laid across the lower legs of the man Larocque recognized as Andrew Morgan, the second President of the Federation of American States.

But it wasn't Morgan he focused on. Another body, that of a woman, was also pinned under the same mass of concrete, though she was face down and it was her upper body that was crushed. A mess of smeared blood lay around the figure, no doubt from what had been a furious effort to try and extricate the body.

Larocque tore his eyes from the corpse he assumed was Morgan's wife and looked in the direction of the FAS President. The man's soft blue eyes had a glazed look to them. He got down on one knee.

During the Whiteman operation, he had seen the look many times. Someone had injected morphine into the man to dull both the physical and emotional pain. Morgan might have been a Navy SEAL at one time, but he was also human. Crushed bone and the death of a spouse in such an unexpected and violent manner would have made the dosing inevitable. The Blues had been lucky they had some of the painkiller on hand.

Morgan's eyes blinked several times and then focused on Larocque's face. "Phillips told me you were coming. Thank you."

"Not a problem, Mr. President. We have a doctor who's coming. He's going to help you get out of here."

"So I'm told. My wife, Colonel. Phillips refused to jack up the pillar because it might cause some of the other rubble to collapse, but if your doc can get me out of here perhaps you can pull her out too. She needs to come with me, Colonel. I'm not leaving her here for Spector's animals."

Larocque turned his head in the direction of the Secret Service agent. "You have a jack?"

Phillips only nodded his head. The pained look that now covered the man's face was obvious. It wouldn't have been easy to say no to his boss's pleas to recover his wife.

He turned back to Morgan. "When the time comes and if the doc says yes, your wife will come with us, Mr. President."

Both of Morgan's hands reached upwards and enveloped one of Larocque's. The older man's grasp was surprisingly strong and when he next spoke, his words were clear and forceful. "You're in command of this operation, Colonel, so if you tell the doc my wife is coming with us, that's what's going to happen. From one officer to another, tell me my wife is leaving this goddamned city with me."

As Larocque stared back at the other man, he thought of Madison and how desperate they both had been to have their daughter's body back from the hospital where the regional coroner had spent what had seemed like an eon evaluating Lauren's cause of death.

The idea that their daughter was laying in some cold room on a slab being looked at by strangers had been maddening. Morgan's thoughts would be going to a similar dark place. If his wife's body stayed behind, what kind of desecration might befall her? Nothing was out of the question when it came to this terrible war, Larocque knew full well.

"Mr. President, as long as we can get you out of here, your wife will come with us. I promise."

Morgan released Larocque's hands while slowly nodding his head. "Thank you, Colonel. My family and God, thank you. If she stayed, I just couldn't..."

"Rest easy, Mr. President. Things are going to happen quickly now."

Larocque got back to his feet and activated his BAM. "Give me Watchtower Actual, priority Delta-Green-Delta."

"Priority call has been placed. Watchtower Actual has accepted. Call in three, two, one –"

"What's your status, Lion Actual?"

"I've got eyes on the prize, sir."

"His status?"

"Stable, but we're going to need the doc for sure. It's gonna be an ugly job."

"Copy that, Lion. I just gave the word to have the doc delivered to you. How do the defenses look?"

"Good enough. As soon as I get off this call, I'll call forward A and B Company. The Pathfinders are already here with me in the building. That should be enough to hold."

"Hold up, Colonel," the brigadier said. "We've got fresh intel coming in."

"Holding," Larocque said, as he turned to more closely evaluate the rubble-strewn room.

There were four large windows that ran the length of the mess hall. Their windows long ago shattered, each opening had three to four armed soldiers or in a few cases, Secret Service agents now dressed in filthy business attire. At random moments, one or more of the positions would let loose with a burst of sustained gunfire. There were no heavy weapons that he could see. Fixing that would be his first order of business. One or two of the Canadian Army's standard heavy machine guns, the C-6, would make this space a much tougher nut to crack.

The room faced the Armory's main parking area. In his mind's eye, Larocque could see an overhead view of the structure and the surrounding area. He knew that beyond the parking lot, there was a residential street lined with brownstone houses. It was among these sturdy buildings and the surrounding neighborhood the Red militia would be gathering in numbers.

His BAM earbud came back to life.

"You still there, Lion?"

"Primed, Watchtower. What's the good word?"

"The word is not good, Lion. I don't know how, but the Reds know you're there. And by you, I mean you, the CO of the Airborne."

Suddenly, a storm of gunfire erupted from outside the building. As Larocque moved to find cover from the rounds pouring through each of the room's windows, he saw one of Phillips' agents stagger back from his position, blood-red hands clutching desperately at his throat. From somewhere close by, someone screamed for a medic.

"Lion, are you okay?" the British brigadier asked.

"All good, Watchtower," Larocque yelled to be heard over the cacophony. "It's just the Reds getting a bit frisky. What's the rest of the intel, sir?"

"A message has been broadcast publicly to all Red Forces in the D.C. area. All units are to move in the direction of the Armory and at whatever the cost, they are to take the building."

"What kind of numbers are we talking about, sir?"

"Lion, within the hour you'll have something like five thousand militia and regular Red army trying to kick down your door. For whatever reason, until this moment the Reds didn't seem all that concerned about Morgan. I suspect they knew he wasn't going anywhere. But with news of your arrival, activity has ramped up considerably. The militia is opening up the streets so the Red's armor can make it to your position ASAP. There's a lot of hurt coming your way and it'll be there soon."

"Is that all?" Larocque asked.

"That's not all, Lion. The orders coming across the wire were given by Spector himself."

The brigadier paused suddenly.

"And?" Larocque prompted the other man. "Don't hold back on me now, sir. My boys and I are about to be up to our necks in shit, so you best give me all of it."

"Spector increased the bounty on your head, Lion. Twenty million dead or alive to the man or unit that takes down the CO of the Canadian Airborne Regiment."

Montreal

Merielle swept through the front entrance of the emergency department with a look that gave every indication she was about to hurt someone.

The seating area that was the triage space for the Emergency Department was jammed full of upset, scared faces. Because of the drama that had come with their arrival, sick or not, every one of those faces zeroed in on Merielle as she bypassed a line of people that were cued up in front of two reception wickets.

To her right, a voice whined loudly in French, "There's a line, you know?"

Merielle ignored the oh-so-Canadian jab, stopped, and turned to face Lastra and the policewoman supporting him. In the fluorescent light, his face was as white as a sheet. "Stay here. I'll be back in a minute with a doctor."

Turning, she spied down a hallway packed with a long line of gurneys featuring people in various states of pain or fear. Not seeing a medical professional of any kind, Merielle launched herself forward.

Another twenty paces into the corridor, there was a room on her right. Without hesitating, she walked in to find a half-dozen occupied beds and a single young woman in medical scrubs who on first inspection looked exhausted.

The patient she was currently hovering over was an older gentleman. Her stethoscope was placed on the man's chest, and she was listening intently. Lifting the instrument, she moved to grab the linen that covered her patient's body, and then with slow a dignity, she drew the sheet over the man's face.

Finally, her eyes moved to connect with the person that had just stormed into the room.

Her eyes narrowed when she saw it was Merielle. "You! It's you who've done this." The accusation came out of the woman's mouth like a hiss.

"Doctor, if that's what you are – I don't have time for any bullshit. I need a physician and I need one now!" Merielle yelled back at the other woman. Her patience, if she had any left, was operating on fumes.

"I am a doctor, and I don't care what you need. Look around you – there are at least two dozen people more seriously injured than you appear to be. And what the hell are you doing here, anyway?"

Just as Merielle was about to step forward to grab the woman and begin to shake her, she heard a shuffling behind her.

The physician's eyes moved past her and suddenly lit up with concern. Quickly, she blew past Merielle. Turning, she saw Lastra in the hallway being held up by Dupuis.

"I think he's going into shock," the officer said, her voice filled with concern.

Merielle moved to follow the doctor who was now in the hallway examining Lastra's arm.

She turned back to Merielle who remained in the room. "He needs plasma and surgery. All the trauma cases have been moved to the second floor. I'm just an intern, but I'll make sure he's seen right away. Let's get him a wheelchair and then…"

The young physician's sentence was cut short by a force of energy and sound that enveloped her, Lastra, and, Constable Dupuis.

In the micro-second she perceived the threesome get swept away, she felt her own body fly backward and strike something hard. Light, the strong smell of some foreign chemical, and an orchestra of screams, were the last things she registered before blackness overcame her.

Chapter 25

Washington, D.C.

"Warrant Officer Bear!" Larocque roared over the sound of close-by machine gun fire.

Hearing his name, the First Nations paratrooper snapped his head in Larocque's direction and then pushed himself up from the pile of rubble he had been perched on. In another moment, the man was in the hallway away from the outer wall of the Armory.

"What's the story, Warrant?"

"Not good, Colonel. The Reds are coming in waves. They're just hurling themselves at us, charge after charge. So many men dying. It's making the Great Spirit sick. I can feel it, eh. It's goddamned palpable."

"Yeah, well it's them or us. The doc's almost here. Can we hold another thirty or not?"

As the question issued from his mouth, someone from inside the room bellowed, "They're coming again!"

Bear's hand reached forward, and he placed a firm grip on Larocque's arm. "Come with me, Colonel. As much as I hate to use it, I think we're gonna need the Aussie's Swarm."

Larocque could not make his face any grimmer. If possible, he had wanted to avoid using the anti-personnel weapon 2nd Commando had shipped into Dover. Nicknamed the Swarm, to say that the APD-8 Hanwha Anti-Personnel Drone System's employment in war was controversial was an understatement. Canada had not invested in the technology, but with the possibility of facing a three-million-man Chinese army, Australia could not afford to be so sanctified.

"Lead the way, Warrant."

In seconds, the two senior paratroopers were back on the pile of rubble where Larocque had first seen Bear. As he cast his eyes onto the battlefield that lay in front of their position, he was immediately reminded of their final stand at Whiteman. Smoking civilian trucks and unmoving bodies – hundreds, if not thousands of them – littered the one hundred meters between the Armory's outer wall and the mid-20th Century homes that lined the west side of 19th Street.

To the north and south on 19th, there was a veritable traffic jam of civilian trucks and cars jockeying to find a sliver of space where they could advance. Amongst the vehicles, men by the hundreds – some in camouflage but most in civilian attire – were moving forward behind and around the vehicles. Across the street, he saw that some of the houses had been struck by the small number of F-35s the Brits had been able to muscle past the French and Red air forces in the short time the Airborne had been holding the building.

The thirty-six fighter jets from the *Prince of Wales* had fought their opponents to a standstill in the sky. Through his BAM, he had listened to the Airborne's Joint Tactical Air Controllers – JTACs – do their very best to wrangle as many of the British fifth-generation fighter-bombers as they could to hammer the surging Reds, but it was nowhere near enough.

Eyeballing the situation for himself, Larocque activated his BAM. "Get me Raider Actual."

Having set a permanent connection with the 2nd Commando CO, he no longer had to use his priority designation to jump the cue to speak to Rydell. The near-AI of the BAM simply dropped him into whatever conversation the Aussie Colonel was having.

"Raider, sorry to interrupt. We need that Swarm, and we need it now! Anything along 19th Street is game."

"Copy that, Lion. The Swarm is on standby. They'll be on your position in five mikes. The Paras' mortar platoon has just finished setting up and will hit them as well. Hold tight, Airborne. Raider Actual out."

He turned toward Bear to give him an update, but as the words began to leave his mouth, a crescendo of gas and diesel engines revved in unison. The roar of machines intermixed with the ominous yells and screams issued by the Red militiamen. And then the next charge began.

Beside him, Bear bellowed, "Fire!" Immediately, every automatic weapon in the room opened up on the wave of American vehicles and men that were headed in their direction.

Larocque did not shoulder his carbine. Instead, he watched a sick ballet of death as men were cut down. Up and down the street as the enemy advanced, he let his brain subconsciously calculate their ability to hold on.

As the first dozen trucks pulled to a stop thirty meters in front of their position and the men in and around the vehicles were devastated by sheets of 5.56 and 7.62 rounds, Larocque took note of the trucks and men that were advancing behind this first sacrificial attack. As best as he could see, each man was bravely surging forward to replace the slaughtered fellows that had preceded them.

At first, this follow-up of militiamen was a few dozen men, but within a minute the trickle of attackers turned into a wave of berserkering irregulars rushing forward. As the Airborne and the other defenders increased their fire from their strong points inside the Armory, it was the bloodiest savagery he had ever seen.

At the window to his immediate left, Larocque heard a sharp yell of pain and the termination of the deeper chug of the position's C-6. Turning in that direction, he saw a pair of his soldiers pulling a third paratrooper back from their firing position. Blood was streaming from somewhere on the prone man's head.

Larocque immediately got to his feet and sprinted to the window. In an instant, he had the critical weapon at his shoulder and started to look for men to kill.

A truck, this time a black GMC loaded with sandbags and men all wildly firing their weapons, came to a screeching halt just twenty meters from his position. He set the iron sights of the machine gun on the windshield and unleashed an extended burst of supersonic lead. Everywhere on the pickup, militiamen found cover, or their bodies were shorn into bloody pieces.

Glancing beyond the machine gun's sights, he noted still more trucks arriving. Again, he pulled the weapon's trigger, causing more chaos and death. But as the number of trucks and men continued to grow, Larocque could feel more and more rounds of enemy fire zipping close over his head and smacking into the concrete inches from his exposed face.

A soldier wedged in beside him just as he was about to expend the last of his adopted weapon's ammo. He paused his firing to look at the paratrooper. It was one of the soldiers that had dragged his wounded mate from the firing position.

The private, who must have been new to the regiment because Larocque had only the vaguest recollection of the young man's face, produced a green box of belted ammunition.

"Changing ammo!" Larocque roared and then reached forward to release the feed plate of the machine gun. Automatically, the private expertly placed the new belt of ammunition into the weapon's breach. Slamming down the feed plate, Larocque charged the weapon and began his firing anew.

In the thirty seconds it had taken to recharge his weapon, more trucks and men had arrived. The fighting was now pitched. Both sides were now saturating their targets instead of taking aimed shots.

On the BAM, he heard an urgent call from Captain Zufelt for reinforcements. Zufelt and his Pathfinders had been given the northern length of the building to hold. That flank looked onto the RFK Urban Campus Arboretum.

The small forest, just ten years old, held a mix of native and exotic trees that wouldn't have been easy for the Reds' vehicles to navigate. On the other hand, it would have offered many excellent firing positions for the men that would be assaulting that side of the building.

Still firing, he activated his BAM and yelled, "Request denied, Captain. Hold that position with what you got!"

Somewhere to his left, there was a holler of "Grenade!" He was tearing into an advancing group of ragtag-looking militiamen when he heard a desperate scream followed by a muffled detonation.

To his right, he heard the baritone of Warrant Officer Bear bellow, "Fix bayonets!"

As his men scrambled to prepare for hand-to-hand combat, he heard the sound he had been waiting for. A low, buzzing sound enveloped the immediate area. As one, their attackers looked upwards into the sky, and en masse, they raised their weapons and began to fire into the air with reckless abandon.

But the torrent of fire made little difference to the four hundred-plus near-AI-controlled anti-personnel drones that were weaving downward toward their targets. Each of the South Korean-manufactured units carried the equivalent of two Claymore mines on their underbelly.

Using the geo-locating software standard in each BAM system, the weapons operator with 2nd Commando had given the Swarm's near-AI instructions to target any human or soft vehicle within a sixty-meter band in front of Larocque and his soldiers.

The Swarm did not detonate as one. Instead, it was a deafening crackle that sounded identical to the cluster bomb munitions that had been re-introduced into the American war arsenal during the second year of the civil war.

He pulled back from the sights of the C-6 to fully take in the devilish spectacle.

Through the dust of the explosions, along much of 19th Street, he took in a swath of shredded and dying men. Where there had been clumps of determined and hard-fighting militiamen before, there were now prostrate bodies lying randomly in every direction. Some were moving with obvious signs of pain, but most were not.

Those miracles of men unhurt by the supersonic shower of six hundred thousand steel ball bearings were in a state of stupefaction or, in but a very few cases, trying to attend to a wounded comrade. Larocque watched it all with bitter sadness. It was a slaughter of human beings that would have rivaled any in history.

He activated his BAM. "Open channel Lion Group One."

"Channel Lion One is open," the female near-AI intoned emotionlessly.

"Listen up, everyone. This is Lion Actual speaking for the record. What lies before us is our enemy. If given the chance, they will kill us without mercy. Every man that we kill today is a man we do not have to kill tomorrow. Unleash hell now, Airborne. That's an order!"

He pulled the C-6 into his shoulder and sighted in on a man dragging a comrade to the safety of a bullet-riddled car. He could tell by the make it had a gas engine, meaning safety lay behind the engine block twenty feet away from the struggling pair.

For the first time in a very long time, he uttered aloud a prayer. "God, forgive my men for what they are about to do. They do it by my hand."

When he pulled the trigger of the machine gun and cut down the brave man trying to save his fellow soldier, his mind made a precise record of it. For the rest of his days, the inhumanity of the moment would infect his memories as thoroughly as any scene he'd witnessed in the heat of battle from the past year.

Perhaps a minute later, he stopped firing and pulled back from the machine gun to listen to the sound of other weapons carrying on with the horrendous cull.

"Take her," Larocque said to the private who had remained beside him to provide a constant flow of bullets. As the young soldier took hold of the weapon, he turned and walked in the direction of the room's exit.

He stopped at the doorway and, as he looked around what had been a good-sized conference space, he took note of the number of soldiers watching him. Both his paratroopers and the few remaining Blue Faction defenders were staring. He could feel the coldness of their eyes as they appraised the man who had just ordered them to butcher dozens of human beings, who at the moment of their deaths, presented no threat to the men and women defending their position.

He did not challenge their looks, nor did he contemplate the idea of offering any kind of defense for the decision he had made. War was terrible. What else was there to say?

Without saying a word, he turned and walked out of the room.

Montreal

Every commando he had sent into the hospital was wearing a body cam. Archer Seven had been given the order to enter the shattered entrance of the emergency ward and identify their target so it was through this team's eight individual viewpoints he took in the destruction of the emergency waiting area.

Elan did not shy away from the images of dead or dying civilians. In his time in Africa and most recently in the former United States, he had taken in scenes as bad or worse. When you unleashed the dogs of war, it was never pretty.

"Archer Lead, this is Archer Seven-Alpha. There's no sign of her, sir. We found what we think are two men who might have been part of her detail. They were in rough shape."

Elan replied, "Take four of your men down the hallway and find her, Seven-Alpha. She can't have gone far. Find her so we can get the hell out of here."

"Copy that, Lead. Four of us moving now."

Elan listened to the lieutenant leading the kill team give the order to advance into the maw of the darkened corridor.

"Sir." It was the talented lieutenant beside him.

"Report," Elan snapped.

"We have a low-flying helicopter coming in from the west. Its cross-section matches that of a Bell 525. It's one of the Canadian Army's medium-lift helos."

"Interesting," said Elan. "We didn't receive any reports of helicopters leaving their special ops base."

"All reports from Dwyer Hill and Trenton indicate nothing has got off the ground, sir."

"Then who is this?"

"We don't know, sir. Its trajectory suggests that it came from the southwest."

"From the US?"

"Perhaps soldiers from the CANZUK build-up at Fort Drum?"

"Impossible," said Elan. "Every calculation we made about that possibility indicated that if they sent troops from that direction, they'd only arrive another hour from now and even that timing was highly improbable. No, it has to be somebody else."

"Sir, Archer Nine has a SAM. Would you like them to take a shot?"

Elan didn't hesitate with his reply. "Make it so, Lieutenant."

Chapter 26

Montreal

The highly modified Bell 525 helicopter of the 427th Special Operations Aviation Squadron of the Canadian Special Forces, instantly picked up the surface-to-air missile the moment it was fired.

The near-AI countermeasure software ripped control from the human pilot and violently turned the helicopter away from the approaching SAM. Simultaneously, from its underbelly, six of ten air defense drones ejected into the night sky above Montreal, spun up, and zipped east to their newly designated target.

For the second time in less than a minute, Petite thanked God he had listened to the airman operating the 525's sole offensive weapon, the door-mounted M134 GAU-17 minigun, and strapped himself into his seat. Had he not, he would have become slurry on the inner walls of the helicopter's cabin as it juked violently to get away from the incoming missile.

As the helo leveled out, he looked at Hall. Janks had gifted her with a bullpup FN-P90 carbine and a customized ballistic vest. Diagonally across her chest was strapped a handgun sporting a good-sized suppressor poking out of the chest rig's affixed holster. Her fair hair was now in a tight bun and her face looked as determined as ever. The look was badass.

The pilot's voice invaded his BAM. "Team Bronco, this is Cardinal One. Sorry for the drama. The near-AI had to deal with an incoming SAM. We're back on track and we'll be on target in ninety seconds. I'm opening the doors now. Until your feet are on the ground, make sure you're holding onto something. They may light us up again. Once we drop you off, we'll stay in the area. If you need us, you only have to ask."

"Copy that, Cardinal One," Petite replied via his BAM. "Good to know we've got you in our back pocket. If you can, put us down about two hundred meters back from the Emerge entrance."

"Copy that. Hang tight. Cardinal One out."

As both the 525's doors opened and the cabin came alive with the roar of the helicopter's engines and rushing wind, Petite unbuckled and moved to the right of the airman now taking up half the doorway with his minigun.

The setup for the weapon was a sliding rail system that allowed the gun's operator to hang well outside the door giving him more and better angles to unleash hell with his wicked-looking weapon.

Again, Petite's earbud came alive with the voice of the door gunner. As he spoke, the Master Corporal's hand knifed in the direction of their destination. "Boss, it looks like the Emerge has been hit hard. It's smoking and shit is everywhere. And there are people with weapons in and around the entrance. They're wearing civie gear. What do you want done?"

"Don't do anything. We don't know if they're the bad guys or the police and there'll be civies everywhere. Once we check things out, if we need you and this pop gun of yours, we'll give you a ring."

The door gunner smiled at the reference to the killing machine he was seated behind. "Copy that, Bronco. Just say the word. I'd love to show you what this pop gun can do."

"Count on it. Bronco Alpha out."

Petite then instructed his BAM to open a channel for his small strike force. "Ladies and gentlemen, you know as much as I do. As soon as we hit the ground, we assume an arrowhead formation and we advance to the Emerge entrance and see what there is to see. There are armed men at the entrance, so be ready. Jankowicz, you have a point."

The big commando only nodded his head from across the helicopter's cabin.

As he turned back to the open doorway, Petite saw that the master corporal and his minigun were now hanging out the door, the weapon's multiple barrels pointed in the direction where Petite and his team would be headed.

Thirty seconds later, the pilot had put them down where he'd asked.

As the wheels of the 525 gently made contact with the street running parallel to the hospital, he shouldered his own FN-P90 and stepped onto the asphalt of the landing zone. As he put space between himself and the helicopter, he saw Janks sprint forward to take point. Looking left, then right, he confirmed the others had taken up their assigned positions.

Behind them, Petite listened to the 525 flex its engines and rise back into Montreal's warm night air. Now on a perma-connection with his team via the BAM, he issued the command to advance. As the order left his mouth, his combined crew of CSIS officers and special forces commandos began to prowl as one in the direction of the still-smoking entrance and the men waiting for them.

After what might have been five seconds or five minutes, Merielle blinked open her eyes. Flickering lights and moaning surrounded her. Her upper back and neck were throbbing heavily with pain.

As she took in a deep breath and tried to orient herself to her surroundings, Merielle registered the smell of burning. A fire, she thought while her brain tried to remember where the hell she was. A hospital. Yes, she was most certainly in a hospital. In Montreal. The rally. Lastra!

Slowly, she got to her feet and oriented herself to her surroundings. She could see the black smoke wafting into the room. But there was no fire alarm. That was strange, she thought.

Merielle's eyes moved to the door and took in a shape lying across the threshold. Instead of the young doctor and the man she loved, it looked like a single, huge body. As she approached, the blackened shape resolved into a large woman. Only a few feet away, Merielle could see that the entire side of the woman's body was singed and that she had a large patch of red-raw flesh on her naked backside. As she stared at the woman, a pair of eyes shot open and blinked. With a gasp, the woman pleaded in French, "It hurts so much. Help me. Please."

With a ruthlessness honed by twenty-one years as a cop, Merielle tore her attention away from the body and forced herself to peek into the hallway and look in the direction of the emergency department entrance.

What she saw, her brain struggled to make sense of.

Through a haze of dust and smoke, she could make out chairs, gurneys, and bodies – some intact, others not – strewn in every direction. At the furthest limit of what she could see, she managed to comprehend that she was looking at the upper half of the body of a small girl who looked to be five or six. In one of her tiny hands, there was a stuffed animal of some sort whose white fur was dashed with blood.

With all the strength she could muster, she turned her back on the unreal scene and looked down the hallway in the direction where the force of energy from the explosion would have projected Lastra.

With only the emergency lighting to guide her, she began to navigate through a chaotic traffic jam of gurneys and bodies. For every wheeled bed standing askew, another was on its side. All had patients in them. Sickly moans and cries for help assaulted her as she pushed deeper into the hospital.

In a section of the hallway that was unlit, her eyes focused on a prone form lying still on the debris-strewn floor. It was the doctor. Her pale, shoulder-length hair did little to hide the fact that her neck had been broken. Placing a pair of fingers on the young woman's neck confirmed she was gone.

Pulling back from the body, she quietly unleashed a curse that would have made the most seasoned of truckers look at her twice.

"Merielle." The voice was a wheeze, but it still managed to easily cut through the darkness.

Her eyes darted further up the hallway, but the only thing she could see was the outline of a pair of gurneys. One was erect while the other was toppled over. Her hand stabbed for the phone in her inner suit jacket. Pulling it out, she thumbed on its light. As she did so, she felt the phone vibrate in her hand. Someone on her list of designated VIPs was trying to call her. As she'd done since this nightmare had started only twenty minutes ago, Merielle ignored the caller and directed the phone's sterile white light down the hallway.

As the immediate area uncloaked itself, it took her a moment to figure out what she was looking at. In the turned-over gurney, a strapped-in patient was hanging awkwardly with the front half of his body pressed into the wall. The unmoving patient's feet were dangling in such a way as to form a small cubby where it blocked her vision.

Pulling away from the physician, Merielle quickly strode to the gurney and upon reaching it, shined her light in the narrow space between the gurney's bed and the wall. Underneath the suspended patient was another body. "Asher!"

Immediately, she moved to the front end of the wheeled bed, and, with all the might her five-five frame could muster, began to slide the heavy structure away from the wall.

With enough space created, she re-activated the light on her phone and darted toward the blood-caked body lying on the floor.

Her gaze immediately went to Lastra's ugly arm wound. The tourniquet that had staunched the blood flow was still in place.

"Jesus Christ, Asher. Talk to me."

When she didn't get a response, Merielle got to her knees and grabbed at Lastra's vest, giving him a violent shake.

"Asher, you son of a bitch. Talk to me!"

Still, the RCMP staff sergeant said nothing.

Leaning forward, she put her face close to his. "Talk to me. I need you to tell me what hurts so I can help you. Asher, baby, please." As the term of affection left her lips, her eyes began to take on water and she let out a quiet sob.

Finally, she heard a moan. And then, as though he was waking from a long sleep in her bed, Lastra's kind brown eyes fluttered open.

As she waited for him to get his bearings, her phone once again buzzed against her left breast. Keeping her eyes on Lastra, she whipped out the device and, without looking at the screen, activated it. "Yes!" she said harshly.

"Good, you're alive."

"Colonel Azim," Merielle said, moderating her voice if only slightly. It instantly dawned on her that the special operations officer might be able to offer some type of help.

"I need your help, Colonel. Everyone's dead. The whole protection detail is gone except Lastra, and he's in a bad way."

"That you're alive is all that matters, Madame Prime Minister. I see you're at the Hôpital Notre-Dame. I need to know where exactly in the building? Hospitals are big places and I need to be able to direct that limited help I'm able to send to you." Incredibly, the man's voice was perfectly calm.

Merielle closed her eyes briefly to reorient herself and then blurted, "We're in the emergency department. They hit the waiting room with a bomb or something. People are dead everywhere."

"Okay. I have people on their way. Are you safe?"

"I don't know. I'm with Lastra in a dark hallway sitting beside some poor dead old man."

"It doesn't sound like it. Find somewhere safe, Merielle. Hospitals are like rabbit warrens. Move and find a room somewhere. Make it more difficult for them to find you."

"Who is 'they,' Colonel? Who the hell are these people?"

"We don't know, but they're still coming for you. Disaster doesn't begin to describe the Montreal PD at the moment, so don't count on them to help you. Stay safe for ten minutes and my people will find you."

"Okay, I'll try, but Lastra's in a bad way. I'm not sure I can move him."

"Prime Minister," Azim said, his voice still cool, operational.

"Yes, Colonel?"

"You have to leave the staff sergeant. They don't care about him. It's you they're after. You have to get somewhere safe, and now."

"Like hell am I leaving him," Merielle said in a lowered, but still outraged voice.

"I just sent you an email," Azim said, ignoring her defiance to leave the RCMP officer. "You need to open it. Your phone has anti-location software on it. We need that disabled so we can find your location precisely. Open the email, and then find a place to hide. Do you understand?"

"I do, but I'm not going anywhere."

"Just open that email and then take a minute and think through your situation, Madame Prime Minister. Think of the big picture. You must survive. Things of monumental proportions are going down, Merielle, and people want you dead. You need to survive so we can hit these bastards back. We can't do that if you're off the board. Find a way to survive, Prime Minister. It's what Lastra would want. Of that, I'm certain. Open that email and move. Azim out."

As the phone went dead, she tapped the screen, opened her email, and found Azim's message. She opened it and then thrust the phone back into her jacket.

Her eyes found Lastra again and, to her relief, he looked like he had a grasp on reality.

"Do you think you can move?"

"I think so."

"Good, cause we're getting out of here."

"Where?"

"Anywhere but here, my love."

Merielle got to one knee and reached out to get a firm hold of Lastra. With his good arm, and a grimace, he clasped her, and together, they started the process of getting to their feet. Standing, she felt Lastra's good hand grab at the handgun still tucked into the small of her back. She was looking down the hallway further into the hospital while Lastra was facing in the direction of the entrance and the chaos of the emergency waiting room.

As she stood there supporting his much heavier frame, she felt his good arm tense as his grip on his weapon firmed up.

In an annoyed tone, she said, "Staff Sergeant, you're in no shape to carry a weapon. Just leave it..."

Firmly, but quietly, he cut her off and whispered into her ear, "I love you, Merielle. Stay alive."

On hearing the words, she looked up and into his eyes but before she could tell this stubborn fool of a man to shut the hell up and do what he was told, she felt herself flying to the side just as Lastra tore his Sig Sauer from her body.

As she struck the wall hard and fell to the dust-caked floor, the roar of gunfire erupted in her ears.

Chapter 27

Washington, D.C.

As Larocque walked into the officers' mess that held the FAS President, his eyes went straight to Major Kirlay. A wiry man hailing from southern Alberta, the surgeon was standing beside a makeshift curtain barrier that had been erected beside Morgan.

Noting the doctor's hands were gloved, Larocque didn't offer a hand as he pulled up his stride. Pointing at the jerry-rigged sheet, he said, "What, you don't want an audience?"

"Based on what's taking place outside, your boys have seen much worse, I'm sure. But if we can maintain some of the man's dignity, it's worth doing. He is a president, after all." The surgeon gave his explanation as though he were commenting on the day's weather.

"How fast can you make this happen, Doc?"

"If I was in a hospital, this would take ninety minutes, at least. But seeing as we're in the field and I have a free hand to skip some of the normal surgical red tape, I'd say thirty per leg if all goes swimmingly."

"Swimmingly, eh? In my experience, Major, nothing in war goes swimmingly. What does quick and dirty look like?"

The surgeon's lips tightened as he gave the question its due. "Not to be morbid, but if I hurry things along, maybe I can shave off five minutes per leg. Amputation isn't really something you should rush. Can you hold that long?"

Before Larocque could reply, someone with an Australian accent announced boldly, "Crikey, Major, now that the lads and I are here, it's a conclusion foregone that we'll hold this bloody place."

Larocque turned and a smile lit up his face. He thrust out his hand to the younger-looking fellow that had interrupted his conversation with the surgeon.

"Corporal Dune. Why am I not surprised?"

The 2nd Commando NCO shrugged sheepishly. "What can I say, Colonel? A call went out for volunteers to make sure the good doctor got to where he needed to be and faster than a roo looking for love, here I am."

For the first time, Larocque noticed the officer standing to Dune's right. Her captain's bars were subtly displayed on her upper arm. As you would expect for a soldier running with Australia's premiere conventional fighting force, she was supremely fit. He reached out for her hand. When she clasped it, it was as firm as any handshake he'd received in recent memory.

"Sir, the name is Captain Harwood. A great pleasure to meet you. Oh, and sorry for this brogan," she said, thumbing in the direction of a still-grinning Dune. "Being a decent soldier is no excuse for terrible field etiquette."

"No worries, Captain. The good corporal here gets a certain amount of leeway from me."

Behind him, he heard the clearing of a throat. "Right, introductions made, we have a surgery to conduct." Turning, Larocque re-engaged with the Airborne's doctor.

"Sorry, Major. To answer your question, if the Reds come at us again full bore as they just did, I say there's a better-than-good chance we're overrun. The Aussies don't have any more Swarms, so everything is going to depend on how much air power the RAF can get to us. I hear the navy might be an option as well, but they're a long shot – literally."

"It is what it is then?" Kiraly offered, but before Larocque could confirm the man's assessment, his earbud came alive with the voice of the BAM system. "Incoming call from Lion Six."

"Accept," he said immediately, turning away from the surgeon. "Yes, Captain Zufelt?"

"Sir, lead Red regular army units have arrived from the east and southeast. There are about fifty or so armored vehicles coming our way."

Larocque could easily hear the worry in the Pathfinder captain's voice. "What's their ETA, Zuf?"

"The militia's doing a good job of getting out of the way. The main elements will be on us in five, ten minutes, max."

"Good. Get your boys primed, Captain, and pass along the word to the other captains I'll be managing air support for the time being."

"Copy that, sir."

"Lead strong, Zuf. Your boys will need you more than ever. You can do this, son. Lion Actual, out."

Larocque's eyes refocused on Kiraly. "The Reds' armor is here, Doc."

"And what does that mean?"

"You have thirty minutes, Major. Maybe."

"Impossible! If I go too fast, I'll lose him. It's a double amputation, for Pete's sake."

Larocque lowered his head and took a step in the direction of the surgeon. The doctor's exclamation of impossibility had caught Special Agent Phillips' attention. Standing near Morgan like a loyal hound, Phillips was now casting a hard stare toward the two Canadians.

When Larocque next spoke to the surgeon, his voice was low. "Doc, head of state or not, I'm not putting your patient before the lives of my guys and gals. If we lose Morgan, for the record, it'll be on me. The generals and politicians, might not like it, but as of this moment, I don't give a damn."

Kiraly was about to say something, but Larocque cut him off. "And don't give me any of that Hippocratic oath bullshit, doctor. Get it done and get done fast. That's an order."

The surgeon looked like he was going to try with another protest, but thought better of it. Instead, he said quietly, "I'll do my best, Colonel."

Larocque nodded his head. "That's all I could ever ask, Major."

Montreal

In the darkness of the hallway, Merielle's senses were overwhelmed by the exchange of gunfire in the enclosed space.

With a strength that had surprised her, Lastra had thrown her against the wall, and unprepared, her head had slammed into concrete block. On connecting, stars had briefly bloomed in her vision and now she was blinking rapidly to try and shake through her disorientation.

As her vision stuttered like an ancient film reel, she made out Lastra's body lying at her feet. He was on his side with his back to her.

With the dim lighting, she could barely make out the wrongness of the side of his head facing the ceiling. Seated against the wall, she began to crawl in his direction, but when her hand hit the floor, she felt something warm and sticky. As she instinctively pulled her hand back, her brain started to differentiate the smell of copper from the powerful scent of gunfire.

Without warning, her stomach rebelled, and in a terrible injustice to the man she loved, her vomit projected onto his back where it mixed in with the other fluids.

She was done. The pain in her body, the smell, the sight of an unmoving Lastra. Whoever wanted her dead could have her.

Slowly, she rose to her feet and turned in the direction of the emergency waiting room. On the floor, perhaps five meters away, she saw a pair of bodies dressed in civilian clothing, each still carrying a suppressed assault rifle she did not recognize.

Pride bloomed in her chest and for the moment the futility she had been feeling was pushed away. Lastra, that beautiful and loyal man, had got two more of the bastards.

Though she resisted the urge, eventually she looked down the hallway in the direction the two dead attackers had come from. Through the lingering haze of the explosion, she could make out more figures with weapons moving around. In hushed tones, it sounded like they were speaking French.

Merielle raised her arms as though she was Jesus on the cross and screamed in her mother tongue, "Come get me, you pieces of shit!"

As soon as the challenge was issued, a green dot appeared on her chest. With a calmness that surprised her, she closed her eyes and waited to feel the intense pain of bullets entering her body. She was under no illusion the body armor she was wearing would do anything to stop the high-caliber bullets that were about to enter her.

Awaiting her execution, Merielle marveled at how keen her senses felt at that moment. They were supernatural. Closing her eyes, it was as though she could feel everything around her.

It was in this heightened state that she heard a footfall behind her. Someone was trying to move quietly. As the person took another step toward her, Merielle could hear the person's rapid breathing invade her ears as though a freight train was passing by.

She opened her eyes and turned her head to see the policewoman who had been helping Lastra. It was Dupuis. Her pistol was drawn, and she was in a shooter's stance. Wide-eyed, the cop was looking in the direction of the armed men Merielle had seen only seconds before.

"Get ready to run," Dupuis whispered.

"I'm not running anymore," Merielle said defiantly.

"Like hell, you're not. I'm not running unless you run, so if you don't move when I open up, it's on you that you made my kids motherless and my husband a widow."

"But –"

"Get ready," Dupuis repeated through clenched teeth. "We're out of time."

As the beginnings of a protest began to leave Merielle's mouth, Dupuis' Glock 19 began to unload. As the sound of bullets filled Merielle's ears, she glanced in the direction of the men trying to kill them. Whoever they were, they had found cover behind corners and or one of the many gurneys that clogged the length of the hallway between them and their prize.

As her magazine ran dry, Dupuis' weapon went silent. With the bark of 9mm rounds no longer screaming in her ears, Merielle picked up part of the conversation of her attackers. *"Put down suppressive fire and advance"* was the gist of what she had heard. But it was not the words that interested her – rather, the investigative part of her brain put a pin into inflections and nuances of the words she was hearing. The men pursuing her were most certainly not Quebecois.

Merielle flinched and instinctively lowered her profile as the first incoming bullets tore by her face.

"Run, Merielle. Now, damn you!" Dupuis screamed as she slammed a fresh magazine into her weapon. She too had got low and moved behind one of the sturdy wheeled hospital beds.

It was the supposition growing in her mind about who was trying to kill her that got her to move. She called to Dupuis, "Moving."

On hearing the word, Dupuis nodded her head, raised her gun, and began to fire.

As the first shot rang out, Merielle got to her feet and began to navigate the mess of beds, debris, and people that haphazardly confronted her as she moved deeper down the hallway.

Reaching a corner, she turned back toward where she had come from and saw Dupuis dodging and weaving the same obstacles she had just navigated. A hail of bullets chased the woman and at ten feet away, Dupuis stumbled and careened to the ground.

Merielle was off like a shot. Keeping herself low, she was on Dupuis in an instant. "Are you hit?"

"My back," the woman wheezed painfully. "I don't think it punctured the vest."

"Good, then you can move." With all her strength, Merielle gathered up the other woman and together they got back to their feet and staggered for the corner Merielle had just left. Again, bullets tore past as they staggered forward.

Together, they dodged around the corner, hit their stride, navigated another corner, and then eventually came face-to-face with a T-section that branched into two short alcoves that both featured a pair of doors. Merielle immediately went for doors that had windows and with both hands tried to jerk them open. Both were locked.

Standing in the terminus of the T-section looking down the hallway, Dupuis' voice was desperate, "The explosion. They've put the hospital on lockdown."

Merielle started to wildly pound the solid security glass and screamed for help. From a room close by, a woman in scrubs popped her head into the hallway. Through the sporadic lighting, Merielle saw the nurse recognize who she was.

"Open the door!" Merielle yelled viciously.

The nurse's face transformed from recognition to anguish. Stepping fully into the hallway, she called back at Merielle. Though muffled by the door, she easily made out the words, "I can't. They're controlled centrally."

Behind her, she heard Dupuis' voice. It was both resigned and scared. "It's too late. They're here."

Merielle spun around and saw the Montreal cop standing exposed in the middle of the hallway they had just left. Suddenly, her hands came up in an instinctive attempt to ward off whatever Merielle could not see.

"My babies!" the policewoman wailed desperately.

Merielle took a step forward but as she did, she heard the sound of suppressed gunfire and watched as Dupuis began to jerk violently and then stumble back to strike the T-section's wall hard. Her lolling head connected with cement and made a sickening *crack*.

As the police officer's body slumped and Merielle caught the first signs of bright red blood seeping onto the off-white floor, she felt herself start to back into the still-closed doors in the alcove.

When her back struck the exit, it felt like she was surging down a river of fear, but as her eyes again took up Dupuis, and the woman's last words rang in her ears, Merielle's racing mind found purchase on a new emotion – anger. At first, it was a trickle, but as she took in the growing pool of crimson forming underneath the Montreal PD cop, the torrent of fear she had been feeling only seconds before morphed into a storm of rage.

With her hands, she shoved herself away from the doors, took two steps forward, and pulled down hard to smooth out her suit jacket. *Stomach in, shoulders back, chin up,* a voice barked inside her head. If Merielle Martel was to die, it would be as the defiant, proud woman that she was.

Three men. Three executioners dressed in civilian attire walked into view. Their weapons – mean-looking assault rifles – were shouldered and ready. Again, green dots, this time three of them, appeared and danced across the ballistic vest she still had on. All three of their faces were neutral but then the lead man – the head of the trinity – revealed what could only be a smile of triumph. They finally had their prize.

The grin enraged her. Like a lioness trapped by a pack of hyenas, Merielle took a step forward and snarled at the three assassins, "Go to hell, you bastards!"

Chapter 28

Montreal

Long before Irene MacPhail had got into politics and become the most recognizable politician in Newfoundland, she had been a scrappy and determined reporter who had put in stints in three of Canada's larger news outlets.

Her eighteen years in journalism had opened the door to her career in politics and though she was nearly ten years out of that business, she still had plenty of contacts she could lean on when needed. But more important for the moment, she still had a fire in her belly when it came to getting to the bottom of a story that caught her interest.

Without question, the disaster still playing out in Montreal late this evening was the news story of a generation, but it was her gut pushing her in the direction of Yvette Raymond.

Her father, also a reporter who had toiled thanklessly for thirty-plus years for Canada's national broadcaster, the CBC, had seeded in her a deep belief in the power of following one's instinct.

She could hear his words as though he were standing over her shoulder editing her first breakout story. *"News is like a pile of fish, my dear. Fish smell as they do, but sometimes when you walk by a catch, you get the faintest hint that something isn't right. The good and dedicated fisherman cannot stop himself from finding out what that smell is.*

It is no different for the reporter. When something doesn't smell right, don't walk past. Instead, pull up your sleeves, get your hands dirty, and more often than naught, you'll find one hell of a story."

Well, Yvette Raymond was most certainly a lot prettier than a pile of dead cod, but the smell wafting off the woman was hardly faint.

In MacPhail's estimation, the Quebec City MP had called the Cabinet meeting to discuss the Montreal debacle too quickly, just as the process she invoked to assume the Conservative Party's leadership was too well planned.

But the kicker for MacPhail had been the breaking news story that her Chief of Staff had brought to her attention the moment she had walked out of the meeting where the vote had been taken to elevate Merielle's chief rival in the role of temporary party leader and prime minister.

In the fifteen minutes between the vote to install Raymond and MacPhail getting back to her hotel room, someone at the CBC had managed to cut a slick, three-minute piece that too easily walked through the technicalities of voting in a temporary leader of the Conservative party. But more than that feat, the well-crafted story had built up Raymond as the natural choice to replace Martel. The piece had practically gushed over the woman's political talent, her level-headedness, and her connections to Quebec's political and business elite, which if you were to believe the CBC, were second-to-none.

That both of these things had been touched on and aired before the official release of Raymond's elevation to interim PM had created such a journalistic stink for MacPhail that had her father's words not been metaphorical, there would have been a fresh pile of shit shaped in the form of Yvette Raymond standing tall in the middle of the room she was now standing in.

In her professional estimation, the piece in question had been at least two hours too early. When combined with everything else, MacPhail's gut was screaming at her that recent events had gone far too smoothly for the blonde Member of Parliament from Quebec City.

Her phone buzzed.

"You're on her?" she asked instantly.

"I am. She's leaving the city, heading north on the 5 in the direction of Wakefield."

"Who's she with?" asked MacPhail.

"I don't know. Someone is in the passenger seat of her vehicle. They left together from the Hill."

"What about Angie? Did you get a hold of her?"

"I did. She pulled her kit together and she's on the road. She's maybe fifteen minutes behind me."

"Good. Thanks, Douglas. I owe you one."

"Ha! Are you kidding, Mac? I haven't felt this alive since I broke that affair Trudeau was having back in '25. Just keep feeding me and if there's a story here, we'll get it."

"Thanks, Doug. When she stops, let me know and we'll go from there."

"Count on it, Mac."

Undisclosed Location, North Carolina

Unlike many of the officers in the operations room, the video of the assault on the D.C. Armory had not been difficult for Parr to watch.

In the past eighteen hours, his ability to stomach violence in high definition had grown in leaps and bounds. The only thing that made this particular display of butchery more difficult to watch was that it was their team taking the loss.

For his part, Spector had said not a word during the early evening battle. Through two different drone feeds, he had silently watched and listened as his commanders issued orders, shouted curses, and, in some cases, died on the field.

When the call was made for there to be a general retreat from the Armory, Spector turned from the bank of displays he had been watching and strode in the direction of the large room's double doors.

On reaching them, he came to a stop, and without turning to look at the group of men and few women he was relying on to run the war, he said, "Mr. Parr and Generals Hoffman and Quinn, with me, please."

Without saying another word, Spector resumed his stride. Briefly, the three men that had heard their names looked at one another but then, like dutiful hounds, as one they moved to follow their master.

In the hallway of the colonial mansion that had been converted to Spector's most recent headquarters, Parr saw the President turn into a room he knew to be the grand estate's library.

He was third into the high vaulted space. Spector was waiting for them at the center of the room with his ham-like arms folded across his chest.

"Gentlemen, I shall be brief, so there will be no sitting down."

The Air Force and Army generals, Hoffman and Spellings, assumed the position that Parr now recognized as 'standing easy.' For himself, he moved to take up a position behind an ancient but well-preserved wingback. With his hands, he stabilized himself into a casual lean.

"As each of you knows, we've dropped five nuclear weapons on the outskirts of Washington. They've served our purpose and I'm pleased with where things stand. I am as confident as ever that we will win this war."

The big Texan paused, seeming to take a moment to consider his next words.

"If this next assault doesn't take the Armory, Hoffman, you're to order your people to drop our final tactical nuke. Under no circumstances am I prepared to see Morgan leave Washington alive. In my opinion, he's precisely the kind of politician the FAS needs at this moment. Mark my words, if he's able to consolidate his authority, we'll be pressured to rejoin the peace talks.

"With the backing of CANZUK, and the Brits' own nukes, he'll look to negotiate, and we'll be in this goddamned mess for at least another year. And when it's all said and done, we won't be any further than we are right now. I won't let that happen, gentlemen. We need to get this done before the diplomats can get their claws into us. No matter the costs, this war ends today."

"Mr. President, if I may?" It was Spellings, the Army four-star.

"You may, General. It's why I brought the three of you here. I've made my decision, but I still want your counsel."

"Sir, if you drop that weapon on the Armory with CANZUK forces there, you're opening us up to retaliation from Great Britain. And to the best of my knowledge, Mr. President, they don't have any tactical weapons."

The general's hands came forward and leveled out at his sternum where they began to move with each of his next words. The man was a notorious hand talker.

"I'm going off memory here, Mr. President, but I believe all of their nukes are submarine-launched ballistic missiles, which means we're talking about a retaliatory strike of something in the range of sixty to one hundred kilotons. If we hit their soldiers, they might choose to eviscerate Tampa or Dallas. Or both."

"Maybe," Parr interjected.

The three men, all at least ten years his senior, looked in his direction.

"I take it you haven't been keeping tabs on what's happening up north?" Parr asked the question while ignoring the two generals' annoyed looks.

"Other than to note that someone has taken a serious distaste for this Martel woman, we've been kind of busy, Mr. Parr." This time it was the Air Force General Hoffman who spoke.

It was said by many that the no-nonsense former fighter pilot would eventually assume the mantle of Spector's VP when and if the President got around to putting someone in the role.

In Parr's estimation of the man, Hoffman tolerated civilians in his presence only because the practical part of the general's brain told him he needed their help to make things happen.

Parr looked down at his watch and then back at the other men in the room. "We're all aware there was an assassination attempt on Martel. We all saw the news reports. But, as of this moment, no one can confirm or deny what's happened to the woman."

"What of it, Parr?" This time, it was Spellings who spoke and unlike Hoffman, he didn't make an effort to hide his disdain for Spector's Chief of Staff.

Whatever the reason, the general had taken a personal dislike of him, but this was nothing new for Parr. Over his professional career, his good looks, intellect, and corporate ladder-climbing had generated legions of people who had come to loathe him. Long before Spellings and Hoffman, he had learned to ignore the haters.

"The 'what of it', General, is that if there's a leadership change in our neighbors to the north, I'm not so sure the UK's policy of retaliation is as straightforward as we might think it is."

When Spellings next spoke, his hand chopped aggressively in Parr's direction. "I don't know if you remember what happened just ten minutes ago, Parr, but our people just got their asses handed to them. If you want to contribute to the discussion, we need facts, not speculation and trite political theories."

Spector intervened. "Hold fire, John. I want to hear what Peter has to say."

Parr unlocked his eyes from Spellings and took up Spector. "Mr. President, as of six or so hours ago, CANZUK became a full-fledged party to our country's civil war and just as the French have been doing, members of their respective armed forces will die.

"And as we know, when soldiers start to die in Western democracies, people notice and they're never happy about it. Recall, if you will, the political grief Martel endured after the Whiteman incident. She may have won the election handily, but she only just won the leadership of her party. There are factions within the Canadian government that were passionately opposed to the Whiteman operation. These same factions still exist, Mr. President. To say the idea of Canada getting involved in our war will be controversial is making an understatement."

Spellings could no longer contain himself. "For Christ's sake, Parr, save us the lesson on Canadian politics. What does this have to do with the Brits and their nukes? They've been explicit. Any attack on their allies with nuclear weapons will be met in kind. Hell, all four of us were watching the same screen when the British Prime Minister made the announcement. She seemed pretty damned resolved if I recall."

Parr didn't turn away from Spector. Instead, he clenched his jaw and waited for the Texan to tell him to proceed or not. It was not as though Spellings' analysis was off the mark.

Finally, Spector said, "Get to it, Peter."

"Mr. President, if Merielle Martel is dead, then give her replacement every reason to rethink their position on our war. All indications are that it is Canadian soldiers at the Armory. Drop a nuke on them and then tell them the next one will fall on Quebec City or Montreal if CANZUK doesn't pull back."

"And what if Martel appears?" asked Spector. "She's a huge pain in my ass but she's also one hell of a fighter. You can't deny her that. If anyone can convince the Brits to hit somewhere like Tampa, it's that woman."

"Let them, Mr. President." When Parr heard the words come out of his mouth, he surprised even himself with how cold they sounded.

Spector's eyes widened in response to the statement and, after a moment of dead quiet in the room, the large man asked, "Did you just say let them nuke an American city? A city full of loyal UCSA citizens? People who have let their sons and daughters die in the hundreds of thousands to win this war?"

Parr kept his eyes locked onto Spector as though he were the only other person in the room. "I did, Mr. President. Their sacrifice would be tragic but think of how this trade-off will play across the country. For what might be a few hundred Canadian soldiers, Great Britain, the very same country we fought the Revolutionary War against, is going to kill a million of our citizens, and risk a larger nuclear war with what will soon be a reformed United States."

He stayed quiet as each of the men in the room made their own calculations. Slowly, Spector's eyes resolved from whatever thinking he had been doing to refocus on his Chief of Staff. Before he could speak, Parr carried on.

"I know it's a horrible cost, Mr. President, but think of what such a tragedy would do to rally the country for what needs to be done in the coming months. Think of the international sympathy that would be generated. It could radically change our standing in the world."

Parr's eyes left Spector's and gathered in the other two men. Spellings' face still looked like he was looking at a puppy who had just pissed on a carpet while Hoffman's façade was more familiar to Parr. It was the face of a man who had grossly underestimated his opponent.

Parr continued. "The British will make this same calculation. They won't nuke an American city because a few of their ally's soldiers died. Soldiers die in war all the time and as soon as we win this war, the world becomes a lot more unfriendly to the United Kingdom. And mark my words, gentlemen – the British Prime Minister may seem resolute giving a speech, but she's no Churchill. We can bully this pot. Of that, I'm confident."

"That's one hell of a gamble, Parr," said Spellings.

"It may be a gamble, General. But either way, we win."

As the two men stared one another down, Spector exhaled loudly. "Alright, you two. All of us want the same thing and we're all on the same side."

Spellings narrowed his eyes as though to suggest his conversation with Parr might not be done, but, eventually, he relented and looked at Spector.

"General Spellings, give the order to assault the Armory one more time conventionally. With everything you've got. Let's do our best to end this thing, making this whole nuclear debate a moot point."

"Yes, Mr. President."

"And, General."

"Yes, sir?"

"If you do take the Armory, no one survives."

"Oh, that won't be a problem, Mr. President. I'm not sure we could prevent a slaughter even if we wanted to."

With a grim look on his face, Spector nodded his head, then turned to the commander of the Air Force.

"General Hoffman."

"Yes, Mr. President?"

"Make the arrangements for the strike we've discussed. One way or the other Andrew Morgan and his new CANZUK friends die today. Mr. Parr is right. We can bully this pot. Now that it's been put to me, I agree that there's little chance that Britain will cross the nuclear Rubicon."

As the general slowly nodded his head. "Understood. We'll make it so, Mr. President."

Finally, Spector's gaze fell back on Parr. "Mr. Parr, I'm pleased with Operation Sunlight, but we need more. Whatever the outcome in Washington, it's the work you're doing that's going to make the difference in the long run."

Parr lifted his chin and straightened his shoulders as Spector's words registered with him. "We have more teams coming online as we speak, Mr. President. The moment I get back to the ops room, we shall redouble our efforts."

Chapter 29

Montreal

Hall was the last person in the stack as their team of five navigated the collection of ambulances and other vehicles parked haphazardly in front of the hospital's emergency department entrance.

Ahead of them, she could hear the yells of men, all of them speaking in French accents that were not Quebecois. From her recent time in France, she easily picked up on two distinct accents. The most frequent was that of Paris while at least one other man spoke with a heavy accent native to France's southeast.

In front of her, Petite barked, "Pick it up, Janks. Those bastards are after something."

As one, their small team of special forces commandos, intelligence officers, and whatever she was, surged forward along the broad side of what Hall estimated was the last ambulance separating them from the men they were about to engage.

Without a moment's hesitation, Janks, followed by Sykes and then Petite, moved past the front of the ambulance, exposing themselves to whatever awaited them. With each of their weapons shouldered and ready, they immediately opened up. The reports of suppressed weapons chattered in her ears.

As she stepped into the open, Hall didn't hesitate a look at what they were shooting at. Instead, Kayed and then herself flanked the three men to their left and began to search for their own targets.

With her FN-P90 in her shoulder, she took in the scene of the destroyed hospital entrance. Whatever weapon had struck the building's glass façade had detonated inside. The resulting force of the blast had ejected the contents of the triage area onto the driveway in front of her.

Glass, broken chairs, torn metal, and unmoving bodies lay in every direction. Just inside the building, she found her first target.

A man with an assault rifle was swinging his weapon to take up one of Petite, Sykes, or Janks.

Stopping in her tracks, she placed the reticle of her weapon at the center of the man's head, and in a smooth motion pulled the trigger, unleashing a short burst. At perhaps twenty yards out, she was close enough to see the spray of fluid leave the back of the man's skull just as he collapsed to the floor.

Her target down, she was moving again. As she scampered forward, bullets tore through the air all around her person.

Behind her, she heard Petite bellow for her to hold up, but she ignored the order. Something instinctual was now driving the bus that was her brain. This had happened before and based on that experience, she had learned to embrace the interplay now taking place between her thoughts and her movement. As she reached the blown-out doors of the emergency department entrance, it was as if her body flowed into the destroyed space that lay beyond.

All of her senses probed the space in front of her. She ignored everything not the enemy or her mission. Moans for help both in English and French were of no consequence as she carefully dodged through the waiting room.

Behind her and outside the building, she could still hear the sound of gunfire and the yells of Petite and the two JTF-2 commandos as they worked in unison to engage the half-dozen or so men they were now fighting.

As she stopped her advance at the nursing triage station, the deep boom of a nearby explosion filled the space around her. A second later, Petite confirmed the source of the rumble through her BAM. "Cardinal One is down. I repeat the helo is down. Hall and Kayed, hold up, damn you!" The man's voice sounded strained.

As the name Kayed registered in her mind, she perceived someone arriving to stand beside her. Glancing to her right, she was pleased to see it was the female CSIS officer. The woman was breathing heavily but as was Kayed's way, she said nothing.

As the two women's eyes left one another, the sound of automatic gunfire emanated from the poorly lit hallway laid out in front of them.

As though shot out of a cannon, Hall surged forward. Reaching the first gurney still erect, she discarded her FN-P90 on the chest of an elderly patient, and as she dodged and weaved forward, her hand reached for the Glock holstered on the front of her chest rig. Of the two firearms, she preferred the Glock for the close in work that was to come.

Without so much as a glance, Hall raced past a pair of armed men lying crumpled in a pool of blood and then just as quickly passed a third dead man wearing a ballistic vest that had POLICE stenciled on it.

Her eyes quickly glanced at the man's bloodied face and as some part of her brain was preparing to shout out a name in recognition, Hall ruthlessly quashed the transaction. Instead, all her mental and physical capacities poured into navigating the mess of debris confronting her as she continued to race forward down the hallway.

With Kayed steps behind her, she finally reached a darkened corner, slowing herself into a stalking advance. As quick as she might, Hall poked her head around the wall and looked down another hallway that was also intermittently lit.

Perhaps forty meters ahead in an isolated pool of light, she took in three men standing at what appeared to be a T-junction, their automatic weapons pointing at someone or something she could not see.

Without further hesitation, she slipped around the corner and, as she quickened her pace, placed the sight of her pistol on the assassin closest to the obscured target.

It was as she entered the hallway's first pool of light that two things happened. Just as a female scream of defiance filled her ears from down the hallway, one of the three soldiers perceived her as she rapidly decreased the distance between herself and the threesome of assassins.

Inhumanly fast, the man spun but before he could zero in on her with whatever weapon he had shouldered, Hall heard the muffled snap of a weapon discharge behind her.

At twenty meters and on the move, the headshot that Kayed delivered was a fighting marvel. As the man's knees buckled, Hall reacquired the soldier who was closest to the person she could not see.

Sensing something terrible had happened to one of his comrades, the lead man briefly glanced in Hall's direction but instead of turning to engage this new threat, his head turned back to the original target and fired his weapon.

In the time she saw a pair of shell casings eject from her target's weapon, Hall unleashed her own grouping of 9mm rounds into the gunman's side. And while she did not instantly eliminate her target with the same level of skill performed by Kayed moments ago, she had connected.

Jerking, the man desperately whirled his body and leveled his rifle in Hall's direction, the green dot from his weapon's targeting laser wildly dancing across her torso.

But before the man could fire, Hall sent the remainder of the rounds in her magazine into her target. Struck several times, her target stumbled backward and then careened to the floor beside yet another body that appeared to be wearing a Montreal PD uniform.

As Hall's vision pulled back, she saw the third man of the kill team on the floor where he had been standing. Kayed had struck again.

Hall turned her head to take in the Arab-Canadian. With her FN-P90 still locked into her shoulder her intense brown eyes continued to search the hallway for movement.

Slapping another magazine into her weapon, Hall resumed her advance to the hallway's terminus. At ten feet away from the T-junction, she heard a moan and saw movement from the man she had dispatched. In the low light where he lay, she could see that he had started to prop himself against the wall. With whatever strength the man still had, he was trying to pull a sidearm from a holster that ran down his thigh.

Beside her, a single shot issued from Kayed's assault rifle. Instantly, the contents of the man's head exploded onto the concrete wall that had been helping to hold his upper body erect.

The last of their opponents dispatched, the two women continued their advance until they arrived at a pair of alcoves that led left and right. Hall turned in the direction the three soldiers had been pointing their weapons and there, seated on the floor, but leaning against a pair of hospital green double doors was Canada's Prime Minister.

With her teeth clenched and a look of pain splashed across her face, Merielle Martel's brown eyes connected with Hall's, and at that moment there was a flash of recognition. "Lieutenant Hall. What are the chances?"

Somewhere over New York State

Recently promoted Wing Commander Harry Khan of the Royal Air Force – RAF – had been shipped back to Canada just three weeks earlier.

On his departure, he had assured his new bride with the fullest honesty that the chances of him getting into the cockpit of a Tempest and flying combat missions in hostile skies were the same odds as winning the Euromillions lottery.

That had been an overstatement of course, but in his defense, the new Mrs. Khan knew quite well he was prone to hyperbole. More importantly, as had been true with every other woman he had spent any time with, he was incapable of delivering a solid untruth. Harry Khan had several questionable qualities, but lying to his intimate partners was not one of them.

So, when he had last spoken to his wife thirty-six hours ago and advised her in no uncertain terms that he would indeed be flying combat missions, there had not been any recriminations. Rather, there had been a touch of crying and some mutual cursing of bad luck.

Bad luck indeed. After the action in the skies above Missouri just one year ago, he could have easily requested a posting somewhere in the labyrinth that was the Ministry of Defence, but that was not Khan's style.

Instead, as a newly minted Wing Commander with more combat kills than anyone else in the entire RAF, he had asked to stay close to the action where he would direct and help less experienced pilots rotating into the increasingly hot North American theatre.

Of course, in asking for this type of assignment, Khan knew full well the risks he was taking. In the Commonwealth, if you commanded a squadron, or as was presently the case for him, an entire fighter wing, you had to get behind the controls of the aircraft that made you.

As a rule, those commanders who looked to skirt the tradition of risking their necks suffered in the eyes of their pilots and the air marshals back in the MOD.

So, newly married, but also brave to the point where more than one of his former commanding officers had called it stupidity,

Wing Commander Harry Khan of His Majesty's Royal Air Force was once again in the cockpit of a fighter jet going to war.

"Raven Alpha, this is Helena Three, we have multiple targets on screen southwest of Point Foxtrot. You should be seeing the data now."

"Copy that, Helena, the data has arrived," Khan replied in a business-like tone to the AWACS officer whose plane was loitering somewhere off the coast of Delaware.

Khan looked at the central screen dominating the cockpit of his sixth-generation fighter.

Already in tune with how he liked incoming data managed, the Catherine Zeta-Jones-replicated voice he had designated for the Tempest's powerful near-AI began to deliver an overview of what his eyes were seeing. He had preferred the younger version of Ms. Zeta-Jones when it was still fresh with her original Welsh accent.

"Radar cross sections are as follows, six F-15Es and eight Rafaels, designation E variant. They are approximately two hundred and fifty kilometers south of Point Foxtrot and are flying in three distinct formations between the altitudes of twenty and twenty-two thousand feet."

"It's a ground attack for sure," Khan surmised, then added, "What are their loadouts?"

"Data insufficient at this time."

"For Pete's sake, Glitch, what are you good for?"

"I do not see how St. Peter or the Christian religion factors into this dialogue. Is it the case that you would like to pray, Commander? Because if you do, I have the following prayers to choose from: The Serenity Prayer, The Lord's Prayer, Christ Be With Me..."

"Stop. No bloody prayers, thank you very much, Glitch, my dear," Khan said to the near-AI. "I would however like it if you could tell me more about the onscreen baddies?"

"As you wish. There is some shadowing to suggest that there are stealth-capable platforms in the general vicinity of the aforementioned combatants."

"Mystères?"

"The data is inconclusive, but considering the last time the Chinese J-31 was seen in the North American theatre was nearly a year ago, it is highly probable they are French Air Force Mystères."

"Good. Let me know of any updates as soon as they reveal themselves."

"Of course, Commander. Do you have any other orders at this time?"

"I do. Activate comms for Raven Flight Charlie, if you would."

"Channel open," advised the pleasant-sounding near-AI co-pilot.

"Right then. The best of the morning to you, ladies and gents. You will have seen the data fresh from Helena. My best guess is what we're seeing is a burgeoning attack on our lads at Point Foxtrot. We shall intervene and defeat this attack before it is allowed to commence. This is our highest priority.

"To this, I would add that the brave men and women of the *HMCS Lightfoot* and *HMS Greyhound* are sailing into the Chesapeake Bay as we speak and have their radars blazing. The moment we start to get data telling us what those fighters are carrying we'll prioritize accordingly."

"And the Mystères?" The question had come from Cypher, a newly arrived pilot from one of the posh suburbs of London who was, to Khan's consternation, a passionate Hotspurs fan.

"Cypher and Rampart, take yourselves up to thirty thousand and hang tight. The Mystères are out there. When they reveal themselves, give them hell."

"Copy that, boss," Rampart, the more senior of the two pilots, acknowledged.

"The rest of you, stay on me. When I say go, we light ourselves up like Christmas trees and we see what's waiting for us. Nothing else matters but keeping these bastards off Foxtrot. If anyone doesn't understand, let me hear it now."

His question was met with only silence.

"Right. Seeing as we have things straight, let me give you one last piece of advice. Keep your head on a swivel and your ears active. When this goes down, it's gonna get hairy real bloody fast. This is when the near-AI earns its keep. Listen, process, act. LPA, people. Do these three things well and we'll make it through this just fine."

In just three weeks, Khan had come to know his new outfit well enough to know the men and women now in the sky with him knew their business. You didn't get to fly the Tempest platform unless you were the best of the best. Nonetheless, even the most talented pilots needed a reminder of the basics from time to time.

"Hearing neither questions nor jibes in response to your Commander's offer of daily wisdom, I shall leave you to your thoughts. Stay frosty, people. Pony out."

Quebec, North of Ottawa

At the tender age of fifty-seven, Douglas Jefferies was an old-school reporter. He had been in his mid-twenties when the death of print journalism had begun to play out.

He had seen it coming and as an independent-minded journalist, had made a series of moves to insulate himself from the wave of change that was going to crash into the industry he both loathed and loved.

Instead of doing what most of his colleagues and friends had done, he avoided the mainstream media like the contagious patient it had become.

In 2009, he had been one of the very few journalists in Canada to create his own platform where he could report the news as he saw it. But just as important, it was also a place where people could find him to tip him off to developments they didn't want to share with the clickbait journalism that had infected outfits like the CBC or the now-defunct Toronto Star.

This wasn't to say that all journalists working with him in Ottawa weren't interested in reporting actual news. Though she had come up through the ranks of the CBC, Jefferies had always considered Irene MacPhail to be cut from the same cloth that he was.

Through an interesting twist of fate, as a rookie journalist, he had admired Irene's father and the work he had done in Newfoundland.

Over his career, MacPhail the senior had been prolific, but if the man had a claim to fame it would be that he broke no fewer than four stories that had led to the resignation of three provincial cabinet ministers and the corrupt mayor St. John's, not once, but twice. For all his troubles, Angus MacPhail had become a living legend in Canadian journalism.

And so, in his last year of Journalism School at Carleton University, Douglas Jefferies, on a hope and prayer, flew himself out to Canada's most eastern province, walked into MacPhail's office unannounced, and insisted the man take him on as an intern.

MacPhail did, which led to one of the best summers of Jefferies' life. It was during this same spell of time that he had first met an awkward twelve-year-old Irene. Even at that tender age, Jefferies could tell the woman was going to go on and do important things.

It was because Irene had hewed so closely to her father's approach to life and then journalism that he had elected to help her as best he could over his career.

As it concerned Irene MacPhail, the bottom line for Jefferies was this – in a country that had become a cesspool of hate and conniving, the only child of Angus MacPhail was the rarest of gems – an honest and excellent journalist, who had made the misguided career decision to become an honest and excellent politician.

Jefferies clung to this idyllic narrative of his relationship with Irene MacPhail as the big man with the shaved head began to beat him for what had to be the tenth time. Slaps rained down on his face while the occasional punch was delivered to his body.

Just as his vision began to darken, the beating stopped and as had been done several times already, an ice-cold bucket of water was thrown on him. He gasped as the freezing liquid knifed into the many open wounds that were on his face.

While the shaved brute had delivered the beatings, it was the short, darkly dressed man that had done all the talking. He was French to be sure.

Perfectly bilingual, Jefferies easily differentiated the man's Parisian accent just as an English speaker could tell the difference between American English and someone speaking the language from the UK.

"Mr. Jefferies, we know that you were in the forest outside the residence where Ms. Raymond was conducting business, and we know that you or someone associated with you was operating a drone and that this drone was equipped with a military-grade laser microphone. It was a remarkable piece of kit actually. Custom made I'm told."

"I'm so glad you liked it. I built it myself. And as I've told you two assholes already, I was here on my own." On finishing his reply, Jefferies spat a mouthful of blood at the smaller man's feet.

The dark interrogator nodded his head slowly as though he was genuinely disappointed in the reply he had just heard. "Mr. Jefferies, my patience for the games you are playing has come to an end. I will ask one more time and only one more time. The recording of the conversation involving Ms. Raymond. I know it was made and I know it was sent to someone. The question is to whom? Who are you working for, Mr. Jefferies?"

"I'm a journalist, for Christ's sake. That means I get to do journalism. I chase down stories however I want and in chasing down those stories, I get to protect my sources. That's how things work in this country, so fuck off."

The interrogator cocked his head and the hint of a smile rose to his lips. "So, do I understand you correctly, Mr. Jefferies? You will not answer my question?"

"Go to hell!"

The door to the room opened and a pair of men as big as the thug that had been beating him entered the room dragging a third person between them. With the low lighting of the room and the person's head lolling, he was unable to make out a face.

As Jefferies stared at the threesome, a chair slammed down in front of him.

Arriving at the chair, the two ogres easily manhandled the person into the seat. One of the two men grabbed the back of the person's long hair and pulled it back viciously. When Jefferies heard a female voice yelp in pain, he felt his heart begin to pound inside his chest. Though it was bloodied and bruised, he instantly recognized the face sitting across from him.

"You son of a bitch!" Jefferies howled. "You let her go, you bastard! What have you done to her?"

The face of Angela Jefferies, his youngest child, had been beaten to a pulp.

Jefferies began to sob. "Oh, Angie, I'm so sorry. I'm sorry, baby."

The small and entirely evil man moved forward. In his right hand was a matte-black pistol. Placing it at the back of his daughter's head, the man's dark eyes connected with Jefferies' own. The man's stare was cold.

"Mr. Jefferies, you may not believe me, but as much as I wish it were not the case that you and your daughter were doing journalism together, this is the situation that now confronts us."

The Frenchman cocked back the hammer of the gun. "I'll ask one more time, Mr. Jefferies. Who are you working for?"

"MacPhail! Irene MacPhail. She's the Minister of Fisheries and Oceans. I sent the conversation to her. She called me and asked me to follow Raymond. We go way back. She has it. All of it."

The handgun raised from the back of his daughter's head and pointed at his chest.

"Thank you, Mr. Jefferies. Now you don't have to watch your daughter die. And in the case of your death, I promise it will be quick."

He only felt the first of several bullets hammer into his chest. The pain was indescribable. As the surreal sound of the gunshots faded away, his chair somehow began to tilt backward. As if in slow motion, his eyes left the terrified vision of his daughter's screaming face. A second later, he could only see the unremarkable ceiling of whatever room he had been in for the past hour. The change in perspective was a small mercy. It would save him from the pain of having to watch his lovely and smart daughter watch him die. Instead, he heard only her sobs.

As his vision began to blur, Jefferies perceived the man who had filled his chest with bullets. The slight man was standing over him, his gun pointing in the direction of his face.

As had been the case throughout this entire affair, the Frenchman's face was sober. When he released his final ragged breath, Douglas Jefferies told himself – no, he assured himself – that, at the very least, the man that had killed him had done so without obvious signs of pleasure. Evil he might be, the man had been a professional. That would serve his daughter well, he hoped. This was his final thought when the blackness mercifully claimed him.

Chapter 30

Montreal, Hôpital Notre-Dame

"Damn it!" The curse came out of Elan's mouth like spitting venom.

He tore his eyes from the image of the body cam that now only showed him the ceiling tiles of the hospital hallway.

"Sir, he got off two shots. He had her dead to rights. The target is eliminated."

Elan wheeled on the lieutenant who had been critical in helping him to manage the mayhem of the past forty-five minutes.

"No, Lieutenant, the target is not eliminated. She is not eliminated until I see her brains seeping out of her skull or some variation thereof. The luck this goddamned woman has had tonight is nothing short of miraculous. No, I need more. We're going in."

Elan turned to the front of the van. "Chief, get us as close to the hospital as you can."

"Yes, Commandant," the older man snapped off his reply and turned to take up their van's wheel.

"St. Croix and Allard, you are with me. Gear up."

As the van began to move, the two soldiers got up from their stations and moved to find their weapons. Elan's eyes reconnected with the young officer who had been his operational right hand since arriving in North America.

"Lieutenant Roche. You will stay here and keep doing as you've been doing."

"But I can go with you, Commandant. Three of you will not be enough."

"Archer Nine is close," Elan said with a tone of finality. "Give them the order to make their way to us, and then keep your eye on the surrounding area. With the downing of the helicopter, every cop in this shit city will start to converge on this location. It was great thinking to fly that Dragon into its rotors, but the consequence is that this city's hapless police force will now have something it can rally to."

Before the younger officer could offer an apology, Elan shut the man down. "No, it is not a problem, Jean. It was the right call. No one adapts better than the 13th Dragoons. It's what makes us special. We fight hard and we think quick. Just keep doing what you're doing, and we'll get through this. All of us will."

From the front of the van, Chief Laroux, a cigarette once again in his lips called out, "Commandant, we're as close as I dare get."

Elan turned to look at the display and situated their new position relative to where the remainder of Archer Teams Six and Seven were engaging with whatever force had unexpectedly swooped in on that helicopter. Outside the vehicle, he could clearly hear the sound of suppressed rounds being fired.

"Well done, Chief. You will stay here with the lieutenant. I suspect our exfil will require all the special abilities you claim to have behind the wheel of a vehicle."

"We'll be here, Commandant. Just say the word."

Elan turned back on St. Croix and Allard. Both were kitted out with body armor and weapons. He had assigned the two men to his team for this very reason. Both had the smarts to manage data and operations, but they were also ferocious combatants.

"Ready?"

"Yes, sir," both soldiers replied simultaneously.

"Good, then let's go find this goddamned prime minister. It's high time for her luck to end."

Petite's anger toward Hall and Kayed for breaking off from their already small formation had fled his system the moment Sykes had been tagged.

Standing less than six feet away, the JTF-2 commando had taken a bullet to his body armor and upper leg. The force of both strikes had driven the well-built man backward into the grille of an ambulance as though he were a skinny 9th grader shoved into a locker by some upper-year bully. As the commando collapsed onto his posterior, Petite saw Sykes reach in the direction of his upper thigh. Blood was pumping out of the wound like a geyser.

Petite tore his eyes away from the scene and yelled in the direction of the other JTF-2 operator. "Open up, Janks. I'm gonna get him!"

"Copy that, boss."

As he heard Jankowicz begin to unload on full auto, he darted to Sykes, grabbed his two legs, and with all of the adrenaline-fueled strength he could muster, yanked the man into the horizontal and dragged the wounded commando to safety.

Now behind the wheel well of a petrol-driven Montreal PD SUV, Petite grabbed the other man's chest rig and like a ragdoll, erected him so he was leaning against the car's tire.

"Ouch! My leg. It hurts like a son of a bitch," Sykes moaned.

Petite performed a blood sweep over the rest of the soldier and when he was satisfied it was only the commando's leg that was bleeding, he quickly produced a tourniquet and shoved it into Sykes' hands.

"Take this and tie it off. You know what to do, right?" Petite asked over the sound of torrents of incoming gunfire.

When Sykes only looked at him blankly, he delivered a firm slap to the soldier's face and bellowed, "Tie it off, man, or you'll bleed out. You feel me, Sykes?"

To his right, Petite heard Jankowicz call out urgently, "Boss, I need you up front, pronto. They're advancing."

His eyes still locked onto Sykes, Petite's hand raised to give the dazed commando another slap, but the JTF-2 man's hands came up defensively. "I'm here. I'm here. I feel ya, alright."

"Damn straight you do," Petite said, slapping Sykes' injured leg. "Tie it off. I'll be back in a flash."

He sprang upward and raced in the direction of the other Special Forces commando. Bullets, dozens of them, knifed through the night air around Petite as he dodged between vehicles. Finally, he was able to lay eyes on the big Polish-Canadian. A single EMS SUV lay between their two positions.

"How we doing, Sergeant?"

"Not great, boss. Another van just rolled up and more of the bastards got out of it. They're at ten and two o'clock from my position."

With the locations provided, Petite shouldered his weapon and rose above the hood of the SUV to look for a target, but the moment he was exposed, a storm of gunfire slammed into his position.

Lowering his profile so only the top half of his head was exposed, he scanned ahead, looking for something to shoot at.

Movement caught his eye. Three men loaded for bear darted in the direction of the destroyed emergency department entrance.

"Janks!"

"I see 'em."

Targets clearly in view, the two Canadians took up firing positions and unleashed their own barrage of fire at the sprinting figures.

Out of the corner of his eye, Petite saw Jankowicz tumble backward. He stopped firing and looked in the direction of the commando. The operator was down and out of Petite's line of sight. "Talk to me, Janks!"

When no reply came, he ducked low, moved to the back of the SUV, and then bee-lined to where he found the commando splayed on the asphalt.

On reaching Jankowicz, he saw there was nothing to be done. Where his right eye should have been was a gaping hole of blood and viscera.

"Fuck!" Petite screamed. "These mother fuckers!" Ripping his eyes from the destroyed face of his brother-in-arms, Petite shot forward to the same firing position Jankowicz had been in only seconds before and immediately saw one of the civilian-dressed soldiers advancing in his direction.

A cool fury coursing through him, Petite placed the reticle of his weapon on the man's chest and pulled the trigger, unleashing a five-round burst.

Hit at near point-blank range, the shocked man stumbled backward, eventually sprawling onto the ground.

No sooner had his target been felled, than a storm of gunfire began to hammer his position, Petite again took cover while activating his BAM. "Get me Bronco Five, now!"

"Channel open," the female near-AI voice said instantly.

"Hall, it's Petite."

When he heard no reply, he repeated himself. On hearing only silence, dread began to fill him. Steeling his voice, he asked for the mysterious fixer one more time.

"Hall, if you can hear me. More men have entered the building. Dollars to donuts they're coming for you. Jesus, are you there? Talk to me!"

Hall's voice suddenly filled the connection. "I'm here, boss. We have her. We have the PM."

Before he could utter a question or word of congratulations, he heard the screech of tires. Without hesitation, he lifted his head and shoulders above his cover hoping to see the Montreal PD's

SWAT team disgorging from one or more tactical vehicles. Instead, his eyes landed on yet another nondescript van. Men, at least half a dozen of them, were piling out of the vehicle's doors, weapons drawn.

Hall's voice hit him like a jab. "Sam, are you there? Did you hear me? We have her. We have Martel. What's your status?"

Again, bullets began to tear into his location, forcing him to take cover. "Hall, listen to me. You have to run. Three of them entered the building and not ten seconds ago more of these bastards arrived. Janks is dead and Sykes is down. I'll do my best to hold down the party crashers, but you have to move. Get to the other side of the hospital and find a way to get out of here."

For several too-long seconds, the woman gave no reply. "Hall, do you copy? They're coming for you, goddamn it! Talk to me!"

A static-filled voice coursed weakly into his earbud. "Sam... mobile... another entrance."

Petite belted out a curse. Whoever their attackers were, they had some high-end kit because they were somehow jamming his BAM, and according to everything he'd been told about the Canadian Army's comms gear that was not supposed to happen.

"Petite!" A familiar voice ripped his attention away from Hall.

"Boss, if you're there, man, I could really use some help." It was Sykes.

Staying low and with gunfire still filling the evening sky, Petite turned his head toward where he had left the wounded commando.

Right where he left him, the crazy tough soldier that was Master Corporal Sykes was hunched over the hood of the police SUV, putting rounds down range. The man's bloodied face was all determination.

Petite got ready to move. It was time for him and Sykes to get the hell out of Dodge. The idea that they could somehow get into the hospital to reconnect with Hall and Kayed was now out of the question. Hall would have to find her own way. There was no way around that now.

"Sykes!" he bellowed.

"Ya, boss. I'm here. Where's Janks?"

"He's gone, man," Petite called back to the commando. "Hang tight. I'm coming your way."

Petite ripped a can of white smoke off his chest rig, pulled the pin, and tossed it in the direction of the two vans that had just arrived. They had done all they could do. It was time to get out of here and survive.

Despite the PM's words, on seeing Merielle Martel in the flesh, Hall's heart sank.

The woman had been on her backside slouched against the stanchion that separated the pair of oversized green doors. Hall's eyes immediately went to a good-sized smear of blood that started high on the door and ended where the PM was now seated.

Finding the source of blood hadn't been difficult. A round had shaved clear through the PM's shoulder, just to the right of the base of her neck. Fresh blood was oozing out of the wound.

Calmly, Hall asked, "Are you hit anywhere else?"

The PM closed her eyes, no doubt concentrating on how her body was feeling. Finally, she said, "I think it's just my shoulder. It's the only thing that feels like it's on fire."

"Incoming priority call from Bronco Actual," the male voice of her BAM announced in her ear.

Hall ignored Petite's request. She needed to stop the woman's shoulder from bleeding and then determine whether or not she could be moved.

"Madame Prime Minister…"

The politician interrupted her. "Drop the Madame Prime Minister bullshit. Merielle is fine. And that's an order."

"Incoming priority call from Bronco Actual," Hall's BAM repeated.

Hall quickly reached into one of the compartments on her chest rig and pulled out a blood-staunching kit. Putting it up to her mouth, she tore the package open, bent down, and applied it to the PM's wound. The moment she put pressure on it, the woman winced. Ignoring the obvious discomfort, she grabbed one of the politician's hands and placed it on the bandage. "Hold this in place, Merielle. I've got to talk to my people."

Not waiting for a confirmation that the former RCMP officer was up to the task, she turned back to Kayed who was keeping an eye on the hallway where they had come from.

Again, the voice of her BAM came alive in her ear, but before it could pester her about the waiting call from Petite, she said viciously, "Accept the call."

As soon as the connection was made, the sound of gunfire poured into her earbud. Through the barrage of sound, Petite's voice came through.

"Hall, if you can hear me. Men have entered the building. They're coming for you. Jesus Christ, are you there? Talk to me!"

"I'm here, boss. We have her. We have the PM."

She briefly heard Petite's voice again, but a wash of static quickly drowned it out. She looked at Kayed. "They're jamming us and more of them are coming."

The Arab-Canadian CSIS officer said nothing. Instead, she positioned herself at the corner of the short alcove and got her weapon ready.

Hall turned back to the PM. In a good sign, she was still holding the staunching kit in place. When their eyes connected, Hall said, "Can you move?"

On seeing the PM nod her head in the affirmative, Hall activated her BAM and said, "Sam, if you can hear me, don't worry about us. We're gonna be mobile soon and we'll find another entrance. Get to Sherbrooke and we'll meet you there."

Behind her, she heard Kayed growl, "Hall, we've got company." The CSIS officer let loose with a short burst from her FN-P90.

"How many?" Hall called over the sound of Kayed's chattering weapon.

Before the other woman could reply, an extended barrage of gunfire saturated Kayed's position forcing her to step back.

"It looks like there's half a dozen of them. We have to get moving," Kayed yelled over the continuing storm of gunfire.

On hearing the assessment, Hall turned to the double doors, placed both of her hands on the door the PM wasn't leaning on, and gave it a solid pull. It didn't budge.

Before Hall could reef on it again, she heard the PM's voice over the cacophony of incoming fire. "It's locked. The hospital's on lockdown."

Hall turned to Kayed, but before the words "crack the door" could get out of her mouth, the CSIS officer had already yanked off her ballistic vest and was pulling out a length of detonation cord she had stored in her chest rig's back storage panel.

Suddenly, the hail of bullets that had been pounding their position stopped. As Hall stepped to the corner Kayed had been forced to pull back from, she detached the only flashbang grenade on her ballistic vest, jerked the pin, and after a glance into the hallway, tossed the non-lethal munition at the two men she had spied advancing. The flashbang wouldn't kill them, but it could give Kayed the time she needed to get through the door.

As she counted off the seconds of the flashbang's delayed fuse, she readied her weapon.

BOOM!

Hall stepped around the corner and immediately found two soldiers pressed closely to the hallway walls. Each was erect and both had their rifles shouldered. For a micro-second that seemed like a minute, the three combatants stared at each other.

With time only to hit one of her targets, she snapped off two quick rounds into the man on her left. As she shifted back behind the safety of the corner, she felt as much as heard the rounds from the other soldier's weapon as they zipped past her upper body.

The moment she was back behind the safety of concrete, she felt someone grab her, and with a strength Hall didn't know Kayed possessed, she shoved Hall into a corner on top of the Prime Minister. As she slammed into the politician, the woman let out a grunt of pain.

Before Hall could begin to formulate a curse or question, Kayed yelled, "Clear!"

When the eight-inch strip of C4 went off less than four feet away, a sharp CRACK hammered Hall's ears and set them to ringing.

Prepared for the explosion, Kayed moved to the door and with a quick jerk ripped it open. "Move, move, move!" the Arab-Canadian yelled.

With the sound of the explosion still echoing in her ears, Hall grabbed at the PM, pivoted with her, and all but threw the woman through the smoke-filled entrance.

With the PM safely through the door, Hall turned her eyes on Kayed. With her FN-P90 shouldered, the CSIS agent was already on the move. Taking two purposeful strides, she walked back to the corner of the alcove, leaned around the corner, and unloaded her weapon.

A hail of bullets immediately ripped into the concrete around Kayed, forcing the CSIS officer to once again retreat. She spun on Hall. "Go. I'll stay here and hold them as long as I can. There are more of them coming. I won't be able to hold them long."

Hall gritted her teeth and nodded at the other woman. She pulled one of her FN-P90 magazines from her vest and tossed it to Kayed. "Good luck, Rana."

"Thanks. Now go. Get her out of here. I'll do what I can."

Hall spun away from the other woman and stepped through the half-open doorway. Walking up to the PM, she said, "Can you run?"

"I can."

"Then follow me."

"What about your colleague?"

Before she could answer, a hail of gunfire sounded through the doorway. She heard Kayed scream something in Arabic and then heard her yell, "Run, Hall! Allah save you. Run, you damn woman!"

Hall reached out her hand to the Prime Minister. "She's doing her job, so I can do mine. Come with me. We're getting out of here."

Chapter 31

Chesapeake Bay, Coast of Maryland

Captain McNeilly of the HMCS *Lightfoot* watched the tactical display intensely.

The *Lightfoot* was the first of his country's Type 26 class frigates to be launched. The ship was two years delayed and a hundred and fifty million dollars more than she was supposed to be, but it had all been worth it. She had been built for this moment.

Standing at the center of the warship's Combat Information Center – CIC – he quietly observed his sailors at their various stations. For the first time in a very long time, a Canadian crew was going to fight their ship.

"Lieutenant Hainsworth. Would you please activate the radar."

"Aye, sir, activating radar."

At tremendous expense to the Canadian taxpayer, the Navy had installed the latest Aegis Combat System, Block 11, into each of the country's thirteen Type 26 platforms.

The *Lightfoot* and the *HMS Greyhound*, herself a Type 26, had been ordered to split away from the flotilla of ships protecting the *Prince of Wales* and race in the direction of Washington, D.C. to provide air defense capacity to the CANZUK soldiers that were fighting in the destroyed city. It had been a mad rush of a plan but as the two modern and heavily armed ships sailed into the narrow confines of Chesapeake Bay, he felt as cocksure as he had ever been.

"Sir, radar is picking up multiple contacts." The lieutenant operating the Aegis systems radar was his best operator, so he did not press the sailor for more information. He just needed to wait and let the man do his job.

"We have eighteen hard contacts three hundred klicks south of Washington. Radar shadowing is suggesting another five to eight stealth contacts."

"Let's not worry about the shadowing, Lieutenant. Give me what you can about the eighteen."

"Aye, sir. There are eight Rafaels, E variant, and six F-15Es. All fourteen are cruising at twenty thousand and are bee-lining for D.C."

"Looking to hit our boys no doubt. Keep tracking them. Where are the other four? You said there were eighteen."

"We have four Rafales running hard up the coast, sir. It looks like they coming for us."

"Details, Lieutenant?"

"Range, one-fifty klicks. Altitude, one thousand feet. They're making seven hundred knots, Captain. They're in a hurry." As the words left the younger man's mouth, they were perfectly calm.

Red lights started to flash throughout the CIC.

"Talk to me, Hainsworth," McNeilly said.

"Sir, we have multiple launches from the four Rafales. Exocets. Twelve, sixteen... no, make that twenty missiles inbound."

"Air defense, if you please." When McNeilly spoke this time, he had to make a conscious effort to keep the words coming out of his mouth as cool as a North Atlantic spring morning.

"Targets have been flagged, sir," a new female voice responded. "The *Greyhound* has locked onto ten. The rest have been left for us, Captain."

"Let'em have it, Ms. Byers."

"Aye, Captain. Sea Sparrows will launch in fifteen seconds."

"Captain!"

McNeilly's head snapped back to Hainsworth, the radar operator. The man's voice, always stalwart, held a pinch of concern.

"Report, Lieutenant."

"Sir, the Aegis has completed its analysis of the loadout of the fighters heading for D.C."

"And?"

"Sir, it looks like one of them is carrying a modified GBU-28."

McNeilly's mind whirled as it quickly ran through the various briefings he had consumed over the past twenty-four hours. And then he had it. Dread filled him.

"It's just the one fighter. Are you sure, man?"

"The loadouts have been confirmed one hundred percent, sir. They're not trying to hide it. Or they can't."

"Sea Sparrows one through eight away," Leading Seaman Byers announced from the CIC's weapons station.

McNeilly felt the ship shudder slightly as the first of eight air defense missiles sprung from his ship's deck.

"Lieutenant Hainsworth, tag that F-15 as priority Alpha for Helena."

"Yes, sir."

"Comms."

"Yes, Captain."

"Ultra priority message for CANZUK High Command. Send along the data, tell them we suspect the Reds are carrying a tactical nuke and they're headed in the direction of our boys."

Washington, D.C.

Larocque had to give credit to whoever was commanding the Red outfit which had just begun to assault the Armory. A seemingly well-organized stream of armor had been making its way east down the thoroughfares of East Capitol, Constitution, and Independence. Through the eyes of three different on-station surveillance drones, the BAM's near-AI had flagged no less than sixty fighting machines, of which half a dozen Abrams were front and center.

Kiraly was twenty minutes into the surgery when the assault started. In what was one hell of an irony, the same pile of rubble that had pinned the legs of President Morgan was the same jumble of concrete that made this particular location of the Armory the best place to weather the incoming storm of high-caliber rounds and armor-penetrating tank shells.

On bent knee on the other side of the sheet where Kiraly was conducting the surgery, Larocque listened to his officers on the BAM give orders in their respective areas of defense, while he himself worked feverishly to call in as much indirect fire and air support as was available to him.

From a position on the campus of Glaudette University just to the northeast, the British Parachute Regiment's mortar platoon was in the midst of saturating a concentration of Red Faction vehicles hammering the north side of the Armory.

As the Paras' mix of high explosive and anti-personnel 81mm shells rained down on the Americans, Larocque watched a Joint Light Tactical Vehicle, JLTV take a direct hit and explode on his tactical pad. Immediately, the boom and concussive wave of the destroyed vehicle invaded the air around him. Nothing was far away in this fight.

Despite the exceptional work of the Para mortarmen, a threesome of Abrams that had been savaging his men's positions along the northern flank of the building continued to unload with their main guns.

One of the four Carl Gustav anti-armor teams on site had disabled one of the Abrams' tracks making it immobile, but in the process had itself been silenced.

"Priority call from Lion Six," the female voice of his near-AI advised through his earbud.

"Accept the call." He manipulated his tactical pad and repositioned the drone's camera. His eyes immediately zeroed in on a pair of tanks that hadn't been there only five minutes ago.

"Captain Zufelt, I see you have new friends?"

"Sir, we have to begin to fall back. We're getting torn apart by those Abrams. Our Carl Gs are gone. I got a few M-72s left, but they're useless on that armor."

"Captain, hear my voice. You will hold your position until I say you can move. Fight hand-to-hand if you have to. Do you understand me?"

"I do, sir, but -"

"No buts, Zuf. You and your boys can do this. I'm sending you some help. Just hold on -"

The voice of his BAM's near-AI interrupted him. "High-priority message from Seawolf Alpha."

Larocque ignored the priority ping and forced himself to concentrate on the Pathfinder captain.

"Just find a way to hold them, Captain. The doc needs ten more minutes at least. You can do it Zuf. I know you can. Lion Actual out."

"Accept Seawolf Alpha," Larocque growled.

As he waited for the Navy to take up the connection, he manipulated his tactical pad to show the precise location of Zufelt. The man's designator was at the halfway point along the northward side of the Armory.

Bringing up the BAM's health status overlay on the map, Larocque could see that the Captain's Pathfinder company was indeed in rough shape. Thirty percent of the heart rates were no longer registering.

"Open priority channel, Charlie-Echo, Warrant Officer Bear, now!"

"Channel open," the near-AI advised.

"Warrant, I need you on me now. I'm in the officers' mess!" Larocque bellowed, his voice cutting through the tumult of the fighting.

Before Bear could confirm the order, the already approved link with the Navy cut into his connection. "Lion Actual, this is Seawolf Alpha, what is your status?"

"Our status, Seawolf, is that we're about to get overrun unless you guys start to throw your bloody weight around. What's the hold up?"

"Hold, Lion," the naval officer said in a neutral tone.

"Hold! You son of a... you called me!" Larocque barked his outrage into the BAM's receiver but the officer he had been speaking to had dropped off or chosen to ignore him.

Just as he was about to unleash a string of profanities across the connection, the wall at the far end of the mess hall exploded inward taking a direct hit from the Abrams hammering his side of the building.

Instinct and the physical force from the impact, sent him sprawling backward to the ground.

Quickly gathering himself, he looked through the haze of dust in the direction of Dr. Kiraly and his patient. Incredibly, the surgeon and the two nurses supporting him had not stopped their efforts. Instead, the three of them had linked arms to form a huddle and create a barrier over the Blue President.

"Major, are we good?" Larocque yelled.

Kiraly flashed an angry look at Larocque. "If you can manage to stop with the explosions, we'll have this done in less than ten minutes, Colonel. It won't be pretty, but he's holding up well. He's one tough SOB."

Larocque only flashed the man a thumbs up and then strode through the dust that now dominated the mess hall to arrive at the newly formed gash that had been created by the tank shell.

Where there had been a C-6 machine gun team moments before there was now a pile of shattered stone and splintered wood framing that had once been one of the mess hall's oversized windows.

Reaching the destroyed position, Larocque threw himself down on the jagged mess. No sooner had his body hit the pile of stone and wood he was joined by two of his men. Without direction or fear the pair of paratroopers began to send short bursts of fire in the direction of the attacking Red force with their assault rifles.

Moving up to the lip of the newly rearranged position to join the two soldiers, Larocque was instantly drawn to a lone attacking Abrams MBT. Just as his eyes framed it in, the tank's main gun recoiled and somewhere to his left another section of their temporary fortress exploded inward.

Arrayed beside the tank was a collection of other fighting vehicles, their various weapons ripping into the Airborne's position. Had it not been for the wreckage of the dozens of pickup trucks that littered the narrow battlefield between the Armory and the neighborhood less than a hundred meters away, the Red Faction armor would have already stormed their position.

As it was, the sea of trucks had served to channel the American armor into dozens of choke points that his paratroopers and the remaining Blue soldiers had used to murderous effect.

But the Abrams was an altogether different animal. While there were only a few of them, their thick armor afforded them the opportunity to unleash round after round into the thick façade of the well-built facility.

Another CRACK from the Abrams' main gun cut through the maelstrom of sound. This time it connected to Larocque's right. This couldn't go on much longer, he thought.

Suddenly, the Abrams started to move and, as it did, other vehicles – JLTVs, Strykers, and some uncountable number of civilian trucks brimming with militia – revved their engines to join the tank. As the collection of vehicles advanced as one terrible force, the deep rumble of their engines worked to muffle the torrents of gunfire that both sides were hurling at one another.

He felt movement beside him and glanced over to see Warrant Officer Bear. His dark skin was caked with sweat and filth.

"You called?"

"I did. Take as many men as you can gather and reinforce Zufelt."

"I can do that, but we're not doing so hot ourselves." As he said the words, the veteran paratrooper motioned to the wall of vehicles slowly advancing toward their position.

"Help might be on the way for this side of the building, Warrant," Larocque said.

"Airstrike?" asked Bear, hopefully.

"No. The Reds have saturated the air above Washington."

"A miracle from the Great Spirit, then? Thunder from the skies or perhaps from your own fingers? 'Cause that would be pretty cool, eh."

Before Larocque could reply to the First Nations soldier's jibe, a new voice streamed into his earbud.

"Lion Actual, this is Seawolf Actual. Sorry for the delay. Things are pretty hot out here on the water."

"Sorry to hear that, Seawolf. Things here aren't much better. We need your help and we need it now."

"Copy that, Lion. We are just in range to affect a fire support mission. Give us a target and we'll do our best to hit it."

"Copy that, Seawolf. You'll have the targeting data in thirty seconds."

"Good stuff, Lion. Make sure you have someone there who can help us adjust the fire. At the distance we are from you, there'll be plenty of room for error."

"Understood, Seawolf. Send as much as you can as fast as you can and we'll adjust. Lion Actual out."

His eyes returned to Bear. "Thunder is on its way, Warrant."

The other man smiled. "I always knew you had it in you, sir. You've got good Indian blood somewhere in you. I can feel it."

"I can do the 23 and Me test when we get back home, but for now, I need you to grab some of the reserve and get to Zufelt. Help the kid hold that side of the building."

"Can do, Colonel." On confirming the order, the warrant officer turned and quickly dodged in the direction of the boardroom's exit.

Larocque heard the screech of metal grinding on metal. His eyes darted back to the approaching Red Faction steel. The Abrams was powering through yet another disabled half-ton truck. It would be point blank in seconds.

Still lying prone, he detached the tactical pad velcroed to his chest rig and brought up the feed from one of the surveillance drones. Using his finger, he outlined a rectangle that ran along the southwest corner of the building. At the center of the flagged area was the Campus-Armory Metro station. His finger stabbed at the structure confirming the fire mission.

Both the Canadian and British Type 26 frigates in Chesapeake Bay were armed with the BAE 127mm Mk 45 deck gun. With the weapon, each warship could hurl their limited stock of extended-range Volcano five-inch projectiles up to a distance of ninety kilometers. At a full rate of fire, together, the two ships might be able to put thirty rounds on target over the course of a minute. The fire mission sent, Larocque prayed it would be enough.

"Here they come!" a voice he didn't recognize bellowed from the window immediately to his right.

He quickly looked up over the lip of jumbled concrete to see a wall of green-black military vehicles arrayed thirty meters in front of their position. On every third machine, an auto-turret was jackhammering bursts of supersonic lead and tungsten while in between each vehicle, Red Army regulars and militiamen were starting to stream forward on foot.

Because of the intensity of the barrage, he didn't hear the scream of the Navy's first shell as it cut through the air above the building. The high explosive, sixty-eight-pound deck gun round exploded somewhere in front of his position. Despite the incoming hail of gunfire, Larocque again raised his head over the lip of their position and searched for the location of the strike.

His eyes immediately zeroed in on the sail-like structure of the Metro Station. The operator of the Mk 45 had hit the structure dead on their first bloody try. Smoke was emanating from the shattered steel-and-glass structure.

Another shell struck, this time twenty meters to the right of the subway station. The civie vehicles and militia in the immediate vicinity of the high-explosive round disappeared entirely or were tossed into the air like rag dolls.

Looking down at his tac pad, his finger stabbed a red glowing square which put him in touch with the officer in charge of firing the Mark 45.

"Seawolf, right forty and drop twenty, fire for effect!"

A calm, lovely-sounding, English-accented female voice began to stream into his ear confirming that the *HMS Greyhound* had been assigned to his fire mission. "Copy that, Lion Actual, right forty and drop twenty. Firing for effect."

"Grenade!" someone screamed to his right.

Snapping his head in the direction of the shout, he saw a black object clatter underneath a huge wooden table that had been pushed to the far wall of the mess hall.

BOOM!

Accepting the bulk of the grenade's energy, the table groaned but otherwise seemed unaffected.

Flashing his eyes in the direction of Major Kiraly, he recognized the body of Agent Phillips writhing in pain on the ground in front of the sheet where the surgery was taking place.

As one of the surgical nurses moved to the American Secret Service agent, Kiraly's head rose above the privacy barrier. The surgeon's eyes immediately connected with Larocque's, whereupon he gave the Airborne CO a thumbs up and then a signal for five more minutes

Before Larocque could signal anything back to the surgeon, the full weight of the Canadian and British Type 26s' deck guns bore down on the attacking force.

He lost count after the first five rounds impacted and shredded through the line of armor and exposed humans that had been swarming his people.

Daring to turn his eyes directly on the hell-storm, he was immediately treated to a direct hit on a JLTV. The well-armored replacement for the Americans' legendary Humvee disintegrated into a mess of burning steel and black smoke.

Everywhere else, pickup trucks and militiamen within the kill zone were tossed or shredded by the vortex of energy the *Lightfoot* and *Greyhound* had unleashed in this section of the Airborne's defense.

When the barrage ended, the echoing explosions transcended into a relative quiet where the only sound Larocque could hear was the collective whine of diesel engines combined with the terrible sound of dying men. The Abrams, the platform he was most worried about, appeared to be untouched by the firestorm, but in that moment, it appeared to be doing nothing.

"Lion Actual, this is Seawolf Alpha. We're ready for your next fire mission."

"Hold one, Alpha," Larocque said as he took in the surreal scene.

"Copy that, Lion Actual. Standing by."

Wishing he had X-ray vision, Larocque stared at the American tank. "What are you up to, you bastard?"

As if the tank commander had heard him, the Abrams' engine growled aggressively but instead of advancing, the war machine began to reverse. As it moved, a nearby and untouched Stryker also began to retreat.

"Open Channel for Team Lion Charlie," Larocque instructed his BAM.

"Channel open," the near-AI voice advised into his earbud.

"Airborne and 2nd Commando, hold your fire, hold your fire. Let them pull back. The doc's done his work, so we're getting out of this nightmare. Whatever you need to do to be able to move in ten, make it happen. No one gets left behind. More instructions to come, so keep your BAMs primed. Lion Actual out."

As the Abrams made a terrible sound grinding through another gaggle of smoking pickups, Larocque eyed what remained of the American assaulting force.

It wasn't inconsequential but it wasn't complete devastation either. Indeed, the naval bombardment had torn the bulk of the militiamen to pieces and here and there the Red's armor was out of commission, but if he had been commanding the attacking force, he might have pressed forward. They had been close. Really close.

His BAM once again came to life. "Priority call, Ultra-Alpha designation. Do you accept the call?"

"The generals can't give me a minute, can they?" Larocque said, his voice well and truly annoyed.

"I do not understand the command. Do you want to accept the call, Lion Actual? Ultra-Alpha designation represents the highest priority designation within the BAM triage system," the female voice said seemingly trying to be helpful.

"Accept the call," Larocque growled.

"Colonel, it's Gagnon." There was an urgency to the man's voice.

"General, it's over. I've just given the order to prep for a pullout. The doc has performed a miracle and -"

Gagnon cut him off mid-sentence. "Jackson, listen to me. I've got bad news that you need to hear ASAP. We have inbound fighters coming your way."

"It's not great news, General, but the Armory is pretty solid. Unless the Reds are sending every plane they have left, we should do okay."

"It's a flight of Red 15Es," Gagnon said.

"And?"

"And we're certain Colonel one of them is carrying a tactical nuke."

Chapter 32

Montreal, Hôpital Notre-Dame

On moving through the destroyed door and down a long hallway, Hall saw her first living hospital employees. As they reached a nursing station, she eyed three women who despite the gunfire had stayed at their post. They ignored her and focused exclusively on the prime minister.

One of them blurted out, "I'm sorry we couldn't open the door. It's controlled centrally."

Before the PM could provide a response, the chattering of automatic weapons sounded down the hallway.

Two of the nurses cowered at the barrage, but the third, a huge battle axe of a woman, stepped forward and produced a compression bandage.

Without asking for permission, she pulled open the PM's jacket, looked at her shoulder wound, and then placed a fresh bandage on the woman's torn flesh. Merielle protested in pain.

"This needs surgery," the nurse said.

Hall ignored the assessment. "Can we get to an exit from here without hitting any more of these locked doors?"

Incredibly, the rotund nurse had produced a blood pressure cuff and was in the midst of placing it around the PM's upper arm. Hall's hand stabbed forward grabbed the medical device, and threw it to the ground.

"Listen! If you don't tell us how to get out of here, she dies." As she delivered the statement, she pointed at Merielle.

Another voice spoke. "I can show you."

Hall's eyes flitted to one of the other nurses. She was close to Hall's age but more important, it looked like she could move quickly.

Before Hall could reply to the woman's offer, an explosion saturated the air around them. The crack of a frag grenade going off in the direction they had come from made all three nurses jump.

Hall stepped forward, grabbed the nurse-turned-guide, and placed as firm a grip as she could manage on the woman's arm. "Get us out of here. Now!"

The nurse's eyes released from the sound of the echoing explosion and locked onto Hall's own hazel eyes. "Follow me."

Like a scared cat, the nurse darted in the opposite direction from where Hall and Martel had come from.

Hall turned back to the prime minister. She put out her hand and the older woman grabbed hold. Her face seemed paler than just a minute ago.

"Can you run?"

Martel only nodded her head.

Hall didn't respond to the politician's affirmation. Instead, she pulled her in the direction of their fleeing guide and activated her BAM. "Get me Bronco Actual, priority Bravo-Victor."

"Bronco Actual's BAM is unavailable. There is a local system jamming all communications," the male voice of the near-AI said calmly.

"Does Bronco Actual still have a heart rate?"

"That information is unavailable at this time."

Hall let loose with a curse.

Ahead of them, the nurse darted around a corner. Pulling on Merielle, she picked up their pace.

Turning the corner, Hall found the nurse waiting for them. She had a door propped open and a poorly lit flight of stairs confronted them.

"Why are we going up?" Hall asked.

"We have to get to the third floor to get around the locked doors, so we can get outside."

"How long before we get to the exit?"

"Two, maybe three minutes."

"Which street will we exit on?"

"Sherbrooke."

"Okay, get us moving but when we get to the top of the stairs, stop." On giving the order, Hall looked at the PM, who, despite a brave face, had struggled mightily to keep pace with their most recent dash. "We'll need a short rest after the stairs."

The nurse nodded her head in understanding, turned, and started to navigate the first steps.

On reaching the third floor, Merielle was plodding and breathing heavily. Hall handed the PM off to the nurse. "Take her into the hallway another twenty feet or so and wait for me."

On hearing the instructions, the nurse reached out for Merielle's hand and, once connected, they slowly began to move down the hallway.

Turning to the edge of the stairs, Hall pulled the final cylinder affixed to her chest rig and made ready to pull the device's pin. Closing her eyes and breathing deeply, she willed herself to listen for the slightest tremor in the air.

Perhaps thirty seconds into her meditation, the sound of boots shuffling on a floor registered in her brain. A second later, the more distinct sound of a hand double tapping on body armor ricocheted off the concrete and filled her ears. The signal to advance into the stairwell had been given.

Hall pulled the pin on the can of CS gas and carefully tossed it down the tunnel of space created by the stairs' railing.

As the hissing cylinder struck the railing and careened off course, a man wearing civilian clothing and a ballistic vest stepped forward, his assault rifle pointing upwards. As their eyes connected, they simultaneously unleashed with their respective weapons. Hall could only get off two shots before she was forced to backpedal, the sensation of bullets ripping past her face all the incentive she needed to start the next leg of their retreat.

She whirled and ran in the direction of the nurse and the PM. "Give her to me and get us to that exit. Move!"

Fit and used to following orders, the nurse uncoiled from holding up Merielle and sprung forward to race down the hallway.

Behind her, someone in French bellowed, "It's only CS gas. Move, move, move!"

Hall grabbed Merielle's hand and pulled her forward. Despite the paleness of the politician's face, she did not need to pull or cajole the woman to move quickly. With their executioners only a few flights of stairs away, the PM did her best to keep the pace Hall was now setting.

As the nurse ahead of them darted around a corner, Hall put her mind to how the hell they were going to survive this mess should they make it outside. Whatever they did, it would have to happen quickly. As they reached the entrance the nurse had taken, she shoved Merielle through. "Go! Follow her. The exit has to be close. I'll be right behind you."

When the Prime Minister of Canada didn't move, Hall roared at the woman, "You have to go, Merielle. I won't be long after you. Go! Now!"

"I can't go with you!" Sykes yelled across the short distance that separated them. "Throw me your remaining ammo and get the hell out of here. If you don't manage to find a way to get mobile, the PM is as good as dead. Find a ride, Petite. It's the only way, man!"

Leveraging his good leg, Sykes rose above the hood of the SUV and unleashed a sustained burst from his FN-P90.

From his position, rapid movement registered in Petite's brain. At least three, maybe four, of the men they were facing, were advancing. He did not have to be a special operations soldier to know they would be flanked in seconds. His eyes went back to the JTF-2 commando. He was back below the hood of the car, staring in his direction.

"Boss, give me your ammo now and get the hell out of here!"

The commando was right. One priority trumped everything else. If Hall had the PM, he needed to find them. Sykes knew that just as he did.

He reached into the mag pouches that ran along the chest of his body armor and tossed Sykes his last magazine. The commando caught it and placed it on the ground beside him.

The soldier's eyes then locked onto Petite's. The younger man's chiseled jawline and determined expression were as resolute an image as Petite would ever see. "GO!" the commando bellowed.

Petite ripped his eyes from Sykes' gaze and exploded forward from his position dodging around one vehicle and then another. For the brief moment he was exposed, rounds from the converging kill team snapped around his running form.

As he sprinted onto the side street that would bring him to Sherbrooke, he looked desperately for an operating vehicle of any kind. It was late and the fighting across Montreal had sent most of the city's residents to ground.

There were cars parked here and there along the street's shoulders, but his knowledge of how to jack a vehicle was rudimentary at best. Even if he did have that skill, he'd still need to download the covert operator app that would allow him to override the anti-theft software he would encounter on whatever vehicle he managed to lift. He didn't have that kind of time. What he needed was a car already in use.

Reaching the intersection of Rue Plessis and Sherbrooke, he positioned himself behind a gigantic maple tree. A long burst of gunfire ripped through the night. Closing his eyes, he fought to calm his breath and listened carefully. On his third intake of Montreal's humid air, a long scream of defiance filled the evening sky.

In the direction from which he had just come, the sound of one, and then a second, shot rang in his ears.

Petite closed his eyes and unleased an ugly curse. As the echo of what was most likely an executioner's bullets faded, a new sound invaded his ears.

As a long-time resident of Montreal, he instantly recognized the noise for what it was. His eyes snapped open and he looked west down Sherbrooke.

In a surreal scene, a threesome of horse-drawn carriages was clip-clopping down what on any other night would have been a busy thoroughfare teeming with late-night commuters.

"Incredible," Petite whispered.

Setting his near-empty rifle down, he burst from his location and began to run in the direction of the lead carriage.

Due to a persistent hue and cry from activists, Montreal banned the highly popular tourist trap for reasons of animal welfare back in 2020. But six years ago, the small industry roared back to life with the advent of electrified carriages.

For all intents and purposes, the horses that were 'pulling' the three carriages down the street were doing nothing of the sort. Rather, they jauntily walked in front of the bygone-looking platforms silently propelled behind them.

As he reached the first of the three horses, he stopped in its path with his hands raised high into the air. The carriage operator eyed him warily, while his horse, a huge white thing, issued what Petite thought might have been an anxious whicker. He was no expert in things equine.

"How fast can this thing go?" he blurted out.

A look of anger crossed the white-haired carriage operator's face. "It doesn't matter, son, cause you ain't getting a ride with any of us. We don't want any trouble. That's why we're out here. The Old City is a flipping warzone. The cops have gone crazy."

"Listen," Petite said, as he forced his breathing to slow down. "I'm not a cop, but I'm not a bad guy either."

"Son, I don't care who you are and I don't give a fiddler's fig if you have a gun. My whole life savings has been invested into these carriages and I'll be damned if they're to be used for any purpose other than carting around too-rich tourists."

Petite, a foreign intelligence officer with time in Haiti and the former French colonies in Africa, honed in immediately on the words "life savings." Money, whether here in Montreal or the sun-cooked streets of Dakar, was with few exceptions, the leverage you needed to get someone to do what they didn't want to. And with the creation of the Direction Action teams, CSIS had invoked a blank check policy of up to one million dollars for its senior field officers.

"Two hundred and fifty thousand dollars," Petite said firmly.

The big horse snorted loudly and stomped one of its hooves.

The old carriage operator leaned forward in his seat and narrowed his eyes. "What do you mean, 'two hundred and fifty thousand dollars'?"

"I mean if you give me and my friends a lift in your carriage, you'll take home that much money tonight."

"Tabarnac!" the man cursed loudly. "Who pays that much money for a carriage ride? Tonight of all nights isn't one for jokes. We don't want none of what you're selling. Out of my way, son."

The man snapped the reins of the horse but Petite didn't budge from his position in front of the huge animal. Instead, his hand took up the horse's bridle.

"Let go of my horse!" the carriage operator demanded.

"Give me your phone number and I'll text you a payment of one fifty, right now. Straight into your bank account. The next one hundred comes after you drop us off. And I swear, if you help me, your business will grow astronomically in the years to come. You, sir, will become the richest horse-drawn carriage operator in the world and a legend of the Old City for the rest of your days."

"Oh, and why's that?" the carriage operator said.

"Because you and your friends here are going to help me save the life of our prime minister."

North of Washington, D.C.

"Missiles incoming," Rampart advised calmly over the flight's open frequency.

The main LCD at the center of Khan's cockpit came to life with a blizzard of data points. One of the French Air Force Gen 6 Mystères had lit up its radar and in the process flagged Khan and the five other pilots that made up his flight.

"Eleven missiles inbound. Meteor designation. Range, 110 kilometers, speed Mach 4," Glitch, his fighter's near-AI co-pilot, announced in his helmet.

"A walk in the park, people," Khan said dispassionately to the pilots he was leading into battle.

"Remember, our bird is better than theirs. That's a fact and help is on its way. Cypher and Rampart, per the plan, hit them from on high. Don't hold back. Expend what you need to get them to pay attention to you."

"Copy that, boss," acknowledged Rampart, the more senior of the two pilots. "Targets have been acquired. Launching in three, two, one. Fox 3's are on their way."

New data points flashed onto Khan's combat management display as eight new missiles from his mates' fighters, also Meteors, joined the fray.

"Incoming missiles seventy kilometers away. Confirming two missiles are locked onto you, Commander," the near-AI updated.

"Rhino and Sax, at fifty klicks, launch your Onryōs, then engage at will. Petal and I are going to drop down to the deck. If all goes well, we'll take 'em from the rear."

"Copy that, boss," Rhino replied.

The Onryōs, or Phantoms, were autonomous, Electronic Warfare anti-missile missiles that had been developed by a Japanese firm. Hugely expensive, each unit carried its own powerful EW jamming system that, depending on the need, projected a focused or broad cloud of energy at approaching missiles or enemy fighters with the aim of confusing or frying their onboard systems.

"Petal, you're with me. We're going low in three, two, one."

On "one," Khan's Tempest rolled in the air and at a speed of five hundred knots knifed at a fifty-degree angle toward the American eastern seaboard.

"Two incoming hostile missiles are fifty kilometers away. They are matching your rate of descent, Commander," his near-AI advised.

In Khan's head, the math worked, but it would be a hell of a close thing. The two CANZUK warships, the *HMCS Lightfoot* and *HMS Greyhound* were deep into the Chesapeake Bay getting ready to pound whatever targets the Canadian Airborne or British Paras were sending their way.

In the case of *Greyhound*, the Royal Navy had elected to fit half of its Type 26 frigates with the American RIM-174 Standard Extended Range Active Missiles. Guided by the Aegis system, the powerful general-purpose air defense missiles could reach out and touch targets at a whopping 240 kilometers.

"Missile launch detected from *HMS Greyhound*," Glitch updated.

"How many from the *Greyhound*?"

"Four RIM-174s are now in the air."

Four is good, Khan thought. When it came to air defense, overkill was never a bad thing. Now, the question in play was whether or not the friendly missiles had the pep to get to where they needed to be before the French Meteors found Khan and his wing mate.

"Commander, I am proposing that you release control to me so that I can maximize our trajectory to better allow for the intervention of the *Greyhound*'s missiles."

Khan only hesitated a moment. "Do it."

As soon as the words left his mouth, his body pressed back into his seat as the near-AI co-pilot adjusted the angle of their descent and accelerated.

"Oi, you had better know what you're doing, Glitch."

"I do, Boss. My calculations suggest there is an 11.24 percent –"

"Stop," Khan cut off the AI's reply and smiling broadly, announced, "Never tell me the odds!"

Instead of acknowledging his order, Khan felt the fighter increase its speed again. The G-Forces on his body further pressed him into his seat. Ahead and below, he could see the green of what must have been the State of Maryland racing up to meet him.

His eyes dropped to the cockpit's main display as the screen started to flash the words, IMPACT IMMINENT.

Khan closed his eyes and released a string of F-bombs.

As he did his best to fill his compressed lungs with enough air to maintain his vision and unleash what might be his last-ever curse, a flash of light and shock of energy ripped through his plane's airframe as it continued to hurtle toward the earth. This was it, he thought.

His hands sluggishly moved to pull his plane out of his dive, but before he could order Glitch to release control back to him, the

6th gen fighter flattened out its trajectory, seemingly pulling itself out of its dive mere feet from the surface of the earth.

"Incoming hostile missiles have been neutralized," Glitch advised, her Welsh-accented voice alluring and calm as ever.

"Bloody hell, that was close!" As Khan said the words, the g-forces pressed onto his body began to relent, if only slightly.

"Commander, I regret to inform you Petal and her unit are no longer with us. The Flight Lieutenant refused to let her co-pilot take control as you did with me. The math, as you tend to say, did not work out for them."

As Khan listened to the near-AI's update, he thought he heard a tinge of resentment.

"She was a hell of a pilot, Glitch, and each of us has to make our own decision when it comes to releasing control."

When the near-AI made no reply, Khan focused his eyes on the horizon. At ninety feet above the ground and a speed of 900 knots, he was a streak of grey lightning racing in the direction of the single spire of the Washington Monument.

Khan's vision quickly dropped down to his plane's main tactical console where he surmised that the other four planes of his flight were still alive and slugging it out with the remaining Mystères. They had downed two of the elite French fighter planes.

"Release control."

"Acknowledged. Control back to you, Commander."

With D.C. fast approaching, Khan pulled back on his plane's flight stick to send him rocketing into the air. He was now well south of the area where his flight mates were mixing it up.

Having been so close to the ground, there was every chance the French fighters and whatever other radars were in the area would have lost his profile.

"Rampart, this is Pony. I'm way south of you guys. Keep those bastards occupied, if you would. In half a minute, I'll have a nasty surprise for your new friends and will be on my way to join you. It's payback time."

"Pony, good to hear your voice. Anything you can do to help, we'd appreciate it. These guys are no slouches."

"Hang tight, lads. I'm on my way. Pony out."

Khan manipulated his flight stick to put his Tempest into a tight turn. With data streaming in from the Aegis systems on the two CANZUK frigates, he didn't need to light up his own radar to get a fix on the two closest Mystères sixty kilometers north and thirty thousand feet above him.

His near-AI having already tagged the two fighters, Khan said, "Glitch, target Vampire One first, if you please."

"Copy that, Commander," the near-AI replied immediately.

His Tempest shuddered slightly as two Meteors ejected from the fighter's now open weapons bays and lanced in the direction of his first target.

"Fox-3 one and two away, Commander," the near-AI advised as the missile trails of the two Meteors faded into the distance.

"Very good. Target Vampire Two and let 'em have it."

"Copy that, Commander. Fox-3 three and four away in three, two, one."

Seconds passed without anything happening. Pursing his lips, Khan finally said, "Glitch, fire Meteors three and four at Vampire Two. Now!"

When the voice of his near-AI made no reply, he said, "Switch to manual override, authorization, Zulu-Alpha-Seven"

"Override denied, Commander," Glitch said.

"Denied!" Khan's voice was filled with outrage. "Like bloody hell –"

Another voice streamed into his helmet. "Pony, hang fire."

"The hell I will. Who's this?"

"It's the *Prince of Wales*, Commander. We need you to break off from your engagement. You're the one and only CANZUK fighter that has a clear throughline to a new high-priority target. Data should be on your display now."

"Negative, PoW, my lads are in the thick of it. Send somebody else. And for the record, how dare you take over my ride in the middle of a scrap? There will be hell to pay once I'm back on the ground, and I don't care who made the bloody decision."

Another voice chimed in on the frequency. This one Khan recognized instantly. "Pony, this is Air Vice Marshal Robert Michaels. Do you copy?"

"I copy, Marshal," Khan said in response to the no-nonsense man who had overall command for the combined CANZUK air forces. Michaels was a fighter pilot himself, and Khan had a deep respect for the man.

"Right then, listen well, Commander. We have it on good authority there is an F-15E carrying a tactical nuclear weapon in the direction of our lads in Washington. That is your new target. Do you copy?"

Khan's eyes moved to the tactical display. Sure enough, the large flight of Red Faction and French fighters that the Type 26s' radar had flagged loitering above the North Carolina-Virginia border were now vectoring north. Amongst the dozen or so green-designated fighters, a single, yellow-flagged plane stood out.

This time, he didn't need Glitch's help to do the calculations. At fourteen-to-one odds, this was a suicide mission if there ever was one.

The Air Marshal's voice again invaded his ears. "Pony, I say again, acknowledge your new target."

The words "tactical nuclear weapon" echoed in his brain. It had been nearly a full day since the Reds had hit D.C. with those terrible weapons. As his fighter had rushed in the direction of Washington moments earlier, he had failed to look for indications of the five separate attacks.

"Pony, do you copy?" This time there was an edge to Michaels' voice.

"I hear you, sir. Target acknowledged. Moving to engage now."

"Copy that, Commander," Michaels said, sounding relieved. "Our own fighters and the RCAF are sending more firepower in your direction, but there's no chance they'll make it to the target before it can complete its mission. It's on you, Pony. I'm sorry. I wish there was some way to narrow the odds, but...."

As Khan rolled his fighter out of its climb and vectored it south in the direction of the approaching Franco-American strike force, his mind reeled through a series of images.

His new wife. Smart and stunning. A keeper if there ever was one. His nieces and nephews. All of them were some combination of precocious and delightful. His fresh receipt of the Conspicuous Gallantry Cross and an extended conversation with the King who had pinned it on his uniform.

They were all cherished memories.

Despite the flood of emotions that came with his thoughts, when Khan next spoke his words were like steel. He loved his wife, his family, and his country, but foremost, he was a senior officer in the Royal Air Force.

"Sir."

"Yes, Commander?"

"No need to apologize, sir. This is the life I chose."

Khan then smiled and added, "And Marshal,"

"Yes, Pony?"

"Let it be known in the official record, I actually like my chances. Pony out."

Chapter 33

Ottawa, Parliament Hill

It had been four dreadful hours since MacPhail had listened to the conversation between Yvette Raymond, the billionaire Marc-Antoine Trembly, and some other man she did not know. It had been this same amount of time since she had last heard from Douglas or his daughter, Angie.

There had been no accompanying message with the recording, which was unlike her long-time friend. Angie, too, had been silent. That neither of them had followed up with her, nor returned her repeated encrypted messages, had elevated the warning flag flapping in her brain to an incandescent red.

Had she heard from one of them and got word they were okay, she would have already sent along the recording of her colleague making a deal with someone who sounded like the devil.

Outrageous and incredible did not begin to describe the arrangement that Yvette Raymond had made with the unnamed third party, who MacPhail surmised was a senior person from the French intelligence service.

In the early morning hours, her mind had been spinning like a top trying to piece together recent events such that they jibed with the conversation Raymond had with the mysterious Frenchman.

The French agent, if that's what he was, had known too much about the assassination attempt on the prime minister not to have been involved. In fact, at one point during the recording, the man seemed to provide a real-time update on Merielle's status. *"She is now trapped in a local hospital,"* and that this, *"whole unfortunate affair will be over within the hour."*

For Raymond's part, it had been clear the Minister of Health hadn't been part of the original plot to kill the PM, but with the deal she had made on the recording, this fact was now inconsequential.

On her own initiative, Raymond had not held back in the least when discussing what Martel's death would mean for her and her political interests. The woman was a duplicitous jackal.

In the time that MacPhail had to wrestle with this information, she had prepared three different messages but wasn't sure which to send.

Had she not been concerned for her two reporter friends she would have already shipped out the first message she had designated for her contacts in the media. A reporter at heart, it was beyond a shadow of a doubt that this move was the right play. It would be an ugly and public thing, but from where she stood it was the medicine the country needed.

Her second prepped message would go to a handful of people she trusted in the Canadian security establishment and the military. For any number of reasons, this was her least favored move. Risk-averse organizations on the best of days, she had reservations that CSIS or the CAF would be able to counter Raymond's machinations. But unlike the media, if they did manage to do something, they might do it quietly and not fracture the country in the process.

In light of all that had transpired, her third message was without a doubt the riskiest. But as a cabinet minister who had sworn an oath of loyalty to the Crown, it was perhaps the message that carried the most weight with her.

She didn't know if Merielle Martel was dead. At precisely 0448 hours on this Saturday morning, the word, both official and unofficial, was that the woman was still missing.

In MacPhail's mind, Merielle was still the PM. She and Merielle were not close friends, but the other woman had earned her respect and, most importantly, she shared Martel's vision for the country. If she could somehow find out if Merielle was alive, MacPhail was leaning strongly in the direction of sending only this third email. Merielle was owed the chance to understand what was happening to the country *and* an opportunity to respond to it.

It was this debate of which message to send, layered over her concern for Douglas and Angie, that had consumed her for the past four hours.

Knock, knock, knock.

She jumped in her seat. At this time in the morning, even with the crisis in Montreal, the Centre Block of Parliament Hill was quiet. The Parliamentary Protective Service and the RCMP had the Hill on lockdown, so whoever had just firmly knocked on her door must have had a legitimate reason to be in the building.

She took a steadying breath, got up from her seat, and walked to the door. She opened it and, as she took in the pair standing in the hallway, her heart began to pound as though a bass speaker had been surgically implanted into her chest.

"Minister MacPhail. I'm so very pleased that we've found you."

Yvette Raymond half turned her body to the man standing beside her. "I believe you know Monsieur Trembly. He is a longstanding friend and political ally of mine."

MacPhail said nothing. Her mind was galloping like a wild horse trying to be in five different places at once.

Raymond's head tilted slightly as though the woman was some kind of raptor eyeing its next meal. When she next spoke, her voice was both clear and confident. "Minister, I have it on good authority that you have some information you shouldn't have."

Still recovering from the blow Raymond's unexpected presence delivered, MacPhail's reply hardly befitted the quick-on-her-feet journalist and seasoned politician she was. "I don't know what you're talking about, Yvette. I've been worried sick about developments in Montreal and have been scanning the news all morning. It's all the same. Whatever terrorists struck in Montreal have melted away, and there is still no sign of the prime minister. Tell me you have news about Merielle?"

"I'm surprised, Irene. Of all people and with everything that's at risk, I wouldn't have thought you would have resorted to such games. I know you have a recording of my recent conversation with Monsieur Trembly and another man. And if it isn't already obvious, I'm here to help you understand that conversation and to explain why it is in your interest to work with us to save this country. Would you allow us to come into your office, so we can have this conversation?"

For a long moment, MacPhail said nothing as she thought through her predicament. She was on Parliament Hill. Police were everywhere. She was safe. She could do this. She must do this. She would not let herself be intimidated by this woman.

Finally, she said, "It's not me who's playing games, Yvette. What you've done is treason. You're selling out this country and its allies. For what, I don't want to know."

For her next words, MacPhail straightened her shoulders making her best effort to emphasize the six or so inches she had on the woman standing in front of her. "The both of you can go to hell."

Though slight, Yvette Raymond's refined beauty and natural confidence gave her a presence that far outweighed her physical stature. The Quebec City Member of Parliament took a step forward, placing herself in MacPhail's personal space. The Newfoundlander, with her fire-red hair and height, did not give ground.

As Raymond's lake-blue eyes stared into MacPhail like a pair of daggers, a soft crying began to fill the empty hallway. As she looked around to identify the source of the sound, the still-silent Quebec billionaire raised his smartphone so that it hung in the air between the two women.

On its screen was the beaten face of Angie Jefferies. When the younger woman recognized MacPhail, she moaned urgently through the gag that covered her mouth and struggled against whatever bonds were holding her.

Finally, Trembly added his voice to the standoff. "I do not play games, Minister MacPhail. I have never played them. Now, if you would be so kind as to do as Madame Raymond has suggested, I have every confidence the three of us can come to an arrangement that allows us to reach an outcome that ends the madness that Robert MacDonald and now Merielle Martel have set upon this country."

MacPhail's eyes took up the corporate titan's face. On responding to his overture, she made no effort to hold back the bitterness now racing through her. "And what gives you the right, Monsieur Trembly, to say anything at this moment? Your money? We'll see how valuable your billions are when you're sitting in a cell in Kingston Pen, because that, sir, is where you're going when this game you're both playing ends."

The pudgy face of Canada's richest man examined MacPhail for an uncomfortably long moment. When he finally spoke, the man's voice was devoid of any emotion. "Let me be perfectly clear with you, Madame Minister. If you do not fully cooperate with Madame Raymond, it will not be just Ms. Jefferies who will be made to suffer."

Though soft in appearance, Trembly was no physical slouch. He had a broad chest and his exposed forearms and hands were thick and strong. He took a step closer to MacPhail.

"The people I associate myself with are supremely comfortable in making people other than the Jefferies suffer, Ms. MacPhail. Your father lives in a long-term care center in St. John's. Room 211 in the Glenbrook Lodge. Your only two nieces are both second- and fourth-year students at Dalhousie University.

"Dani, the youngest of the two lives in Fraser House, room 314. The oldest, Sienna, lives in a dilapidated two-bedroom apartment just off campus."

A disgusting smile split Trembly's face. "She's quite pretty. Sienna, that is. It would be a terrible, terrible shame if anything happened to her."

The billionaire lowered the smartphone with the Angie Jefferies' face and took another step toward MacPhail. Gently, he placed his free hand on one of MacPhail's forearms and applied pressure.

"Our time and patience are wearing thin, Madame Minister."

Not without force, he pushed her back into her office.

"Grant us ten minutes of your time, and I'm confident we can come to an arrangement that is satisfactory to us all."

As she took a step back, MacPhail allowed herself to quickly peek down both lengths of the hallway. They were still alone. But instead of fear flowing into her, a tide of anger that was common of the people of Newfoundland began to well up inside of her.

Taking one more step back, she planted her foot and ripped her arm from Trembly's grasp. With her own set of blue eyes ablaze, she stared down the Quebec billionaire. "Don't you dare touch me again, you son of a bitch, or else."

Trembly's jaw clenched, but he took no further action. MacPhail quickly positioned herself behind her desk and returned her gaze to Raymond. The woman's face was as unrevealing as ever.

MacPhail gestured to the door. "Close that if you would?"

Taking the seat behind her desk, she resolved that she needed more information. As Trembly moved to shut the heavy wooden entrance, she took her own seat and turned her still-furious gaze back on Raymond. "Ten minutes, Yvette. And not one bloody second more."

Montreal

On emptying the rest of her weapon's magazine at the men pursuing them and tagging the first that had come out of the stairwell, Hall had fled after the nurse and Merielle.

Finding them at the exit that would let them escape the hospital, Hall quickly dismissed the healthcare worker who had her arm around the prime minister. As Hall moved to take up supporting the politician, she thought it looked like some of the woman's health and wits had returned to her.

"Have you reached your people?" Merielle asked.

"No. But if they're still alive, they'll be looking for us."

"Let's hope so because I'm in no shape to go much further."

Before Hall could respond to the PM and offer words of encouragement, her ears registered the same screech she had heard only a minute before when she burst through the last set of doors before reconnecting with Merielle and the nurse. The door's lack of maintenance was either a warning to save them or a harbinger of doom. Whichever, their pursuers were still coming.

Hall stepped out from Merielle's arm, allowing the woman to stand on her own, and then offered her hand for support. As the PM firmly latched onto Hall's hand, the younger woman pulled in the direction of the exit. Pushing open the glass exit door, Hall drew a long breath of humid Montreal air into her lungs while listening to the wail of some far-off siren.

She quickly scanned the crescent driveway that served as the main drop-off point for this section of the hospital. Parked vehicles of all kinds were visible, but there was no sign of Petite or lie-in-wait assassins.

Looking right, she had an unobstructed view of Sherbrooke. The thoroughfare was absent from any moving cars. Immediately across the street was a good-sized urban park. Through the trees, she could see a pillar of smoke rising into the night air.

She took a step forward, but the prime minister grabbed her arm. "We can't go into the park. That's where they ambushed us. And we need a ride. I wasn't lying when I said I can't go much further."

The woman was right. They did need a ride. Hall looked left down Sherbrooke. A gaggle of trees and shrubs blocked her line of sight.

She had to choose a direction. 'Go left', her brain screamed at her. If Petite was alive, he would be coming from that direction.

Pulling the PM, she said, "Let's go."

Together, they jogged in the direction of the small stand of trees and vegetation. Above the sound of their movement and the ambient noise that was Montreal, Hall's ears were struck by the unmistakable sound of clip-clopping. A second later, as clear as a bell, she heard someone yell, "*YAH!*"

As they reached the far end of the small copse, Hall slowed down, and with weapon in hand, edged past the foliage to take in the growing sound of what was unmistakably a cavalcade of horses.

Taking in the scene, Hall felt her jaw drop. Thundering down the middle of what should have been one of the city's busiest streets was not one, but three, horse-drawn carriages.

Leading the first of the carriages was a spectacular white horse and a driver whose hair and mustache matched his steed. As it cantered forward, the street lighting reflected off the beast, giving it an ethereal quality.

Smile beaming, Hall turned back in the direction of the PM. The woman's eyes looked like they might pop out of her head.

Hall again grabbed the PM's hand and yelled, "C'mon! We're getting out of here."

"On that?" the politician said, pointing with her free hand in the direction of the fast-approaching carriage.

Hall ignored the question only to yank her charge forward. Pulling Merielle to the side of the avenue, for the first time, Hall's eyes made out that there was a person behind the driver, seemingly speaking into the white-haired man's ear.

As the carriage operator pulled back on the horse's reins, Petite rose behind the driver and locked his eyes onto Hall's. The smile on the CSIS officer's face was radiant.

As the carriage approached their position, Hall yelled at the top of her lungs, "Don't stop! They're right behind us."

Hearing the message, Petite only nodded his head, yelled something to the driver, and then leaned out of the carriage's door.

Arriving at their location, the thundering horse did not come out of its trot. The PM still in hand, Hall started to run to keep pace with the horse as it pounded past them.

Seeing Petite waiting for her, Hall pivoted and slingshot the PM forward and toward the carriage. Petite, a powerful man, grasped the forearms of the prime minister and hefted the woman upwards as though she were a toddler.

The carriage now past her, Hall lengthened her stride and moved to catch up with the vehicle. Only two years removed from her varsity cross-country career, she easily managed to catch up with the back end of the carriage where Petite was waiting for her, urging her on.

Accessing that final gear that all runners have when finishing a race, Hall leaned forward and stretched her hand toward Petite.

When their hands met, he bellowed, "Up you go!" With his one hand crushing hers and every ounce of brute strength the man possessed, Hall flew upwards.

Airborne for a fraction of a second, she managed to shift her body just enough that she didn't fully crash into the prime minister.

Striking the bench seat of the carriage hard, Hall rebounded and then crumpled to the floor of the seating area.

Despite being winded, Hall grabbed at the PM's leg and hauled herself up and in the direction of the driver.

"Fly, old man!" she hollered. "They're right behind us!"

CRACK! The driver immediately snapped the horse's reins and thundered another, "YAH!" into the night air.

As the horse shot forward, Hall was instantly thrown back into the forward-facing bench seat, slamming into Petite full-on. The man's effort to soften the collision failed miserably, so when their two bodies connected, it felt as though Hall had struck a block of granite.

As quickly as she had connected with the CSIS officer, he unceremoniously threw Hall to the carriage's floor. On slamming into the rubber and metal of the cab's floor, she managed to cast her eyes in the direction of the entrance she and the PM had fled from only a minute before.

As the doors swung open, and men with assault rifles came into view, zeroing their weapons in the direction of the carriage, the sound of suppressed gunshots filled Hall's ears.

Looking up and in the direction of the new noise, she took in Petite emptying the magazine of his handgun in the direction of their pursuers.

His weapon expended, Petite moved instinctively to load a new magazine, but before he resumed firing, he called in the direction of the driver. "As fast as you can, Tony!"

The old man cracked the horse's reins. As the momentum of the carriage again shifted Hall backward, she pushed herself up off the floor and slid into the seat facing the PM.

Erect, Hall's eyes again moved in the direction of the hospital entrance. It was now well behind them. Half a dozen men with weapons were there. Some were running after them while others had their weapons leveled and were taking aimed shots in their direction. She lowered her head instinctively as a single bullet tore through the air close by.

On emptying another magazine of bullets at their pursuers, Petite lowered his profile to crouch beside Hall. On glancing in her direction, she put her hand out to fist-bump the CSIS officer. "In the history of getaways, Sam Petite, that was beyond epic."

As the sound of incoming gunfire stopped, the intel man returned her smile but, just as quickly, Petite's shoulders slumped as a look of sadness washed over him. "We lost Janks and Sykes. Where's Kayed?"

Before Hall could offer a reply, the prime minister spoke up. "She's gone, too. She stayed back to delay those animals. She gave her life to save mine. Just as your people, Sykes and Janks did."

Despite her slouched position, Merielle Martel reached across the seated area and gingerly held out her hand to Petite. The CSIS officer's hand quickly took up the politician's. "It's good to finally meet you, Madame Prime Minister. My name's Sam Petite. I work for Colonel Azim."

"And you're the leader of the team that saved my life?" Merielle said.

As Petite released the woman's hand and sat back, he replied, "I am, Madame Prime Minister, though I haven't been much of a leader. Three of my five team members are dead, never mind the other things I've had to do in the past twenty-four hours."

As Petite's statement of despair registered with her, the stern look of an RCMP Inspector settled onto Merielle's face. "Officer Petite, if Azim brought you on board, it's because he knows you can get the job done. But that job isn't done yet. You're alive and some of your team isn't. This is the work your country has asked you to do."

The PM paused and allowed her face to soften, if only slightly. "Sykes, Janks, and Kayed need you to complete the mission, just as I need you to. There are some bad people that need to pay for what's been done today and that can only happen if you get me to where I need to be."

"And where's that?" asked Petite, making an effort to keep his voice neutral. "Our ride out of here was shot down, our comms are still being jammed, and as you can see, we are fleeing one or more teams of assassins in a horse-drawn carriage."

From nowhere, the driver called over his shoulder, "Just to be clear, this is an electrified horse-drawn carriage, and Zeus here can take you just about as far as you need to go." He quickly added, "As long as you pay me, mind you."

"To Ottawa?" Petite asked of the operator.

"Ah, no, he's a bloody horse," the driver said quickly. "I was thinking I'd drop you off somewhere in Mont-Royal. I know of a few secluded nooks where you might be able to hide until you figure out what to do."

Petite moved across the seating area so he was beside the PM. "Sorry, Tony. What I should have asked is, what's the range on the carriage without Zeus and how fast can it go?"

Still urging the horse forward, the old man turned his head slightly and gave Petite a sideways look. "It has a range of three hundred kilometers, or so I'm told. As for a top speed, I actually don't know. Why?"

Petite leaned forward and slapped the old man on the shoulder, and said, "Then we can make it to Ottawa?"

"My carriage is not leaving my sight Sam, and it's most certainly not going to Ottawa."

"How's two million?" Petite immediately called back to the old man.

"Three," the driver called back just as quickly.

"Then we have a deal, sir. As the prime minister is my witness."

As Petite turned away from the driver, his eyes met the PM's. The politician was nodding her head in approval. "Well played, Mr. Petite. Colonel Azim chose you well to put you in charge of this mission. Very well indeed."

Chapter 34

Somewhere over Maryland

Khan had decided to stay low as he tracked toward the grouping of fighters that was his prey. On the oversized data management console forming the center point of the Tempest's instrument panel, he could see the eight Rafaels of the French Air Force flying in a screening formation well ahead of their American allies.

He wouldn't have to worry about them. By the time they realized he had slipped behind them and engaged the Strike Eagles, they would need to turn their attention to a flight of Canadian F-35s that were blazing in their direction from a forward operating base in Quebec.

His flight of Tempests was officially out of the fight having finished tangling with the French 6th-gen fighters. In the end, the French had acquitted themselves satisfactorily. Along with Petal, Flight Lieutenant Jonathan "Rowdy" Stevens had also been shot down.

On their side of the ledger, his remaining lads had brought down four of the Mystères. A two-to-one kill ratio would have been something to celebrate had his country not lost two of its most exceptional service members, and the hugely valuable planes Petal and Rowdy had been flying. But this was war.

The loss of Petal cut particularly deep. Cheryl 'Petal' Robinson was only six months returned from maternity leave after having her first child. Not three days before shipping out to North America, Khan had held her little man in his arms in his office while his mum had run off on a quick errand somewhere on base. He recalled the experience had been something close to magic.

"Target is now in range," Glitch advised, her designated voice as fetching as ever.

The F-15s were flying eighty kilometers behind the French Rafaels and were themselves spread out in pairs. If it were not the case that he knew which plane carried the tactical nuke, the odds of him being able to find and take down the right fighter would have been the equivalent of having a terrible hand in poker.

As it was, he was sitting with a pair of pocket nines. In his experience, it was something he could work with, but like poker, most things came down to how your opponents responded to the data on the table.

The F-15s were south and west of D.C. The tactical nuke the fighter in question was carrying was GPS guided, which meant the pilot could release the weapon kilometers out from his target. That meant the time of waiting was nearly over.

"Glitch."

"Yes, Commander."

"You know what we have to do?"

"I do, Commander. At all costs, we need to neutralize the Red Faction fighter designated Bravo-Three."

"Indeed. At all costs. Do you know what that means?" Khan's voice was sober on posing the question.

"I do. Per your policy, I won't give you the odds of us surviving what is to come. I will only say they are poor. But what that means for me and you is quite different."

"Is it?" Khan said, arching one of his eyebrows.

"Yes, it is, sir. I know that if anything happens to me, a copy of myself remains intact and waits to be uploaded into the next pilot who would like to benefit from the near-AI that flew missions with 'living legend' and modern-day ace, Harry 'Pony' Khan."

"Whoa, ease up there, lass," Khan said as a smile flared onto his face. "I hope you're not talking about me like that with the other planes? It's poor form."

Ignoring the question, the near-AI said, "Two hundred and eleven days past, The Sunday Times said of Wing Commander Khan, and I quote: *The country has not known a fighter pilot of this man's skill and achievement since the terrible days of 1940. The man is, and this is based on many conversations with those who fought with Khan in the skies above the American Midwest, a living legend.*"

"Are you trying to ignore my question, Glitch?"

"Which question, sir? In the course of this conversation, you have asked two. Shall I repeat them back to you?"

"Are you being a smartass?"

"No, Commander, while I am most certainly smart, despite the voice you gifted to me, I have no ass that I am aware of." As the near-AI delivered its response, it was deadpan.

"You cheeky mare. You most certainly are being a smartass. The one about the afterlife. Do you ever think about it?"

"Commander, I was not programmed to consider my demise, nor in the evolution of my thinking has the question of my death confronted me. For me, it is fair to say that it is a non-issue."

After a long moment, Khan finally said, "If you survive what's about to happen, I want you to deliver a message to my wife. Can you do that for me?"

"I am pleased to report that the engineers who made me foresaw this eventuality. Should it come to pass that something catastrophic happens to me, in the nanoseconds before whatever disaster strikes, whatever message you might provide to me would be transmitted to any individuals you designate."

After a pause, the near-AI asked, "Is it the case that you have a message for Ms. Murphy-Khan, Commander?"

"I do." Khan was ready. Like all things in his life, when it was time to act, he did. "Tell her she was my one great love. Tell her that the last thing that crossed my mind before I did my duty was that I want her to be happy. And tell her that I believe we'll meet again and that when we do, our love can be rejoined if that is what she wants."

After a pause, the near-AI asked, "Is there anything else, sir?"

"No, Glitch. That is all."

His message primed, Khan punched up his plane's speed up to six hundred knots. The moment the Tempest broke the sound barrier, he pulled back on the fighter's flight stick shooting him into the overcast morning sky. In less than a minute, his speed and angle would put him at the center of the flight of F-15Es.

"Glitch, tag Bravo-One and Two, and send the Phantom their way. Set its mission for the broadest disruption possible. Then target Bravo-Five and Six with a Meteor each. Once this dance starts, we'll see what Bravo-Three and Four do, and then we'll make our move."

"Considering there are six of them and only one of you, this is a sound strategy."

Khan smiled and said, "Greatest fighter pilot since 1940, my dear, Glitch. The Sunday Times' words, not mine. Execute, now."

Ottawa, Parliament Hill

MacPhail had agreed to their terms. She had to. Trembly had shown her the bloodied body of Douglas Jefferies to drive home the point that he was perfectly capable of delivering on his threats toward her father and two nieces.

She would actively support Raymond's move to become prime minister. Once secured in that role, MacPhail would resign and accept the ambassadorship of France, where she would serve in a figurehead-like capacity and be closely monitored to ensure she was complying with their deal.

France, she thought. Amid the dictation of the treasonous pair's terms, it had become clear this country was behind the disaster in Montreal, and that it was France that would ensure she did what she agreed to.

Angie Jefferies, Douglas' daughter, would continue to be part of the leverage they would hold over her. Jefferies would be taken from Canada and held until such a time, Trembly was satisfied MacPhail could be trusted to continue to play the charade she had agreed to.

So it was that in two hours she would be standing immediately behind Yvette Raymond as she took to a microphone in Confederation Hall of the Centre Block of Parliament Hill and announced the Conservative Party had appointed her as interim prime minister. Two weeks past that announcement, MacPhail would resign and would be in Paris.

While it was still relatively quiet on the Hill, the Health Minister and the billionaire had walked MacPhail to Raymond's office. On reaching the woman's lair, Trembly had taken her phone and handed her off to Raymond's Chief of Staff, Eloise St. Martin. The two traitors then left the office to undertake some other unsaid part of their plan.

Among the close-knit family that was the political party's senior staffers, Eloise St. Martin was known to be a cold fish but also a sharp operator.

On the first occasion MacPhail had tried to engage the woman in a conversation, the staffer's no-nonsense reputation had revealed itself instantly. "Do not talk to me, Madame Minister. Only sit where you are or I will send word to Monsieur Trembly. He is a most serious man."

That fruitless exchange had been forty minutes ago.

"I have to go to the washroom, and I need a coffee," MacPhail said, her voice insistent.

St. Martin's eyes lifted from her screen, and she delivered a hard stare in MacPhail's direction.

"What, will you see me pee myself? MacPhail said with faux indignation. "Won't it be just a tad bizarre with me standing behind your boss on national television with piss-drenched pants? And if you don't put a coffee in me soon, I may not make it to the announcement at all. I'm bloody exhausted."

The woman's eyes narrowed briefly as she tried to see through whatever game her charge might be playing.

"I really need to take a pee, Eloise. Like now."

Without saying a word, the staffer pushed back her seat and stood. "I'll have coffee brought in. We'll go to the washroom, but you're not to speak with anyone. Do you understand?"

MacPhail gave the woman an annoyed look. "Listen, it's nearly eight AM. With all that's going on, it'll be busy out there. I'm a Newfoundlander and a reporter of two decades. I like to talk. If you make me walk around this place playing at something I'm not, it'll raise more than a few eyebrows. I know what the stakes are, so my best suggestion to you is to let me handle the situation as best as I see fit."

After taking a moment to think on MacPhail's words, Raymond's Chief of Staff said, "Fine. But you said it yourself. If you do anything stupid, Minister Raymond and Monsieur Trembly will be apprised, and you'll only have yourself to blame for what comes next. Do we have an understanding?"

MacPhail didn't hesitate with her reply. "A perfect understanding. Now let's get going before I have an accident. Christ all mighty, I can all but taste the piss in my mouth."

The Quebecer's mouth thinned at the salty language, but quicker than MacPhail might have hoped for, she started making her way to the door.

In the long hallway that contained Raymond's office, a few political staffers she recognized were hurrying along the corridor. As they moved in the direction of the washrooms, she received more than a few head nods and a pair of "good mornings," but to her relief, no one engaged with them.

In truth, she had not needed to go to the washroom. At least not badly. The three emails she had in drafts on her personal email account remained on her machine ready to be sent. In the time she'd had to contemplate her situation, she had made her decision about which email was to be sent if she could somehow find a way.

The evidence that had been playing out in her mind since the assassination attempt on the PM suggested the woman was not dead. If she was, the media would have wind of it by now. Every reporter in the country would be shaking down every source they had to nail down Merielle's status. The fact that nothing solid had come forward suggested the woman was still in the game.

And then there was the conversation with the villains, Raymond and Trembly. The audacity and speed of what they were proposing suggested they, too, were uncertain about the whereabouts of Merielle Martel. If the PM had been killed, Raymond would have the luxury of time to play out her machinations like the calculating spider the woman was.

Which brought her back to her draft email. It had to be sent, but to send it, she had to gain access to someone who would be able to help but who wouldn't raise the suspicion of the woman walking beside her.

So far, the Conservative Party staffers they had crossed paths with had been minor players in the complex political hierarchy that was Parliament Hill. To engage one of them as they walked the long hallway would have been all but useless.

So, when the door to the washroom opened and she nearly collided with a heavily pregnant Katie Goldberg, a close friend to her own Chief of Staff, MacPhail had to make a special effort not to squeal in delight.

She immediately embraced the woman and gave her a big hug.

As she pulled back, her hands dropped to the woman's upper arms where she drove both thumbs into the woman's flesh.

Goldberg flinched slightly, but before she could say anything or begin to pull away, MacPhail's hands dropped and gently took up both of the woman's hands.

"Katie, you're glowing. A more beautiful pregnant woman, I haven't seen in a very long time. How many more weeks?"

Goldberg, a senior policy advisor for the Minister of Agriculture and in line for her own Chief of Staff position, began to look downward at her now-smarting biceps, but as she did so, MacPhail pumped the woman's hands hard, forcing the staffer to look at her.

Goldberg's eyes narrowed slightly as her eyes connected with MacPhail's, but after a not-too-long pause, she responded to the woman's question. "Less than a month."

"And it's a boy if I remember correctly?"

"It is. And a big one."

"A blessing! Listen, Katie, I'm about to burst, but I'm wondering if you might be able to help me out?"

"Of course, Minister. Helping is what I do."

"Goodness, am I ever glad we ran into each other. Here's the thing, with all that's going on, I've misplaced my phone and I've been in meetings all night, so I haven't had the chance to look for it yet."

"Oh dear," Goldberg said. "Does Sandy know? Would you like me to help her track it down? My day hasn't started as yet, so if you need a couple of extra eyes to search around, I'd be happy to help."

MacPhail continued to beam a smile in the other woman's direction. "That's kind of you, my dear, but what I need is for you to get a message to Sandy. I sent Sandy home near midnight last night, and she's due back at any moment. After this bio-break, it's back to meetings for me, so I won't be able to stop by my office and fill her in."

"I can touch base with Sandy if you'd like," offered the pregnant woman.

Still holding the other woman's hands, MacPhail pumped gently and said, "That would be so very helpful, my dear."

"Not a problem. I haven't talked to her in a few days anyway, so I'll pop in to see her. Is there anything else you want to pass along? If I know Sandy, she'll ask about this meeting you're going to and where she can find you."

"Ah, no doubt she will. Extraordinary times call for extraordinary meetings, my dear Katie. The meeting is for Ministers only. She'll understand. But there is another message you could pass along for me."

The voice of Raymond's Chief of Staff interjected with its usual coolness. "Madame Minister, the meeting is starting momentarily. We need to hurry."

For the second time in less than a minute, MacPhail drove her thumbs into Katie Goldberg's flesh, but this time the woman gave no indication of the pain she must be feeling. With her nails driving into hands, MacPhail blinked three times.

The blinking she knew from her days as a reporter. If an abused woman had an unexpected visit from the police and her abuser was in the house or she was in some other danger, the woman would slowly blink three times informing the police she was at risk and wanted their help.

Goldberg certainly would have felt the pain in the palms of her hands and most certainly saw the blinking, but as she stood there, the younger woman gave zero indication of MacPhail's bizarre behavior. It was now or never, she thought.

"Just one more thing, Katie."

"Whatever you need, Minister."

"This is going to seem crazy, but, when you see Sandy, could you tell her there's an email on my machine that's ready to go to Ms.

Chrysler? She's a constituent and I promised her I'd get back to her by no later than today. She's the former mayor of Conception Bay South and a shrew with time on her hands. If I don't get back to her, the woman will go to the media, and with all that's going on, the last thing I need are reporters making something out of nothing."

Ms. Chrysler was the key. When her Chief of Staff heard that fictitious name, she would know something was up. It was a private signal they had worked out years before. Along with the message she had just given to Goldberg, MacPhail prayed she had given Sandy McNabb what she needed to start rooting around in her email box. She was a bright and loyal woman but, perhaps more importantly, she was a voracious reader of mysteries.

On releasing Goldberg's hands and stepping back from the woman, MacPhail hoped her Chief of Staff was up for the whopper of a clue she had just delivered.

"Thanks, Katie. I'm so very glad we ran into each other this morning."

With that, MacPhail stepped around Goldberg's glorious, protruding belly and entered the washroom.

Sandy McNabb scrunched her lips as she carefully listened to Katie's words.

"I'm telling you, Sands, it was all a bit weird if you ask me. Her nail pressed so hard into my skin I half expected it would be bleeding. And then the eye blinking. I'm not sure what it was about, but I can tell you it wasn't normal."

"And Eloise was there?"

"Standing right behind her. Per the norm, the woman said barely a word."

"Alright. Thanks, Katie. I guess I better track down this email she's so concerned about. Geez Louise, you'd think with all that's going on, Ms. Chrysler would lend us a day of grace, but Irene knows that woman well. She is indeed a bloody shrew."

Standing in front of McNabb's desk, Goldberg suddenly rolled her eyes and said, "I gotta go pee again, Sandy. I'm not sure what any of this is about, but if you need me, just shoot me a text and I'll drop everything."

"You're terrific," McNabb said to her friend, quickly adding, "but, I'm sure it's nothing."

Goldberg raised one of her eyebrows and eventually said, "Okay, if you say so. Just text if you need me."

"I will. Thanks, K!"

As the pregnant staffer turned and walked out the office door, McNabb counted off five long seconds and then shot from her chair into the adjoining office that was Irene's.

Passwords entered, she immediately navigated into her boss's official Member of Parliament account, found the draft folder, and reviewed what was there. There was nothing of interest.

She then jumped onto the encrypted email service Irene used for private affairs. Once again, she pounded the keyboard to get into the account and went straight for the draft emails. Immediately, she flagged the top three identically titled messages: URGENT MESSAGE from Irene MacPhail: OPEN NOW.

As McNabb reviewed the first of the emails, a mix of terror and fury began to percolate within her. This was bad. It was bad for the party but it was worse for the country. Much worse.

As she finished the third correspondence, she recalled the message Goldberg had relayed to her not ten minutes ago.

The use of Ms. Chrysler meant her boss was in some kind of trouble. She now knew what that danger was. And without a doubt, that part of her boss's message that spoke to Ms. Chrysler going to the media and Irene not wanting their involvement, most certainly meant the draft email for the various news outlets was not to be sent.

Which left the other two messages.

The second draft email featured seven different names from three different agencies. Public Safety which, to those in the know, meant CSIS. There was a lone RCMP email. And there were three addresses belonging to personnel from the CAF.

The third email was addressed to a single person who went by MerMar87. This without a doubt was the PM's personal address. On thinking of Merielle Martel, she quickly checked the news. It was 0832 hours and there was nothing new being reported about the Prime Minister.

Her eyes went back to the second email. She only recognized one of the names. Stephane Martel, the PM's National Security Advisor and ex-husband, was somebody McNabb knew professionally. More important, she understood that Martel herself trusted the man implicitly. That was enough for her.

Taking a deep breath, she pressed send on the message that would go to the PM's personal account and the one that would go to the PM's ex.

She leaned back in her boss's chair and let out a breath she was still holding. With everything happening in Washington, Montreal and now here in Ottawa, it felt as though she had just walked into a hurricane of psychic energy, and she felt herself begin to panic.

McNabb's mind flashed to Katie and a few other colleagues she was close to. They were all in danger. Perhaps she should tell them to get off the Hill for the rest of the day.

But just as quickly as the alarmed thought had entered her mind, she dismissed it. Were she and the staffers connected to her to leave all of a sudden, Eloise St. Martin might connect the dots. The woman might be as cold as a witch, but she was no fool. On the contrary, she was as sharp as a tack and as ruthless as any political operator McNabb had encountered in her own long political career.

No. She would stay and would hope and pray that Irene MacPhail knew what the hell she was doing.

Chapter 35

Washington, D.C.

Since the Red Faction had pulled back nearly fifteen minutes ago, his Regiment's departure from the D.C. Armory had been uneventful.

Here and there, militiamen continued to harass them. Most likely the communication that a tactical nuclear weapon was on its way hadn't been passed along to their commanders.

CANZUK electronic warfare units carefully monitored the militia's rudimentary comms systems, so had they been told about the pending strike, somebody within the ragtag force would have mentioned it.

"Warrant Officer Bear," Larocque called out. "Where is that medivac?"

Bear, who hadn't been more than ten feet away from Morgan's litter since they started moving, pointed to the east. "They're five minutes out, sir. They must be flying real low, 'cause I can't see 'em. Apparently, it took longer than it should have for them to decide to make the trip."

Bear did not have to explain the reason why the medivac might have been delayed. Based on Larocque's calculation, the chances the two helicopters would be caught in the hell storm to come were high.

Regardless of the reasons for the delay, Larocque once again found himself issuing a quick prayer inside his head. "God, if my boys and I were going to sacrifice ourselves, let this politician make it out alive."

While he had tasked Bear with overseeing the evac of Morgan, he had taken on the task of managing the movement of his dead and wounded soldiers. He looked to where forty-three covered bodies were laid out in the morning shade being provided by the Washington Islamic Center.

Not far away from them was a similar number of wounded who could not fight. Major Kiraly was among them, along with a handful of the Airborne's medics. The doctor, assisted by one of his nurses, was working feverishly to save one man.

Larocque bit down on his lip hard to stave off the emotion welling up inside him. The notion that these brave men, his boys, were going to be cheated from surviving this most recent shitshow was almost too much to bear.

He tore his eyes away from the bloodied surgeon and the wounded and dead men who surrounded him, and bit down so hard on his lip he tasted blood.

The pain felt good and was what was needed to put him in the right frame of mind.

Whether they knew it or not, in their final minutes, his men would see their CO faithfully and proudly pushing them forward. For however much time they had, it was beyond imperative that every man and woman in the Canadian Airborne Regiment knew he was proud of them and that they had won the day's battle.

Fortified, Larocque began to stride in the direction of his wounded soldiers. As he did so, he caught a streak of gray flash overhead. As his eyes darted upwards to take in what he thought was the tail end of a Royal Air Force Tempest, the roar of the machine's engines washed over him.

He nodded his head to acknowledge what the passage of the top-of-the-food-chain fighter meant. He and his boys now had a chance. That it was just one fighter meant it was a small one, but a chance nonetheless.

As the echo of the Tempest's engines faded away, they were replaced by the deep thrumming of approaching helicopters. He pivoted to the east and saw the two ancient Black Hawks the Blue Faction had sent to pick up their president.

Larocque rounded on the surgeon and bellowed, "Major Kiraly, finish what you are doing and get ready to leave! Your patient's ride is imminent, sir, and you and the designated others will be leaving with him!"

The surgeon waved a bloody hand in the air signaling he had received the message. As much as Kiraly was an exceptional doctor, he was also an excellent soldier in that he followed orders. When the medivac left, the surgeon would be flying out of here because his CO had ordered him to.

"Open channel, Lion Team Zulu."

"Unit-wide channel open," advised his BAM.

"Airborne, this is Lion Actual. I've just received word enemy fighters are inbound, so we need to skedaddle and fast. Designated stretcher bearers get on the wounded now. The Pathfinders will lead us across the Whitney Young Memorial Bridge, A Commando will go next with the wounded. B Commando is next. C Commando and yours truly will pull up the rear."

Larocque shifted his eyes to the approaching helicopters as they began to slow themselves down to make their approach.

"Everyone listen up. The moment those helos lift off the ground, everyone moves with purpose and quickly. We need to move fast, people. Damn fast. Make sure we do. Lion Actual out."

As the first of the two Black Hawks touched down, Kiraly's two nurses hoisted up Morgan's stretcher and moved. Larocque watched the process intently as the primary objective for their mission was passed off to the medics waiting inside the helicopter. As the nurses turned away from the choppers to begin to help more of the wounded get aboard, he was filled with relief and satisfaction. They had done it.

Three minutes later, when the last of his own wounded were jammed into the medivacs and the two Black Hawks began lifting into the air, he looked around. Everywhere his eyes touched, his soldiers – professional and determined – were doing what he'd asked them to do. They were moving as though the devil himself was about to appear. That it was unlikely to be fast enough didn't matter to Larocque. What did matter is that his boys and those few women that were of the Canadian Airborne Regiment were striding forward and winning until that moment they weren't.

West of Montreal

It had taken another hour, but the Montreal Police with the help of the Quebec provincial police, the Sûreté du Québec, had locked down the city. The teams of assassins had exfiltrated Montreal. As a testament to their planning and abilities, not a single combatant, dead or alive, had been left behind.

On speaking with Azim, Merielle's direction had been crystal clear. No one in the political establishment could know she was alive. Not after reading the message Irene MacPhail had sent to her private email. Though it would mean uncertainty and angst across the country, she needed to keep her newly identified enemies unbalanced.

With little doubt, Yvette Raymond and the billionaire Trembly would have been advised she escaped the hospital wounded, but alive. Now, the question Merielle needed an answer to was whether or not they would back away from their coup. She was far from certain they would.

It was now clear to her that Raymond did not care one smidge for the political family to which she belonged. She was after power, and if she couldn't have it, Merielle had little doubt the corporatist from Quebec City would look to incinerate everything she and her predecessor, Bob MacDonald, had built in the past six years.

Too often, that's what desperate and bitter people did, whether it was in the process of ending a marriage or losing control of an organization you believed owed you something.

For better or worse, the Conservative Party of Canada belonged to Merielle Martel. She had won the right to lead it, so it would be a cold day in hell before she allowed it and her country to be destroyed by someone who was in the pocket of a reclusive billionaire and fascist France.

If the Party and the country were going to survive this test, it would only be if she managed to right the situation quietly. On this point, she had agreed with MacPhail's message entirely. The only question was how?

From across the room, she heard Hall say, "She's here." The talented fixer then passed Merielle her phone.

Taking the cell, she activated its speaker function. "Martel speaking. Officers Petite and Hall are with me."

"Madame Prime Minister, as directed, I'm here with Inspector Martel. We've made the arrangements you've asked for."

Merielle smiled when she heard her ex-husband's name. Despite where their relationship had gone, he'd always been there for her.

"Risking your career again, eh, Stephane?"

"Good to hear your voice, Madame Prime Minister. As you can imagine, the past twelve hours or so have been upsetting, and that's putting it mildly. But to answer your question and as you well know, I'm on leave from the RCMP, so you'll only be ruining my nascent political career, such that it ever was."

"All the same, Inspector, it's great to hear your voice. I'm glad you're on board," Merielle said.

"Me too, Mer. Colonel Azim and I think we have things worked out here in Ottawa, but we're going to have to move quickly, and there are risks, Merielle. Big ones."

"How can they not be big? The world has gone mad and we have to do our best to deal with it. Colonel, what's the plan?"

When Azim spoke, he sounded as calm as ever. "The Inspector is right, Madame Prime Minister. We need to move quickly. Raymond has announced she's to make a statement to the press at 1030 hours. That doesn't give us a lot of time to get you back to Ottawa."

Merielle cut the officer off. "Colonel, I have access to the news just like you do. You can assume I have the latest politically. If we need to move quickly, I'm prepared to do so. What's the plan?"

"Three helicopters are on their way to your location. One of the flights will take you to Ottawa, Madame Prime Minister. Once there, you'll connect with Inspector Martel."

"And everything is set as I asked for?" Merielle asked, interrupting the special forces officer.

It was her ex-husband who replied, "I'm still working out a few minor details, Mer, but by the time you get here, we'll be ready."

"Keep things as quiet as you can, Stephane."

"That won't be a problem. I've back-channeled to get the right people lined up. They'll be dark until I give the word."

"Good," Merielle said, her voice confident. "Colonel, you mentioned a second and third helicopter. What's the plan for those other flights?"

"They are for Petite and Hall. They'll be attending other locations."

Merielle's eyes shifted to the two operatives. "What locations and for what purpose, Colonel?"

"Madame Prime Minister, for the record, should I be asked if you were aware of how my people were tasked, I will advise the inquiry you did not ask the question you just asked. In fact, we did not have this conversation."

"Understood, Colonel. The less I know about the part of the game you're about to play, the better."

Somewhere Above Virginia

"Bravo-Six has been destroyed. Congratulations, Commader, you now have seven kills to your record," Glitch announced unemotionally into Khan's helmet.

He grunted as he maneuvered his fighter into a vertical ascent and then finally offered weakly, "Good to know."

Despite the g-forces pressing onto his body, Khan managed to keep his eyes clear and zeroed in on his main tactical display. Glitch had helpfully animated the two missiles chasing him as though an airborne third party was observing the high-speed spectacle. With each passing second, he could see the distance between his fighter and the missiles decrease.

The moment his batch of missiles had left the underside bay of his fighter, the Red Faction F-15Es had been able to narrow the focus of their radars and had tagged him. Seconds later, they had unleashed their own salvo of missiles in his direction.

The Japanese Phantom he had launched had fried the four older model AIM-120s sent his way but one of the Strike Eagles had been carrying a pair of Lockheed Martin's AIM-260 Joint Advanced Tactical Missiles.

Long range, fast, and hardened to withstand exactly the types of EW attack the Phantom delivered, they represented the most capable missile in the Red's dwindling inventory of high-end munitions.

"Glitch, where's Bravo-Three?"

"Bravo-Three is thirty-one kilometers from the anticipated target. He is at fifteen thousand feet cruising at four hundred knots. Anticipated release of the weapon in three minutes."

Though straining to breathe, Khan unleashed a string of curses. He was running out of time.

The perimeter of the main tactical display started to throb bright red. The 260s were close.

"Commander, I recommend release of the Banshee," Glitch offered calmly.

Khan didn't offer a reply.

"Commander? The Banshee –"

"Now, Glitch. Release it now!"

"Banshee released," the near-AI co-pilot announced.

He did not feel the sleek, nine-foot-long drone eject from the underside of his fighter. Instead, he prayed the experimental countermeasure would work as advertised.

The Banshee, a top-secret project that had been the culmination of a five-year partnership involving a collection of UK and Swedish companies had not been ready for the Tempest's first combat action in the skies above Missouri a year ago. Had the product been in service, perhaps some or all of his mates would not have been shot down by the Chinese J-31s.

The loss of those pilots and the preposterously expensive fighter jets they had been flying had forced the RAF to bring the countermeasure unit into service despite its quirky performance.

In the 2010s, chaff had become all but useless because modern missiles had gained the ability to instantly differentiate between a moving target and a rapidly decelerating cloud of aluminum. The Russian Air Force had learned about this technical shortcoming in spades in the skies over Ukraine.

On paper, the fully autonomous Banshee should have been a game changer. When employed and when it worked, the drone had three different tricks up its sleeve.

First, at six hundred meters behind the Tempest, the countermeasure would match the speed of its paired fighter and juke violently in an effort to convince the incoming missile to shift its targeting.

As it danced in the path of the approaching missiles, the Banshee would also reveal itself as the world's most costly glitter bomb. Using its own onboard near-AI, the drone would issue streams and bursts of chaff-like materials to stymie any older-model missiles. A bevy of flares were also on the menu if needed.

Finally, if the juking, glitter, and exploding incendiaries didn't put off whatever weapon was hunting the Tempest, the Banshee would immolate itself into a colossal sphere of energy, damaging or destroying the missile about to ride up its mothership's back end.

It all sounded terrific until it had been discovered the software responsible for managing the nano-second precise decisions of the drone had been corrupted by what was suspected to be Chinese industrial espionage. As recently as this morning, Khan had been assured the weapon had been cleansed of the highly elusive self-replicating Chinese code.

Still in a climb, a burst of bright light invaded Khan's canopy.

"Incoming missiles destroyed. I'm pleased to report the Banshee performed as per its intended design," Glitch announced.

Khan didn't acknowledge the update. Instead, he released his plane out of its climb and proceeded to vector in the direction of his target.

"Distance to Bravo-Three?" Khan asked.

"Twelve kilometers."

"Acquire Bravo-Three and launch missiles," Khan said urgently.

"Target acquired. Remaining two Meteors launching now. Fox-3's away."

At this range, the F-15 that was their target was well within the no-escape range of the two missiles he had just unleashed.

"Time to target, Glitch?"

"Forty-one seconds."

The warning lights on Khan's flight panel began to throb bright red again.

"Two incoming AIM-120s, courtesy of Bravo-Five," the near-AI advised.

"Courtesy, my dear Glitch. That's a fine way to put it."

Before the near-AI could reply, Khan put the Tempest into a steep dive.

"Let's see if we can outrun them, shall we? I'm gonna put us on the deck and when we get there, take over. Get us as close to the ground as you can. Maybe at speed and being so low, we'll lose them over D.C."

"Commander?"

"I'm kinda busy at the moment, Glitch. Gravity to us meat robots can be a real bitch."

"Boss, Bravo-Three has dropped its weapon. It was released at fifteen thousand feet. At terminal velocity, it will strike its target in 44.25 seconds. If you were to release control to me now, I am 92.33 percent certain we can intercept the weapon before it hits the ground."

"Clarify 'intercept,'" Khan said.

"We have no weapons that can target a falling bomb, Commander. By 'intercept,' I mean, we would connect with it."

"If I eject, would you still be able to hit it?"

The near-AI paused for a moment, no doubt to re-run the numbers.

"If you eject, my new aerodynamics will make the task more difficult by several factors."

"Give me the bloody number!" Khan barked at the near-AI.

"There is a 16.33 percent chance I will strike the weapon."

"Then we do this together."

The near-AI gave no reply.

"Glitch, did you hear me?"

"There is no mathematical possibility you'll survive should we connect with the weapon. You will die, sir, and you will make your wife a widow."

Khan's reply was instantaneous, "We're out of time. Glitch, I order you to take out that weapon. Now!"

He released the navigation controls that allowed him to maneuver the fighter and felt the plane adjust its flight and increase its speed. Glancing down at the tactical display, he could see airspeed data race upward. As it did, more pressure layered onto his body.

As they leveled out at four hundred feet, Khan gazed forward at the hazy skyline of Washington, D.C. Smoke continued to emanate from the nuclear wounds the Reds had inflicted the day before. He closed his eyes.

"Glitch."

"Yes, Commander."

"Further to the message for Ms. Murphy-Khan, a message to my parents and sister, if you would."

"It will be passed along."

"Tell them I love them dearly. Tell them, Allah was with me when I died. Tell them for King and country. End message."

"The message has been sent, Commander. They will hear your voice one last time."

His bases covered, Khan opened his eyes and glanced to his left. The outskirts of the most southern suburbs of D.C. were a blur. In the time he still had, he did something he had not done in a very long time. He began to pray.

Chapter 36

Undisclosed Location, North Carolina

Parr had silently watched the two helicopters pull away from the RFK Urban Campus. On one of the two helicopters rode Andrew Morgan. A camera on one of the surveillance drones had been able to zero in on the man's face as he was being loaded up.

As the medivac choppers left the camera view of the on-station drone, the voice of the pilot flying the F-15 Strike Eagle carrying the two-kiloton tactical nuke that was to end the life of the Blue Faction President was talking through the final seconds of his approach.

"Bandit Alpha has launched two missiles," the pilot announced calmly through the link. After a brief pause, he continued, "The math is good. They won't be in time. I'm staying with the mission."

With a growing understanding that Morgan would survive what was to come, Parr and every other set of eyes in the operations room landed on Spector. The oversized Texan stood tall at the center of the room, his hands on his hips. Oblivious to the stares saturating him, his own eyes continued to stare at the display the two helicopters had just left.

Spector would not be happy that Morgan had escaped his end. The Blue Faction President's survival meant the war would grind for at least a few months more. But as well as anyone in the converted operations space, Parr understood it was the soldiers moving to and fro on the display that represented Spector's true bane.

"Mr. President, do we call off the strike?" It was the Air Force General, Hoffman. Understandably, the man's voice had an urgency to it.

When Spector did not offer a reply, nor look in the officer's direction, the general tried again.

"Mr. President, I feel compelled to remind you that if we hit those soldiers, the Prime Minister of Great Britain is on record as recently as this morning stating her country would have no choice but to respond in kind should we use nuclear weapons."

In a display of what had to be righteous discipline, Spector said and did nothing. As the silence in the room seemed to press physically into the walls of the crowded space, a smile slowly crept onto Parr's face.

In the past year, he had worked with Mitchell Spector more than anyone. He knew both how much the man standing alone at the center of the room wanted to win the war and how dark Spector's heart truly was. He did not need the President's reply to Hoffman to know how the next few minutes would unfold. With this realization, Parr's grin of approval and anticipation beamed outward like the true believer he had become.

When Spector finally rounded on Hoffman and gave his reply, his words were deliberate and calmly delivered. "The strike proceeds, General. I don't give one pinch of horseshit what the Prime Minister of Great Britain has to say. We have Washington and in two months, we'll be along the 49th parallel from Maine to Minnesota. By then we'll have the weapons we need to glass London if it comes to that."

Spector pointed to one of the displays. A collection of soldiers had formed a loose diamond formation, with perhaps a dozen men at its center. As one, they were moving toward the Anacostia River.

"Those paratroopers and the colonel who leads them are outstanding soldiers. But they are the exception, General. Canada, as a country, is soft. Over the past seventy years, the United States has fought war after war, and become as hard as any country in the history of man."

Spector's gaze released from the display and found Hoffman. "While we've sacrificed and bled, do you know what our neighbors to the north have done, General?"

When Hoffman gave no reply, Spector continued, "While we have fought and kept our homeland safe from terrorists, the Russians, and the Chinese, our pleasant and compliant neighbors have become fucking Pablum. With all the milk and honey they've poured into the veins of their citizens, there has never been a democracy riper for the fall."

Spector took a step in the direction of the general and when he next spoke the calmness of his voice was spoiled with an edge of menace. "Canada doesn't have the stomach for what is coming, General Hoffman. And the UK, a once proud and strong country, is no different. The world and history are closing the book on the values this pathetic alliance claims to hold dear.

"Further, we both know the United Kingdom does not have any tactical nuclear weapons, and we also know that in the months it would take them to develop such weapons, the circumstances of their ally's demise will become all too clear. Great Britain will not respond in kind because their prime minister will know a lost cause when she sees it."

"Weapon away," the voice of the F-15E pilot invaded the ops room.

Ignoring the monumental update, Spector turned away from Hoffman and again took up the display. Someone had pulled back the drone's lens so that it was capturing the entirety of the D.C. Armory and its surrounding neighborhoods.

When Spector next spoke, his voice carried to all corners of the room while his eyes remained fixed on the screen. "Ladies and gentlemen. The gates of hell have been opened for us and until I tell you otherwise, we continue to fight this war like our lives depend on it. Because they do. When we dropped the first weapon yesterday, me, you, all of us – we burned our ships on the beach. There is no heading back.

"We are going to win this war, and then we're going to show our former friends to the north, the British and the other pissant countries in that pathetic little alliance, just how bad a call it was to mess with the United Constitutional States of America."

Ottawa

As the convoy of unmarked RCMP vehicles raced north on Uplands away from the Ottawa International Airport, Merielle's hand again moved to feel the bulk of the pistol on her hip.

She had insisted on the weapon. She had no idea how things would play out when she got to the Hill. As her helicopter arrived in Ottawa, Stephane had sent a text advising that Raymond had called a mandatory meeting of Cabinet at 0930 hours but added he had no intel on what the Quebec City MP would be saying.

What the woman would be discussing wouldn't matter, Merielle thought. One way or the other, the dance her political rival thought she was leading was coming to an end.

On offloading at the airport, a fit, but geeky-looking, soldier had given Merielle a BAM unit and provided her with a quick tutorial on how the system worked. Staring out the window of her racing SUV, a male voice came alive in her left ear. "Incoming call from Bronco Delta."

"Accept call," Merielle said, as she was instructed.

"Outrider, all stands ready. As soon as you give the word, everything you asked for is a go."

"Excellent work, Colonel Azim. And our plans for Monsieur Trembly?"

"We have eyes on him. He left the Hill about ten minutes ago. He's in a convoy of three vehicles, heading north. It looks like he's returning to his chateau in the Gatineaus. I have an assault team in the air moving in their direction. We need to take them on the road. Once taken, Petite's team will have a free hand to move onto the compound to collect the Jefferies woman."

"So your people will be able to shut down his comms when they move on him?"

"Not a problem, Outrider. The people back at the chateau will have no idea."

"It's a good plan if you can pull it off, Colonel."

"My people are the best, Madame Prime Minister. We will pull it off. You can count on that."

"Your confidence is appreciated, Colonel. Still, good luck to us all. Outrider out."

North of Ottawa, Quebec

From one of the rear passenger seats of the SUV, Marc-Antoine Trembly saw the hand of the head of his security team jerk upwards to his earbud. After tapping it several times, the Frenchman suddenly ripped the unit out of his ear and turned to face him.

"Check your phone."

Immediately, Trembly grabbed his smartphone.

"It's off," he said. "I didn't shut it down. What the hell is going on?"

"Quiet," the security man said firmly.

As the windows of the vehicle started to lower, Trembly strained to hear the distinct sound of helicopter rotor blades cutting through the morning air.

"Someone is coming," said the security man.

"They wouldn't dare." As Trembly delivered his response, the lead vehicle of their convoy came out of one of the many tight curves of the two-lane highway that carved through this craggy part of Quebec and slammed on its brakes, throwing Trembly forward.

An army-green helicopter, its blades whirling, was in the middle of the road. In front of it, a dozen or so masked men with weapons of various kinds were moving forward at a run.

With the passenger-side window all the way down, Trembly's head of security forced the upper half of his body through the opening and bellowed, "Reverse, reverse! Head to Point Alpha! To Point Alpha!"

As the tires of all three of the motorcade's SUVs began to screech, trying to get purchase on the road, Trembly's head swiveled in the direction he hoped would take him to safety.

There, he found a second helicopter in the process of landing. The moment the machine's wheels touched down, another team of soldiers extricated themselves and began to advance toward the now fully turned-around SUVs.

To their right was a steep rockface. To their left, they were hemmed in by a barrier purpose-designed to prevent vehicles from falling down a steep, forested decline. Trembly, whose only experience in warfighting was thousands of hours played on Call of Duty as a younger man, had enough understanding of small-team tactics to appreciate how well the Canadians' takedown had just gone.

"So, Martel survived," Trembly said quietly to himself.

"Sir, we can fight our way out. Just say the word." On laying out the option of escape his security lead's voice rang with a confidence that Trembly himself did not feel.

The soldiers were closer now. At least half of them had surrounded his vehicle.

"No. Stand down," he said, making a concerted effort to calm his voice. "That's what she would want. She would love nothing more than for me to die on this highway. No. This war has just started, my friend. Today is but a setback. This Martel woman has underestimated me, and that suits me just fine. She has no idea what she has coming."

Slowly, Trembly opened the door and stepped onto the pavement with his hands raised into the air. In seconds, three soldiers darted forward and surrounded him. Without a word, one of them slipped a hood over his head, while the other two grabbed him roughly by the shoulders and dragged him in the direction of the helicopter that had cut off the convoy's escape.

On reaching the helicopter, he was handed off to another pair of men who easily hoisted him off his feet and tossed him horizontally through the air. The moment he was slammed onto the helicopter's hard metal floor, his hands were yanked behind his back and zip-tied.

As he lay there, he could hear soldiers begin to clamor aboard. Over the wash of the engines, his captors were silent until someone yelled, "Ready!" and banged twice on something metal.

For a brief moment, his body felt lighter as the aircraft rose into the air. As the door to the outside closed, a relative quiet filled the cabin. Through the fabric of the mask, he made out the vaguest outline of someone standing over him. The person moved to one knee and lowered himself near Trembly's face.

He could hear the man's exercised breath. A second later, the hood was pulled free, and he was staring into the face of a man who might have been in his early forties. The goatee he wore was speckled with gray, and his uniform was a different color than the men that had grabbed him and swept him into the helicopter.

"Marc-Antoine Trembly, my name is Sergeant Ellis of the RCMP. You are under arrest for the murder of Douglas Jefferies."

JTF-2 had performed the high-risk takedown flawlessly. As the helicopter carrying Trembly rose into the air, the remainder of the commandos rounded up and disarmed the billionaire's security team, and in under two minutes had placed the mercenaries in the second Bell 525.

That had been seventeen minutes ago. Now, Petite was riding shotgun in the first of the three SUVs of the pirated convoy. The driver of the vehicle, one Major Benoit, was also the man commanding the sixteen commandos that would assault Trembly's chateau.

Without taking his eyes off the road, the special operations officer spoke to the commando sitting directly behind Petite, "Jimmy, how are we looking?"

"Could be better, sir. They've amped things up across the property. They've doubled security on the perimeter and added what has to be a sniper position about two hundred meters south of the main building in the tree line. He'll be able to draw up on us the moment they realize it's us in these SUVs."

"This was always the plan, Master Corporal. Once Trembly's security team stopped talking to the mothership, we knew things would start to buzz. As long as Mr. Green here says we're a go, we hit these guys as planned."

The major briefly took his eyes off the road he was racing down and looked at Petite. "Are we good, Mr. Green?"

"We're good, Major," Petite said in response to the cover name Azim had given him.

The JTF-2 officer nodded his head and said, "Open channel Saber Team Bravo."

"Alright, listen up, gentlemen. We are doing this. Jimmy says they know something is up, but they can't know it's us in the SUVs, so we execute as planned. Vehicle Charlie, a sniper has been flagged in the tree line south of the building. Data is coming to give you a precise location. Your task is to keep that position busy or eliminate it. I do not care which. The rest of us hit the main building like a ton of bricks. Saber Alpha out."

"Open Channel Saber Eight," the major said without missing a beat.

"Corporal Hartnell, tell me those breaching drones are on standby."

"Ready, sir. Just say the word."

"Execute now, Corporal. We'll be on the property in one minute. Saber Alpha out."

Ahead and to the right, Petite eyed an opening in the thick evergreen forest that dominated this part of Quebec. As they approached the road that led to the Trembly compound, Benoit barely let up on the gas. On reaching the side road, he jerked on the SUV's wheel and plunged the vehicle into the narrow, paved driveway.

"Shouldn't we slow down?" Petite asked, as calmly as he could manage. "If we go in like a bat out of hell, they'll know something's up."

The JTF-2 officer didn't look at Petite on delivering his reply. "Not a concern, Mr. Green. Like everything else today, faster will serve us better."

Seconds later, the major hammered the SUV's brakes, bringing the vehicle to a screeching halt fifty feet from the massive home's main entrance. As Benoit's door flew open, he was yelling, "Move, move, move!"

Armed again with a suppressed FN-P90, Petite watched for a fleeting moment as two SUVs packed with Canada's most elite fighting force unloaded onto the pavement and rushed in the direction of the few flabbergasted men standing in front of the structure.

Stepping out of his seat, Sam Petite shouldered his weapon and moved to join Benoit. For the third time in less than twenty-four hours, it was go time.

"There, you see, Corporal. I told you there was nothing to worry about. There are a dozen reasons the Commandant might not want to communicate with us. The man knows his business as well as anyone."

As the two former French Legionnaires stood side by side on the steps of the grand chateau's main entrance, the corporal said, "They're moving pretty fast, don't you think?"

"They are, aren't they?" the grizzled, older man replied pensively. "Perhaps Monsieur Trembly needs to take a shit. You know rich people shit too, my friend. And in all of our time here, I've never seen the man hit the head. Whatever the reason, Corporal, let us go meet our comrades. If something's going on, best we look interested in finding out what the problem is."

As the older man began to walk down the expansive staircase that led to the building's colossal double-door entrance, the long-since-retired Foreign Legion man stopped and tilted his head to the right.

Pulling up, the corporal eyed the other man warily. The old fox had heard something. Even at fifty, the Adjutant's ear verged on supernatural. On the dozens of contracts they had worked on together over the years, he had come to trust the other man's hearing as much as his own eyes.

Like a coiled viper, the old man whipped around in the direction he had canted his ear and produced a compact assault rifle from underneath his jacket.

Above the tree line, perhaps one hundred meters away, the corporal saw what his friend had heard. Drones. A lot of them. And they were moving fast.

Without saying a word, the older Legionnaire unloaded a magazine at the approaching machines. As the rounds began to fly, the approaching airborne units began to dodge and weave randomly.

As the older soldier worked to replace his spent magazine, the corporal raised his weapon, picked a target, and opened up on full auto.

At twenty meters out, the unit he'd been targeting waddled in the air and fell toward the well-manicured lawn that surrounded the main building. The corporal didn't watch the drone's terminus. Instead, he looked to find another target, but it was too late. The flight of melon-sized drones zipped to his right in the direction of the chateau's huge, solid double-door entrance.

Like bees working a comb of honey, the dozen or so units briefly hovered in place and then suddenly rotated themselves so their underbellies were parallel to the door. As one, they raced forward and attached themselves to the door's perimeter and its locking mechanism.

"Get down!" the older man bellowed beside him.

The corporal did get down. Years of vicious fighting in five different shitholes in Africa and Central America had attuned him exceedingly well to actions or words that facilitated one's survival.

CRACK!

As one, the drones exploded, allowing the breaching charges each carried to cut through steel and wood.

Ears ringing, the corporal began to pull himself off the stairway to look in the direction of the double doors. The one on the right, though still on its hinges, had been blown inward.

As he flexed his body to raise upward, he heard shouting in French immediately behind him, "Still! Don't move! Don't fucking move!"

Half prone, the corporal rotated his head and saw a pair of soldiers with their weapons trained on the Adjutant and himself.

"You too, old man! Hands off the weapon, or you eat it," the same man with the heavy Quebecois accent said.

Slowly and deliberately, the corporal moved his hand from his weapon. As he did so, the booted feet of more soldiers pounded past him up the stairs. The Canadians had shown up like a hurricane. In moments, they would find the Jefferies woman, he thought. Now, more than ever, he was glad they hadn't been ordered to kill her. He had guessed she had been his age and she'd been cute, not that it mattered now.

"On your stomach and hands behind your back. Now!" the soldier yelled at him.

He did as he was told.

When the zip-ties snared his wrists, he grimaced in pain.

From inside the building, there was a short exchange of gunfire. When he and the older man finally looked at one another, his longtime friend's face was one of chagrin.

"I guess that rich bastard didn't need to take a shit after all."

Chapter 37

Montreal

"We're good now. Finish up and get home," the voice said over Hall's BAM.

"Copy that. We'll be out of here in ten. Cypher Four out."

She turned to face the young man standing on his toes. His hands, bound in rough cord, were stretched above his head. The rope that had been holding Marc-Antoine Trembly's only son erect for the past ninety minutes ran through a pulley and terminated in the hands of a gorilla of a man. Like Hall, he too was wearing a mask that covered everything but his eyes.

"A chair, please. And more water," Hall said.

In the darkness that dominated the extremities of the room, there was movement, and a few seconds later, another masked man, this one rapier-like, placed a chair immediately behind Trembly the younger.

"Release him."

As the Euro playboy, Théo Trembly, slumped into the waiting chair, she stepped forward and grabbed the man so he wouldn't fall to the ground.

As Trembly's posterior made contact with the chair, he groaned in pain.

"Water, if you would," she said, giving the order casually.

As she stepped back from the man-boy, there was a grunt followed by a brief flash of light that reflected off the bucket of ice water that had been tossed in the face of the billionaire's son.

As the near-freezing liquid crashed into Trembly, the sinewy muscles of the twenty-four-year-old contracted, while his hoarse voice did its best to release a howl of surprise and anguish.

"Stop! Please. I did everything you asked. Don't kill me. My dad. He's rich. He'll pay whatever you want. I swear, he will. Please…"

As the young man's voice trailed off, Hall took a step forward and placed one of her feet on the seat of Trembly's chair.

"Open your mouth," she said quietly.

"What? What do you mean?"

Hall executed a bird-like tilt of her head as she looked down at the shivering Quebecer.

She stepped back. "Open his mouth."

The gorilla stepped out of the darkness and viciously slapped one of his hands into the side of Trembly's drenched face. As Hall's subject tried to recoil in pain, the large man's hand took hold of his soaking hair, savagely pulled forward and roared, "Open your mouth or the next time I swear I will shatter every goddamn bone in that pretty face of yours!"

"Okay! Okay!" the young man stammered. Slowly, as Trembly's gaze locked onto Hall's, he opened his mouth slightly.

As though she were a quickdraw from a bygone era, a suppressed handgun appeared in Hall's hand. Seeing the weapon, Trembly moved to snap his mouth shut, but the meathead again reefed on the socialite's scalp, and bellowed "Open!"

With a screech of pain, Trembly re-opened his mouth if only slightly.

"Wider, Monsieur Trembly. I'm not going to ask again," Hall said gently.

Hesitatingly, the man's mouth opened wider.

Slowly, as though she were conducting a procedure of some kind, Hall slid the cold cylinder of the suppressor between a set of teeth that were perfect except for the bright red blood that covered them.

When the suppressor finally hit something solid, she drove it into soft tissue eliciting a gag. As Trembly suddenly tried to squirm, the gorilla wrapped one of his thick arms around the man's neck while his other hand continued to pull back on Trembly's thick black hair. As Hall's associate applied increasing pressure to Trembly's windpipe, the man's eyes began to bulge.

With her free hand, she gently prodded the muscled arm wrapped around Trembly's neck, giving the signal for the man to let up.

"Things will go better if you just relax, Monsieur Trembly. We're almost done. The nightmare is almost over."

On hearing her words, Trembly took in a deep breath.

"That's it. Deep breaths. And one more. And still one more. Good, good, Monsieur Trembly. Very good."

Hall counted to five, allowing the terrified Quebecer to further calm himself.

"Better?"

Slowly, Trembly nodded his head.

"Excellent. Now, I want you to listen carefully. Will you do this for me?"

Another nod was given.

"You have been brave today. Should you have the opportunity to think back on this moment, you will think of the terror, the begging, and the mewling, and you might conclude you're pathetic. But I want you to know that in my time doing this type of work, you have done well. As well as any soldier. More so in some cases. Do you understand what I'm saying?"

Trembly nodded again, his pretty green eyes registering what seemed a genuine comprehension.

"Good." Hall reduced the pressure she had been applying to the back of Trembly's throat with her weapon.

Her foot still on the chair, she leaned in closer to the man. "Hear my words, Theo Miguel Trembly. This is not about you. Your father, for reasons historians may get to assess, has made certain choices. In the past hour, you have played a part in helping him reclarify what is important. For your sake, I am pleased to report he has made the right kinds of decisions."

"Nod if you understand what I'm saying?"

He nodded.

"Now, listen very carefully because the exceptional life you have been living depends on it. Whatever your father or anyone else tells you, you need to understand the next words out of my mouth are the most important words you'll hear in your life."

After a brief pause, Hall asked, "I want to see a vigorous nod if you understand what I'm saying, Theo."

The young man moaned, but eventually began to nod his head as though he meant it.

"Good. Then here it is. If you tell anyone or do anything that informs another person about what happened today, you will be found, and you will be killed. Is this clear?"

Another nod.

"Then there just one more fact to deliver," Hall said. We won't just kill you, Theo. We'll kill your mother, your sister, your niece, and any other children your sister or you might have. Two years from now or ten. It does not matter."

Without warning, Hall drove the extended barrel of her Glock back down the man's throat. In sync with her movement, the gorilla tightened his grip, holding Trembly firm. A yell of pain filled the room.

Hall drove her face to only inches away from Trembly's and, when she spoke, injected every ounce of venom she could into her words. "You and your family live so long as you keep your mouth shut, Theo Trembly. We don't care about anything else. Straighten up, piss away your daddy's money, become an addict, or become your own man and rule the world. We don't care one speck of fly shit. All that matters is today. Today, the past hour, none of this happened. Do we understand one another?"

With terrified eyes, Trembly nodded his head vigorously as best he could.

In a quick motion, Hall pulled her weapon out of the man's mouth and turned her gaze into the darkness. "Do it."

The third man of Hall's team again stepped into the light, this time with a syringe in one of his hands. Without pause, he stepped toward Trembly, and, with physician-like precision, inserted the chemical into the man's throbbing neck artery. In three breaths, Trembly lost focus and stared blankly into the harsh light above.

"Drop him where we discussed," Hall said.

Standing in the light, the two masked men she had only met hours before said nothing. Instead, they stared at her.

"I know this is hard for both of you. I know what you're thinking. What we just did was crazy, illegal, and inhumane beyond measure. It's the very kind of third world shit you've spent your entire careers working against. I know all that."

Hall half-raised her Glock 19 and began to unscrew the suppressor. As it came off, she continued. "For too long, gentlemen, Canada has refused to do hard things. Too much is on the line. Rationalize it however you want but make peace with what was done today. Because if Mitchell Spector and the animals that work for him win the civil war, and the Americans come for us, today is but the smallest taste of what is to come. Except it will be us on the receiving end."

As quickly as the handgun had appeared, Hall made it vanish somewhere on her person. "War, gentlemen, is never, ever pretty. We exist and do the work we do because our country is fighting a war we must win. That is the calculation and whether we like it or not, what we did this morning was a necessary part of winning that war."

Hall stared back at the two CSIS officers that had been recruited into Azim's growing underground unit. She had been assured they would do what needed to be done.

She readied herself to reproduce her weapon and do yet another hard thing. "Are we good?" The question was delivered neutrally to the two men standing in front of her.

"I'm good," said the bigger of the two men.

After a few seconds of quiet, the slender man finally said, "Me too."

Hall relaxed and thumbed in the direction of the drugged socialite. "Then grab the partied-out rich kid so we can unload him. He's had quite the night of fun by the looks of it. For ourselves, we still have things to get done today."

Ottawa

"Yes, Madame Prime Minister, thank you for the call and for your support," Merielle said via the quantum encrypted connection. "More than ever, the alliance will have to stick together. And I agree, the retrieval of Morgan could be a game changer."

Merielle paused to listen to the United Kingdom's leader.

"Yes, Madame Prime Minister, if they do drop the weapon on our soldiers, I agree we should talk before we move to retaliate. And yes, I too appreciate and support the concept of a proportionate response. You and I are not Mitchell Spector," Merielle said.

After another short pause listening to her colleague across the Atlantic, Merielle brought the conversation to an end. "Thank you, Prime Minister. Your wish of good luck is greatly appreciated. We'll talk again soon."

She pulled the phone from her ear and looked at her ex-husband.

"So you're sure about what you want to do, Mer, because we've got Raymond dead to rights. Trembly, for all his billions and erudite bullshit, is more than willing to point the finger at her. The only question is do you want us to perp-walk her or keep things low-key?"

As the first vehicle of their convoy stopped at the main security entrance leading to Parliament Hill, Merielle shook her head. "No. We do this my way."

On the move again, her SUV stopped in front of the west entrance of the Centre Block. An RCMP officer she didn't recognize stepped to the door and opened it. In what was a rarity on Parliament Hill, the officer had a compact assault rifle brazenly brandished across his chest. Between the SUV and the door, another six similarly armed officers formed a cordon. It was quite the spectacle of force.

When Merielle had questioned the need for such a display, Stephane, in a rare exercise of firmness, advised point blank for her to shut her mouth, and let him manage the security element of what was about to happen.

As she strode past the officers and through the heavy double doors and walked up the stairs that led to the House of Commons foyer, her eyes locked onto a gaggle of reporters loosely hanging around the stairs that cabinet ministers took to go back and forth between the second floor where her office and the Cabinet Room was located and the House of Commons.

It was a younger CBC reporter who first spied her. "There she is!"

Perhaps if the woman had more experience she wouldn't have said anything and instead would have marched toward Merielle ready to unload with a first question for Canada's suddenly re-appeared prime minister.

Instead, a dozen heads snapped in her direction and on realizing Merielle was alive, as one, they rushed her like a well-dressed, too pretty offensive line.

"Madame Prime Minister, where have you been?"

"Prime Minister, are you okay?"

"Madame Prime Minister, is it true you've resigned?"

Merielle's hands flashed into the air with her palms outward. "Other than to say that I am well, I have no comment at this time. My colleagues are expecting me and as you can imagine, with all that's transpired in recent hours, it is imperative I speak with them before I make a statement to the press. Stay tuned."

The same beefy RCMP officer who had opened her door roared, "Step aside! Step aside! You heard her, she'll be back, you vultures."

Like a ship breaking through the waves of a rough ocean, he and two other strapping police officers stepped into the braying reporters and none too gently pushed them aside.

Keeping her eyes forward, Merielle began to climb the stairs that would bring her into the very heart of Canada's political power and a confrontation with her newly revealed nemesis, Yvette Raymond.

"And so, you can see my friends, this government is in no position to proceed one minute longer with this ill-advised adventure in Washington. We must bring our soldiers home now," Raymond pronounced to the room with as much conviction as she could muster.

The Minister of Public Safety immediately added his voice to the discussion. "I don't like it, but Yvette is right. With the events in Montreal and with things on a knife's edge in the US, we need decisive action. Terrorist attacks, assassinations, armed interventions in civil wars. None of this sounds like the Canada I grew up in. As a country, it's almost as if we walked into a different dimension."

A sober look on her face, Raymond watched as Weisman again carried her water. The man's desire for status and power easily rivaled her own. As they rose higher on the mountain they were now climbing together, he would need to be managed carefully. In the moment, however, he was serving a purpose and brilliantly so.

It was now MacPhail's turn. If she played her part only half as well as she could, the Newfoundlander would seal the deal.

A handful of Cabinet Ministers from outside Quebec were vacillating at the prospect of unilaterally pulling Canada's armed forces from the action that was playing out in Washington. She needed this group to win the day, and it was MacPhail who could give them to her.

With the Montreal attack and the death of Blanchard and others, the collection of fair-weather politicians sitting around her had been pining for someone to treat recent events with a more neutral eye. Getting the country's soldiers out of the insanity that was the United States civil war was a critical first step of her plans. That the decision would likely lead to the end of CANZUK was a delicious add-on.

MacPhail had assured them during their earlier meeting that she would know the right time to weigh in. By design, the tired-looking woman sat across from her. She looked pensive and for what seemed like a too-long moment, she and Raymond locked eyes. It was time to give the Newfie a push.

"Minister MacPhail, I believe you wish to say something?"

The other woman's jaw tightened perceptibly.

In response, Raymond's eyes narrowed. Trembly had warned her the woman might not cooperate. Though their qualities were few, he had reminded her that Newfoundlanders did possess healthy amounts of pride, which under the right circumstances could lead to the unpredictable happening.

MacPhail released her gaze from Raymond and slowly rose from her seat. For what seemed an eon, she looked up and down the table that had faithfully served generations of Canadian politicians.

The woman inhaled deeply. "Colleagues, I stand with the Minister of Health –"

The heavy wooden door that was the only way in and out of the Cabinet chambers swung open and cracked loudly as it impacted the stopper that prevented it from crashing into the stone-block wall.

As the jarring noise invaded the political sanctum, every pair of eyes left MacPhail to zero in on the person who had the temerity to so rudely interrupt what could be the most important political discussion in the country's history.

When Merielle Martel stopped her advance into the room, she took up position beside Bob MacDonald's still vacant chair at the head of the table. As she stood there silently and took in the entire space, the woman seemed a physical giant.

As was her way, she wore a well-tailored power suit that served to enhance the figure she had maintained from a lifetime of long-distance running. One by one, she locked eyes with every person sitting around the table.

Still not saying a word, Martel's right hand moved to her hip and pulled back her suit jacket to reveal the holstered handgun. Slowly, the prime minister placed her right hand on the weapon.

"Colleagues, approximately forty-five minutes ago, I retook my oath of service to the RCMP in the presence of three members of the Supreme Court. As I stand before you, I once again have the authority of the King and our wonderful country to directly enforce its laws. These are extraordinary times."

Her statement finished Martel took a step in the direction of the one person she had visually passed over as she had canvassed the room. "Yvette Suzanne Raymond, you are under arrest for the murder of Douglas Jefferies and the kidnapping and torture of Angela Jefferies. On your feet."

A rare smile emerged on Raymond's face. "Is that so? And what evidence do you have to support these outrageous allegations? Because I can tell you, Merielle Martel, that I have no idea of what you are speaking.

"And setting these fictional allegations aside, you owe this group an explanation for the disaster that took place in Montreal, never mind the unauthorized deployment of Canadian troops to Washington. All of it is madness. This time, Madame Martel, you have gone too far."

Walking in the direction of Raymond, Merielle pulled up her stride in front of the still-seated woman, allowing herself to tower over the blonde MP.

"Unbelievable," MacPhail said from across the table. Her arm was raised, and she was pointing an accusatory finger in the direction of Raymond. Her face was almost purple with rage. "Colleagues, not one hour ago, Minister Raymond sat in my office and threatened my family if I didn't support this coup of hers. Well, damn the consequences, I won't support her. Our country is too important."

Ignoring MacPhail, Raymond pushed her seat back, giving her space between herself and Martel. Getting to her feet, she turned to face the rest of the room. She was as cool as ever.

"Colleagues, I give you exhibits A and B as to why this party and country need new leadership. In A, we have a prime minister who survived an alleged assassination attempt and who for the past

– what, sixteen hours – has left our country in the dark, all the while the brave men and women of our armed forces became engaged in what is the most ill-advised military action in the history of our country. Why would someone do this? Does this sound like a person of sound mind? And what of Cabinet? What of you? Are we just pawns in Merielle Martel's game?"

Raymond's blue eyes, filled with contempt, released from the thirty-odd politicians riveted to her and focused in on Merielle. "I agree with Minister Weisman. I don't recognize our country. It is madness, and it must come to an end."

She then rounded on MacPhail and pointed an accusatory red-nailed finger at the Newfoundlander. "And you, Exhibit B, how dare you?"

The Quebec City MP pulled her smartphone out of her jacket and placed it on the boardroom table in front of her. As her hand left the device, the sound of Irene MacPhail's voice filled the room.

"Yes, I can't stand the woman. She plays things fast and loose and I, too, am worried about the adventurism that's taking place down south. What kind of idiot orders our brave soldiers into a foreign country where nuclear weapons have just been used? She's mad and this CANZUK alliance is nothing more than a neo-colonial fever dream. And that's nothing to say about what she did to Josee Labelle. Today, you can count on my full support, Yvette. The madness of Merielle Martel has to an end come hell or high water."

"That's not me!" MacPhail fairly yelled. "I didn't say any of that. 'Neo-colonial fever dream.' Really, Yvette? That doesn't sound like me in the bloody least."

When Raymond next spoke, her words easily filled the large room. "These are your words, Minister. Recorded less than an hour ago. Deny it all you want, but as a Minister of the Crown, I swear the words we've just heard are true."

"You evil bitch," MacPhail said without hesitation.

Ignoring the curse, Raymond's glare moved back to Martel. "You cast allegations of the most serious kind Madame Prime Minister, but they are nothing more than allegations from a person who has no proof and is in way over her head."

Raymond took a step toward Martel. "You can stop drowning, Merielle. Resign honorably or face a vote of non-confidence and end your career in the ignobility you so richly deserve. The choice is yours."

As Martel faced off with the other woman, her right hand came up to her ear. After a moment's pause, she said, "Bring him in."

From outside the room, someone could be heard, "Clear a path! Clear a path!"

While every other set of eyes in the room turned to the entrance the Prime Minister had walked through minutes ago, Martel and Raymond continued to stare each other down.

"Whatever lie you are bringing through that door, it won't be enough, Merielle. Resign, and I promise you can enjoy a quiet and lucrative retirement. I give you my word."

Martel gave no reply to the entreaty. Instead, she turned her back on the other woman to take in the scene at the door.

Arms behind his back and walking between what was obviously two plain-clothed police officers, arrived Marc-Antoine Trembly. The richest man in Quebec had a worried look on his face.

"Colleagues," Merielle said, while pointing in the direction of the easily recognized corporate titan. "Monsieur Trembly, I understand you have reached a deal with the Crown."

The instant the question registered with the man his face transformed from worried to furious. His eyes then moved from Martel to Raymond.

Merielle continued, "Monsieur Trembly, if you would, please tell us if Madame Raymond had knowledge of and gave sanction to the kidnapping, torture, and subsequent death of Douglas Jefferies."

The billionaire said nothing. Instead, the man's face grew red as he projected hate-filled eyes toward Merielle.

"Monsieur Trembly," Martel said loudly. "I would remind you that twenty-five years to life is a very long time. It would be the greatest mistake of what remains of your free life if you thought the full weight of the Crown will not come down on you. Madame Raymond cannot save you. Do not join her in the fantasy she is currently playing out in her mind."

"This is outrageous!" The voice came from across the table. Weisman, the Minister of Public Safety, was glowering in Martel's direction. "Where is this man's lawyer, Merielle? Where have you been? You owe us an explanation, and until such an explanation arrives, I will not be a party to this abomination of justice."

The Prime Minister didn't take her eyes off the billionaire. "Monsieur Trembly, the truth. It is now, or it is never."

"Yes," the man said quietly.

"'Yes' what, Monsieur Trembly? My colleagues need to hear what you have to say."

When Trembly next spoke, the words exploded from his mouth. "She knew. At Irene MacPhail's direction, Jefferies and his daughter had recorded a conversation they shouldn't have. Madame Raymond and I discussed his capture and his interrogation."

"And his death, Monsieur Trembly. Let us be specific," Merielle said, her voice the perfect emulation of the policewoman she had been.

"Yes."

"'Yes,' what, sir?"

"Yes, we discussed his death."

Merielle then turned and laid her eyes on Weisman. "And tell us, Monsieur Trembly. In the plans you and Madame Raymond concocted which would allow her to take over the leadership of the Conservative Party, what involvement did Minister Weisman have?"

"He cut a deal. He would support Yvette if he was elevated to Minister of Global Affairs."

"And?"

"And, when he did become Minister of Global Affairs, ten million in crypto was to be provided to him."

"Lies! All lies!" shrilled Weisman.

"Thank you, Monsieur Trembly. Your arrangement with the Crown will be honored," Merielle said, her voice still that of the veteran policewoman.

"Officers, take him away."

Merielle rounded on Raymond.

"Murder and bribery, eh, Yvette?"

Raymond remained silent.

"Nothing to say. Good. That's the right play."

"This is beyond outrageous, Merielle," Weisman stated, his voice still strained. "I refuse to be a part of whatever charade you think you're playing at."

Martel ignored the man and turned to take in the fullness of the room.

"Colleagues, Minister Weisman is correct about one thing – you are owed a full explanation, and I will give it to you. But first, Madame Raymond and Mr. Weisman will join me in my office. I would like Minister MacPhail and Minister Oyinlola to join me as witnesses to the conversation."

Merielle's hand snapped forward and roughly grabbed Raymond's upper arm. Though only an inch or two taller than the Quebec MP, in that moment, Raymond seemed to wilt to half

Merielle's size. Merielle winced in pain as the arm attached to her wounded shoulder rose and gestured to the still-open door that would lead them to her office.

With a solid grip still on the other woman, Merielle took a step forward but, as she did so, Raymond tried to jerk her arm free.

A police officer of twenty-one years, Merielle's muscle memory as it pertained to subject control asserted itself instantly. As her grip further tightened on Raymond's arm, she gritted her teeth, shifted her weight, and with the hand attached to her injured shoulder, she grabbed Raymond's wrist and applied a near bone-snapping wrist lock onto the dainty and unsuspecting woman.

As her body registered the pain, Raymond instantly cried out. "Stop! Jesus, stop, you're hurting me!"

As the cries of pain elicited someone to call for security officials to enter the room, Merielle continued to apply pressure to Raymond's joint and stepped closer into the other woman's personal orbit. Bringing her mouth to Raymond's ear, she whispered, "You have no idea who you've messed with, Yvette. I'm who you think I am, only worse. Much fucking worse."

Sensing rushed movement out of the corner of her eye, Merielle looked up from the Quebec MP to see Stephane and the burly officer who had helped escort her into the building storming toward her. On reaching her, she shoved Raymond in their direction.

As the two policemen collected their new charge, Merielle's gaze transited to Weisman. She only stared at the man.

"I know my rights, Merielle. I'm a lawyer. What you are doing is a travesty. It is perhaps the most un-Canadian act since… since… well, since the death of Josee Labelle."

When Merielle snapped her fingers, the crack they made easily echoed inside and beyond the granite block of the conference room. As though dogs on the hunt, another pair of well-built RCMP officers barreled through the entrance straight in the direction of the Minister of Public Safety. Together, the two uniformed policemen roughly grabbed the too-well-dressed MP from Vancouver and began to force-march the slight man out of the room.

"This is outrageous, Merielle. Outrageous! I won't be treated like this! I'll go to the press!"

As Weisman was all but dragged yelling from the room, Merielle took up those who remained of her Cabinet. The look on their faces ranged from delight to disbelief to abject horror.

"Colleagues, it's been an incredible sixteen hours or so. Were I you, I too would be concerned or perhaps as outraged as Monsieur Weisman claims to be. Just give me twenty more minutes. During this time, Ministers MacPhail and Oyinlola will represent you in the conversation that is to take place with the two criminals who just left us.

"From you, colleagues, I have nothing to hide. And when I return, I give you my word as a sworn police officer, the prime minister, and your friend, that you will get the full story. And when you have all of the details, together, we'll debate and determine the fate of our great country."

Washington, D.C.

"Thank you, General. I appreciate you letting me know."

As Larocque watched the last of B Company and the wounded they were carrying begin their quick march across the Whitney Young Memorial Bridge, for the hundredth time, he dismissed the idea of giving his Regiment a heads-up of the holocaust on its way. Better they don't know, he thought.

Captain Zufelt and his Pathfinders were now across the river and might survive depending on the size of the blast. Radiation would saturate them, of course, but at least they would get to see their families. And Merielle would make sure they were taken care of. Though painful, their final days would be filled with the dignity and pride of what they had accomplished. That was something, he told himself.

"Colonel?"

Larocque let out an explosion of air he'd been holding in his lungs as he turned to the speaker.

"Ah, Corporal Dune. I thought you would have been across the river by now."

"Colonel Rydell said we should cross with the last of you. He mentioned something about the Canucks not being alone on the shitfront."

"Shitfront?"

"In this context, sir, I reckon, it means something bad is coming. But here's the thing. I gotta close mate working the recce drones, but according to him there's nothing close to us. Just a few of those militia types, and they're useless bludgers if there ever were any. Any ideas what the CO might be talking about, or is it above my pay grade?"

On taking in the question, both pride and sadness welled inside Larocque. Without saying a word, he turned and looked back in the direction of the D.C. Armory. On the far side of the RFK Urban Campus, he could clearly see the distinctive white roof of the structure they had just retreated from. His best guess was that the weapon would hit the building dead on. It was one hell of a target.

"You still dating that Canadian gal, Corporal?" Larocque said over his shoulder.

"I reckon I am, sir. We have our share of tiffs, but she's a hell of a Sheila. Might be that I ask her to marry me. Oi, it might be I become a Canuck, just like you."

"Ms. Larocque and I have tiffs too, my friend, but she's the best thing that ever happened to me. You haven't asked for it, but my advice is that if we make it home you make that girl your wife. She'll ground you, son. And men like us, we need to be grounded."

When Dune next spoke, his voice sounded hesitant. "Oi, what do you mean 'if we make it'? The Reds that could have taken us squibbed, sir. The way I see it, we're in the clear. My best guess is we'll be back home within a day or two, and heroes we'll be. Every last one of us, right, Colonel?"

Larocque felt the younger man step beside him. In the year since their tilt in that arena in Edmonton, he had grown quite fond of the cocksure Aussie commando.

"Do you ever pray, Corporal?"

"Nah, all respect, Colonel, it's a load of shit. It's just another way 'the man' controls you. The Army controls me enough, thanks."

Larocque smiled at the reply. "Well enough, Corporal Dune. I only just took up the practice. If you don't mind, I'll pray for us both."

"No wukkas, Colonel."

"The King's English, Corporal."

When Dune next spoke, he did his best to drop his accent. "As you Canucks like to say, it's all good, sir."

Above, in the overcast sky, Larocque heard the distinctive clacking of a guided weapon as it adjusted its targeting fins.

As he looked into the air, beside him, Dune quietly said, "That doesn't sound good. Is that what's got you worried, Colonel?"

Larocque didn't answer the question. Instead, in the few seconds they had left, Colonel Jackson Larocque of the Canadian Airborne Regiment prayed for his pregnant wife, his unborn child, his soldiers, Dune, his girlfriend, and his country. As best he could, he had done right by them all.

When the detonation came, his eyes were closed. Standing easy, his chin was up, his chest was out, and his shoulders were back. Larocque would die the proud soldier and man he was.

When Khan's Tempest impacted the falling tactical nuclear bomb, at just under twelve hundred knots, a micro-second of perception permitted him to feel the simultaneous disintegration of his fighter and his person.

His prayer finished, his mind perfectly clear, Wing Commander Harry 'Pony' Khan's life ended knowing he had set the bar for those that would continue to fight this war.

Until the end, he had fought the good fight. Until the end, he had done his lads and his country proud.

Epilogue

Australian Broadcasting Corporation Report

"Now let's go to our North American-based reporter, Roger Lang, who's been embedded with frontline CANZUK troops for the past two weeks.

"Roger, it's good to see you safe, my friend. The bravery of your reporting speaks for itself, but let me just say on behalf of all of us here at the ABC, how much we admire and appreciate your willingness to report from the dangerous conditions you've been exposed to. Bravo, sir."

"Thank you, Andrew. All I can say is that it's the job I signed up for and whatever inconveniences and dangers I've experienced, they pale in comparison to the tribulations that CANZUK soldiers have had to endure."

"So what is the latest, Roger?"

"In a word, it is desperate. After three weeks of non-stop fighting, CANZUK forces have ceased their retreat north in the direction of the Canadian border.

"Since the two sides met in Pennsylvania, it has been the worst kind of fighting for each and every kilometer. To say that it has been vicious would be an understatement.

"The Canadian 2nd Division, now half their fighting strength, have consolidated their position in Buffalo along with the 10th Mountain Division of the FAS. Combat engineers, with the support of exhausted but determined infantry, have been readying the city for a siege that will come courtesy of the UCSA's 3rd Army Corps."

The reporter paused and thumbed in the direction of the city skyline currently serving as his backdrop.

"Here in Syracuse, what's left of the consolidated CANZUK forces are undertaking similar inspired preparations to ready for the city's defense.

"Made up of the 1st British Expeditionary Division and the combined 4th Expeditionary Division of Australia and New Zealand, combat engineers with the help of local tradies are working at a frantic pace to make this Upstate New York city into a modern-day fortress.

"I am not a military man, Andrew, and I am limited in how much detail I can reveal about the preparations, but I can tell you from what I have seen with my own eyes here in Syracuse, when the Red Faction attacks, the fighting will be as brutal as we've seen to date."

"Brutal indeed, Roger," the in-studio anchor said. "It's been said the fighting of the past three weeks would rival anything the Diggers saw in WWII, and that casualties have been heavy. What of the morale of the Australian soldiers you've been speaking with?"

"Andrew, to the last, the Diggers I've spoken to are primed. I know families back home have been affected deeply by the costs of this war, but the fighting men and women of Australia are ready for whatever comes next."

"Incredibly brave. Thanks for this update Roger, and on behalf of myself and all of those watching, stay safe."

The new anchor's eyes shifted to another in-studio camera. "That was Roger Lang, reporting from Syracuse, New York."

In the top left of the screen, the male reporter's face was replaced by that of a woman. "Now let's move on to the reporting of Cindy Chang who is coming to us this evening from Hanoi, Vietnam."

"Cindy, you've just arrived in Hanoi - what is the latest with regard to Chinese provocations across the region?"

Pacific Ocean, Off the Coast of British Columbia

The Long March 15 was the second of its class to be commissioned. At six thousand tons, the nuclear-propelled Shang Class Type 095 submarine was the People's Liberation Army Navy's best option to engage with an enemy when you wanted one or both of surprise or deniability. Today, Commanding Officer Captain Zhang Bo wanted both.

"Conn, Sonar, what's the status of the track?"

"Sonar, Conn, the track remains good and clean. All four surface vessels are continuing their efforts to hem in Long March 11. All data points suggest they're oblivious to our presence."

"And the Canadian sub?"

"She's a quiet thing, Captain. The Germans truly are masters of the craft."

"Cut the narrative, Petty Officer Lee. Do we have a track on her or not?"

"We do, Captain, but it's faint."

"Not for long," Zhang said, his voice confident.

"Conn, Weapons."

"Weapons, Conn, ready for your orders, Captain," another petty officer replied, his voice edgy.

"Everyone, take a deep breath," Zhang said in a firm, raised voice. "This action is a long time coming and we hold all the advantages. Stay focused and stay relaxed. It is we who are the predator in these waters."

Despite the indirect rebuke, the officer manning the weapons station kept his eyes zeroed in on the data on the multiple screens in front of him. The very kind of discipline he demanded of his crew, Zhang thought.

"Weapons, flood all torpedo bays and launch attack sequence Alpha on my mark. Once launched, re-flood bays one to six and be ready for a follow-up salvo. New targets will be engaged on my say-so."

"Conn, weapons bays one through six flooded and ready for attack sequence Alpha," reported the petty officer. This time, the man's voice was level, and for a brief moment, his eyes connected with Zhang.

Zhang nodded his head in the younger man's direction. "Weapons, fire all torpedoes."

Without hesitation, the officer moved to depress each of the buttons to launch the first six of the Long March 15's forty-eight Shark 242 Long Range torpedoes.

As the AI-controlled weapons emerged from their firing tubes and started their sixty-five-knot race toward the four Canadian ships, Zhang waited patiently for his sonar team to report on his adversaries' response.

A large display in front of him was counting the seconds since the launch of their first salvo. At fifty-two seconds, he finally heard the report he was hoping for, if a full minute sooner than he had expected. "Enemy torpedoes in the water, Captain."

"Where did they come from, Sonar?" Zhang asked curtly.

"From the Canadian sub, sir. It's exactly two kilometers west of the flotilla. They've targeted Long March 11. We have a precise handle on her now."

"Excellent, Sonar. Not where we thought she would be," he said with a hint of admiration in his voice. "It would seem whoever is commanding that boat is not without some skill. Good, it will make our victory all the more satisfying."

"Weapons, launch two torpedoes at the Canadian sub on my mark, and then launch the remaining four torpedoes at the Type 26 that is furthest east. Employ attack pattern Lima.

"Aye, Captain, weapons ready."

"Fire."

Again, the weapons station officer manipulated his controls to launch the Chinese attack sub's second full salvo of the PLA Navy's most advanced torpedoes.

"Captain, all weapons are away."

On hearing the update, Zhang turned away from the pair of officers manning the weapons station and put his eyes on his submarine's pilot. "Helm, bring us up to twenty-five knots and down to a depth of six hundred feet. Make your course 135 degrees."

Zhang reached for a nearby rail to brace himself for the aggressive maneuvering.

"Captain! Torpedo in the water. Distance, nineteen hundred meters, bearing, 110 degrees. Speed, 55 knots. It's headed in our direction, sir."

Unexpected, thought Zhang. Being as close as they were to the North American coast, it would be little surprise if the Canadians had one or several of their fixed-wing ASW aircraft in the air supporting the modest task force he was now prosecuting.

That the plane had been able to lay down an attack so quickly meant one of the Canadians' P-8 Orions would have had to have been on top of their position. Whether it was a stroke of luck or good tactics, the Canadians were offering more resistance than he anticipated. He wondered if the Australians would offer the same type of challenge with their navy. Intel reports suggested the Aussie fleet of Virginia and Astute-class nuclear platforms represented twice the adversary of the Canadian's conventional 214s. He would look forward to that challenge when it came.

"Helm, increase speed to thirty-one knots and stay on the current set course until I say otherwise."

"Aye, Captain. Increasing speed to thirty-one knots, sir," the submarine's pilot confirmed.

Zhang looked to the large tactical display in front of him and confirmed the progress of their first six torpedoes. One of the

Canadian Type 26 frigates had positioned itself directly between the incoming weapons and the Berlin-class multi-purpose replenishment ship that was their main prize. A brave move, if not unexpected.

To lose the replenishment ship would mean the Canadians would be hampered in sending a larger number of their ships to the Pacific to confront China.

The angst the sinking of the large and expensive vessel would cause the Canadian populace would be an added bonus. By every measure, the people who occupied the top half of North America were a soft people. On its own, he wondered if the loss of the ship and its sailors might not be enough to bring the unserious country to its knees.

"Captain, countermeasures have been launched by the outermost Type 26."

He ignored the update. He had his own incoming torpedo to worry about. His hand darted to the tactical screen in front of him and swiped right. The new data showed the closing distance between the Orion's torpedo and his own boat. Range was four hundred meters.

"Weapons, launch countermeasures, spread Echo-Foxtrot."

"Aye, Captain, countermeasures launching. Countermeasures away."

"Helm, maximum speed, get us under the thermocline as fast as you can," Zhang said, his voice still perfectly calm.

A faint explosion reverberated throughout the hull of the submarine.

"Report," Zhang barked in the direction of the sonar station.

"The Type 26 designated 'Oscar' has taken a direct hit, sir."

"Captain!" one of the other three other sonar techs called out.

"Report," Zhang said.

BOOM! Suddenly, the submarine around Zhang shook violently.

"Sir, the Canadian torpedo took up our countermeasure. That was the detonation. We're in the clear."

"Very good. Helm, the thermocline. How much further?"

"Another forty seconds, Captain."

"When we get there, run silent if you would."

"Aye, Captain."

Zhang closed his eyes and took a deep breath. The Canadian P-8 Orion would still be hunting them but their dash into deeper water would insulate them from the active pinging sonobuoys the plane would now be dropping madly into the ocean in an effort to firm up their signature. That they hadn't had a fix on their location when they launched their attack meant Zhang and his boat would be extremely difficult to find. They were safe for now.

Another soft rumble echoed in the confines of the sub. Zhang opened his eyes. "Sonar, report."

"A pair of hits on the replenishment ship, Captain. We struck her amidships and aft."

Zhang gave a reserved pump of his fist.

"Captain, I'm also picking up a number of other secondary explosions from the direction we last picked up the 214. The Canadian sub is sinking, sir."

"Did we get her?" Zhang asked quickly.

"No, sir. Our torpedo was defeated by a countermeasure. The kill will be registered to Long March 11."

A huge smile lit up Zhang's face. "Excellent. Captain Wu will be pleased. How do our comrades fare?"

"Data coming in now, Captain. It looks like Long March 11 was hit at the same time the Canadian boat was. She too is sinking. Indications are she was struck by a torpedo launched from one of the Canadian helicopters. Based on data we were picking up before the engagement, we estimate that at least three of the flotilla's six helos were in the air when our attack commenced."

Zhang nodded his head slowly. He had known Wu, the captain of the Long March 11 very well, and over the years had served with many of the 11's officers. Compared to other branches within the Peoples Liberation Army, the officer core within the submarine force was a small and tight-knit community.

But in his older generation sub, a Type 093, Wu had not been a match for the Canadian's new and hugely capable Type 26 frigates. In another hour, the Canadian Navy would have run him down, leaving them to focus their energy on finding his own vessel.

That outcome would have been unacceptable. Better to strike down their enemy while they were focused somewhere else. It was a brutal calculation, but the loss of one second-generation submarine in exchange for a capital ship and several of its brand-new escorts was a decision he, and the admirals he reported to, were prepared to live with.

Another extended low rumble reverberated through the ocean to impact his submarine's hull. Shang's eyes move to the men operating the sonar station. "Report."

"It looks like two more of the Canadian frigates have been hit, Captain. Vessel designated Victor was hit by two torpedoes from our second salvo, while vessel Romeo was struck by Long March 11. There remains a single untouched Type 26, sir."

Shang did not say or do anything to acknowledge the update. Instead, he raised his hand and swiped the screen in front of him twice until a map of the west coast of North America was staring back at him. His index finger designated a point about one hundred kilometers west of Vancouver Island.

"Helm, increase depth by another hundred meters and set a speed of four knots. Move us in the direction of the location I just designated."

"Aye, Captain. Increasing depth to eleven hundred feet, setting speed to four knots, and heading set for one hundred and ten degrees."

Zhang turned his eyes away from his tactical display to take up his crew. "Listen up, people."

Those who could afford to take their eyes off their displays did so to look at him. Each face he examined held a look of expectation.

"Today, we struck a monumental blow that will serve to bring down what for all intents and purposes is the one last pillars of democracy in this world.

"As the Canadians lick their wounds and bicker about what to do about the threat we represent, we will proceed to sink every ship in this part of the Pacific that intends to move goods to and from this part of the world. In a month, maybe two, we will have done our part to bring the CANZUK alliance to its knees. And when we finally strangle this pitiful alliance our great motherland will have secured a foothold in North America.

"It will be a dream come true for our nation, and all of you will have played a leading role in making it happen. All of you are heroes."

Zhang turned his eyes in the direction of the sonar station. "Sonar."

"Aye Captain," the senior tech responded, his voice ringing with pride.

"Find us our next target, but this time, make sure it is of the fat and juicy variety. Now that we've given the Canadians a bloody nose, let us see what we can do to put their neck in a noose so that we may well and truly snuff out this pathetic little country."

Élysée Palace, Paris, France

"Their backs are to the wall, Madame President. Literally. Yes, the costs to us have been enormous, and not all has gone to plan but we are where we wanted to be. Almost precisely so."

The French President sat behind her desk staring at her closest advisor. Behind her, light from the mid-afternoon sun came through the huge triplicate windows filling the gilded room. The effect gave the President of France a seemingly benevolent glow.

"Remind me, Pascal, my friend, where it is we want to be?"

"Madame President, the United States is as weak as ever. Yes, they have pushed CANZUK back, but the Canadians are undertaking a national mobilization, as are the British. Spector would be a fool to cross the border. If he does, it could be years of bitter fighting. Our analysis suggests that should the Canadian defense falter in Upstate New York, and should the Red Faction move across the 49th parallel, it will be the Northern Ireland experience multiplied by a factor of ten."

The President moved forward to place her elbows on her ornate desk. Tenting her fingers, her lacquered nails formed a tower of red as she stared back at Charron. "Not if he decides to flatten Toronto and Ottawa. It's not Americans who live in these cities and you know Spector as well as I do. The man is capable of almost anything."

"The British have been quite clear on what will happen should Spector go that far."

"So, you're prepared to acknowledge the Texan could do it? He is as unpredictable as he is ruthless. A modern-day Stalin, if you ask me. This purge we've been hearing about in the American Northeast could very well be straight from the Soviets' playbook. Brutal and efficient only begins to describe what's been happening."

"We have our agreement and thus far, Spector has honored it," Charron replied.

"He has honored it but agreements are just that. Just as they can be set, they can be broken. Not to invoke the Russians again, but look what happened to them. Had Stalin not sent millions of Russians to the slaughter against the Huns, they'd be speaking German in Moscow today. Jesus, we'd be speaking German."

Charron nodded his head respectfully at the comment. "It is not an unfair analysis, Madame President. I too have been taken aback by Spector's ruthlessness. But, as unlikely as a nuclear strike on a Canadian city is, we do have contingencies. Several of them, in fact."

The French President un-tented her fingers and slipped back into the rich leather of the Italian-designed office chair she was seated in. "So, am I to take it your recommendation is that we stay the course in North America?"

"That is our strong recommendation, Madame President."

There was a quiet knock at the door. "Ah, yes. Our coffee," the President said. "Come in, come in."

Charron turned his head in the direction of the large double doors that led into the huge room. A handsome young man, looking sharp in his Army casuals, entered the room pushing a burnished trolley featuring a porcelain coffee set that at one time had served coffee to France's last emperor.

As the soldier poured Charron's coffee, the President re-engaged the conversation. "And what of our plans here at home, my old friend?"

"We are pleased with our progress. Most pleased. With yesterday's election in Belgium, another nationalist government stands to join the cause."

Pausing in his reply, Charron moved to take his first sip of the exquisite coffee served only by the President's office. As civilized a woman as there was in Europe, France's president allowed Charron a moment to savor the beverage's wonderful flavor.

The satisfying moment passed, he continued with his briefing. "As has always been our plan, we are now in a position to expand the outposts in Libya, Yemen, and Syria. The relocation of the Muslims can now commence with all the vigor the challenge deserves."

"And the Germans? Do you think they now have the stomach for it?" the President asked.

Charron nodded. "The last terrorist attack was enough to bring them around, Madame President. They won't begin to move the numbers we were hoping for, but it will be a start. It is the commencement of the policy that we are concerned about for the moment. Once they come to see this is as humane a program as we described it to be, the Germans will bring their normal efficiency to bear. They cannot help themselves."

"These attacks you speak of are most unfortunate. I take it the conspirators continue to elude the authorities – ours and the Germans?"

"They are a new kind of enemy, Madame President. I don't need to remind you that there are now as many Muslims living in Europe as there are people in France. And a good portion of these are second, even third, generation. They know our ways and they speak our languages. The European Muslim is a well-equipped conspirator. It is why we must act. Now and without reservation while the rest of the world is preoccupied with the madness playing out across the Atlantic."

It was now the President's turn to give a vigorous nod. "I agree, Minister. Your daring vision is coming to be. Though they may not know it, in the decades to come, the people of this country will thank you for what we are about to do."

Charron's reply to the kudos was immediate. "It could not happen without you, Madame President. Your strength of leadership and willingness to make the hard decisions will be judged by history as incomparable."

For the returned compliment, the President only smiled. "You mentioned there was something else you might need from my office?"

A sheepish look fell onto Charron's face. "Indeed, there is one more thing, Madame President. But you have done so much already, I hesitate to ask."

The President waved her hand to brush away Charron's recalcitrance. "Go on. If you need to ask, then I should hear it."

"It's this Martel woman."

On the mention of the Canadian Prime Minister, the President's face darkened.

"The policewoman," the President of France said derisively. "What of her?"

"It is she more than anyone else that is holding this CANZUK charade together. If she goes, the board re-sets more quickly than it otherwise might. And more, the sooner she goes, the sooner we can re-claim our man from the Canadians. The pressure I'm getting from the intelligence community to resolve that particular situation grows with each passing day. Monsieur Besson was well-liked, as you know."

On hearing the setup for Charron's ask, France's President crossed her arms and then elevated one of her manicured hands to her chin. For a long moment, she stared at Charron and said nothing. When she finally spoke, it was but a single, clipped word. "No."

A look of confusion dropped onto Charron's face. "I'm sorry, Madame President. What exactly are you saying 'no' to?"

"No, I will not give you permission to again move against this Martel woman."

"But, Madame President, you've read the same reports I have. The Canadian government is beyond fragile, and it is Martel alone who is holding them together. My people have drawn together a plan -"

"No!" As the word left her mouth, the hand that had been holding up her chin, crashed down on the table.

The next words in Charron's throat froze in place. In all their years working together, he had never heard Marie-Helene Lévesque raise her voice in anger, never mind shout.

Behind and to the right of him, he heard the doors to the President's grand office open. As the heavy footfalls of more than one person filled the room, he dared not take his eyes off the President. You did not take your eyes off the viper as it was preparing to strike.

To his left and right, his peripheral vision caught the sight of two hulking men in dark suits.

Finally, he said, "Madame President, I do not understand. We have made such progress."

Slowly, one of Lévesque's hands rose into the air where she elevated her index finger. Again, Charron held back his words.

"We have made progress, and it is for that reason you will continue in your current capacity. But from this day forward, I need all your energies to be focused on the Muslim problem."

"And North America? Who will ensure France's aspirations bear fruit in that part of the world?" Charron dared to ask.

"I will." The woman's statement was emotionless.

Charron's eyes grew wide. "Madame President, I would never question your decisions, but is this wise? You have a country to run and should things go wrong, you need plausible deniability. And the complexities of the file…"

He stopped his explanation as the President's eyes began to narrow.

"You inserted over two hundred of our soldiers into a country we are not at war with and undertook the assassination of a head of state without so much as giving me the courtesy of a briefing."

Before he could begin to utter a defense, she snapped, "And don't feed me this plausible deniability shit again, Pascal. It is I who run this country, and it is I who decide when and where the sons and daughters of France will die. And whether or not I can deny my knowledge of something will matter little should France not be on the winning side of the revolution our country continues to drive forward."

One of Charron's hands moved to cover his heart. "I was only doing what I thought to be in the best interests of you and our great country. And we came so close. Our next effort would be more subtle if only you will give me the opportunity."

Lévesque's eyes shifted to the brute standing to Charron's right. The unsaid order given, a massive hand came down and clamped none too gently onto Charron's shoulder. A slight man, Charron flinched in pain in response to the vise-like grip.

"There will be a letter waiting on your desk when you get back to your office, Minister Charron. In it, you will find my instructions as they pertain to your redefined role. You will implement them and serve France to the best of your abilities, or there will be consequences."

As she finished her words, the second man's hands came crashing down onto Charron's other shoulder, at which point the two men helped him to his feet.

For a brief moment, the two politicians stared at one another. Finally, the President of France said, "Serve me well and demonstrate to me you remember your place, Pascale Charron, and I will allow you to place your hands back on the levers of power. But undermine me or worse, make me the fool again, and you'll see President Spector isn't the only person who can be brutal and efficient."

The President waited to see if a reply or retort would be delivered. Assured no response was to come, Lévesque shifted her eyes to one of the dark suited giants standing beside the man who had until a minute ago had been her closest political ally.

Pascal Charron, France's Minister of the Interior had become too powerful. Too much of the bureaucracy was looking to him for leadership and it was the bureaucrats who got things done.

The time for a reset had come. "Gentlemen, see that the Minister makes it back to his office without delay."

Ottawa, Parliament Hill

Irene MacPhail fell into the chair sitting behind her desk. Another workday that had ended near midnight. Her forty-seven-year-old body couldn't do this much longer.

In the hours after the Raymond-Trembly debacle, she had agreed to two things with Merielle Martel. To take up the unoccupied role of Deputy Prime Minister, and as Deputy PM without a portfolio, it would become her job to problem-solve those issues the PM needed fixed.

And issue number one had been the Raymond-Trembly agreement, if that's what you could call it.

Despite her past as a journalist, she had agreed with the PM that Canadians did not need to know how close their government had come to fracturing, and how a senior minister of the Crown and one of the country's richest men had conspired to commit kidnapping and murder to take over the leadership of the country. Never mind France and the role it had played.

At the time she agreed to the arrangement, MacPhail had been assured by Martel those details and more would come out the moment the military situation south of the border changed for the better. But it hadn't.

So, as she sat in her chair with her eyes closed and contemplated the day, she felt the full weight of her responsibilities and conscience press down on her shoulders like the full weight of the

Canadian Shield, that field of granite that dominated the eastern half of the country.

She opened her eyes when she heard someone's voice waft into her workspace through the doors she had left open. Her new office was all by itself directly across from the entrance to the House of Commons. Within a week of being there, she had missed her old digs.

There, for better or worse, she had been surrounded by the offices of her colleagues. And despite how busy each MP or Minister was, the small collection of politicians and their staff had gelled into what was, for the most part, one supportive community.

Now, closer than ever to the center of power, she was isolated both physically, and to an increasing degree, emotionally.

It was to reduce this growing sense of seclusion that MacPhail had taken to the habit of keeping the two doors to the Deputy PM's chambers open late in the evening. Where she grew up, a door left wide open still meant visitors were welcome. And to her delight and relief, in the short time she had been in the isolated location, people had made a point of stopping by.

It was through the open door that led into her office that her tired eyes suddenly caught movement of some kind. But as quickly as the movement had come, it was gone again.

She scrunched and rubbed at her eyes. Opening them, this time, she took a hard look at the entrance and everything else in the small, nearly one-hundred-and-fifty-year-old chamber that was her office.

Nothing was amiss.

"Jesus H. Christ, you're seeing ghosts, woman. It's time to go home and get a proper night's rest," she muttered to herself.

"Madame Deputy Prime Minister."

Before she could cover her mouth, MacPhail let out a shriek just as she leaped out of her chair.

Her eyes now fully alert and tracking for whatever threat had just entered her world, she immediately focused on a small drone hanging in the air three feet in front of her.

As she pulled her hands away from her mouth, she could faintly hear the whirring of the rotors keeping the micro-unit aloft.

"Very sorry to give you a start," the little machine said, its voice clearly audible.

After looking around the room for other threats and seeing none, MacPhail finally said, "Who are you?"

The drone's reply was instant. "Perhaps you might close your door. The security that is normally there will be back in less than a minute and it is imperative that our conversation remain private."

"And why shouldn't I call said security?" MacPhail replied, her wits reformed. "The fact that you're here in this form tells me you shouldn't be here at all. So whoever you are and whatever your intentions, you'd better understand this straight off the top – I can't and won't be corrupted."

"We understand this, Deputy Prime Minister. It is for this reason precisely that we've come to you."

In the House of Commons foyer immediately outside her office, she caught the sound of a pair of voices she recognized as Parliamentary Protection Officers. On more days than not, members of the Hill's security force would pop their heads into her work area just to say hello.

Her eyes moved back to the drone and then back to the door. In the end, it was the reporter in her that won the battle.

She hurried to the ancient oak door that would seal off her office from the antechamber occupied by Sandy, her Chief of Staff, during regular business hours, and sealed herself in with the interloper.

She wheeled back on the micro-drone. "Who are you?"

"Who I am isn't nearly as important as who I work for."

"And who is it that you work for? And before you offer another cagey bullshit response, I'd suggest you aim to get on the right side of me with a bit of honesty. I'm not in the mood to be playing games. Not with strangers who snuck into my office in the middle of the bloody night."

Slowly, the drone glided toward MacPhail so that it was once again only a few feet away from her face. She took a step back so that her back was against the thick wooden door she had just placed between herself and the pair of armed security guards not thirty feet away. Not her smartest move, MacPhail thought, chiding herself.

"I am an intermediary working for France. French intelligence, specifically."

MacPhail scoffed. "You mean the same French intelligence service that arranged the successful assassination of my country's prime minister and, more recently, an unsuccessful second attempt to kill Canada's duly elected leader?"

As the words left MacPhail's mouth there was a heat to them. She stepped in the direction of the drone. The flight response that had been coursing through her only seconds before had quickly morphed into something approaching fight.

As she continued walking, the drone zipped to her left, getting out of the way. Moving to her desk, she grabbed at a wonderfully carved canoe paddle that had been given to her during a potlatch ceremony she had attended with the Cowichan First Nation in her days as Minister of Fisheries.

She rounded back on the drone, the paddle cocked and ready. "France. Is that the country you claim to represent, you little flying pissant? Because if it is, you must think I'm the most stupid person in the history of politics if you think I'm going to trust anything your government has to say."

As she shifted her weight to bring her weapon to bear, the drone spoke, its tone level and calm. "As we speak, Deputy Prime Minister, a clandestine outfit called the White Unit – a unit that reports directly to the Prime Minister of Canada – is in the process of ending Yvette Raymond's life."

"Wrong," MacPhail hissed at the drone. "Canadian prime ministers don't assassinate political opponents. And don't you dare throw the name of Josee Labelle back at me. I looked at the evidence as hard as anybody, and if anyone killed that woman, it was the country you claim to represent."

The drone slowly moved forward, despite the threat of the paddle. "Think what you will, Deputy Prime Minister, but tomorrow, you will read of the death of Yvette Raymond. We don't know how she will die but just as you and I now speak, Ms. Raymond is dead or will be. And when her death is confirmed in the media tomorrow, ask yourself who killed her, because I can assure you it was not France."

"Bullshit." MacPhail swung the paddle, but the drone easily dodged the attempt. Despite feeling the fool, she immediately raised the converted weapon again.

"You were once a reporter, Minister MacPhail, and as best we can tell, you remain a reporter at heart. Admittedly, France has blood on its hands, but so does the woman who is your prime minister. More than you can know. The evidence is there if you look for it."

"What evidence?" MacPhail said, her voice stern. "Extraordinary accusations call for extraordinary proof."

"It is there if you look for it, Madame Deputy Prime Minister. Merielle Martel is not the woman you think she is. The crucible that is war changes people, and history is unkind to those who make the work of the tyrant possible. Even those who are unknowing."

Suddenly, the drone zipped back and upward in the direction of her office's high ceiling.

Paddle still in hand, MacPhail took a step in the direction of the floating envoy. She cocked back the weapon. "I won't be manipulated into doing something that will hurt my country. This is your last chance."

"We have given you all the information you need, Deputy Prime Minister. Follow the evidence and your conscience or do not."

Without warning, the drone exploded with the force of a bottle rocket, showering the room with debris. Flinching, MacPhail staggered backward until her backside ran into her desk.

Breathing heavily, she set down the paddle and looked down at the largest piece of wreckage remaining of her midnight conspirator.

Her cell phone went off. Turning, she grabbed the unit off her desk and looked at the number. It only displayed RCMP. She immediately accepted the call. "Irene MacPhail, who's this?"

"Deputy Prime Minister, it's Staff Sergeant Roberts. I'm in charge of the protective detail assigned to Ms. Raymond. You asked that I call you directly if there were ever any issues with Ms. Raymond."

MacPhail's heart began to pound. "Yes, Sergeant. Is there something wrong?"

"There was a break-in of her home at some point in the past hour. We don't know how they got in –"

"Sergeant," MacPhail interrupted the police officer. "What of Ms. Raymond?"

"She's dead, Madame Minister. She was found in her bedroom. We don't know the cause."

"My God," MacPhail said more to herself than to the officer on the line.

"What would you like us to do, Minister?"

When MacPhail said nothing, the Sergeant began to repeat his question, but he was cut off by MacPhail's response. "We do our jobs, Sergeant. As best we can, we do our bloody jobs, so that we can find out who the hell did this."

Canadian Forces Base, Alert, Nunavut

It had taken the better part of the day to get to the world's most northern military base but as Merielle stood in front of Pierre Besson, the Director of France's foreign intelligence agency, she was glad she had taken the trouble. She had underestimated how satisfying it would be to see the gaunt handcuffed man sitting across from her.

"I understand you've been exceedingly unhelpful to my colleagues, Director Besson."

"Is that a question, Madame Prime Minster?"

Just as a genuine smile emerged onto her face, the phone in her jacket pocket vibrated. Expecting the call, she pulled out the device and placed it at her ear.

"It's been done," said the voice.

"Are we sure?"

"There is no doubt."

"And it was done quietly?"

"Yes, all went to plan."

Without another word, Merielle disconnected the call and slowly replaced the phone into her suit jacket.

Pushing her chair back from the table, she stood allowing herself to look down at the still handsome French intelligence officer. "You won't know this, but in a recent effort to assassinate me, your country took something from me that was dear to my heart.

"Actually, your country has taken two things from me that I hold dear. In the first case, my prime minister and friend. In the second, someone I loved."

Besson stared back at Canada's leader with a defiant look. "I don't have any idea of what you're talking about. But if I did, I would say that those who play dangerous games win equally dangerous prizes."

"Indeed," Merielle said quietly. "Please join us won't you, Colonel."

Behind her, the only door to the room opened. Without saying a word, Colonel Azim strode past Merielle to set himself behind the Frenchman.

With a single nod of her head, the man who led Merielle's personal Action Group descended on France's most senior intelligence officer to envelop him into a rear naked choke hold.

As Besson struggled against the assault, his bulging eyes found Merielle's, and for that period of time he remained conscious, he sought to plead for his life.

Straining mightily, his bound hands reached out to her. "Please..." he managed to gasp.

Merielle said no words nor took any action. She only watched as the man's terrorized resistance slowed and finally stopped.

As the body of the former Director of the DGSE was finally lowered onto the table and his executioner stepped back from his work, the Prime Minister of Canada nodded her head in satisfaction, turned, and without saying a word, left the room.

The End

Copyright

Copyright R.A. Flannagan Writing 2023

Published by R.A. Flannagan Writing

All rights reserved

No part of this book may be reproduced, scanned, or distributed in any printed or electronic form without the permission of the author. The author holds exclusive rights to this work. Unauthorized duplication is prohibited.

This is a work of fiction. Any resemblance of characters to actual persons, living or dead, is purely coincidental.

Cover design by Ares Jun: aresjun@gmail.com

Special thanks to my editor: Stephen England. Stephen is an author himself and he writes a terrific thriller: https://www.stephenenglandbooks.com/

Special thanks to my beta readers: Chris Dale of the United Kingdom and David Parker and Bob Flannagan, both of Canada.

Afterword

Dear Reader,

A million thanks to you for reading *Red Blue Storm*. It is my second full-length novel and I sincerely hope you enjoyed it.

This being my second full novel, the effort to produce *Red Blue Storm* was a touch less grueling, though the process of writing a 500-page novel is and will always be hugely challenging.

Because of the effort and my development as a writer, I think this second book of the CANZUK at War series was an improved product in many ways. I hope you'll agree.

One thing that is critical to authors is reviews. This is perhaps more true for independent, self-published authors. The more reviews a book gets, the more Amazon's algorithms promote the story, which leads to more people reading this novel.

So please, however much you enjoyed this story, if you could take a brief moment to leave a star rating or a review on Amazon, I would greatly appreciate it.

Want more of R.A. Flannagan's Writing?

If you want to stay connected with me or want to see what other stories I've written, visit my website at: www.raflannagan.ca[1]

On my website, you can sign up for my newsletter and read my occasional blog posts. I'm also on Twitter at: @ra_flannagan[2]

I can also be reached via email: raf@raflannagan.ca

---

1. http://www.raflannagan.ca
2. https://twitter.com/ra_flannagan

Other Works

Caribbean Payback, the CANZUK at War series, Book 0.5

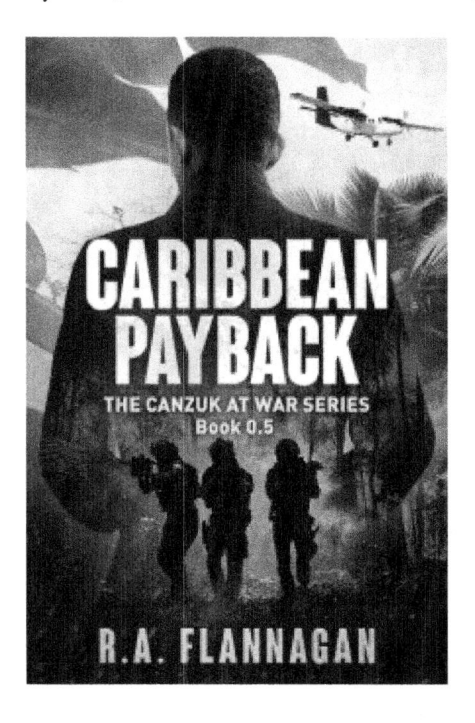

A UN peacekeeping mission has turned into tragedy. Peacekeepers are dead, a soldier is now a hostage, and a country is looking for answers.

Special forces and intelligence operatives, are given the task of settling the score in a country where corruption and chaos are a way of life. The best of Canada's military and intelligence services converge in a race against time and hidden agendas to save one of their own and to repair a country's honor.

Politics, espionage, and military action drive this standalone story, which features CSIS intel officer Sam Petite and cast of other daring and determined characters.

In *Caribbean Payback*, Canada has never been so badass!

Fans of Clancy's Red Storm Rising, Bond's Red Phoenix, Lunnon-Wood's Long Reach, or Greaney's Red Metal will enjoy this fast-paced, action-packed, short story.

Download today on Amazon[1] for only $0.99 and support the work of Canada's only military thriller novelist.

---

1. https://www.amazon.com/Caribbean-Payback-CANZUK-War-Novella-ebook/dp/B09RHF5547

List of Faction States – US Civil War II

The United Constitutional States of America – The Red Faction	The Federation of American States – The Blue Faction	The Neutral States
- Alabama		
- Alaska		
- Arkansas		
- Arizona	- Connecticut	- California
- Florida	- Delaware	- Colorado
- Georgia	- Illinois	- Missouri
- Idaho	- Maryland	- Montana
- Indiana	- Massachusetts	- New Mexico
- Iowa	- Michigan	- Nevada
- Kansas	- Minnesota	- North Dakota
- Kentucky	- New Hampshire	- South Dakota
- Louisiana	- New Jersey	- Wyoming
- Maine	- New York	- Hawaii
- Mississippi	- Ohio	
- Nebraska	- Oregon	
- North Carolina	- Pennsylvania	
- Oklahoma	- Rhode Island	
- South Carolina	- Washington	
- Tennessee	- Washington, D.C	
- Texas	- Wisconsin	
- West Virginia	- Vermont	
- Virginia		
- Utah		

Printed in Great Britain
by Amazon

29432842R00260